VIVIAN VAUGHAN

SUNRISE SURRENDER

ZEBRA BOOKS
KENSINGTON PUBLISHING CORP.

ZEBRA books are published by

Kensington Publishing Corp.
475 Park Avenue South
New York, NY 10016

Copyright © 1993 by Vivian Jane Vaughen

All rights reserved. No part of this book may be reproduced
in any form or by any means without prior written consent
of the Publisher, excepting brief quotes used in reviews.

If you purchased this book without a cover, you should be
aware that this book is stolen property. It was reported as
"unsold and destroyed" to the Publisher and neither the Au-
thor nor the Publisher has received any payment fro this
"stripped book."

Zebra, the Z logo, and the Lovegram logo are trademarks of
Kensington Publishing Corp.

First Printing: September, 1993

Printed in the United States of America

To Elaine Raco Chase

"Words, once my stock, are wanting to commend

. . . so good a friend."

John Dryden
"To My Friend Mr. Motteux"

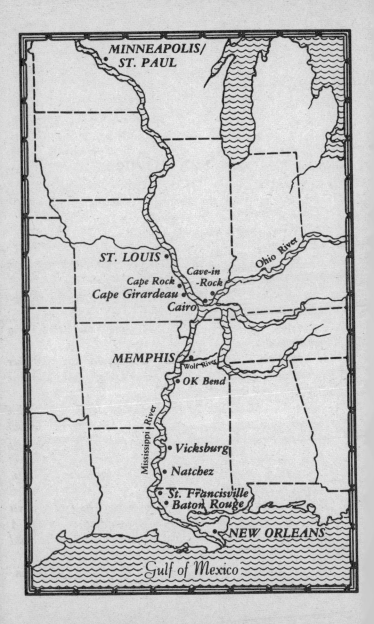

Chapter One

St. Louis, Missouri
June 1879

The ship tossed on an angry sea, rocking the narrow bunk where two lovers lay locked in a heated embrace.

"Ah, my love," he whispered, "you have lost none of your passion with time."

"And you, 'tis true, have kept your word. You have had no other woman but me."

He belted out a laugh as he plunged again and again into her receptive body. "God's bones, so I have. And you have been true to yours, no other lovers."

The woman stared into his face, most of which was hidden in the dimly lit cabin. His dark hair was but a darker shadow now, and his eyes were black, eyes she knew to be the color of the sky on a cloudless summer day. She wondered whether the wee seed growing inside her womb would have the same blue eyes. She hoped so, as she hoped for a son.

She had not told him of the coming babe. The idea was yet so new and strange she had difficulty accepting it herself. A child on a pirate's ship. What right had they to rear a child thus?

And yet they must. For this life was the life they had chosen.

7

Leaving it now, even if they fancied to, would result in a hangman's noose for the both of them.

As he drove his lusty body faster and faster into hers, all thoughts of babes and pirate ships and hangman's nooses receded, swept to sea on a wave of passion so potent that when it crested she cried out, drawing him to her bosom, holding him protectively in sweat-laved arms, while the crying of a babe echoed in her ears.

"Delta, are you up?" Ginny Myrick's voice filtered through the closed bedroom door.

Awakened by her sister's call, Delta Jarrett sat up in bed. Then the dream came back, stunning her with its sense of foreboding. She clutched her head, squeezing her temples between the heels of her hands, while the colorful patchwork quilt danced like a whirling rainbow before her dazed vision.

She knew the truth of the dream. Anne Bonny, one of her own ancestors, had borne the child in her womb, not the son she wished for but a girl. Anne had been scheduled to hang immediately after the delivery. Although the details were uncertain, at best, some claimed she had been released from prison and had disappeared with her child. Jack Rackham, Calico Jack they called him, had been hanged for piracy on the high seas without ever learning of the child Anne was to bear him.

Ginny stuck her head through the doorway to Delta's room. "Hurry and get dressed, Delta. The boat leaves before noon."

When Delta didn't move, Ginny crossed the room to sit beside her. "Whatever is the matter? You haven't changed your mind about this journey to New Orleans, have you?"

Delta lowered her hands. "That dreadful nightmare. I dreamt it again."

"Oh, baby." Ginny folded her arms around her younger sister's shoulders, drawing her near. From the other room children's voices clamored for breakfast. Ignoring them, Ginny patted Delta's back. "That's what this trip is all about, ridding you of that needling dream. Get dressed and come eat breakfast. By the time you reach New Orleans you'll be in fine spirits again."

Delta shook her head. "The dream is so depressing, Ginny. And repetitive. It's as if our ancestors are trying to tell me something—to warn me of something— but I don't understand what." She raised stricken blue eyes to seek reassurance. Ginny, eleven years her senior, had been more mother than sister to Delta, having taken her in as a youngster even before their mother died three years back.

"Why do I dream of intimacies between my ancestors?" Delta wailed. "Why, Ginny?"

Ginny smoothed Delta's mass of brown wavy hair back from her eyes. "Could be you're right," she sighed. "Perhaps our ancestors are trying to tell you something. At twenty-five a girl's body is ready for marriage and a family. It's no wonder your brain is barraging you with such things, considering all the offers you've refused."

"You mean prissy Tommie Babcock?"

"Among others," Ginny acknowledged. "If Tommie is too dandified to suit your taste, what about Karl Horner? He's a farmer, and a successful one, at that."

Delta sidestepped the familiar argument. "If I'm dreaming about marriage, why don't I dream about a respectable marriage? Yours and Hollis's, for instance."

Ginny's face reddened.

"I don't mean about your love—" Delta pulled away, running fingers through sleep-tangled hair. Desperation replaced her embarrassment. "Why do I dream about people who lived a hundred years ago, who led terrible lives? Why do I dream about pirates?"

Ginny stood, shaking her head.

"It's a warning," Delta persisted, pressing both hands to her heart. "I know it. I feel a heavy, awful sense of foreboding, as if something terrible is about to happen and I'm supposed to prevent it, but—"

"I don't believe in such things." Ginny crossed to the doorway. "For my money your nightmare is a combination of things. First, you've had this dream ever since we returned from Summer Valley. Seeing Kale and Ellie so much in love stirred tender yearnings inside you. Word about Carson's unexpected marriage in Mexico added fuel to the fire. Then there's the winter. Winters always depress folks, and this one was especially harsh. By the time you reach New Orleans, magnolias will be in bloom, mockingbirds will be singing, and you will be yourself again. You'll have a fine time with Cousin Brady, and when you return, you'll be ready to consider an offer from one of the young men who have been pestering Hollis for your hand."

Two little faces pushed through Ginny's skirts, their dark eyes shining.

"Mama, I'm hungry."

"Mama, the bacon's burning."

"Mama, is Delta gonna meet a pirate on the Mississippi River? Can I come too? I want to meet a pirate."

Ginny rested a hand on each twin's head. "No, Joey, you know pirates don't travel the Mississippi. You've

10

lived in St. Louis all your life. Have you ever seen a pirate set foot on our docks?''

"No, but I want to.''

"Me, too,'' echoed his twin, Jimmy.

Delta shook her head to clear it of premonitions and went to kneel before the children. "I'll make you a deal. Help your mother with breakfast while I dress, and if I meet a pirate on the Mississippi River, you'll be the first to know.''

Joey's little face brightened. "Oh, boy, a scoop for Papa's paper. We get a scoop.''

"A scoop,'' Jimmy repeated.

Delta dressed carefully in a gray faille traveling suit, its long fitted jacket and draped skirt liberally flounced with claret. In the months since the dream of her ancestors, pirates Anne Bonny and Calico Jack, began to plague her she had tried every method she could find to deal with the debilitating emotional pall the nightmare cast over her. To keep her mind in the present and away from dreams, she focused on the smallest details of daily life, such as the scent of violets when she powdered her body, the feel of filigree buttons when she did up her jacket.

Her eyes fell on the open steamer trunk she had packed the night before—snatches of blue cashmere, of yellow watered silk, of delicate white lace peeked from hangers and drawers. Mama Rachael had worked for weeks sewing her wardrobe for this journey, a wardrobe that closely resembled a trousseau.

Ginny had all but said she wished it were.

The trip had been Ginny and Hollis's idea jointly, Delta knew. Ginny thought this voyage aboard the *Mississippi Princess* would provide the sort of respite Delta needed to shake the burdensome nightmare. Victor Kaney, captain of the fancy new showboat, had

11

offered his vessel to serve as St. Louis's flagship in a procession to honor the opening of South Pass at the mouth of the Mississippi below New Orleans sometime in July, the exact date to be determined by the completion of the jetties and their subsequent success in removing the sandbar that had blocked river traffic for the last forty years.

The St. Louis city fathers had gladly accepted Captain Kaney's offer. Not only was James Eads, the embattled engineer of this project to restore commercial river traffic to the entire Mississippi Valley, one of St. Louis's most prominent citizens, but many of the major stockholders in Eads's South Pass Jetty Company were also citizens of St. Louis and had agreed to travel to the festivities aboard the *Mississippi Princess*.

Hollis Myrick, publisher of the *St. Louis Sun*, had been delighted with his wife's idea. "You can serve as the *Sun*'s official reporter for this momentous event," he had told Delta, adding, "and send us travel and human-interest stories from every port along the way."

Ginny's only hesitation had been for want of a chaperon. She certainly couldn't leave her duties at the paper and the constant job of mothering four young children. Then Hollis had hit upon the solution. His mother, known to all as Mama Rachael, could accompany Delta as far as Memphis, where she had been longing to visit an old friend, Maud Wadkins and her spinster daughter, Hattie Louise. The Wadkins women had fled to St. Louis to escape the yellow fever epidemics that hit Memphis a while back and had insisted on Mama Rachael visiting them as soon as it was safe to travel to their beleaguered city.

Hollis convinced Ginny that by the time the boat reached Memphis, Delta would have become acquainted with the crew and could travel under their protection the rest of the way to New Orleans.

If not, he reasoned, Cousin Cameron Jarrett, who worked for the Pinkertons and was stationed in Memphis where the boat was to remain in dock for three days, would note the situation and find a suitable replacement for Mama Rachael.

Delta agreed to the trip, although the prospect of dealing with her nightmare away from the security of home and Ginny's support terrified her. It *had* been a harsh winter, she acknowledged, and she would like a change of scenery. Her brother Kale Jarrett and his wife Ellie were supposed to travel to New Orleans in July, as were another brother Carson and his new bride, Aurelia, whom Delta had yet to meet.

And Mama Rachael would make an agreeable traveling companion. Having lived with the Myricks almost as long as Delta had herself, the squat little woman with her snow-white topknot was as much grandmother to Delta as to the young Myrick children.

Pulling her hair well back from her face, Delta wrapped the length of it into a loose twist at her nape. No topknot for her. With her height, inherited from the lanky Jarretts, she didn't need extra inches. She added a low-crowned straw bonnet decorated with sprigs of silk thistles that complimented the red highlights in her hair, securing it to her mass of hair with several steel hairpins.

Examining herself in the looking glass, she adjusted the prim white collar that peeked above the gray collar of her jacket, added a pair of small pearl loops to her ears, and pronounced herself ready for the adventure ahead.

But when she caught her own eye, she realized that more than their color was blue. The melancholy inside her tainted her mood, bringing grave doubts that a simple journey down the Mississippi River, even if it were on a grand new showboat, could chase the demons from her head.

Ginny believed it was possible, though, and Delta prayed her sister was right. She knew Ginny was not right about the other—she would not return to St. Louis and agree to marry any of the men who had offered for her hand.

She would rather remain a maiden aunt than become some tiresome man's miserable wife.

They heard the steamboat's calliope before they finished packing the wagon. Hollis loaded the last trunk—Delta had two, Mama Rachael only one—and took the valises and bandboxes the children clamored to hand him. He had returned home from the newspaper office in time to drive the family to the docks to see his mother and Delta safely aboard the *Mississippi Princess*.

"Hurry, Hollis," Mama Rachael encouraged her son. "Whip up this old nag and let's get on the road. Don't make us miss the boat."

Unlike Delta, Mama Rachael had no misgivings about the trip. She had been packed and ready to go for over a week, and had talked incessantly about the voyage, to the end that the family had given up conducting a conversation on any other topic.

Today, however, Hollis had other things on his mind. He assisted the women onto the two-seated wagon, then stepped up beside Ginny. For once the children did not have to be prodded to climb aboard.

Hollis pulled the team into the road and headed for the Market Street docks. Above the clatter of horses' hooves, the creaking of the wagon, the chatter of the

14

children, and the beckoning tones of the distant calliope, he proceeded to issue last-minute instructions to Delta.

"Your first stop will be tomorrow at Cape Girardeau." He spoke with one eye on the road, his head cocked around toward Delta. "You should be able to write an article on the theatrical troupe in time to post it upon your arrival. I've already spoken with Captain Kaney. He's working up an itinerary you can use to set up interviews at each stop down the river."

"For shame, Hollis," Ginny scolded. "You make this voyage sound like a dull business trip. Delta's supposed to relax and enjoy herself."

Delta grinned at her brother-in-law who had served as her surrogate father the last few years. Like Ginny, Hollis had trouble accepting the fact that Delta had grown up. "Don't worry, Ginny. I know what Hollis is up to. He thinks if I post an article from each stop, he can keep track of my whereabouts."

"Delta—" Hollis objected.

"I don't mind, Hollis," she conceded with a feigned grimace. "But as long as I stay on the boat and the boat stays on the river, I doubt there's much chance I can get lost."

When the sternwheeler, *Mississippi Princess,* came in view, all tongues ceased to wag. Ginny found her voice first.

"It looks like a wedding cake."

Delta gave her a disgusted shrug.

"It doesn't look like a pirate ship," Joey wailed.

"No. it doesn't," Jimmy agreed.

"It isn't a pirate ship, stupid," ten-year-old Katie retorted. "Mama told you there are no pirates on the Mississippi River."

"Delta said she'd find us one," Joey returned.

15

"Both of us," Jimmy added.

While the family babbled in animated abandon around her, uneasiness stirred inside Delta. She strove to concentrate on the magnificent steamer. It did look like a wedding cake—five tiers of glistening white, each wrapped in a confection of fanciful grillwork, draped in red, white, and blue bunting, and topped by two bright red smokestacks and the largest American flag she had ever seen. A banner strung between the two stacks proclaimed, "Jas. B. Eads, Pride of St. Louis." The boat's name, *Mississippi Princess,* was painted in red and gold on a sign above the giant red paddlewheel at the stern.

In keeping with the boat's festive attire, the scene around Pier Fourteen where she was docked resembled a Fourth of July celebration. Hundreds of people milled about, the men in polished silk hats and patent leather boots, the ladies in the latest fashions, their parasols creating a rainbow of color up and down the usually drab wharf.

Day-to-day activity at the St. Louis wharves, as old-timers were fond of reminding everyone, did not compare with the bustle before the war. The scant five or six boats lined up at the mile-long wharf on any given day generally served as a bleak reminder of the dozens of boats that had vied for berth space in years past.

But pessimism was not the spirit of the day. Revelry infected the area around the *Mississippi Princess* and all who had come to see her off. The calliope had given way to a brass band that blared from the top deck. Below, near the gangplank, a fiddler, a small man close to Delta's own size, feverishly produced a feisty tune she did not recognize, but one that set her feet to tapping, nonetheless. Loose bow strings flew about his swarthy, angular face.

16

Again her gaze traveled the length of the enormous white boat, while she tried to grip the anxiety building inside her. Already she wished she were staying home. Already, but too late, she admonished. The sweeping wraparound railings and brass and red trim blurred before her troubled gaze.

"We'd better hurry," Mama Rachael urged. Her brown eyes fairly danced with excitement. Delta thought suddenly that she wouldn't be surprised were Mama Rachael to jump from the wagon and take off skipping toward the gangplank.

"I've studied the schedule," the little woman explained, keeping her seat with obvious effort. "If we want lunch, we had best get aboard and unpack our belongings. The brochure says the chef is from New Orleans. I shouldn't wonder if we were served something exotic like crawfish or shrimp for luncheon. Possibly even champagne."

Delta grinned. If she couldn't muster enthusiasm over the journey, Mama Rachael possessed enough for both of them.

Hollis drew the team as close as he could, waylaid the first roustabout who passed their way unengaged, and arranged for their luggage to be transported aboard. Then he led the family up the crowded gangplank, greeting first one citizen of St. Louis, then another, all the while issuing instructions to Delta.

"I forgot to tell you about Louisiana," he said. "Keep your ears open for news of their gubernatorial race. The incumbent, a man by the name of Trainor—William Trainor—is running for reelection on a platform to expel all Voodoos from the state."

"The Voodoos?" Delta questioned.

"Well, their leaders. Primarily, I think, he's targeting Voodoo queens. Folks in St. Louis don't put stock in

17

such things, but they should find it interesting reading. So learn all you can.''

Delta clasped hands with her twin nephews who ran to keep pace on either side of her. ''I may not have time to find you a pirate after all,'' she told them. ''Your pa is more interested in theatrical troupes and witches.''

Suddenly it was time for good-byes.

Hollis pressed a wad of folded bills into Delta's hand. ''Tips for the cabin boy,'' he told her.

Ginny hugged her. ''Remember to arrange for your gowns to be pressed. You can't appear in wrinkled gowns on such a magnificent vessel.''

Delta squeezed her eyes to hold back tears. ''I'll miss you. I wish I weren't going.''

''Now, now,'' Ginny hushed. ''Last minute jitters, that's all it is. You'll have a grand time.''

''That she will,'' a baritone boomed above them. ''We wouldn't be doing our job if we showed anyone less than a grand old time.''

Delta smiled at the robust figure of a white-haired gentleman, clad in a sparkling white suit.

Hollis introduced Captain Victor Kaney. While the rest of the family watched, wide-eyed, Mama Rachael fairly preened for the captain. ''I do hope we haven't missed luncheon.'' She offered her hand, encased in a black mesh glove, which he took and held. ''I've read all your literature,'' she continued, the black plume on her straw bonnet bobbing in tempo with her excitement. ''I can't wait to see what your famous chef has prepared for us.''

''Indeed you haven't missed luncheon, Mrs. Myrick.'' He glanced to Delta, then back to Mama Rachael. ''We sit informally at breakfast and lunch, but

18

I expect the two of you to dine at my table in the evenings."

A sharp whistle pierced the air and the captain dropped Mama Rachael's hand as though he had been burned by steam from his new engine. "That's my cue," he said. "Time to get to work." He stopped a passing cabin boy. "Orville here will show you to your cabin. Stateroom 219 on the cabin deck."

Captain Kaney turned to Hollis. "I'm afraid that's your cue, too. Time for visitors to disembark. I promise to keep a personal eye on these two ladies."

Delta hugged Ginny, then turned to Hollis. The unsettled look on his face brought a smile to her lips. "Don't worry," she whispered as she hugged him good-bye. "I'll chaperon Mama Rachael."

Two more blasts from the whistle sent the straggling visitors scurrying for shore. Delta and Mama Rachael stood at the rail waving to the little group on the dock. While Mama Rachael babbled excitedly, Delta struggled to hold back tears.

"Don't forget your promise," little Joey called to her.

"Your promise," Jimmy echoed.

She adjusted her parasol and waved to them. Oh, to be a child again. By the time she returned from New Orleans, Joey and Jimmy would have forgotten all about pirates. Somehow she doubted her nightmare could be expunged so readily.

One sight of their elegant stateroom and Delta wanted to bolt for shore. Two beds, clad in beautiful green damask, hugged opposite walls, leaving only a narrow walkway between them. A walnut chiffonier with attached looking glass was built into the walnut veneer wall opposite the foot of each bed, again with a narrow passage between bureau and bed. The room contained one window, on the wall facing the rail, which was heavily draped in green damask. Delta stood in the doorway, trying to suppress a suffocating sense of claustrophobia. How would she ever deal with her nightmare in such an enclosed space?

Mama Rachael headed for one of the trunks that had been placed to either side of the bureaus.

"After you unpack," Orville was saying, "a porter will remove your trunks to the storage room."

Delta watched in dismay as Mama Rachael opened the door to one of the chiffoniers, inspecting the interior hanging space and drawers. With the door open, passage about the room was limited to crawling over the beds.

"Ma'am?" Orville inquired.

Delta focused on the cabin boy who stood directly in front of her.

"Will that be all, ma'am?" he repeated.

Quickly she moved aside to allow him to exit the small stateroom. "Yes." She handed him one of the bills Hollis had given her and which she still held crumpled in a tight fist. "Thank you, Orville."

The deck rocked beneath her feet. Her eyes widened.

"We're pulling out," he explained. "As soon as we get underway, the luncheon whistle will sound. Dining room's on the observation deck, two flights up the same staircase we used to reach your cabin. Can you find your way?"

She nodded.

"Delta," Mama Rachael called. "Which gown do you want pressed for dinner? Hurry, child. We mustn't be late for luncheon."

After promising to send someone to fetch their gowns for pressing, Orville hurried down the swaying passageway.

Delta moved into the room, closed the door, and before the whistle sounded for the beginning of luncheon, she and Mama Rachael had unpacked their trunks. Once the bulky trunks were removed, she assured herself, the cabin would not be so confining.

They left their stateroom and headed down the deck with Mama Rachael still babbling, seemingly oblivious to Delta's black mood. "I wonder which deck we should choose for our afternoon promenade?"

The boat was well under way by this time, and although Delta had been concerned about walking on board a moving vessel, the movement was hardly noticeable, nothing like riding in a carriage. To her left she watched the St. Louis shoreline recede. She could still see people on the docks, but was unable to make out individual figures. She turned away, refusing to give in to a wave of melancholy.

They pressed along the deck, which was crowded with people hurrying this way and that. Every one greeted everyone else, creating an air of instant camaraderie. A soft breeze off the river flirted with Delta's cheeks, and she suddenly entertained the surprising inclination to remove her hat and take the pins out of her hair.

She smiled to herself, feeling her anxiety begin to ebb. This voyage might not be so difficult, after all. Then better judgement overtook her emerging sense of euphoria and she sighed. If she intended to enjoy herself, she would have to do so during the daytime when she wouldn't be plagued by that detestable nightmare.

"A promenade after lunch sounds wonderful," she told Mama Rachael. "You choose which deck."

"The vista will be different from every one," her sprightly companion observed. "We must try them all before we reach Memphis. Perhaps we should begin below on the main deck and work our way up. Then again, we could start at the top on the sun deck and work down through the promenade deck and the . . ."

The grandeur of the dining room jolted Delta out of her reveries and stilled, momentarily to be sure, Mama Rachael's tongue. Taking up the width of the ship, minus the outside passageways, and practically its entire length, the enormous room surpassed anything Delta had ever seen. Resplendent with heavy moldings, the room resembled a tunnel fashioned of elaborate filigree work, which one need only enter to arrive in wonderland. The ceiling, constructed of row upon row of intricately carved arches, was hung with a dozen chandeliers that swung ever so gently with the motion of the boat. Two rows of tables, each accommodating eight or ten gilded bamboo-carved side chairs, ran the length of the room with an aisle down the center. Each table was dressed in starched white, and at the head of each stood an equally starched, white-jacketed waiter.

Numerous doors opened at intervals along both outside walls, and diners spilled into the room from them all. At every doorway a steward greeted the passengers. "Take any place you want. Luncheon is informal on board the *Princess.*"

Informal? Delta was suddenly relieved that Mama Rachael had insisted on sending their nicest gowns to be pressed. At the far end of the room, raised above the other tables on a dais, stood a long empty table. The captain's table? Yes, she would need her finest gown to sit up there.

Trying not to gape at those around her, Delta followed Mama Rachael into the room, allowing her now-mute chaperon to choose their table. They were joined by two couples who introduced themselves as the Humphrieses from St. Paul, near Mama Rachael's age, and the Menefees from Dubuque, who might be a few years younger.

If Mama Rachael was disappointed that the entree was roast beef instead of crawfish—and the drink, coffee instead of champagne—she was allowed no time to show it. Talk centered on the nature of the trip itself.

"Derned clever of Captain Kaney," Mr. Humphries was saying. "Combining a showboat with a passenger ship and taking the whole kit and caboodle down to New Orleans to celebrate with Captain Eads."

"And danged considerate of Kaney, too," Mr. Menefee added. "Way I hear it, folks down in Louisiana have been giving Eads such a hard time, it's a wonder the man didn't give up the project and tell them to keep their danged sandbar."

Mr. Humphries nodded, sagely. "The man's a genius, Eads is, even if the Army Engineers don't agree."

Mr. Menefee scowled. "The Army Engineers have had forty years to remove that sandbar and all they've done is talk. After Eads opens the Mississippi to commerce, everyone in the Valley will be singing a different tune."

"From the depths of their full pockets," Humphries predicted.

"Come now," Mrs. Menefee chided. "Whatever the reason for the voyage, we're here to enjoy it." She smiled across the table to Delta and Mama Rachael. "I haven't seen either of you ladies aboard before."

"We're from St. Louis," Delta supplied.

"Have you had a chance to look over the boat?" Mrs. Menefee inquired. Upon receiving a negative response, she continued. "Lottie and I will show you

23

around after luncheon.'' She leaned across her husband to confirm the invitation with Mrs. Humphries.

''Certainly, Dora,'' Lottie Humphries agreed. ''We'll start with the sun deck.''

''And end in the cabin lounge.'' Dora Menefee winked at Delta. ''The cabin lounge is Lottie's favorite place on board. That's where we ladies are allowed to gamble.''

''Gamble?'' Mama Rachael quizzed.

''Cards,'' Lottie explained, her cheeks taking on a flush that Delta decided had nothing to do with the room's lighting. ''After all, we're isolated here in the middle of this big river. Who's to know?''

Delta glanced at Mama Rachael in time to catch the twinkle in her eyes. Between promenades, dinner at the captain's table, and gambling in the cabin lounge, Mama Rachael would be hard-pressed to find time for chaperon duty, not that Delta envisioned the need for such protection on board this magnificent floating palace.

They had finished a dessert of chocolate mousse and macaroons and were enjoying a second cup of a rich coffee that Mr. Menefee claimed was flavored with chocolate, but which Mrs. Humphries insisted was made with chicory, when Captain Kaney stopped by their table.

He exchanged amenities with the Humphrieses and Menefees before favoring Mama Rachael with a radiant smile. ''I hope your stateroom is satisfactory, Mrs. Myrick.''

''More than satisfactory,'' Mama Rachael enthused, her smile vying with the captain's for luminosity. ''We can't thank you enough for such a fine cabin.''

Bowing low from the waist, he turned to Delta. ''This young lady deserves the credit. And I do thank you, from the bottom of my heart. The articles you plan to write about our little boat will provide a wealth of publicity. Least I could do when Myrick approached me was to provide a suitable stateroom for your journey."

He handed Delta a sheet of paper. "Our itinerary. I've jotted down names of citizens at each port for you to consider for interviews."

Delta scanned the list.

"I've also spoken with Zanna, the artistic director for the Princess Players. She and the cast are anxious to talk with you. You're invited to join their rehearsal after luncheon." He glanced up and down the length of the finely appointed dining room. "We need a little time to set this room up as a grand salon and theater."

Delta's eyes widened at the prospect, and he laughed.

"Let me assure you the task looks more formidable than it is. With all hands working, we can accomplish the transformation in less than thirty minutes."

The captain moved away. Lottie Humphries inquired about the interviews—"Not that I was eavesdropping, you understand." Mama Rachael began to explain, and Delta found her eyes suddenly riveted on a solemn face two tables beyond—

A face that captured her attention as though a spell had been cast over her, calling to mind Hollis's discussion of Voodoos. But it wasn't black magic that held her gaze.

It was a man. An uncommonly handsome man. And although he stared at her with a frightening intensity, she did not feel threatened. He seemed familiar, like an old friend.

She struggled to place him in her mind. His face was weathered, with broad forehead and a cleft between his eyes above a long, straight nose. Light from the gently swinging chandeliers skimmed his black hair, causing it to glisten with golden highlights. A shock fell over his forehead, giving Delta the impression he might have been walking along the deck before luncheon. She reached to smooth her own hair back in place.

His dark eyes narrowed in a way that should have alarmed her, but again did not, for their familiarity. His lips remained closed. She could tell they were well shaped. Suddenly she wondered what he would look like if he laughed, and she smiled. He did not.

Was it his solemn countenance, she wondered, that caused him to look so out of place here in this gilded dining room? His oversized physique, his rugged face, even his windswept hair, bespoke a man accustomed to the outdoors. His suit, however, what she could see of it, was surely straight from the city, a fine black jacket and starched white collar above a fancy silk necktie.

She had met this gentleman somewhere before, most assuredly. And he must find her familiar, from the way he stared, she thought, reconsidering her choice of the term "gentleman."

But even the arrogance in the straightforward way he stared at her seemed familiar. They had met before, definitely. She searched her brain for a name, but none came. Hordes of people passed through St. Louis. Many of them came to the *Sun* office for information or directions. That must be where she had seen him.

Strange, though, she had the feeling she *knew* this man, had talked to him. Not just talked, either. Deep inside she felt certain she *knew* him, knew things about his life, personal things, intimacies.

Before she could further probe her subconscious, his eyes narrowed to a mere squint, sending a shiver of alarm down her spine. She watched his jaws clench.

Without warning, he scraped back his gilded chair in an angry gesture and strode from the room, leaving her to stare helplessly after him.

She watched the larger, somewhat older man who had dined with the stranger, rise and follow him from the dining room.

Except that man was no stranger, she thought, stunned by a sudden tremor of foreboding.

faintly across the room as Brett again studied Suzette
any charm from it except... someone must have stitched
it... and she looked... at the neck... Pierre went
"...low as down... a... quarter's... standing...
the... chalds... in the... water... and it... or... from...

Chapter Two

By the time Brett Reall reached the rail outside the
dining room his heart beat against his ribs as relent-
lessly as the *Mississippi Princess's* paddlewheel slapped
into the muddy water to propel the vessel down-
stream. He stared at the roiling brown waves that
fanned out from the side of the boat three decks below, waiting for the steady river breeze to cool him
off. It did not.

Pierre caught up with him. "What was that all
about?" Pierre towered a couple of inches above Brett's
six and a half feet, with muscles to do a keelboatman
proud—which was the reason he had accompanied
Brett the last ten years, notwithstanding the gray in
Pierre's hair and the twenty years he had on his now
thirty-five-year-old nephew.

Brett turned to face his uncle, who filled the bill as
both companion and bodyguard. "Who the hell is
she?"

"Who? The girl with blue eyes, *non?*"

"No," Brett mocked, swiping at the shock of hair
that fell over his forehead, "the wrinkled old crone beside her. *Oui*, the woman with blue eyes. Who is she?"

Pierre shrugged, lifting his shaggy eyebrows. Brett

glared across the river to the western shore. From this distance it looked more like a horizon than a riverbank.

"She's a beauty, for truth," Pierre said at length. "Hair as brown as a beaver pelt, and lots of it from the looks of things, skin the color of fresh-skimmed cream, eyes as big and bright as cut sapphires."

He paused, then when Brett remained silent, continued. "They were tinged with melancholy, those eyes, but that didn't detract from them. Me, I thought it added to the mystery. And her lips—so full, so rosy, so—"

"She knows me."

Pierre halted his discourse, studying his nephew from beneath shaggy black eyebrows. "She could think the same about you, *nèfyou,* the way you stared at her."

Brett whirled to face his uncle. "God's bones, Pierre, listen to what I'm saying. She recognized me."

Silenced, Pierre stared hard into his nephew's black eyes. Even with the age difference, the two men could have passed for brothers. Swarthy of complexion and broad of shoulder with lean torsos reflecting their French heritage, both men had hair black as Hades, at least Pierre's had been until recently when silver streaks began to appear. Brett teased him about being long-in-the-tooth.

"Never you min', *tonc,*" he would tell his uncle in their common Acadian dialect, "you might look like a long-in-the-tooth panther, *oui,* but you know what they say about ol' panthers. They lose their get-up but never their come-along."

Pierre's eyes widened now at his nephew's claim that the woman had recognized him. "Me, I have never seen that beauty before."

"When did she come aboard?"

"At St. Louis," a third man responded.

The two men started at the voice, then settled down when Gabriel, the third member of their trio, sidled up beside them. A short, wiry man nearing mid-thirty, Gabriel carried his fiddle and bow clasped one in each fist. "Ah, *non*, that is one woman you couldn't miss in a bayou fog."

"Is she alone?" Brett demanded.

Gabriel turned his back to his friends at the rail, greeting this person and that, as the passengers began to leave the dining room. He fiddled a few strains of "Arkansas Traveler" while supplying details surreptitiously over his shoulder concerning Delta's arrival on the *Mississippi Princess* accompanied by the Myricks. "She and the ol' lady were all that remained as travelers," he finished.

"She recognized you, *certainement?*" Pierre quizzed.

Brett inhaled a lungful of river-scented air, then exhaled slowly. "No," he replied at last. "No, I'm not certain of it. But she had that look in her eyes—like when you see someone you know but their name slips your mind."

Gabriel raised his bow and played a few bars of "Go, Forget Me, Why Should Sorrow o'er That Brow a Shadow Fling."

"Maybe you take the wrong message, *mòn ami,*" he told his friend. "Maybe she wasn't thinkin', 'I know this man,' but 'I want to know him.' "

"Maybe it was those blue eyes that raised your hackles," Pierre suggested.

"*Oui,*" Brett agreed. "Blue-eyed women have a way of doing that."

Pierre frowned. "I'll ask around."

"No, that would only draw attention." Brett glanced from one man to the other. "Keep your eyes and ears open. Both of you. We'll rendezvous at the usual place around midnight."

Gabriel strolled off down the deck, entertaining the passengers with another lively tune as Captain Kaney had hired him to do, and Pierre turned toward the stairwell. "Want to fortify yourself with a whiskey before your game with the little old ladies?"

Brett declined. "Go ahead. I need some air."

Pierre slapped him on the shoulder. "Don't worry, *nèfyou.* It is clever, your disguise. An' ten years is a long time. No one is expecting you to return by now. Much less would they look for you on a showboat, playing cards with ol' ladies in the afternoon and high-stakes poker with their husbands at night."

After Pierre left, Brett leaned folded arms against the rail and tried to clear his mind of the unwanted image of those clear, blue eyes. Those melancholy blue eyes.

Pierre was right about his disguise as a gambler; it was a good one. But the self-restraint required to carry it off was becoming a chore. He was tired of little old ladies and rich old men. He was tired of expecting danger to leap at him from around every corner of this damned boat.

Oui, it had been a clever idea, but was it a sane one? After ten years in exile was he so homesick he would risk any danger, even the loss of his life, to return to the bayous of Louisiana?

Was it homesickness that drew him back? Or was it a pair of blue eyes that danced in his dreams to the beat of a Voodoo drum?

The decision to return home had been the easy part. Once made, he had been faced with the logistics of such a journey. Traveling horseback through the country would be certain to arouse suspicions, Pierre had

31

argued. They all three agreed that the rails were out of the question with the Pinkertons in operation.

Then he heard about Kaney's new showboat and his trip to Louisiana to participate in the procession to honor the opening of South Pass. It had seemed a perfect solution. The older, wealthier passengers on such a voyage would be unlikely to suspect a fellow traveler of being a fugitive, and at every stop he would have the opportunity to check his waystations. With over a third of the trip elapsed, he had finally become hopeful of its success.

At least he had been hopeful until today at noon when a pair of melancholy blue eyes threatened to topple his carefully laid plans.

He shuddered recalling them. Recalling, too, the dream that had haunted him for six long months. A dream of blue eyes.

That dream had called him home. Until then he hadn't allowed himself to think about returning to the bayou—except perhaps of a cold winter's night. The winters in Canada had been rough. He knew he would never get used to the cold. But all in all, trapping was trapping, whether in the frozen north country or in the steamy swamps of his homeland.

He probed it now, that dream of blue eyes. But it wasn't any clearer in the harsh light of day than in the shadows of the night. Blue eyes and a misty woman of undetermined age and description.

The only conclusion he had been able to draw was that the blue eyes belonged to his mother. Again the blue eyes of the woman in the dining room sparkled before him. *Oui, Maman's* eyes had once sparkled with that same trace of melancholy. But not the day he left her alone in the bayou. They had been dark with fear and sadness that day. Were they still?

Was she still alive, his *maman?* That question had preyed on his mind. That question was pulling him home. The blue eyes of the woman in the dining room danced in his vision. Her eyes and her face. Pierre had been right about the woman's beauty. Her beauty had held him spellbound for a time, her creamy complexion, her full lips that practically issued an engraved invitation to a man to kiss them. But it was her eyes that had captured his attention.

He gripped the rail with both fists. God's bones! He must watch his step, else his attention would not be all that was captured.

Leaving the dining hall Delta hurried to her cabin to fetch a notepad and freshen up for her interview with the cast of the Princess Players. The stranger's arrogance, followed by his angry departure from the dining room, pursued her like an angry cur nipping at her heels as she pressed along the crowded passageway.

Except he was no stranger, she thought for the dozenth time. Not to her. She knew him from somewhere. But where? By the time she reached her stateroom, foreboding, as heavy as a river fog on a spring morn, had settled over her.

Mama Rachael had stayed behind in the dining room, accepting Lottie's and Dora's invitation to tour the boat.

"Meet us in the cabin lounge at three," Dora Menefee had instructed, after Delta excused herself from the dining table. "We have tea and play poker there every afternoon."

"I'll try, Mrs. Menefee," Delta had replied, watching Mama Rachael nearly burst her stays with excitement, "but my interview may not be finished in time."

She felt a sudden need to caution Mama Rachael to watch her money and not get carried away with her betting, but she didn't know how to do so graciously in front of strangers, so she resisted.

Arriving at her stateroom, she let herself in, closed the door behind her, and stood a moment, taking in the room afresh. With the trunks removed, there was definitely more space, and after Mama Rachael left the boat at Memphis, Delta would have all the space to herself. Perhaps it wouldn't be so bad.

But the beds were awfully close, she thought suddenly, and Memphis was several nights away. What if she cried out in her sleep? She would wake Mama Rachael and be required to explain her dreams and—

Delta sighed. She and Ginny had gone over this same thing several times. Mama Rachael was a heavy sleeper, Ginny had insisted. Wasn't it like raising the dead to awaken the woman when on occasion her snoring became intolerable?

That was true, Delta had always countered, but—

"Just wait and see," Ginny had predicted. "Mama Rachael's snoring will probably keep you awake every night. By the time you arrive in Memphis, you'll likely be so eager for a good night's sleep, you'll welcome a nightmare or two."

On a cold day in hell, Delta thought now, recalling her reply to Ginny as she opened the door to her chiffonier intending to repin her windblown hair. She gasped. For instead of her own reflection in the looking glass, the countenance of the stranger glared ominously back at her.

Slamming the door on the mocking image, she tried to laugh at such foolishness, but the sound quivered from her throat. How had the image come so quickly to mind—so clearly—when she had been thinking of something else?

Her heart pounded against her chest. The stateroom became stifling. Inhaling deep gulps of air, she fought to still her racing mind. But the image had appeared so suddenly she began to wonder whether she had any control over her own brain. That, she told herself, was foolishness.

Fiercely she threw open the chiffonier again, this time in defiance of her lack of will power. Perhaps she couldn't control her dreams, but she could certainly control her brain while awake. She glared at her own reflection. No arrogant stranger was going to ruin her daytime hours.

The experience added to her anxieties, however, and she soon became desperate to escape the confining stateroom. With studied deliberation she concentrated on preparations for her upcoming interview.

Recalling Hollis's instructions that an interviewer should never present herself as a threat to her subjects, she removed her hat and carefully stuck the pearl-headed pin in her pincushion, then rearranged her hair in a more casual style, catching her long curls with a claret bow at her nape.

Surveying all she could see of herself in the small looking glass, she decided to removed her suit jacket as well. A simple skirt and waist, she reasoned, would be less formal for an afternoon aboard ship than a suit, although her waist was far from simple. Mama Rachael had outdone herself on Delta's wardrobe. The entire bodice of her white waist was constructed of tiny diagonal tucks, interspersed with bands of the same cotton lace that trimmed the high collar and broad cuffs.

She tugged on her corset, pulled down the tail of her

waist, and smoothed her skirt over her hips. Without warning her attention returned to that despicable stranger. He had been elegantly attired.

She scowled at her reflection, tying her claret sash with such a jerk her breath caught. Even dressed like a gentleman, she countered, the man's rough exterior had been evident.

She thought of her brothers, rough and tough to the man of them. Yet they were compassionate and gentle inside. She had detected no such redeeming qualities in the stranger in the dining room. He had stared at her with a hard, almost cruel intensity.

Why she hadn't felt instantly threatened by such a man, she couldn't fathom. Whatever the reason for his physical similarity to someone she knew, this was assuredly a man a lady should regard from afar. His quick flash of anger proved his volatile nature.

But her persistent brain refused to listen to reason. Leaving her parasol behind, she took up her tapestry portfolio with notebook and pencils inside and retraced her steps to the observation deck. On the way, her mind replayed the drama at lunch, going over every feature of the stranger's face. Perhaps if she could place him in her memory, she could then erase him from her mind. Since she had seen very little of the world— Silver Creek, Texas, and St. Louis and points in between—the task shouldn't be difficult. She knew he wasn't from Silver Creek. So he must be someone she had met at the *Sun* office. Perhaps an acquaintance of Hollis's.

She sighed. Perhaps he merely resembled someone she had known before.

The angry manner in which he had stomped out of the dining room still confounded her. It was as if he had been angry with her, but what had she—?

Her feet came to a halt. Could he have taken offense at the bold manner in which she had perused him? Could it be? She blushed to think so, but, however embarrassing, the idea began to ease her foreboding—a fact that only proved Ginny's theory that once a reason was found for something, the solution would follow.

She would steer clear of this stranger. That should be simple enough. And it would solve the problem, especially if he had been put off by her unseemly, but definitely unintentional scrutiny.

Nevertheless, she mused, he had been staring at her first—

"There you are, Miss Jarrett." Captain Kaney stopped her on the observation deck outside the dining room. "On your way to rehearsal?"

Delta came to an abrupt halt in front of the captain, but her attention focused on the man at his side, while her stomach turned a somersault. "Yes, sir," she mumbled, managing to smile, albeit feebly, at the stranger from lunch before she tore her eyes away.

Her brief glance, however, had been enough to determine that up close his gaze was even more intense. Not as cold and hard as she had thought, but piercing, searching. And his eyes were black.

Eager to move away, she turned to go. "Excuse me, I'm late."

The captain called her back. "Let me introduce you two, since you'll both be guests at my table this evening."

Delta felt her knees go weak. Given no choice, she complied with the captain's suggestion, again making a tenuous attempt to smile. This time, however, she avoided the stranger's eyes, focusing somewhere near his chest. Inanely she calculated its size, which must surely match her brothers' chests, in breadth.

"Miss Delta Jarrett from St. Louis," the captain enunciated each word in a tone befitting the most proper drawing room, "may I introduce M'sieur Brett Reall of Canada."

Canada? She hesitated, belatedly extending her hand. Only then did she realize she had failed to replace her gloves after combing her hair. How stupid, she admonished, feeling weakness grow like warm yeast inside her stomach. She never forgot things like gloves and—

His hand was large and callused and very warm. Hers felt hopelessly damp and small—and it trembled.

She chanced a glance at him.

"Mademoiselle." His voice was rich, his French accent melodious, yet his greeting was uttered without a trace of warmth.

"Mr. Reall," she quipped, quickly withdrawing her hand. "Please, excuse me." She turned to the captain. "Rehearsal is sure to have begun without me."

"The room should be ready by now," Captain Kaney acknowledged, his final words fading in her ears as she fled through the double doors that led to the grand dining room.

Except it was no longer a dining room. The fixtures were the same—swinging chandeliers, ornate arches and moldings—but the dining tables had been undressed and separated into numerous small tables with four gilded bamboo chairs to each. Already a few passengers sat at the rear of the room sipping drinks and gossiping.

At the far end of the hall the captain's table had also been removed from sight. The dais now obviously served as a stage. Sounds of allocutions and instruments warming up drifted her way.

But she had trouble concentrating on them.

The stranger had a name now. Brett Reall. Who was he, this Brett Reall? Her hand still throbbed from his touch. His deep voice reverberated in her brain like soft music.

But his eyes stared, fixed and cold. Somehow he didn't seem alive, made of flesh and blood. But for the warmth of his hand she would have thought him a mannequin like the ones found in Mrs. Doppleheimer's Dress Shoppe.

Her brain still reeled from the encounter, when an attractive redheaded woman not ten years older than Delta herself jumped from the low stage and strode down the aisle, hand extended in greeting.

"Hi, I'm Zanna. Actually, my name is Suzanna, but everyone calls me Zanna. You must be Delta, the journalist."

"Yes." Delta took Zanna's offered hand. She perused the artistic director's personal style, which could be described as creative, at best. Straight red hair swept loosely back from her round face formed a bun at her nape, from which numerous wisps escaped here and there. Her white waist and purple faille skirt were commonplace and could have been found on a woman from almost any walk of life, but the yellow fringed stole tied about Zanna's hips gave her costume a flair all its own, and the double strand of red glass beads added to her gypsy image.

One end of the stole came perilously close to dragging the floor, and one corner of her collar was turned under. In all, she looked harried, as though she were pressed for time and had not had a chance to check the looking glass.

"I hope I'm not interrupting rehearsal," Delta said.

At that, Zanna lifted her palms toward the ornate ceiling then dropped them to her sides in an expression of resignation. "What rehearsal?" She started walking toward the stage and Delta followed. "Look at that. Does that resemble anything halfway organized?"

Delta studied the assortment of actors and musicians assembled on and around the stage, which stood open with heavy draperies pushed to the far walls on each side. It fairly bustled with activity. As Zanna had suggested, however, each of the half dozen actors appeared to be engaged in a different performance.

And the musicians, as well, she noticed. From the orchestra's position to the right of the stage, a trumpet blasted intermittent notes, while a trombone ran the scales, and a drummer appeared to be lost in his own world.

On stage a beautiful young woman with a round face and cherublike body sang to the near-empty salon. Blond hair fell in unrestrained ringlets around her innocent face. A pale blue ribbon was tied around her head, the bow just off center, matching her lovely lawn gown. Tears streamed down the young woman's face, but she paid them no heed. Her voice, as it drifted in and out among the other havoc coming from the stage, was lyrical.

"What is that she's singing?" Delta asked Zanna.

" 'The Fatal Rose of Red,' " Zanna responded.

A man and woman stood a few feet behind the petite songstress, squared off as if in battle.

"No, no, no," the woman was saying. "I said position three, Explosion, not position two. That's Gentle Animation."

The man dropped his hands, immediately drawing criticism from his coach.

"Extend your arms," the woman encouraged. "Fully. Fully."

The man complied.

"Step forward on your right foot."

Again the man complied, his mouth twisted in an expression of disgust.

"Drop to your left knee," the woman instructed.

The man knelt, but in doing so, he dropped his hands.

"No, no, no," the woman wailed, at which the man jumped to his feet and stomped off the stage.

"What are they doing?" Delta asked Zanna.

"That's Iona and her husband Frankie," the artistic director explained. "Iona is forever pressing the positions of elocution on the cast. As you can see Frankie doesn't take well to her instructions."

Nearer the front of the stage, opposite the tearful songstress, a tall dark-headed gentleman faced another portion of the empty salon, but instead of singing, he was declaiming:

> It was the schooner *Hesperus*,
>   That sailed the wintry sea;
> And the skipper had taken his little daughter,
>   To bear him company.

Zanna sighed audibly. "When I told Albert to prepare something from Longfellow," she observed, "I intended him to choose a passage from *Evangeline*. Don't you agree *Evangeline* would be appropriate since we're on our way to the bayous of Louisiana?"

Delta laughed. "Definitely more appropriate than a poem about a shipwreck."

Zanna looked suddenly wary. "Don't get the wrong

idea. It isn't as bad as it looks. We're in the process of changing our production to fit Southern audiences.''

At Delta's curious expression, Zanna explained. "Since the war, some topics must be avoided. For example, we're replacing our treatise on government, with a monologue Albert calls, 'Superstitions of Aboriginal People of the American West.'

Suddenly a young man emerged from behind a stack of tables, jumped off the stage, and headed down the aisle toward them.

"I'm quitting if you don't find a way to cut off that water pump," he stormed. "I refuse to play a love scene opposite a bawling woman."

Delta stared at the almost-too-handsome actor who looked near her own age. His light hair glistened with hair oil; not a stand was out of place. His shirt was fresh, his trousers creased, and his necktie neatly tied. His hazel eyes, set beneath heavy, symmetrically arched brows, focused exclusively on Zanna.

"I'll speak to Elyse, Nat," Zanna assured him. "Here, meet Delta Jarrett. She's the journalist Captain Kaney told us about."

Nat turned to Delta with a terse, "How do you do." Instantly his eyes widened, his manner eased, and his tone changed from one of dismissal to definite appreciation. "A pleasure I'm sure, Miss Jarrett." He offered his arm, which she took after a questioning glance to Zanna.

"Nathan Thomas, our leading man," Zanna said, by way of introduction trailing the two of them down the aisle to the front of the salon.

"Please don't misunderstand, Miss Jarrett," Nat explained, staring at Delta with such a suggestive leer she had trouble keeping a straight face. "It isn't my

42

technique that causes Elyse to cry during the love scene.''

Delta laughed. Although, as a rule, conceited men bored her, something about Nat was refreshing. With his boyish good looks and wry smile he looked more like a little boy playing dress-up than like a man out to seduce a woman.

''May I quote you?'' she asked.

He waggled his eyebrows. ''You needn't take my word. I'll be happy to furnish you with all the research you need.''

''Nat,'' Zanna broke in. ''Get on stage, so we can run through the melodrama. You may feel like sowing wild oats, but my feet hurt.''

Nat shrugged good-naturedly, waggling his perfect eyebrows at Delta, ''Later?''

She grinned, noncommittal, and tried to listen while Zanna introduced the rest of the cast.

''Frankie and Iona,'' she indicated the two at the rear who had ceased their arguing, but obviously had not resolved the dispute. ''Don't worry about their spats,'' Zanna whispered. ''They have at least three a day, on good days. Iona got the upper hand this time, but their arguments are usually over whether Iona will perform a double flip. Frankie usually wins, even though Iona hates to do them.''

''They're acrobats?'' Delta asked.

''Dancers, but we try to liven up the production whenever possible. We all double around here.'' She nodded toward the songstress, who by now had finished her song, or given up, Delta suspected, and was fussing with the bow at her waist. ''That's Elyse, our leading lady.''

''She looks awfully young.''

''Sixteen. That's about average. Audiences like the

43

innocent nature of younger girls, but of course it's harder on me. I end up playing mother.''

"Why was she crying?''

"Who knows?'' Zanna turned palms toward the ceiling. "Nat was right. She cries at the drop of a pin. But she has the sweetest voice this side of heaven. Men love her, and women aren't threatened by her. She's perfect for the family-oriented shows Captain Kaney wants.''

The middle-aged man who had been declaiming when Delta entered the salon, came forward. Bowing over the edge of the stage, he greeted Delta with, "And I, Miss Jarrett, am Albert Renier, the villain.''

"Don't let him fool you,'' Zanna warned. "He's really a pussycat.''

Delighted, Delta shook his hand, laughing at the obvious truth in Zanna's comment. For a villain the man had the loveliest black eyes, soft and kind. Unlike those other black eyes—

"Never fear, Miss Jarrett,'' Albert assured her. "When I comb my hair into a V over my forehead and feathered my brows upwards, I can frighten the bloomers off the most innocent ingénue.'' Speaking, he raked his hair forward with long fingers, narrowed his eyes, and elicited another laugh from Delta.

"You can take notes while we rehearse,'' Zanna suggested, before calling the cast to attention. "Afterwards we'll answer your questions.''

Seated at a table on the front row, Delta tried to concentrate on the melodrama unfolding before her. From the little she had learned so far, the cast of the Princess Players could furnish enough material for articles for the entire journey.

Why did Elyse cry so much? Why was Nat stuck on himself? Why did Frankie and Iona fight three times a day? Why was the villain softhearted, and did it have anything to do with the artistic director?

Yes, Delta mused, the Princess Players would make interesting subjects, even before she examined their acting credits.

After Zanna walked the actors through their steps, she returned to sit beside Delta.

"Our little drama is called *The Saga of Judge Noah Peale,*" she explained. "We considered performing one of the original showboat dramas, such as *The Drunkard* or *The Lying Valet,* but decided to try something related to the West. Maybe something fresh will take folks' minds off the aftermath of the war. Our first performance will be tomorrow at Cape Girardeau."

A few moments later Zanna turned to Delta, a tentative expression on her face. "Are you an artist?"

"I draw a little, but—"

Zanna's smile lit up her face. "I knew the gods were smiling on us the moment I saw your lovely face."

"I'm not an artist, Zanna."

But Zanna would hear none of it. The moment the cast completed a second run-through of *The Saga of Judge Noah Peale,* Zanna dragged Delta backstage where she announced, "Our new set designer."

"Set designer?" Delta gasped.

"Don't worry, all we need is a Western barroom."

Delta surveyed the elegant salon. "Captain Kaney might be able to convert this room from a dining room to a grand salon, but I certainly can't turn it into a Western barroom. Look at all this finery."

"You can do it," Zanna exclaimed. "We'll help."

"You expect me to build a set for a Western barroom?" Delta felt sure she must have lost the essence of the conversation somewhere along the way.

"No, of course not," Zanna corrected. "You design it. We'll all build it."

"Design it?" Delta echoed. "Me?"

Three hours later Delta had to admit, their creation bore some resemblance to a barroom, its crudely constructed bar made from a dining table covered with canvas. Albert offered to paint the canvas to look like planks.

Delta agreed, then added, "We'll need some barstools." She nodded pointedly toward the elegant bamboo dining chairs. "And don't tell me those will do."

Zanna laughed.

"I know." Nat spoke from near Delta's elbow, where he had worked all afternoon. "We'll fetch some kegs from the boiler room."

"Great idea," Delta exclaimed.

Nat reached for her hand. "Come with me. We'll find the captain. He'll tell us who to ask."

She slipped her hand out of Nat's grasp. Across the set she watched Elyse's eyes dim. The girl might cry at the prospect of playing opposite Nat in a love scene on stage, but watching her the last few hours, Delta had decided the girl's problem more likely stemmed from fear of revealing her true feelings in front of a room full of strangers. Elyse reminded Delta of a shy little bird, never speaking, but keeping a keen eye on everyone who came in contact with Nat. If he hadn't been so enamored with himself, Delta reasoned, Nat could have seen the truth.

"No, Nat," Zanna was saying. "Delta isn't here to run errands. You go ask the captain."

"I'll go with him," Albert offered. "We'll get the paint at the same time."

"Will you put the barroom on the playbills?" Iona asked Delta after Nat and Albert left. Along with the rest of the cast, she and Frankie had pitched in to help

46

construct the set without squabbling one time the entire afternoon.

"Am I what?" Delta questioned the dancer.

Zanna blanched. "Oops! I forgot to tell—ah, to ask her." She turned to Delta. "Since you're so good with words—I mean, obviously you're good with words since you're a journalist—I thought . . . ah, we thought you might consent to design the layout for our playbills."

"But I've never—"

"I mean, since you're doing other promotion for the showboat."

"I'm not doing other promotion, Zanna. My articles are—" She stopped short of admitting that the articles were nothing more than busywork intended to take her mind off a worrisome nightmare. Designing sets and playbills should serve the same purpose. Besides, what else did she have to do with her time? "I'll try," she agreed. "But I'll need your help."

The new job worked into the scheme of things quite well, she decided, for by the time Albert and Nat returned with paint and a couple of empty kegs to serve as barstools, she had sketched the playbill and she and Zanna were busy with the wording.

"Here, try it out for size," Nat suggested, offering her a seat on one of the kegs. The moment she sat on the keg, he took the other one, pulling it close beside her.

Delta jumped to her feet. Without giving anyone time to object she took Elyse by the shoulders and guided her onto the keg she had just vacated. "You two rehearse your lines while Zanna and I finish the playbills."

While Frankie and Albert painted the canvas bar, Delta and Zanna finished the playbill design, with Iona, Elyse, and Nat looking on.

Finally Elyse consulted the little gold watch pinned

to her bodice. "Oh, dear, we'd best hurry, else we won't have time to dress for dinner."

Although the words were so softly spoken that Delta wondered whether anyone had heard, the cast immediately prepared to leave.

"Captain Kaney insists we dress for dinner," Zanna explained.

"I should hope so," Delta replied, "in a room as elegant as this one." Following the actors from the salon, she finally summoned enough courage to ask the question she had worried over all afternoon. "What do you know about a man named Brett Reall?"

Zanna rolled her eyes. "I know he's one of the most handsome men I've ever met." As if to demonstrate, she clasped her hands together and pressed them to her heart.

"And dangerous," Nat added.

"Dangerous?" Delta quizzed.

"I didn't mean to frighten you," he added. "You're perfectly safe—with me on board."

"You're safe, anyway," Albert told her. "Other than attending meals and engaging in poker games, M'sieur Reall has not mingled with the passengers."

Nat's words spun in Delta's brain. "Why do you say he's dangerous?" She held her breath for his reply, but Albert spoke first.

Leaning his face close to hers, he quirked his eyebrows. A teasing grin tipped the corners of his lips, forming a half-moon over his goatee. "Some call him a pirate," he announced in a stage whisper.

Delta's heart skipped a beat.

Nat took her arm. "Don't worry your pretty head over that fellow. I'll protect you from him."

Chapter Three

Brett dressed for dinner with special care. Since discovering that Delta was a member of the theatrical troupe, he had relaxed. That explained everything. She looked familiar because he had seen her perform somewhere. It had nothing to do with her blue eyes.

It had everything to do with blue eyes, his conscience needled. But not *her* blue eyes. She just happened to have blue eyes—blue eyes that reminded him of other blue eyes.

Oui, Pierre had been right. Those blue eyes had raised his hackles. For too long now, he had been hunted by authorities and haunted by memories—memories of blue eyes.

He inserted black onyx cuff links into the cuffs of his white shirt, then added a starched wing collar. *Delta Jarrett*. The name played in his mind. Perhaps this lovely blue-eyed woman would provide the chance he needed to rid himself of those memories.

A knock came at the door just as he stepped into his black trousers. At Pierre's call, he unlocked the door from the inside, then proceeded to attach his suspenders.

Pierre bowed to his nephew in mock deference. "Ah, *nèfyou,* what have we here? Evening clothes."

Brett turned back to his toilette while Pierre poured them each a whiskey. "I'm dining at the captain's table," he explained. "Besides, those gaudy vests are getting to me."

Pierre handed Brett a glass of whiskey, downing his own in a couple of gulps. "The pilot, he says we should arrive at Cape Girardeau by ten o'clock tomorrow mornin'. Gabriel will go ashore to check things out. We'll wait here for his signal."

Slipping into a white silk vest, Brett buttoned it, then took a swig of the whiskey. "Take care when you speak with Gabriel," he told Pierre. "He'll make a better sentry if no one suspects he's with us."

"Oui," Pierre agreed.

"We'll need horses," Brett continued. "Cape Rock is several miles out of town."

"You should let me make the inspection, *nèfyou.* You stay on the boat, away from eyes tha' could recognize you."

Brett shook his head. "Gabriel is a good man. He can sniff out authorities like a dog on the trail of a wounded panther." He tied his black silk necktie and gave himself a once-over in the small looking glass, smoothing back unruly hair, before shrugging into a black evening jacket. "I want to meet with our men personally, discuss with them face to face where we're going to take this business when we return from the bayou."

At the door Brett clapped Pierre on the shoulder. "After dinner I must sit in on that private poker game the captain has arranged. I will see you tonight at our rendezvous."

"Fortunate, your *maman* raised a gambling man, *oui.*"

Brett grinned. *"Oui."*

Pierre stopped him. "You are still concerned about that blue-eyed *pichouette, mon nèfyou?*"

"She's no little girl, Pierre, or are you going blind? And no, I am no longer concerned. The captain introduced us this afternoon. Her name is Delta Jarrett. She's with the acting troupe. An actress. We must have seen her perform somewhere."

Pierre grinned. "Perhaps we will again, my nephew."

Some call him a pirate.

The words had echoed through Delta's brain while she hastily dressed for dinner, closing out even Mama Rachael's enthusiastic recital of her own afternoon's experiences.

Orville had returned their pressed gowns by the time Delta returned to the stateroom from rehearsal. Mama Rachael was almost ready to leave.

"Hurry, child. We can't tarry in this room when there is so much going on outside."

Delta stripped to her corset and pantaloons. "Tell me about your afternoon," she suggested. Filling the small bowl with water, she added a splash of violet-scented cologne and began to sponge off.

Mama Rachael giggled, drawing an inquisitive frown from Delta.

"We toured the ship," the excited little woman said.

"All five decks?" Delta removed her stockings, bathed her legs, then pulled on a fresh pair of stockings. Without removing her corset, she replaced her full gathered petticoat with a foulard that had a straight paneled front and rows of ruffles down the back. Over this she slipped a blue faille gown with fitted princess basque and deep square neckline. An inserted tablier of cream faille draped loosely around her hips and fell in a new shorter quarter-train. Mama Rachael had spent an entire week embroidering poppy leaves around the neckline and along the edges of the train.

"Just the promenade and observation decks," the little woman admitted.

Offering her back, Delta squeezed the sides of her gown together while Mama Rachael fumbled with the hooks.

"We visited the pilot house, and Mr. Sandee, he's the *cal*liope player, he promised to let us watch him play that contraption when we approach Cape Girardeau tomorrow."

"The word is pronounced cal-*li*-ope," Delta corrected. "It's Greek, meaning beautiful-voiced."

Turning Delta around, Mama Rachael fluffed the red poppies she had made from tulle to fill in the decolletage of Delta's gown. "That's what the captain said," she agreed. "But river people pronounce the word *cal*-li-op-e. Else they say steam piano."

Delta eyed Mama Rachael more closely. The feather on her black bonnet tipped precariously over one eye. The bow holding the box-pleated frill of black satin around her neck was partially untied. Face to face now, Delta smelled the unmistakable scent of alcohol.

"Mama Rachael, what have you been drinking?"

"Tea. With a splash of brandy."

"A splash? You're tipsy!"

"No, child, 'twas only a ti' drink. Way out here in the middle of the river with no one to tell on us, what harm can come from having a ti' drink with our ti' game of poker?"

Delta recalled Lottie Humphries expressing the same sentiment at lunch. "How many did you have? And how much money did you lose?"

"Me? Lose at poker? Why, child, I can beat the pants off any one of those rowdy brothers of yours. Do you think I'd let family pride down on this fancy showboat?"

"That's just it," Delta objected. "We're not at home. Playing for matchsticks around the kitchen table is a far cry from playing poker with strangers. How much did you lose?"

Mama Rachael pursed her lips, but finally replied, "I won this." Speaking, she dug into her reticule and produced a ten-dollar gold piece.

Delta's eyes widened.

Mama Rachael's eyes mimicked them. "You wouldn't tell Hollis, would you?"

At length Delta smiled. "Of course not. But you must be careful. We don't know anyone on board." She recalled Nat's claim that Brett Reall was dangerous. "You must take care. We could be overrun with rascals and rogues just waiting to take your money."

"Nonsense," Mama Rachael replied. "You shouldn't look on the dark side of everything. What's wrong with having a ti' drink with our little game? At home I often have a toddy before bedtime."

"I know. But we're not at home," Delta repeated. Straightening the plume on Mama Rachael's hat, she retied the frill. "Let's go to dinner."

On the way Delta considered their conversation. "You're picking up the language of the river fast. What does ti' mean?"

Mama Rachael smiled, so happy with herself that Delta felt her own spirits rise a bit. "That nice gentleman calls things *ti,* " Mama Rachael explained. "A ti' drink, a ti' game. It means small, petite, I believe he said.''

"What nice gentleman?"

"Why the gambler who played poker with us—M'sieur Reall.''

Delta felt the deck pitch beneath her feet. Had the *Mississippi Princess* hit a snag? Surely that must be it, she admonished herself. Why should one more piece of dastardly information about the horrid Brett Reall matter? "M'sieur Reall is a gambler?''

Mama Rachael rolled her little brown eyes. "And such a nice gentleman.''

Upon entering the dining room, which was quickly filling up with people, the first glimpse Delta caught of Brett Reall belied his occupation as a gambler. His appearance fit Mama Rachael's description to a T—a nice man, a handsome man, one who at the moment looked a trifle uncomfortable standing beside Zanna at the captain's table at the far end of the room.

Well, he should look uncomfortable, she retorted to herself, with all the things being said about him.

Delta quickly drew her attention to the room itself, which glittered beneath the lights of the dozen chandeliers. The tables had been reset for twelve diners each, except for three or four smaller tables for two tucked into the corners of the room. Fresh white cloths were centered with brass candlesticks and brass vases held fresh-cut flowers.

"There you are,'' Captain Kaney greeted them. Offering an arm to each, his smile lingered on Mama Rachael. "Come with me. I'll introduce you.''

With Mama Rachael twittering beside him, the captain escorted them down the long aisle to his table. A rush of self-consciousness suddenly washed over Delta. Only with effort was she able to keep her eyes from straying to Brett again.

Instead she concentrated on the cast of the Princess Players who milled around, talking, waiting for the captain to arrive before taking their places.

While Captain Kaney introduced Mama Rachael to the cast, beginning with Zanna and continuing around the gathering, Delta made her way to the opposite end of the table.

Nat suddenly appeared at her side, pulling out a chair with a dramatic sweep of the hand. "Allow me."

This was not what she wanted, Delta thought. Glancing about, she noticed place cards at each setting. The card where Nat tried to seat her read "Elyse."

Nat reached for the card. "I'll exchange—"

"No." Searching for Elyse, Delta found the shy ingénue standing directly behind her, where she was sure to have heard Nat's suggestion. "This is your place, Elyse. I'll find mine."

"Here, young lady," the captain called.

She turned toward him, only to discover that Mama Rachael had already been seated and was leaning across the empty chair the captain held, obviously for Delta, talking to the person who sat on the other side.

Brett Reall. Delta's stomach fluttered at the thought of sitting beside him.

"Mademoiselle." Brett rose in perfect imitation of a gentleman while the captain seated her. It must be imitation, she insisted to herself, feeling him settle back in his own chair. Gamblers were perfidious heathens. Gamblers were not gentlemen.

But when she allowed herself a brief glance at his face, thinking to look quickly away, she was further confused. Instead of reestablishing the man as a rogue, that one glance revealed a perceptible change in his expression.

The captain took his seat on the opposite side of Mama Rachael, and a waiter came to Delta's rescue, moving between herself and Brett to serve the first course.

She studied her tureen of bouillon with earnestness, while around her the diners began to chatter. She could hear Mama Rachael's voice, still prattling, although she could not distinguish the words.

She heard Zanna's animated chatter and concentrated on her soup, trying to close out the words. Inexplicably she feared being drawn into conversation with the man beside her. She heard her name mentioned, heard Zanna mention her appointment as set designer. The waiter removed her soup tureen.

"A set designer? I had you pegged as a songstress."

It took Delta a moment to realize Brett had spoken to her. Without fully intending to, she looked up. Their eyes held. His were warm. What had happened to the coldness she had seen earlier?

She struggled to summon a measure of civility. The best she could manage was a weak shake of the head. Why had her wits suddenly turned to mush?

"I'm disappointed," Brett commented. "I thought perhaps we would hear you warble a tear-jerking ballad tonight."

She smiled at the ludicrous suggestion. "I don't sing."

"Never?"

She thought of the family gatherings where everyone joined in singing old ballads and hymns. "Never around strangers."

At the word their eyes clashed again. Something

about him was so familiar the word "stranger" sounded foreign.

"Delta Jarrett," he mused without breaking eye contact. "Where have we met before?"

The room buzzed around her like a hive full of bees. "I wondered that, too," she confessed. "I don't know where it could have been, except—"

"M'sieur Reall," Mama Rachael interrupted, leaning across Delta to speak. "The captain said perhaps we could have a ti' game in the morning after the ship docks at Cape Girardeau."

Delta watched Brett hesitate before he replied. "Why, madame, do you intend to stay aboard while we're in port?"

"They say there isn't much to see at Cape Girardeau anymore," she replied. "I thought perhaps a little game might be more lively."

His eyes danced, and after a moment, his lips followed suit. Delta felt a rush of heat in her belly just watching him smile.

"Then by all means," Brett replied, "we shall have a ti' game after I return from shore."

The waiter moved between them, placing a plate of fried catfish before Delta, then one before Brett.

Although her desire for food had vanished, she began to eat.

"When we get further south," Brett said, "the chef will likely prepare filé gumbo."

She glanced at him between bites. His eyes were not only warm now, they glowed with geniality.

"Have you ever eaten filé gumbo, m'moiselle?"

"No," she responded.

"It's spicy." Brett raised an eyebrow. "Perhaps you do not like spicy things?"

The challenge in his question both confused and somehow exhilarated her.

"We ate spicy food in Texas."

"Texas? You are from Texas? I thought the captain said St. Louis."

"My brother lives in Texas—one of them."

"One?" He favored her with such a vibrant expression, she began to wonder if she had judged him too harshly. "How many brothers do you have?"

She laughed. "Six. All older than I."

He laughed with her. "I take warning, m'moiselle. You are surrounded by guardians."

"You might say I am," she agreed, thinking of the proprietary nature of not only her brothers, but her cousins, as well. "Especially against men who gamble with little old ladies and feed them liquor."

Brett grimaced, but his eyes remained warm and playful. "You wound me, m'moiselle." He glanced beyond her to Mama Rachael, then in conspiratorial tones, continued. " 'Twas only a ti' game. And believe me, your chaperon holds her own at the card table."

In spite of her misgivings concerning Mama Rachael and the gambler, Delta found herself enjoying his company. "I suppose you should have been forewarned, m'sieur. Mama Rachael has had a lot of practice. She can win the pants off any of my brothers."

Brett laughed aloud at that. "After playing with her this afternoon, I do not doubt it."

"Her words, not mine," Delta insisted, regretting her bold statement. "But she only plays around the kitchen table for matchsticks."

"Believe me, she could whip any of the gentlemen I'm engaged to entertain this evening." Brett's black eyes twinkled with mischief. "Perhaps we should team up, she and I."

"Was that the reason for the drinks this afternoon, m'sieur? To slow down her calculations? Surely, it is unnecessary to ply little old ladies with liquor."

"A ti' drink. That was all. A *petit* splash of apricot brandy in her tea. She enjoyed it, *oui?*"

"I'm aware of that, m'sieur."

Moving his lips closer to her ear, he lowered his voice. "Please, I am not out to win the pants off your chaperon, M'moiselle Jarrett. Nor to inebriate her. But I do intend to try to keep the shirt on my own back." He sat back, displaying again that mischievous grin. The whiteness of his teeth made his tawny complexion appear even darker beneath the sparkling chandeliers. "As well as other articles of my clothing."

"I regret my slip of the tongue," she admitted, speaking now to her plate, feeling her cheeks burn. But in spite of her embarrassment, when he laughed, she joined in.

Suddenly Delta found herself staring into his eyes, thinking how she had never seen eyes so black—black and oh, so familiar.

"You were saying where you thought we might have met," he said.

She nodded.

"On the stage somewhere?" he suggested.

"On the stage?"

"They say everyone doubles." He stared at her mutely, his lips curving into a confident smile. "I thought perhaps set designers might double as actors."

"I'm not a set designer."

He looked to Zanna then quickly back. "But—"

"I have no connection with the Princess Players. I only met them today. Zanna asked me to help with one set."

Brett's eyes narrowed, forming a vertical cleft between his brows. She stared at it as though mesmerized. "I admit to a bit of confusion," he was saying. "When the captain introduced us you were on your way to rehearsal."

"Oh, now I understand." She laughed. "I had an appointment to interview the cast."

"Let me enlighten you, M'sieur Reall," Captain Kaney suggested from down the table. "Miss Jarrett is writing articles relating to the *Mississippi Princess* and interesting people and things at each port-of-call to send back to the *St. Louis Sun.*"

Suddenly Delta felt as though Brett had moved his chair to the opposite end of the table, the distance between them became so great.

"You're a journalist?"

She watched all warmth drain from his eyes. His features took on the stony pallor of a marble statue, reminding her of the way his anger had risen suddenly at lunch. Looking away, he resumed his meal in silence.

Delta picked at her dessert, lemon cheesecake served with a brandy sauce. She wondered what precipitated such erratic behavior in this man. Once started, talk of her interviews took over the conversation. The cast began to throw out topics for her to investigate.

"Cape Rock," Frankie suggested. "It has a magnificent view."

"The postal service's 'Great Through Mail' originates at Cairo," Albert added. "You must look into that."

"Delta," Nat called from down the table. "What about Cave-in-Rock above Cairo? I hear there's a gang of retired outlaws holed up out there." He waggled his perfect eyebrows in a suggestive manner that made her cringe. "I'll be happy to ride out there with you."

Finally the meal was over. Captain Kaney rose to announce that a brief theatrical recital would take place as soon as the room could be converted. Brett was the first person on his feet, and to Delta's surprise he held the chair for her to rise.

Tentatively she smiled. "Thank you, m'sieur."

All she received in reply was another glimpse of that stony expression, before he strode from the dining room by the nearest exit.

He did not reappear for the recital and Delta had trouble keeping her mind on the proceedings. True to form, Elyse sang her ballad, "The Fatal Rose of Red," with tears rolling down her cheeks. Since Nat had taken the bold step to seat himself next to Delta during the performance, Delta didn't wonder. She ignored him as best she could. In fact, she felt like crying herself. She couldn't imagine why, but suddenly everything around her became dreadfully unimportant. Even Albert's recitation on the "Superstitions of Aboriginal People of the American West" failed to hold her interest.

Mercifully the evening's entertainment was short—Elyse's song, Frankie and Iona's dance number performed to the comic instrumental, "Suzanne," and Albert's recitation. Zanna ended the performance with an invitation to all on board to attend the full performance the following night on the docks at Cape Girardeau.

Delta bade good night to the Humphrieses and Menefees and followed Mama Rachael to their stateroom, where she prepared for bed, replying to her still-chirping companion with a mute nod now and again.

Mama Rachael apparently did not notice. "Good night, child," she said after she had snuggled into her berth. "Sweet dreams."

Sweet dreams? For the first time in hours Delta

thought of her nightmare. Well, she wouldn't dream of ancient lovers tonight. Quite possibly she had found a new nightmare to disturb her dreams—an ill-tempered gambler who doubled as a gentleman when the notion struck him. She closed her eyes with Brett's smiling face on her mind. It quickly turned to an icy glare.

The moon shone as a bright orange disk above the pirate ship, Kingston. *The lovers stood on the bridge, Anne's long auburn hair blowing like a sail in the gentle night breeze. Beneath the moon's glow she could see the sculptured details of Calico Jack's face. She traced his lips with her fingers, reveling in the delicious feel of his skin against her fingers, against her breast where her blouse was open to his bare chest, against her thighs where his hands roamed beneath her skirts.*

Often on a calm night when the crew had retired and the moon had begun to wane, Jack would take the wheel and Anne would join him. Often they shared tales of the day, and always they loved.

While her fingers idly trailed across his lips, as though she hadn't already memorized each line and every curve, she felt him clutch her buttocks in powerful hands. She shifted her body to accommodate him, but instead of entering her as she had thought he would, he held her hips close to his, nuzzling her until she squirmed with desire. His lips, creased in a smile, closed over hers, caressing, delving, possessing her as surely as if he had laid her on the deck and thrust himself into her body, leaving her buzzing with unfulfilled desire. Never had she known such lips. They caused a joyous song to leap to life within her heart. Then, as if from a great distance, the song was joined by the mournful cry of a babe.

* * *

Delta sat bolt upright in bed, her body flushed with heat, her heart thumping wildly. The small room was dark, the only sound that of Mama Rachael's rhythmic snoring.

The nightmare had returned. When she had been so sure it wouldn't, the nightmare had returned, but this time in a different form. She squeezed her eyes and rethought it, disquieted by the fact that the dream had changed, certain now that her ancestors were sending her a message. For months she had dreamed the same intimate dream. Why had it suddenly changed? She forced all thought from her brain, struggling to recapture the vision. But only a premonition, heavy and depressing, remained of it. A premonition that threatened to smother her in the confines of this small, dark room.

Fumbling in the darkness she found her white batiste dressing gown, threw it on, and groped her way quietly across the room so as not to awaken Mama Rachael. Once on deck, she leaned against the rail, breathing deeply, staring into the black of night, allowing the night breeze to cool the sheen of heat that glazed her body.

A few stars were out, but the moon was nowhere to be seen. She must be on the wrong side of the boat, she thought in absent fashion. The breeze began to calm her, yet inside she trembled at what the change in the dream could mean. No one, she reasoned, was plagued by dreams from the past without some meaning being attached to them.

One part of the nightmare had been the same, though. Terrifyingly the same. The cry of the babe. Someone was crying for her help. Somewhere, someone needed her. But who? And what did they need?

Gradually she became aware of voices from around

the corner toward the stern of the boat—furtive male voices that drifted toward her in waves, above the steady clop-clopping of the paddlewheel.

She grimaced. The nightmare had invaded her entire life, coloring her every experience with evil portent.

When the voices grew louder, she reluctantly left the rail, recalling the warning she had issued Mama Rachael about rascals and rogues. She would do well to heed her own advice. Belligerent male voices in the dead of night could bode no good. She had almost reached her cabin, when one of the voices rose above the rest.

"She's a newspaper woman, so steer clear of her."

The voice as much as the words stopped her in her tracks. The voice belonged to Brett Reall, she was certain of it. And he was talking about her. Creeping stealthily on bare feet, she peered around the corner.

Even though he stood with his back to her, she immediately recognized Brett, and the bottom seemed to fall out of her stomach. The two men he addressed faced directly toward her. One was the man he had dined with at lunch earlier in the day. The other looked familiar. She shivered, thinking how she'd had her fill of familiar-looking men.

Suddenly one of the men pointed her way, and in a flash she realized she had found the moon. She had crept farther around the corner than she intended and the moon shone directly on her.

In the next instant she turned to leave, but Brett Reall had been alerted. Quick as a lynx he was upon her, catching her arm and turning her roughly to face him.

"God's bones! You're spying on me."

"Spying on you?" She stared, aghast. He had removed his jacket and tie. The neck of his white shirt lay open and glistened against skin that looked nearly black by the light of the moon. "Why would I—?"

"Stalk someone in the dead of night—?" he interrupted. His eyes perused her nightclothes. Hastily he jerked her out of the direct line of moonlight in which she was illuminated. With a brief toss of his chin, he dismissed his cohorts; "Garbed for clandestine meetings?" he added. "I wonder, m'moiselle journalist? A scoop for your newspaper?"

Although his words sounded ludicrous, his tone and manner were menacing. Albert's facetious statement about the man surfaced. Some called him a—

She stared, mouth agape, at his face. His eyes studied her in earnest. His lips—

Some call him a pirate.

Her eyes traced the curve and line of his lips. *His lips—*

She felt her knees buckle. Her arms went limp. The last thing she recalled before he drew her into his arms was the pirate's lips from her dream.

Brett's lips claimed hers fully, roughly, splaying against her mouth, wet and hot. Feverishly he delved and explored, pressing her to him with rugged force. Gone was the gentleman at the captain's table, in his place an unpolished brute.

Her strength returned and she began to struggle. Still his mouth devoured her, his lips harsh. Tears stung her eyes. Behind her closed lids visions of those soft, passionate lips from her dream taunted her.

Finally it was over. Thrusting her an arm's length away, he glared down at her. Again his eyes roamed her now disheveled nightclothes. "Don't look so startled. That's what you came looking for, isn't it?"

His bitter tone added to her mortification.

Chapter Four

"Delta, get up." Mama Rachael tried to rouse her. "We must have our oatmeal porridge before the boat arrives at Cape Girardeau."

With a groan, Delta pulled the covers over her face.

"I want to watch Mr. Sandee play the *calli*—uh, the steam piano, and you have a big day on shore. Get up or we won't have time for our morning oatmeal."

Delta wriggled herself to a sitting position, stretching to bring life back to her limbs. In spite of the early hour and her befuddled brain, she smiled. "I know, Mama Rachael, Queen Victoria convinced the world that the health of Scotland derived from their habit of eating oatmeal porridge every morning."

"Laugh if you want, child, but it's true. Why, that's the way I raised Hollis, and Ginny has taken my advice all these years. Look at their children. Look at you."

Suddenly her encounter with Brett Reall returned, and along with it, her melancholy. Yes, she thought, look at me. She stumbled from bed and peered into the small looking glass on the chiffonier. Mama Rachael had lit the three lamps in the room. The one near the looking glass cast a dark shadow over half the glass. One glance at her haggard face, and Delta wished the shadow covered the entire glass, then she wouldn't be able to see the dark circles ringing her eyes.

She doubted she had slept a wink after returning to the cabin from her encounter with the despicable Brett Reall.

She dressed in the green grosgrain walking suit she had laid out the night before. Sporting a plain basque, the skirt was designed with a tablier that pleated across the hips and tied in ample back drapery above two rows of narrow vertical pleating from her knees down. The walking-length skirt ended just short of the floor, revealing a pair of black patent pumps, and allowing her to walk about town today without her hem sweeping the street.

Torn through the night between visions from her dream and lingering images of Brett's despicable behavior—his brutal lips, rough hands, cold eyes—she had finally formulated a plan she hoped would remove both from her life forever.

If, as she now believed, her ancestors were calling on her to help someone, could they not mean for her to save whoever that person might be from a man as despicable as Brett Reall?

Some call him a pirate, Albert had teased. Nat had called Brett dangerous. And they must be right. From the conversation she overheard the evening before, she knew he feared having something in his life exposed.

Yes, she had decided somewhere near daybreak after even the gentle rhythm of the moving boat had failed to lull her back to sleep, Brett Reall surely posed a danger to someone. The crying child in her dream could well represent that someone. But even if he had no connection to her nightmare, exposing him for the criminal he surely was would grant her a measure of satisfaction.

Completing her toilette, she began to organize her attack into a workable list. First she must talk to Albert and Nat. Perhaps they could guide her to others who knew things about Brett Reall, things he wanted to hide. He had accused her of spying on him, of gathering information for the newspaper. Why not do it?

Formulating a plan of action began to relieve her melancholy. She pinned the green grosgrain bonnet Mama Rachael had stiffened with crinoline on top of her head, picked up her tan-colored gloves, parasol, and portfolio containing her notebook and lead pencils. That's what she would do. She would talk to Albert and Nat. She would discover everything they knew about Brett Reall; then she would expose him in an article for the *Sun*.

The article would rid her of her nightmare, and perhaps if she worked really hard, Hollis would realize she had a talent beyond that which he expected of her: marrying one of the suitors who pestered him for her hand. She sighed. Her rough-and-ready brothers had definitely biased her against city slickers.

As a result of her decision to investigate Brett Reall, breakfast went especially well, even though she failed to see either Albert or Nat.

Afterwards she and Mama Rachael, along with Dora Menefee and Lottie Humphries, followed Captain Kaney to the sun deck—called the Texas or hurricane deck in the old days, the captain told them—to watch Mr. Sandee play the steam piano.

"Stand back," Captain Kaney cautioned. "Can't have you ladies getting scalded."

Even from the distance the music was deafening. But it lent an air of festivity to the day. Dora Menefee tapped her foot, Lottie Humphries hummed, and Mama Rachael clapped in time with the strains of

"Oh, Dem Golden Slippers," a smile of unrestrained joy on her face.

Delta studied the instrument. Shaped like a V with a little keyboard at the open end, the instrument consisted of two rows of graduated whistles pitched to the notes of the scale. It looked like nothing more than pipes and valves. When Mr. Sandee pressed a certain key, steam was released to the corresponding valve and that particular whistle blew.

"We have forty-eight whistles," the captain was explaining. "The number for these remarkable instruments runs anywhere from thirteen upwards to fifty-eight."

Delta watched, amazed at the beautiful tones issuing from such a crude instrument. Steam billowed everywhere, encompassing Mr. Sandee, who wore protective canvas clothing and gloves.

Looking around she expected to find them entering the port of Cape Girardeau, but such was not the case. Forests framed the river on either side, calling to mind Mama Rachael's claim of isolation here on the boat. "Why is he playing before we reach town?" Delta inquired. "Is he practicing?"

"Practicing?" Captain Kaney echoed. "Lawd no, Miss Jarrett. He doesn't need practice, and we don't play the *cal*liope unless we're approaching a town. Other times the steam from the contraption distills our drinking water." His eyes twinkled. "Everyone doubles on board the *Mississippi Princess*, even this fine steam piano."

Mr. Sandee finished "Golden Slippers" and immediately took up another tune, "Turkey in the Straw."

"But to answer your question," the captain continued, "we begin playing the *cal*liope five or six miles out of town. The sound carries even farther than that, up

69

to eight, nine miles given the right weather. Country folk along the way hear the music and know the show-boat's comin'. That gives them time to finish their chores and get to town for our performance.''

Zanna joined the group looking for Delta. "If you want to go into town with us, come on down to the main deck. You can play tuba.''

"Tuba?" Delta stared, aghast.

"Everyone doubles," Zanna teased, repeating Captain Kaney's words. "We'll plug it to prevent stray sounds.''

Captain Kaney clapped her on the shoulder. "Doubling in brass is a common practice, but I'd insist on Zanna finding a more feminine instrument if I were you.''

After Zanna assured Mama Rachael she would look after Delta during their foray into town, the two younger woman headed for the main deck.

"Townsfolk tend to judge the quality of our entertainment by the size of the cast," Zanna explained on the way, "so we muster anyone who's willing to march through town.''

"Whether they play instruments or not?''

"Sure. Half the instruments in the band are plugged anyway.''

"Even Orville?" she quizzed when upon reaching the main deck she recognized the cabin boy who served their room. He wore a blue and gold band uniform and held a battered trumpet as though he wasn't sure what to do with it.

Zanna shrugged, repeating the familiar phrase. "Everyone doubles.''

Albert also wore a blue-and-gold uniform, but his had more braid and his hat rose a good six inches above the others. He stood at the front of the group directing

the loosely organized band of cast members and re-
cruits.

"Don't worry," Zanna whispered from their place
at the rail. "I wasn't serious about the tuba."

But Delta's mind had strayed. Seeing Albert had reminded her of her mission to uncover the truth about
Brett Reall. At the thought, her shoulders tensed. With
furtive glances she looked first left then right, relaxing
only after she made certain he was nowhere in the immediate vicinity.

She chastised herself for such foolishness. At some
point she would be required to have contact with the
man in order to conduct a proper investigation. And
even though she had once thought the ship so large she
would be able to avoid running into him, such had not
proven the case, as witness his presence at the captain's
table and later that evening their accidental meeting
outside her very own cabin.

No, she had little hope of evading the gambler for
the entire trip to New Orleans, assuming of course that
he didn't disembark at some earlier point. She dared
not hope for such good fortune.

She would, however, prefer to postpone an encounter with M'sieur Reall as long as possible. If he should
come within range at the moment, she was afraid she
might spit in his face.

"March along with me," Zanna was saying. "We'll
follow the band and hopefully look like leading ladies
or something even more interesting."

Delta cast her a dubious glance. "I'm not sure I like
the sound of that."

While they laughed, the showboat rounded the bend
and pulled into a berth at the Cape Girardeau docks.

No sooner had the town come into view around the
bend, than the calliope stopped playing abruptly. To

Delta's amazement, the brass band took up the tune without missing a beat.

"More doubling?" she questioned.

Zanna laughed. "If the townsfolk want to think our band is that powerful, we don't mind."

Leaning against the rail, Delta studied the scene before her. Cape Girardeau was a pretty town, but nothing like as large as St. Louis. Brick buildings nestled among and on several summits with unpaved streets running up and twisting around. As she watched, the area came alive with boys of all ages and sizes running for the docks.

"They've got the sickness," Zanna explained. "River fever. Every boy in the Mississippi Valley wants to pilot a steamboat down this mighty river. We'll see most of them between here and New Orleans."

Delta checked her portfolio, making sure she had the article she had hastily written on the cast of the Princess Players to post to Hollis. Quickly she tried to order her thoughts, her purposes. Captain Kaney had related some of the history of Cape Girardeau. If she followed his leads, she could collect enough information for an interesting travel piece with little effort: settled in 1733 by Spanish immigrants led by a man named Jean Baptiste Girardot. A flourishing town before the Civil War, the citizens were trying to reestablish themselves by bringing in several railroad lines.

Using the captain's list she should be able to research an article in short order, then get on to a more serious matter—the mysterious case of M'sieur Brett Reall.

She gripped the rail with a tight fist. Brett's unexpected brutality the evening before had created a chill she could not dispel, one that lingered yet, even beneath the warm rays of the morning sun. Indeed, a sick sort of dread continued to tremble inside her.

While the gangplank was being lowered, the landing party, Zanna's term for the advance team sent into town to publicize tonight's performance, gathered around.

"Time to go. You all know your roles. March behind the band, smile, wave, invite everyone to the performance tonight." Zanna shoved bundles of playbills into the hands of each cast member as they moved in behind the band, waiting for the gangplank to be lowered.

Below them the docks were now crowded with not only eager-faced boys, but with men, women, and children of all ages and descriptions—a dazzled crowd who stared as with one pair of eyes toward the magnificent floating palace.

"We'll perform the free concert at the far corner beyond the Jesuit school," Zanna instructed. "Afterwards I want everyone to fan out. Cover the town and don't return to the ship until you've distributed all the playbills."

The band struck up again. Delta moved onto the gangplank with the rest of the cast. Suddenly she felt the crowd separate behind her. A body wedged into place at her side, the extra weight causing the gangplank to wobble. Reaching up to steady herself, she clutched Nat's arm. She looked up into his smiling face. His eyebrows lifted in invitation.

"Stick with me, Delta. I offered to show you the sights."

"Nat," Zanna called his attention, "find several local boys to post playbills on trees along the roads leading into town. Assure them free admittance for their families—"

"Come on, Zanna," he coaxed. "Let Albert take care of the playbills. I planned to show Delta Cape Rock."

Delta blanched. As much as she wanted to press Nat for information about Brett, she certainly didn't intend to spend a day alone with him and his insufferable ego. She could question him on board the *Mississippi Princess*. Besides, she had work to do.

"I saw Cape Rock when we passed it while ago," she told him. "I need to spend my time making inquiries in town."

"You could write an article on it," he countered. "It's the original site of the old trading post. I'll tell you about it on the way up there."

"Thank you, Nat, but Captain Kaney has already furnished me with everything I need."

"Illicit activities are rumored to still be conducted in the abandoned warehouses." He waggled his eyebrows. "A star journalist like yourself should at least be curious to see—"

"That's enough, Nat." Zanna pushed several bundles of playbills toward him. "Get some of those boys to help you."

Led by Albert, the procession reached the docks, stepping into a semblance of formation as they took solid ground.

Zanna called ahead, "Look happy. Smile. Invite everyone to the performance."

Nat persisted. Shifting the playbills to one arm, he took Delta's elbow with his free hand. She suppressed the urge to pull away. Ahead of them she spied Elyse walking behind the band.

"I have a wonderful idea, Nat," she said suddenly. "After you post the playbills, why don't you show Elyse

Cape Rock? There must be a cafe in town that would fix a picnic lunch for the two of you.''

"And risk my bread getting soggy from her tears? This afternoon is for pleasure, Delta. I want to spend it with you.''

"My company wouldn't be much pleasure today," she retorted. "I didn't sleep well last night, and as soon as I gather information for my article, I intend to return to the boat.''

Nat frowned down at her, his eyes showing his confusion. "What don't you like about me?''

"Nothing, Nat. You're absolutely charming. But you're wasting it on the wrong person.''

"You mean Elyse?''

She nodded. He had turned loose her elbow, but now when they stepped from the gangplank onto the docks, he took it again.

With a tug, he drew her to a halt. "Why are you determined to pair me up with Elyse?''

Beside them the fiddler played in competition with the band. Glancing at him, a sudden wave of recognition passed over Delta. He didn't meet her eye, and she looked quickly away, but the premonition lingered.

"Why, Delta?'' Nat was saying. "Can't you see it's you I'm interested in getting to know better?''

"Thanks for the compliment, Nat, but right now all I have on my mind is conducting the investigations my brother-in-law sent me to do.'' And uncovering the truth about the unsavory character of M'sieur Brett Reall, she added to herself.

"Later?'' Nat queried above renewed vigor from the fiddler who threaded himself in and out toward the head of the gathering, dancing a jig and entertaining the crowd with his lively music.

Shaking her head, she watched the fiddler disappear

into the crush of people. "Give up, Nat. Take Elyse to Cape Rock. I'll make you a ti' wager that she won't cry one tear all afternoon if the two of you are alone."

Zanna nudged them along. "Get going, Nat. These folks won't wait around all day."

Delta fell in step beside Zanna. Lovely brick buildings were set snugly along the river—a school for boys, the captain's notations read. She glanced up the winding clay street. On a knoll above town stood a stately building that closely resembled a brick castle with towers and spires—another school, according to the captain's notes. And in the center of town a brick building surrounded by what must certainly be acres of blooming roses. She could almost smell their fragrance from the docks.

Suddenly a few feet from the boat, a chill coursed unbidden along her back. Her steps faltered. Without warning the image of Calico Jack came to mind—his rugged face, his carved lips. The image was so clear she felt as though she were experiencing his presence. As quickly as it had come, the chill passed and warmth suffused her with the softness of early summer. Inexplicably she turned to stare back at the *Mississippi Princess*. Ginny had been right, she thought. It did look like a wedding cake.

Then she saw him. Brett Reall leaned against the rail on the promenade deck with the nonchalance of a man who hadn't a care in the world. He stared after her. She could feel the intensity in his black eyes, or perhaps she only recalled it, she corrected hastily. His solemn, unreadable expression belied the brutal way he had forced himself on her the evening before.

Turning quickly away she followed the cast in morose silence, Zanna's instructions to smile lost in the maze her brain had become. At the entrance to the Jesuit school, she bade Zanna good-bye.

"I'll meet you at the city hall," Zanna told her, indicating a brick structure in the center of town. "It's the building surrounded by roses. That's where you'll find the mayor."

With difficulty Delta concentrated on her interview with the master of the Jesuit school, and it went well enough. Afterwards she hurried across the street to see the mayor, scarcely daring to look left or right, so afraid was she of seeing Brett again.

Since the city hall stood in the center of town, the entire city could be viewed from the grounds. Several roads fanned from the edge of the beautiful rose gardens like spokes from the hub of a wheel.

Mayor Girardot was a friendly octogenarian, eager to discuss his efforts to bring the rails to town. He confided that he could be a descendant of the city's founder. Then again, he confessed, his family could merely have taken the man's name.

"That isn't uncommon out here even today," the wiry little fellow assured Delta. "Folks change their names at the drop of a hat." He chuckled. "Or the drop of a gun barrel."

The mayor had insisted they enjoy the roses, reminding her not to forget to mention them in her article, so they strolled up and down the pathways, while she conducted the interview. The many-hued roses lent an elegance to the old brick buildings. Their fragrance drifted like sweet perfume on the soft air.

"Fur trade made us great," the mayor told her. "That's slacked off considerably. Everything's slacked off since the war, but we're working to bring prosperity back to town. We'll run it in on the rails, like the war run it out."

Delta wrote furiously, striving to record the man's conversation word for word. His provincial jargon would lend authenticity to the article and make writing it easier.

Which in turn would give her more time to pursue leads on the despicable Brett Reall. At the thought, she glanced up from her pad to see two horsemen approach from the wharf area. Nearing the city hall, one of them drew rein, tipped his hat back with a finger, and stared at her. Her heart skipped two beats. Brett Reall, accompanied by the companion she had seen with him on other occasions.

She stared as though transfixed. The alacrity with which her brain seemed to call forth this despicable man stunned her. His gaze was intense. It penetrated to some unknown place deep within her, violating, the way his lips, his tongue had violated her the evening before. Yet, somehow, despicable though he was, she did not feel threatened. And that fact was the most ominous of all.

When at last he broke their gaze it was as before, with a grim, almost angry toss of his head. Watching him ride away from the city hall, she realized to her horror that she had been smiling at him.

Quickly, she composed herself and concluded the interview, promising to send the mayor a copy of the *Sun* when the article was published.

Snatches of Nat's earlier conversation came to mind. She stared up at the empty road where Brett had disappeared. "Where does that road lead?" she questioned the mayor.

"Cape Rock," he responded. "It's a couple of miles out of town, but I wouldn't advise you to travel there. It's no place for a lady."

"Why's that, Mr. Girardot?"

"Nothing there but a bunch of abandoned buildings and a gaggle of riffraff. We leave 'em alone; they leave us alone. Been that way since the war."

Brett Reall sat easy in the saddle as he and Pierre left the wharf. Gabriel had gone ashore earlier, surveyed the town, and returned to the *Mississippi Princess* with two horses.

Brett had planned with care his excursions into the towns at their various stops. First, Gabriel searched the area for anyone who smacked of law enforcement. If the way was clear, he rented riding stock from the local livery, relieving Brett of any contact with townspeople. Later, if questions arose, no one would have cause to remember him.

The sun showered its early morning warmth over the clay street that led uphill from the docks to a brick building in the center of town, whence other streets angled off in several directions. The building was surrounded by a multitude of roses, and the sun glistened off dew on their petals like the reflection of a rainbow. Then suddenly, there in the middle of the glorious profusion, he saw her.

She stood among the roses, the hem of her green skirt swaying gently in the breeze. Encompassed by the many-colored roses, she was the fairest of them all. Warmth traversed his body, not all of it the physical yearning to savor this woman's sweetness.

That was there, too, of course. Lust. Hadn't it prompted his reprehensible conduct the evening before? Lust was certainly one of the emotions he felt for Delta Jarrett, had felt for her even before the sample he had taken beneath the light of the moon.

But lust wasn't all he felt for her. She touched something inside him that defied identification. Something warm and familiar. Dangerously familiar. Warning bells sounded in his brain with the potency of that calliope.

Delta Jarrett, who the hell are you?

She looked up, saw him, and smiled. In that astonishing moment, the world seemed to glow brighter, as though someone had turned up the flame on a lantern.

Preposterous. Who was this woman? What kind of power did she hold over him?

Who the hell was she? A clairvoyant? A witch?

He scoffed at such thoughts. Those were ideas his mother would have come up with. His mother, who not only believed in witchcraft and all things psychic, but practiced them, although he'd never put stock in the psychic abilities she claimed to possess. Her curative powers derived from her knowledge of herbs and potions, from her skill at diagnosing ailments and prescribing treatments. That's what he had always believed.

He had never believed in witchcraft. But there stood Delta Jarrett, drawing him to her with those melancholy blue eyes, eyes that attached themselves as with a steel trap to his soul and seemed to pull it right out of his body.

No, he had never believed in witchcraft, but he had never before felt himself drawn by some intangible force to another human being, either.

Suddenly the man beside Delta moved within Brett's frame of vision. An elderly man, he noticed, who was talking, nodding his balding head, and waving his walking stick in the air.

The walking stick diverted Brett's attention, but it was Delta's notepad with pencil poised over it that captured it. Delta's notepad on which she took notes to write articles to send back to a newspaper in St. Louis.

A newspaper that could ruin his chances of completing this harmless journey and returning to his Canadian haven beyond the United States border, beyond the authority of United States marshals and courts of law.

Angrily he tore his gaze from her and spurred his mount up the hill Gabriel had directed him to take. He would finish this meeting and he would stay clear of that blue-eyed witch.

He would.

But throughout the meeting with his warehouseman at Cape Rock he found his mind wandering to her eyes, her smile, the taste of her lips, the feel of her curves against his hard and lonely body. By the time he concluded his business and headed back to the *Mississippi Princess,* his mind was clear on how to proceed.

"Ol' Thompson, he seems a capable sort," Pierre suggested, when the two of them approached the showboat. Gabriel stood on the dock fiddling in a wild contest with a local musician.

Brett grunted.

"Good news that he can handle double the number of pelts we've been sendin'," Pierre continued.

"Oui."

"He might suggest someone to handle operations up St. Paul way, *non?"* Pierre questioned.

The two men dismounted at the dock, Brett's mind still worrying with his decision, with implementing it.

"He might—" Pierre began.

"We'll discuss it later. Find me that cabin boy— Orville, I think his name is. I have an errand for him."

Pierre studied his nephew from beneath shaggy

81

brows. "Ah, *mon nèfyou,* your brain, she is still in that rose garden, sure."

Brett glanced back from hitching his reins. He opened his mouth to protest Pierre's remark, then closed it and headed for the boat.

By the time Delta finished her interviews, met Zanna, and returned to the boat, the rest of the crew, who had also returned, were taking lunch in an open-air dining area off the paddlewheel lounge.

Still shaken from her latest encounter with Brett, Delta was determined to pursue her plan to investigate the man. She took the seat Albert dragged up for her and agreed to the chicken salad sandwiches and iced tea the steward suggested. But her mind remained on her target.

Granted, her original decision had sprung from the anger his rough handling had engendered the evening before. But now she was able to see him in a more objective light, she told herself. Here was a man with a devious past to hide. She was sure of it.

Why else had he been so alarmed to learn that she was a journalist? The instant Captain Kaney mentioned her occupation at dinner the evening before, Brett had ceased all conversation with her. Afterwards he had precipitously left the dining room, when earlier he had indicated an intention to remain for the theatrical performance.

Those mysterious actions coupled with his later accusation that she was spying on him left her to draw only one conclusion: M'sieur Brett Reall had a past to hide and he was nervous as a caged polecat that she would unearth it.

But their visual encounter outside the city hall had

left her with a more important reason for uncovering the truth about Brett Reall. He terrified her. More than anything before in her life, more even than those dreadful nightmares, he frightened her deep down inside in a manner she could neither understand nor identify.

It wasn't a fear like of rabid dogs or violent men. Rather, it was a fear of the unknown, of the strange sort of power he seemed to wield over her, as if he could see into her heart, into her soul.

That, she knew, was nonsense. No one could do that. But his penetrating gaze pierced her in a way she had never experienced before. And if her heart didn't see this as a threat, then her brain would have to work overtime to convince it that a man of such mercurial mood swings, a man who managed to materialize at her very thought of him, was a man who represented danger.

She learned little from her afternoon's interrogation. Albert merely shrugged at her question. "You know how rumors grow out of speculation, Delta. None of us *knows* anything about the man. He keeps to himself. His appearance at dinner last evening was a surprise. Since he boarded at St. Paul I've seen little of the man."

Delta ate part of her sandwich, then asked, "Where does he usually dine?"

Albert shook his head. "In his cabin, I suppose. I've seen him and that companion of his in the dining hall a few times—off in a corner, secluded-like. Last night was his first time at the captain's table."

"Perhaps it was the first time the captain had invited him," Delta suggested. She recalled all too well seeing Brett in the dining hall yesterday at lunch—the first time she had ever seen him. *Or was it?*

"Could be," Albert replied.

"You say he boarded at St. Paul?"

"I said that, but you must understand, St. Paul's where we boarded—Zanna, Frankie and Iona, and I."

"What about Nat?" she asked. "And Elyse?"

Albert considered the question. "Come to think of it, Nat did board at St. Paul. Only he wasn't a member of the cast then. He auditioned for Zanna after we got underway."

"And Elyse? Do you remember when she came on board?"

"Sure do." He smiled. "Hannibal. I'll never forget the sight of her. A ragamuffin with the voice of an angel."

"A ragamuffin? You mean she was an out-of-work actress at her tender age?"

"Not exactly. Such cases are fairly common. A pretty young thing dreams of running away from the harshness of life to join a glamorous theatrical troupe on a showboat. Happened all the time before the war. Why, some of our best actresses came into the business that way."

Delta filed this information. Although she had allowed Albert to lead the conversation astray, she wanted to hear more about Elyse. She wondered whether Nat and Elyse had ridden up to Cape Rock. Since neither of them were present at the moment, perhaps Nat had taken her advice, after all.

She sighed. If he had, she hoped it worked out all right. She really should learn to keep her nose out of other people's business. She had enough trouble of her own.

"Put on your thinking cap, Albert," she said, wrapping up the conversation. "I want to write an article on these actresses who started out ragamuffins. You'll be my primary source of information.''

On the way back to her room Delta thought about the things Albert had told her about Brett Reall and the many things he had not known about the man. Even before leaving the paddlewheel lounge, she began to wonder whether she was overreacting to the entire situation.

Brett Reall could well be a criminal of some sort. On the other hand, he didn't have to be. Keeping to oneself and shying away from publicity did not make one a criminal.

And neither did looking at a woman the way he looked at her. She felt a strange sensation in the pit of her stomach at the thought that he might find her attractive. He was certainly handsome enough himself.

But he could also be a brute, as she had discovered the evening before. So she would stay away from him. If she happened to hear anything about him, fine. Otherwise she would avoid him.

In line with that, she merely peeked into the cabin lounge on the way to her stateroom. Mama Rachael was there, along with Mrs. Humphries and Mrs. Menefee and a couple of other ladies she had not met. And Brett Reall was there, sitting at the table with them, smiling, laughing.

Something warm fired inside her at the sight of him. Like at dinner the evening before, he was playing the perfect gentleman. Suddenly she entertained the fear that he would look up, see her, and his eyes would grow cold and hard, as they always seemed to do in her presence.

The moment his head began to turn, she darted past the doorway. By the time she reached her stateroom she was more convinced than ever that she must steer clear of Brett Reall.

Then she opened her door and found the surprise of her life.

Chapter Five

An apology from Brett Reall? Rereading the message that accompanied the enormous bouquet of roses on her nightstand, Delta's hand trembled:

> Please accept this attempt to apologize for my conduct last evening. In an effort to amend things between us, may I escort you to dinner? I will meet you at the lower entrance to the dining hall at eight o'clock. In anticipation of your acceptance I have alerted the captain that we will not dine at his table tonight.
>
> Your humble servant,
Brett Reall

For one brief instant her reservations about the man vanished beneath the romantic nature of his apology. But Brett Real was nobody's "humble servant" and she would be anybody's fool to believe otherwise.

She finished the article on Cape Girardeau—to post from Cairo the following day—and was still in a dither when Mama Rachael returned from playing poker with that scoundrel.

"Delta, child, he's such a nice young man," Mama

Rachael insisted after Delta informed her of Brett's invitation, saying, "He even went so far as to cancel my invitation at the captain's table. The nerve of him! Now I must remain in this tiny cabin and have Orville fetch me a cold dinner."

"There's no reason for you to refuse the man's dinner invitation," Mama Rachael argued. "Land sakes, what harm could he do you in a dining hall full of people?"

He could stare at me, Delta thought, feeling herself warm beneath Brett's intense perusal, even as she envisioned it. Her eyes involuntarily went to the roses and she thought of the startled look in his eyes when she glanced up from the rose garden—startled, yet suffused with a warm, welcoming glow.

She winced. What had turned his mood sour, his gaze to ice?

"M'sieur Reall is a very good gambler," Mama Rachael continued. "And he's a gentleman. Nothing like those slick-fingered, silver-tongued heathens who frequent saloons on shore. Why, you could write an article about him."

Delta smiled in spite of her gloom. The article she had planned to write about Brett Reall would not extol his virtues, but his vices. The article she planned would set the man in his place, once and for all.

Her spirits began to lift at the thought. Why not go ahead with it? If she played things right, asked just the right questions, she might get all the leads she needed from this one dinner engagement. Why not?

"This once," she agreed at length, eyeing Mama Rachael sternly. "But you must promise to find me at the end of the meal. I don't want to be left alone with him after dinner."

Mama Rachael shook her finger in Delta's direction.

"Delta, child, how do you expect to catch a man with an old lady like me tagging along?"

Delta's mouth fell open at the astonishing remark. "I'm not out to catch a man, Mama Rachael." *I'm out to catch a pirate.* The thought raised goosebumps along her arms.

Mama Rachael busied herself pulling garments from the chiffonier. "This yellow gown is perfect." She withdrew the matching yellow wrap, then hastily thrust it back inside the wardrobe. "If your shoulders get cold, he can lend you his jacket."

"Mama Rachael!"

Ignoring Delta's outburst, the little lady continued to flit around the room preparing Delta for her dinner engagement. She found the curling iron and placed it over the chimney of a lamp. "We'll curl your hair and pin in a couple of those lovely yellow roses. My, my what lovely roses. I knew that man was a gentleman. Haven't I told you so all along?"

Delta couldn't believe her ears. "Hollis sent you as a chaperon, not a matchmaker."

"I can be both."

"No, a chaperon protects her charge from the wolf. You're trying to throw me to him."

Mama Rachael huffed and Delta dutifully dressed in the yellow silk gown, thinking all the while that perhaps she should have awakened her eager chaperon the night before. What would Mama Rachael have thought about the way this *gentleman* forced himself on her reluctant charge in the dead of night?

Not the dead of night, her brain rejected. By the light of a golden moon.

Tugging on over-the-elbow white gloves, she heeded Mama Rachael's advice to leave the wrap behind—not because she intended to let Brett Reall drape his jacket around her shoulders. She vowed to return to her own stateroom long before the chill of night set in.

But her knees almost buckled on the last carpeted step leading to the observation deck. Already she regretted her decision to accept this invitation, and she hadn't even looked into Brett's stormy eyes yet. Perhaps he wouldn't show up.

Luck was not with her, however. A crowd thronged about the doors to the dining room, but Brett Reall caught her eye the moment she stepped off the staircase. And the inspection she received was one she recognized instantly. Not the strange, intense perusal of a phantom from her past, this look was purely sensual, one of approval and promises from a handsome man to a woman he obviously found attractive.

She felt her skin glow and hoped her reaction did not show in her own eyes. When he touched her elbow she was glad to have the fabric of her gloves between their skin.

Once inside the door he escorted her to a small table for two snuggled into a far corner from the dais—one of only a few such tables in the entire room.

Desperate to break the tension between them, she struggled to think of something impersonal to say, finally observing, "I understand you and your traveling companion usually dine in seclusion."

Walking around the table, Brett seated himself opposite her. When she chanced a look at him, an amused grin tipped the corners of his lips. His eyes left hers briefly to travel the crowded room. "This is the table Pierre and I usually take, *oui*. I would not have called dining in a room this size filled with prattling strangers seclusion." He shrugged. "But being a journalist, you must know more about words than I."

"I didn't mean seclusion," she admitted hastily.

Unbuttoning the wrist of her right glove, she wriggled her hand from the mitt, then concentrated on tucking the fingers into the arm of the glove, freeing her hand to eat. "They say last night was the first time you've dined at the captain's table."

The conversation was inane, and glancing up again she realized, unfortunate, as well. A discerning smile creased Brett Reall's beautifully shaped lips. His black eyes questioned.

She flushed. "I mean—" Stumbling, she sought some way to cover the fact that she had discussed him with others.

He leaned back in his chair. "They're right," he admitted, then refused to let her off the hook so easily, adding, "whoever you questioned about me. Last night was my first time at the captain's table. The reason, m'moiselle, contains little in the way of intrigue. It was the first time I had been invited."

A waiter appeared with their soup tureens. Delta escaped Brett's arrogant expression by examining the image of the *Mississippi Princess* fired in gold on the bowl of her porcelain tureen. With equal attentiveness she unfolded the crisp linen napkin and pressed it across her lap.

"A bottle of champagne," she heard Brett order. "And none of that bubbly house stuff you pass off on us hapless gamblers in the cabin lounge."

Light danced from the brass candle fixture in the center of their table. Crystal tinkled nearby. A violinist strolled the room. The strains of his instrument added to an atmosphere that was already so charged it closed out the babbling voices around them, enveloping them as in their own private space. In spite of the warm feeling that was beginning to creep up her back, she felt awkward and was sorry she had come. She wanted to run from the room, but dared not. What did he think this was, a party? Why did he think she accepted his miserable invitation?

"Champagne?" she questioned, but her voice cracked somewhere in the middle and she was surprised that he understood.

"You don't drink champagne?"

"You needn't waste it on me. The roses were enough, and—" She wanted to tell him that all the roses ever grown, all the champagne ever fermented could never make up for his actions the evening before. But she didn't. For some reason she was reluctant to spoil the warmth growing inside her, relaxing her, truly relaxing her, for the first time she could remember since her nightmares had begun.

"I suppose you picked them yourself from the beds around the city hall?"

He laughed. It was a soft, rich sound that strummed her senses. Then he sobered. "If I thought it would make up for my appalling actions last night, I would claim to have grown them myself. But the truth is, nothing can make up for that."

His admission shocked her. Her eyes flew to his. He looked sincere, but— First an apology, now an admission of the shamefulness of his actions, both from a man she would have thought too arrogant for either.

She looked away when the waiter brought their champagne. Brett tasted it, accepted it, and after the waiter left, offered a toast.

"To a new beginning."

The rims of their glasses touched as he spoke those words, and her hand trembled, causing the glasses to clink against each other, sending the tinkling sound of fine crystal rippling through the already impregnated air.

Involuntarily her eyes sought his again, and she felt caught in his snare. She wanted to look away, but could not. It was as though he held her by some invisible bond that reached from his eyes to her very soul. As though he had held her like this before, as though he had held her like this forever.

Forcefully she broke their gaze, took a gulp of champagne and again considered running from the table. With great effort she was able to remain in her seat. She started to taste the soup, but had to mentally steady her hand in order to keep her spoon from shaking.

The soup, or perhaps the familiar actions of lifting spoon to mouth, swallowing the liquid, and repeating the process, calmed her. Finally she looked up to find him eating, as well.

"You should have auditioned with Zanna for the role of leading man," she told him.

He studied her, silent a moment. "You're comparing me to that pantywaist who fawned all over you last night and again this morning?"

She laughed at his genuine consternation, then found herself staring at him, wide-eyed, when the implication of his words began to take form. Quickly she diverted her gaze.

Brett shrugged. "I had trouble carrying on a conversation with you at dinner last night while he undressed you with his eyes from across the table."

"He did nothing of the sort," she denied, watching the waiter remove her empty soup tureen and replace it with a dinner plate. Her head spun with a new phrase while she contemplated the meal—fresh catfish and scalloped potatoes. *He had noticed.* This handsome man who for some mysterious reason sent her senses reeling had noticed Nat's attention. Whatever did that mean?

She glanced up. "To answer your question, no, I'm

not comparing you with anyone. You're just a very good actor." She watched his eyes narrow.

"You think this is an act? The roses? The champagne, the dinner invitation—all an act to *what?* Seduce an innocent girl?"

His suggestion caused her food to tumble in her stomach. "Well, you won't."

The crease between his eyes deepened. "You don't even know me, yet you cast me as a villain."

Her brain spun with the mercurial changes in this man. "You forget last night, m'sieur."

He held her angry gaze, his voice soft and dangerous. "No, *ma chère,* I will never forget last night."

She looked away, stared at her plate. The thought of eating with the lump in her throat almost made her choke.

In a manner to which she was becoming accustomed, his voice changed from soft to harsh. "God's bones, what else can I do? I apologized in every way I know how. I can't change what happened, take everything back. But neither can you. Why did you come on deck dressed like you were out to seduce a man? Didn't you know how you looked? Pierre and Gabriel were all eyes. Didn't you care?"

"I—" She bit off her words short of telling him about her nightmare, for that nightmare shot suddenly to mind with the force of a rocket on the Fourth of July. Horrified, she jumped from her chair and fled through the nearest door, running, stumbling along the deck until she felt his hand grasp her arm, bringing her to a halt.

He jerked her into his arms with the same force he had used the evening before. But unlike the evening before he held her tightly against his body, clasped her head to his chest, and let her sob into his fine black jacket.

The nightmare had returned suddenly with the verisimilitude she usually felt upon awakening from it. Beneath their feet the deck gently rocked, but Brett held her steady, never uttering a sound, while she cried against his rapidly beating heart.

When at last her sobs ceased and her heart stopped racing, he drew her back and dried her eyes with his handkerchief.

"Are you finished?" he asked in tones as gentle as the breeze.

She nodded, snuffling.

He held the handkerchief to her nose, ordering, "Blow."

Afterwards he stared solemnly into her face so long she began to wonder what he was thinking. Idly he began to push her gloves down her arms. Then he removed them in the same inadvertent manner. Finished, he tucked them into one of his jacket pockets, and his hands retraced their path, sending showers of warmth along her arms. All the while he looked intently into her eyes, as though searching for answers. When he spoke his voice carried a tone of confusion, of awe.

"We can't begin again, can we?"

Her heart stopped. What was he saying? That this was the end? That couldn't be. She could not, must not, allow such a thing. "Why do you say that?"

The tone of his voice didn't change when he spoke again, nor did the intensity in his eyes lessen. "Because we already are."

"Are what?" She watched his Adam's apple bob above his starched collar.

"We just are," he said. "You and me. We *are*. It's like we have been forever."

She thought about his words, words that made no sense. Yet, they expressed the same sentiment she had felt only moments before. Forcefully she pushed the nightmare aside, into the niche she had created for it in the back of her brain. If only it would remain there.

"Whatever it is you're talking about," she declared, "I don't believe in such things."

"Neither do I. But there's something between us, Delta Jarrett. Something that's been going on a long, long time. I feel it, and you do, too."

Later she thought how if another man had said these things she would have accused him of employing a unique if somewhat bizarre courting technique. But she couldn't accuse Brett of such, because what he said was true.

With studied slowness, he lifted her arms and placed them around his neck, then slid his own around her shoulders. Gradually, gently, giving her all the time she needed to pull away, he drew her closer. But she didn't pull away. Such a thing never entered her mind.

When his lips touched hers, she reached to meet them. And this time they set her on fire. This time they were soft and kind, turning her melancholy into something so poignant tears again filled her eyes. But they were no longer tears of trepidation. She tightened her arms around his neck, feeling her tensed muscles relax even as her body sprang to life with a thousand different sensations—sensations that were all new, yet deeply familiar at the same time.

Consumed by a sense of anticipation, she opened her lips to his and accepted his sensuous exploration by returning his rising passion with passion of her own.

His fingers slipped up her nape, cupping her head,

and each place they touched came alive. The throb of his heart charged hers. The feel of his hard body pressed solidly against her own made her ache to feel his skin against her skin, soft and hot, like always—

Like always. That thought unleashed her nightmare from its cage in the corner of her brain. She drew back, stared into his glazed eyes. Easing one hand from around his neck, she trailed her fingers in a tender line across his neck and up his jaw.

The moonlight shone on his solemn face, deepening his eye sockets, hiding his eyes. His lips felt soft beneath her fingers, as she had known they would. She traced the chiseled outline of his mouth, her eyes riveted on those sensuous, passionate lips, those familiar, oh-so-familiar lips—

From her nightmare.

Some call him a pirate.

Fear returned. Swiftly it swept up her neck, exploding inside her head.

"Who are you, Brett Reall?" she whispered. Her heart beat faster. "What do you want from me?"

Bewitched by the magic of the moment Brett stood stunned by Delta's sudden change in mood. One moment she had been willing and passionate, the next her body went rigid in his arms. He watched fear spread across her face, tightening the once-supple mouth, turning her eyes to rock-hard sapphires.

Like her mood change, her questions stunned him. They had sprung like demons emerging incongruously out of the soft pools of her desire.

"This," he mumbled, lowering his lips. "This is what I want from you, *chère.*" He kissed her again. It took longer to quell her fears than the first time, but finally he felt her relax against him. Her arm crept tentatively back around his neck.

With his hand to her back, he pressed her gently against him, nestling the soft mounds of her breasts into his chest. They tantalized, those breasts, they beckoned him. He ached to touch them, to kiss them, to suckle them like a babe.

His hand swept down her back. He crushed her bustle of yellow silk in a palm and pulled her hips against him, knowing that somewhere beneath his wool trousers and her voluminous skirts they could find fulfillment, sweet and wild as a mountain stream, hot and steamy as bayou water.

What he couldn't do with his body, he attempted with his lips, and soon her mouth opened to his quest. Soon she reciprocated, seeking, he knew, the same wondrous destination as he—a summit where their passions could crest, spiraling them in mutual surrender toward the heavens.

From the dining room behind them voices erupted, finally entering his engrossed brain. Befuddled, he set her aside with trembling arms. He held her shoulders with a firm grip, as much to support himself as to support her.

Diners wandered onto the deck. He released her arms but remained standing too close for propriety's sake. What the hell kind of spell had she cast over him?

His heart hammered in his ears. Her now-puffy lips remained slightly open, inviting. Her wide-eyed, innocent vulnerability only added to his rising passion. And from somewhere deep within him, remnants of his earlier plan began to emerge.

His earlier plan—to keep an eye on her in order to prevent her delving into his business for her damned newspaper.

"There you are." Mama Rachael paused beside them, then started to move off down the deck. "Such a nice night to be enjoying the moonlight. I'll run along—"

"No." Delta's voice quivered.

Brett held her gaze, watched her turmoil.

"You two enjoy yourselves," Mama Rachael insisted. "Take in the performance on the docks."

"No—" Delta began.

Giving her no time to object further, Brett took her elbow in one hand, Mama Rachael's in the other. "Come ladies, we'll take in the performance together."

Later he wondered at his sanity, but at the time his only consideration had been to prolong contact with Delta Jarrett. Why? He could not decide.

It must be self-preservation, he determined, steering the ladies by their elbows through the crowd and onto the docks, where he found them seats on a wooden bench near the front of the area set aside for a stage. With her in view she couldn't very well snoop into his affairs, he reasoned.

But at the moment she wasn't snooping into anyone's affairs. She hadn't uttered a single word since her last attempt to end their evening together.

Lanterns on poles ringed the area. Spectators approached from all sides, only a small portion of them passengers from the showboat. Men stood about in small groups, while women gossiped and children played tag in and out among the bales of hay and wooden benches. The air hung redolent with the hay and soft smells of summer.

Albert wandered among the crowd, selling tickets. Brett dipped into his pocket and paid for the three of them. When Delta objected, he responded.

"This is my evening, remember?"

She blanched. "Part of your attempt to apologize?"

He glowered at her, angered at her readiness to call his indiscretion to mind. "No, Delta. We've moved beyond my feeble attempts to apologize. You know that as well as I do."

He watched a flicker of acknowledgment flash across her eyes before they again took on the melancholy that gave her such an air of vulnerability. He was hard-pressed not to gather her in his arms and hold her tightly against her fears.

He didn't doubt a woman's tendency to fear him. Even though he had never harmed a woman in his life, neither did he usually go out of his way to play the part of a gentlemanly suitor. It rankled him that he was doing so now.

Delta's chaperon chattered on, oblivious to the tension between the two of them. "We will have our little game tomorrow, won't we M'sieur Reall, even though we are scheduled to arrive at Cairo before lunchtime?"

"By all means, Madame Myrick. I wouldn't miss our ti' game."

"We shall have to take advantage of every moment. My journey ends at Memphis, you know."

Something turned sour inside Brett. His eyes darted to Delta's. He held her gaze. "No, I didn't know."

"Not me," she said. "Mama Rachael is staying behind to visit an old friend. I am—" She stopped talking in midsentence and turned toward the makeshift stage where Zanna had begun to introduce the evening's performance.

"You're what?" Brett prompted in her ear.

"I'm not getting off at Memphis," she replied without turning her attention from the stage.

The melodrama began, but Brett continued to watch Delta, trying to sort out, to put a name to his emotions. His body's reaction to a beautiful woman was understandable, but whatever the hell was going on inside his brain didn't make a tinker's damn worth of sense. He had no business getting involved with a woman, any woman.

But Delta Jarrett wasn't *any* woman. And that fact troubled him more than the prospect of running into Canadian Mounties or United States marshals. A premonition clouded his mood. Whatever hold Delta Jarrett had over him would likely not be as easily evaded as the law.

When he saw her run her hands up and down her forearms a couple of times, he removed his jacket and put it around her shoulders.

"I don't need this." She reached to remove it, but his hands stilled hers.

He grinned, hoping to coax a smile from her. "That pantywaist of a leading man is about to come onstage," he whispered. "I don't want him gawking at your bare shoulders."

She smiled at that and he settled down beside her to watch the melodrama, conscious primarily of her body so close, yet so unattainable.

"Such a nice gentleman," Mama Rachael mused, leaning across Delta to pat Brett's arm. "I told Delta you were a gentleman."

Delta grimaced beside him, and he laughed. "Thank you, madame. I can use your help in convincing the m'moiselle of that."

Delta seemed to relax during the performance; she even laughed from time to time. But when the show was over and Mama Rachael announced that she was off to have a nightcap with the Humphrieses and Menefees, Brett felt Delta tense.

"Don't worry about M'moiselle Jarrett," he quickly

assured Mama Rachael. "I will see her safely to her cabin."

"No—" Delta began.

Brett gripped her arm. *"Oui.* I'm your escort for the evening, responsible for seeing you safely back home, which in this case is a stateroom on the cabin deck of the *Mississippi Princess,* a showboat—"

He continued to prattle in an inane manner until they arrived on the cabin deck. Reaching her stateroom, he drew her around the corner to the stern, where they had met so unceremoniously the evening before.

"Now, do you mind telling me what has you running scared?"

She refused to meet his eye. "Nothing."

He gripped both her upper arms, his fists easily circling them. "I'm not stupid, Delta. Something I did offended you. And don't mention last night," he warned. "What we shared outside the dining hall took us far beyond that event, mistake though it was. What we shared outside the dining hall was the beginning of something neither of us will be able to let go unless we explore it further."

When she didn't answer, he pulled her to him and kissed her like before, gently, tenderly, completely. But she resisted, and unlike earlier, he wasn't able to coax her into yielding to the passion he knew she felt.

She didn't outright reject him, however. Her hands crept tentatively up his chest. And when he lifted his face inches from hers, her fingers found his lips, traced them, and he saw tears roll down her cheeks.

He kissed them away. "God's bones, Delta, don't fight it. I'm not some demon from out of the night."

She stiffened in his arms as suddenly as if a bolt of lightning had struck her. She pulled away. At first he

102

thought she intended to turn and run from him, like earlier in the dining room. But she didn't.

Instead she removed his jacket and handed it back to him. "This won't work, Brett. I can't see you again." Before he knew what had happened, she turned and ran for her cabin.

Angrily he headed for his own stateroom on the promenade deck, looking neither left nor right, seeing only Delta's frightened expression. For it was fear he had seen in her eyes. Fear, stark and cold. He couldn't recall ever having frightened a woman before, but that fact did nothing to lessen the guilt that gnawed inside him like a beaver felling a pine tree.

And the guilt angered him. It dredged up emotions he had struggled to put behind him for the last ten years. Had he fled his home, forsaken everything he held dear, only to return with nothing but a heart filled with guilt? The same old sickening, debilitating guilt?

Unlocking the hand-painted door to his stateroom, he flung it open and stomped inside. Pierre and Gabriel lounged in the two club chairs, whiskeys in hand.

"What are you doing here, Gabriel?" he snarled. "Did anyone see you come in?"

"Non." Gabriel exchanged amused glances with Pierre, although Brett could tell immediately that Pierre's amusement didn't extend beyond the fake grin on his face.

"You're getting carried away with this *femme* journalist, *non?"* Pierre questioned.

Brett tossed his jacket across the back of the settee. He crossed the room and poured himself a drink.

Pierre pursued the issue. "It's dangerous, I tell you, exposing yourself on the front row of a public theatrical performance."

Brett emptied his glass in one gulp and refilled it.

Taking a modest swallow, he set the drink aside, loosened his tie, and began removing the studs from his shirt. "Closer we come to Louisiana, the more care I'll take. Right now, I think it's best to keep an eye on her."

"An eye?" Gabriel taunted. With two fingers he grasped the end of Delta's white gloves that peeked out of Brett's jacket pocket and pulled them free. "Keep your eyes on her, *oui*, my friend. And what else?"

Brett jerked the gloves from Gabriel's hands.

Gabriel shrugged, lifting his eyebrows suggestively. "What you think, Pierre? They aren't her drawers, *non*."

"For truth, they will be next time," Pierre muttered.

Suddenly all Brett wanted was to be left alone. Delta's rejection, for whatever reason, had left him defenseless. He needed to regain his wits. He felt as though he had just come off a big drunk and needed to sleep it off.

Motioning to the door, he half-playfully ordered, "Get out of here. Both of you. I need some sleep."

The two men rose.

"What about tomorrow?" Pierre questioned at the door.

"Tomorrow?" Brett asked. "Same as always. As soon as we arrive at Cairo, you, Gabriel, will check out the town. If it looks safe, bring two horses to the docks. Pierre and I will ride up to Cave-in-Rock."

"While I keep my eye on the boat, sure," Gabriel said.

"And on M'moiselle Jarrett," Brett added before he even thought. After a brief pause to consider the plan, he continued. "Keep her in your sights at all times. I want to know if she asks questions about me, what she asks, and from whom she seeks such information."

Delta stood beside Zanna the following morning watching the *Mississippi Princess* round the hairpin curve called Dogtooth Bend and steam into the port of Cairo, calliope blaring. The town sat on the point of a long, flat V of land where the Ohio River joined the Mississippi. The port was crowded with a fleet of great white boats emblazoned with the letters U.S.M.

"The mail packets," Albert explained. "The post office's Great Through Mail has been a big help since the war."

Delta checked her tapestry portfolio for the article she had written on Cape Girardeau. "I'll be glad to get to Memphis where we can stay awhile," she told Zanna. "I'm beginning to feel like a war correspondent, posting articles from a new battlefield every day."

"After a while it begins to feel like a battle," Zanna agreed. "Three days in one place will definitely be a luxury." She handed Delta a basket the chef had prepared for their lunch. "Time for me to go to work."

While Zanna organized the cast for the parade through the streets of Cairo, Delta studied the passing countryside—trees and water as far as the eye could see. She tried to recall the captain's instructions about her interviews. First, she would meet with the postmaster. He—Captain Kaney was certain—could give her names of other citizens of the fast-growing metropolis to interview.

Nat spoke from her left shoulder. "See where the two rivers merge?"

Looking down, Delta watched muddy red and brown waters swirl together like batter in one of Ginny's marble cakes. Her emotions eddied in much the same manner. Nat made her nervous, but she decided it wasn't so much Nat himself, as the thought that Brett might be watching them.

The brass band blared; the boat nudged the dock. Deckhands scurried to lower the gangplank. Nat took her elbow and ushered her into the crowd of cast members.

"You and that gambler were getting thick as thieves last night," he observed following her onto the rickety gangplank.

"We certainly were not."

"I saw him put his coat around your shoulders. I'll bet you let him kiss you goodnight."

She turned to glare at him, but Brett's words when he covered her shoulders came to mind and she smiled in spite of herself. "That's none of your business, Nat." Gathering her wits, she lowered her voice. "If you'd tend to your own business, you wouldn't have reason to worry about mine."

"My business?" he called above the band. "You mean Elyse?"

She nodded. "Did you have that picnic?"

His grip tightened on her elbow. When she looked up to protest, he was grinning. "Now, that's *my* business."

"Good."

"Seriously, Delta, I hate to see you get mixed up with that gambler."

"Why?"

"I told you he's dangerous."

They had stepped off the gangplank onto the dock when he made the pronouncement. Zanna was issuing last-minute instructions for the parade and the concert at the far corner of the city hall. The fiddler had taken up his usual place beside the gangplank, plying his instrument with such vigor that bow strings flew about his face.

Delta stopped dead in her tracks. "How is he dangerous?"

"He just is," Nat hedged. "I can tell a criminal when I see one. Reall's got that hunted look about him."

"Do you know for a fact he's a wanted man?" Passengers jostled her from behind, pushing her toward Nat, who caught her arm.

"Not for fact, but—"

"Then don't spread gossip," she demanded above the cacophony of crowd noise, band music, and fiddle.

Nat grinned. "So, you are taken with him."

"No, Nat, but I won't hear a person's reputation sullied by someone who doesn't know the facts. How would you like it if people spread the rumor that you're a Casanova?"

He squeezed her elbow. "If you see me as a Casanova, Delta, I must be making headway."

Before she could dispute his deduction, Zanna thrust a bundle of playbills into Nat's arms. He scowled. "I wanted to show Delta Cave-in-Rock."

" 'The play's the thing,' as Mr. Shakespeare said. You were hired to be a member of this cast."

"Zanna—" Nat objected.

"We all double, Nat. Since you refuse to don a uniform and double in brass, you'll have to double in promotion."

"What is Cave-in-Rock?" Delta asked after Nat sauntered off and she and Zanna fell into step behind the band.

"It's a large cave in the bluffs outside town. Actually, it's quite a ride, I hear. Indians used to think the

Great Spirit resided there. Recently it's been home to outlaw gangs who raid boats along the Ohio River."

"That's right," Delta recalled. "Someone mentioned it at dinner the other night." She recalled, as well, where the goodly portion of her mind had been during that discussion—on Brett Reall. He had just become morose upon learning that she wrote for the *Sun*. A fact that had led her to believe him to be exactly what Nat claimed—a wanted man. A criminal.

Criminals. Outlaw gangs. She hadn't dared to admit it to Nat, nor to another living soul, but she too felt certain Brett was a hunted man. The things he had said, why, he had almost admitted as much.

She had no business getting involved with such a man. Even though, as Mama Rachael had claimed, he knew how to act the gentleman, no telling what sort of criminal he would turn out to be.

But the truly frightening thing was the way she had begun to connect him to Calico Jack in her nightmare. She knew she shouldn't allow herself to make such an outlandish association. She knew it was only coincidence that his lips were the same lips she saw in her dream, his kisses the same tender kisses as in her dream, that even his curses were uttered with the same oath.

His eyes weren't blue, of course, like Calico Jack's. And he didn't brandish a sixteenth-century cutlass.

But he made her experience the emotions from her dream—frightening emotions that burned with the heat of passion, that pulled her toward some unknown pinnacle like a moth drawn helplessly to a deadly flame.

Some call him a pirate.

Reason told her Brett Reall had nothing to do with her nightmare. But he had brought the dream to life, had given it a physical dimension, a fact that would make it even more difficult to rid herself of the nightmare. No, she had been right to end the relationship before it began.

But it had begun. Following Zanna away from the showboat, she knew as much. Suddenly a familiar prickling tingled along the back of her neck, and she swirled to look back at the boat. Without thinking, she searched the decks for him, certain she would see him standing at the rail staring after her.

But he wasn't there. And she didn't see anything more of him for several hours.

By the time the parade and free concert were over and the playbills distributed, Delta had posted her article on Cape Girardeau to Hollis and conducted her interview with the postmaster in charge of the Great Through Mail. She joined Zanna and the cast on a grassy knoll opposite the city hall, where they spread a blanket and ate a leisurely lunch prepared by the *Mississippi Princess*'s chef—fried chicken, cold potato pancakes, apple turnovers, and lemonade. The sky was blue overhead, the sun warm, and Delta felt her sleepless nights begin to catch up with her. She yawned.

"Why don't you catch a catnap while we set up for tonight's show?" Zanna suggested while Delta helped her return the dirty dishes to the basket to carry back on board.

"I need something else for my article," she objected. "The postmaster told me about an old stagecoach stop outside town. I think I'll ride out there and take a look."

"I'll come with you," Nat suggested.

Zanna shook her head. "We'll never erect the set by showtime without your help, Nat." She glanced around the group, musing, "Who else could ride with you?"

"I don't need a chaperon, Zanna. I'm perfectly capable of hiring a horse and riding about a city as civilized as Cairo by myself. Besides, with the showboat in town everyone will be too occupied at the docks to pay attention to one lone woman.''

''I promised Mrs. Myrick—'' Zanna began.

''Don't fret,'' Delta broke in. ''I'll be back before Mama Rachael finishes her ti' game.''

''If that gambler returns in time to play with those little old ladies.'' Zanna mused. ''I haven't seen sign of him all day.''

''He rode out toward Cave-in-Rock earlier,'' Nat furnished, a satisfied smirk on his face.

Delta thought about that later. It vexed her to hear Nat express the same sentiments about Brett Reall that she felt, even though her feelings and Nat's were worlds apart. She worried that her suspicions might be true; Nat gloated that his were.

The nag she rented at the livery was surely the most ancient horse in all Cairo, she decided, when she couldn't get it to travel faster than a trot.

''He's all I got, ma'am,'' the hostler had told her. ''Seems like ever'body an' his dog wanted a horse today.''

At her request he had pointed her northeast toward the site of the old stagecoach station. She hadn't told city-bred Zanna the entire truth about her little journey. The postmaster had said she might find a docile old man who had been a member of the Cave-in-Rock Gang living in the old stage station. He claimed the oldtimer loved to talk about his experiences. This was an interview subject she couldn't pass up. Hollis would love it. And he would be impressed with her expertise in arranging it.

Although she had set out with more trepidation than she admitted even to herself, she found the way easily enough. A couple of miles out of town the road forked, then a few more miles it forked again. Two turns going, two turns coming. She hadn't been raised with six brothers for nothing. Why she could remember going hunting with Kale when she was still a small child.

She smiled. Kale never complained about taking her, even though her short little legs must have slowed him down. Kale had been her favorite brother when they were growing up, partly, she knew, because he always paid attention to her. At home they roughhoused so much Benjamin was always on them about it.

The eldest of the brothers, Benjamin had raised the entire passle of kids after their mother lost her mind. Benjamin had wanted her to turn out a lady. And thanks to Ginny, she had.

The old stage station was built with mud-chinked logs set against the side of a slight rise, exactly where the postmaster had said she'd find it. The place appeared deserted.

Drawing up outside the front door, she dismounted and hitched her horse to an ancient post. Hoofprints in dried mud showed where other animals had been tethered, but she didn't see any signs of recent use.

Digging her pad and pencil from the saddlebag, she stepped up to the scarred wooden door. When no one answered her knock, she pushed and the door swung open.

Suddenly above the creaking hinges, she heard the metallic clicking of several gun hammers being cocked. Her feet froze on the threshold, her hand still touching the rough wood of the door. Drawing a deep breath, she called out. "Mr. Felton?"

"God's bones, Delta! Hold your fire, men."

111

Chapter Six

Brett's voice knocked the breath from Delta's lungs as surely as if he had backhanded her across the face. He followed his words out of the dusty darkness of the cabin, grabbed her by the shoulders, and dragged her into the room. "Who's with you?"

Her mouth felt as dry as the logs in the old house. "No one."

"You rode out here alone?"

She nodded.

His grip on her shoulders tightened. She expected him to shake her, but he didn't. Light filtered through years of layered dirt on the single window pane. She coughed against the dust.

"You expect me to believe you were brave enough to ride out here all by yourself? You, who are so afraid of me you can't even—" Abruptly he clamped his jaws together. Releasing her, he changed the subject. "Check around," he called over his shoulder.

She heard bootsteps, saw shadows in her peripheral vision. Her eyes remained fixed on Brett. Her heart thrummed with the meaning of finding him here in the nest of an old outlaw.

Fury simmered in his eyes. "I don't need to ask why you've come. You're spying on me again."

She found her voice, and her anger. Jerking her shoulders to free them, she stood her ground. "I certainly am not spying on you. I had no idea you were here. I came to interview a . . . a *former* outlaw."

"What does that mean?"

She glared at him, feeling tears spring to her eyes. It was true, what she had suspected, what Nat claimed. Brett Reall was an outlaw, and she suddenly realized how desperately she had hoped he wasn't.

"Why don't you stay out of my life?" she cried.

"Me? You're the one who rode all the way out here to spy on me. Why the hell don't you stay out of my life?"

Suddenly her nightmare returned, as clear in her head as if it were a melodrama performed on stage. She saw him on the pirate ship, with his cutlass, in her arms. She felt his lips on hers, his hands on her bare skin, his body hot and passionate beside hers, inside—

Tears rushed to her eyes. "I wish I could."

Seconds turned into ages while they plumbed the depths of each other's eyes. Brett wanted to protest the truth of her statement, to argue that she could stay out of his life if she wanted to. That she was nothing but a snooping journalist.

But he knew better. They were drawn to each other. By some inexplicable force, for some unfathomable reason, they were being drawn together. His gut clenched in a knot of fear. Every time he was with her he risked discovery. At the moment he was in no position to probe the reasons or interpret the meaning of it all. If he made it to Louisiana a free man, perhaps he could enlist the aid of his mother to exorcise this beautiful demon from his life. Perhaps, if he believed in such things. But for now—

Pierre stepped through the threshold. "Gabriel's bringing in that actor."

The knot in Brett's gut turned to stone. Fury built inside him as he tore his attention from Delta. Beyond Pierre's bulk, he glared at the Princess Players' leading man.

Brett turned back to Delta. "What the hell game are you playing?"

"He didn't come with me," she insisted.

"He wasn't with her, *non*," Gabriel agreed, stepping to the doorway. In one hand he held the rope by which he had bound Nat's hands. "He was followin' her."

Brett studied the belligerent young actor, then returned his attention to Gabriel. "You're the one I told to follow her," he stormed.

"I was, my frien', but this fellow showed signs of strikin' out on his own. I didn't figure you'd want him hanging 'round."

"You had me followed?" Delta demanded. "Why?"

Brett swung his head around at Delta's question. Her blue eyes danced like a fighter in the ring. Her cheeks were flushed with anger. Strands of hair had escaped the coil at her nape, and a few clung to her neck and face. One strand stuck to her lips.

He lifted a hand to brush it away, then clenched his fingers into a fist and dropped it to his side. She wasn't afraid of him at this moment, he noticed, only mad—fighting mad, like a riled gater in a Louisiana bayou.

"Why?" she repeated.

He cocked his head, squinting at her through narrowed eyes. "Because I figured you'd try to follow me. From the looks of—"

"Then your guilty conscience led you astray, M'sieur Reall."

"Guilty? Of what am I guilty? Of not wanting some meddling journalist sniffing into my private life? Of not wanting to see myself spread all over the newspapers for folks to gawk at over morning coffee? I'm a private man, m'moiselle. Last time I heard we had laws to protect a man against invasion of privacy."

Suddenly she smiled, not a spontaneous smile of joy, however, but a self-satisfied smirk. "Perhaps I was wrong," she purred. "It must have been your arrogance that led you to believe I was following you. I came out here to interview a Mr. Felton."

Brett held her stare while the words sank in. Wint Felton or himself, what difference? It all boiled down to meddling in his affairs.

"Let's get going," he barked. "Gabriel, take that actor back to town, and don't let him out of your sight until you get there." He turned to Pierre. "Finish up here. I'll escort the lady."

When he tugged on Delta's arm, she jerked away. "I made it out here by myself, and I can find my own way back."

"I wouldn't hear of it," he hissed, nudging her out the door.

Outside, Gabriel helped Nat into the saddle, then tied the actor's hands to the pommel. Nat cast her a silent plea just before Gabriel, taking up Nat's reins, led the actor away from the cabin.

Still grasping Delta by the arm, Brett unhitched her mount with his free hand and led it around to the back of the cabin where other saddled horses were hitched. Before he could help her into the saddle, however, she attempted to replace her notebook inside her saddle-bag.

Suddenly curious he took it from her hand. Thumbing through the pages, he stopped at the last entry, studying it with pursed lips, striving to make sense of the situation. Finally, he looked back into Delta's eyes. "Wint Felton?"

She nodded, defiance shining like the morning star from her blue eyes.

Inside him relief began to ease the knot of fear and anger. He knew he should resist the growing desire to trust her, to—God's bones! What was this woman doing to him?

Reaching for her, he crooked an elbow around her neck and drew her face to his. The moment their lips touched, he felt her resistance began to fade. She moved tentatively into his arms, her fingers grasping his shirt for support.

With an audible groan he pulled her tightly against his body, laving her face with kisses. At length, her arms crept up his chest. Desire like wildfire ignited and spread down his body when her fingers touched the skin at the back of his neck. Reflexively, hungrily he deepened his kiss and she responded, leaving him weak and wondering at his own sanity.

What kind of magic did this woman spin that made her so irresistible? Black magic, he was certain. For no other kind had touched his life in ten long years. Delta Jarrett could bring him no good. Not in the long run.

But for now she was the best thing that had ever happened to him. The sweetest, the most desirable. Her skin tasted slightly of salt and of violets. The soft mounds of her body meshed against his hard, hungering frame in a way that aroused a carnal ache deep in his groin. He swept a palm down her back and cupped her padded hips hard against his own, showering him with both ecstasy and pain.

Again and again his tongue pillaged her sweetness. The ache in his lower extremities became acute, throbbing in rhythm to his plundering kisses.

As suddenly as a roll of thunder announces a summer shower, the squawking hinge on the cabin door reminded him they were not alone on some deserted island in the bayou. Lifting his lips, he traced his hands back up her frame, absorbing every nuance of her tormenting shape. He felt her shallow breath against his skin, saw her begging eyes. He cupped her breasts, one in each palm, and watched the fire in her eyes deepen to a hot blue flame.

"You were right to be afraid of me, *chère,*" he whispered, kissing her lips, her eyes, her face. "I want to make love with you worse than I've wanted anything in my grown life."

Although her brain struggled to revive her earlier fear of this man—this pirate, this outlaw—Delta's body felt so wonderfully alive beneath his touch, beneath his gaze, that all she wanted was to remain in his arms forever.

You already have, she thought, as his lips claimed hers for one last demanding, promising invasion. *Every night in my dreams.* But somehow she knew that making love to Brett Reall in the flesh would be a thousand times more exciting than their nocturnal coupling in her dreams.

Then his mood changed abruptly, as she had come to expect. He turned her toward the cabin with a gentle hand at the nape of her neck. "Come," he said in a voice so husky he could have been inviting her to his bed. "If you want to get that interview before we head back to town, we'd best get started."

Astonished by this turn of events, she let him lead her around the corner of the cabin where, after sending

Pierre back to town, he called forth a scruffy old man who tottered down the rickety steps with the aid of a crude cane. Wint Felton's sparse white hair dragged his shoulders, making up in length what it lacked in bulk.

"Wint, meet M'moiselle Jarrett. She wants to ask you some questions about—" Brett turned amused eyes on Delta. "Hell, let her tell you what she wants. She writes for the newspaper."

While the old outlaw settled himself on the top step, Brett guided Delta to a seat below him. After which, he moved opposite her, sitting on his heels at the edge of the steps. He pulled off a stem of grass and stuck it in his mouth, his eyes teasing Delta all the while. "Ask him whatever you like. If he doesn't know the answer, he'll make one up."

Delta sat, momentarily silenced by the alacrity with which Brett had switched from romance to business. While her body still thrilled from his caressing hands, he had set aside the thing he professed to want worse than anything in his grown life—as if they had suddenly come to a fork in the road, and he had chosen the unexpected path. But the way his eyes played over her lips, the rapid throb of the vein in his neck gave him away.

Disconcerted by the knowledge that she had such an effect on this man—and he on her—she studiously opened her notepad, striving to focus on the interview at hand.

Ask whatever you like, he had said. Had he intended to issue such a bold invitation? Fighting back the urge to jump up and run away from the very opportunity she had been seeking, she chanced a look at Brett. "Anything?"

The vertical cleft between his eyes deepened as her

challenged registered. He cocked an eyebrow. "Anything," he agreed.

With pencil poised she turned to Wint Felton. "I'm preparing articles for the *St. Louis Sun*. The postmaster in Cairo said you might be willing to relate some of your experiences on the river . . . ah, and with the Cave-in-Rock gang." When she mentioned the gang, her attention shifted to Brett, who still stared at her. His thoughts were unreadable.

The old man's flaccid features took form. He hooked a thumb around each of his suspenders and cast her a sagacious glance before staring off into space somewhere in the region of the hitching rail. "He be right."

Delta waited, but no elucidation followed. As an interview subject, she hoped he would improve soon. "You were a member of that gang?"

"Yep."

"Could you describe your most daring adventure?"

"Was all of 'em darin' in them days, lady," the old man replied. Delta held her tongue, while he spat off the side of the porch, then turned his attention back to the hitching rail.

Brett came to the rescue. "Tell her about that keelboat affair back in twenty-two, Wint."

Without changing expression, the old outlaw resettled his wad of tobacco in the opposite cheek. This time when he glanced at Delta, she could tell the dam had been breached. His memories gushed forth and an hour later were still flowing strong.

At the beginning Delta wrote swiftly, recording the ever-changing number and names of men in the gang, their feats in robbing the ships that plied the Ohio and the Mississippi, the cargo they stole, the fights they engaged in. She tried to capture his phraseology, which she knew would lend authenticity to the article.

According to Wint, one gang member had muscles enough to "t'ar the hide off a wildcat," another could "out-sw'ar the devil," and still another could "sear the bark off a Injun at fifty yards just by smilin' at him."

"Then thar's ol' Swifty Reynolds," Wint added. "He weren't no member of the group, min' you, but he was a man to reckon with. I seen the time he cordelled a flatboat loaded with booty over ever' snag, sawyer, and sandbar from Natchez to Memphis, single-hand'. Outrunnin' the law, o' course."

"That's keelboat talk," Brett explained. "Cordelling was the way keelboatmen got their boats back upstream after selling their goods in New Orleans. Six or eight men worked along the shore, physically pulling the boat upcurrent by means of a stout rope."

Delta studied the old man's withered form. "That's why keelboatmen were known for their muscles," she mused.

Brett nodded. "Wint here was one of the best."

As Wint continued, Delta became so engrossed in the tales the old man spun one after the other that she forgot to write them down. Brett kept the monologue running, prompting from time to time as each story ran its course.

"Tell her about Mike Fink."

"Tell her about Bill McCoy."

Finally, when the sun had begun to sink in the sky and the old man seemed fairly spent, Brett called a halt with, "If you've got enough information, Delta, maybe we should mosey on back to town. Wouldn't want to keep you out after dark."

Her eyes had been on her notebook when he made the statement, and she kept them there. After his earlier confession concerning how badly he wanted to

120

make love to her, she dared not think what being out after dark with him could mean.

Girding her courage, she responded with what she had been planning from the beginning, "I have a couple more questions." Started thus, however, she hesitated to continue. Like plucking a seedling from the soil that nurtured it, would her questions destroy this fledgling relationship she felt growing between them?

At length she knew she must seek answers, even though they most likely would be answers she did not want to hear. She focused her attention on Wint Felton. "How long have you known M'sieur Reall?"

Across from her Brett chuckled, but she resisted the temptation to look at him.

"You mean, ah— *him?*" Wint questioned.

Delta nodded, finally chancing a glance at Brett, who still sat on his boot heels, still chewed on the same stem of grass. A bemused look creased his lips. Studying those lips a lump rose in her throat.

"Nigh onto all his life," Wint responded. "His pappy and me, we run many a broadhorn on Old Muddy and even over on the Ohio. And 'fore that, we run traps in the Louisiana bayous. His pappy and me, we go back a long ways."

"Is he a pirate?" The question escaped Delta's lips before she realized it had formed in her mind. Involuntarily her eyes flew to Brett's. The stunned expression on his face echoed her own.

But the old man slapped his knee and hee-hawed. He spat again off the side of the steps, unhooking a thumb long enough to wipe his mouth with the back of his hand before clutching his suspenders as before. "A pirate, you ask? A pirate? Lordy, sweet lady, ain't we all?"

* * *

"A pirate?" Brett demanded after they were well out of earshot of the cabin. "God's bones! What century do you live in?"

She caught her breath at his oath—and at the question he posed. Lately she'd begun to wonder the same thing. She considered responding that the answer depended on whether he meant in the daytime or at night.

Clutching the reins in sweaty palms, she glanced at him. He didn't belong here in the daylight. He belonged to the night, to her dreams—his strong body, which she knew as well as she knew her own, his tender lips, the intense way he had of looking into her soul, even the way he cupped her breasts in his palms, the longings he stirred, the passions he enkindled. His favorite oath. All these belonged to her dreams.

He didn't belong in the daylight. He didn't belong in 1879. *Did she?*

They rode in silence and after a while her thoughts settled down. Finally as they neared Cairo she decided he deserved an explanation. "Have you ever heard of Calico Jack?"

"The pirate?"

She nodded.

"Sure, I've heard of Calico Jack. What about him?"

"He was one of my ancestors."

A quizzical expression narrowed Brett's brows. After a moment, he retorted, "Congratulations. Everyone has at least one black sheep in the family. Glad to know you're no different."

"You look like him."

"I *look* like him? How do you know such a thing?"

Desperately she tore her eyes away and concentrated on the ruts in the road. She started to tell him about the dreams, then and there. She needed to tell him. "Descriptions," she finally mumbled. "Descriptions passed down through the family."

"Descriptions?" he echoed. "You're comparing me to descriptions of a man who's been dead more than a hundred years?"

She swallowed the lump in her throat, wishing she hadn't started this conversation. He would think her demented, witless. With great effort, she shrugged and tried to laugh it off.

"They call you a pirate."

In one ferocious movement he reached for her reins and jerked both their horses to a halt. "Who calls me a pirate?"

She stared at him, wide-eyed.

"Who, dammit?"

Her mind raced vacantly. Once more she had aroused his anger. This time she knew why, or supposed she did. No outlaw wanted to be found out. Suddenly her head became so jumbled with the present and the past she didn't know who she was, where she was.

"God's bones, Delta, are you stark, raving mad?"

Tears glazed her eyes. She fought to keep them back, but they rolled down her cheeks anyway. All she could think was that now she had driven him away. He thought her mad. Now she would have him only in her dreams.

Before she realized it, however, he was leaning across the space between them, kissing her lips. Gently, soundly, then hungrily.

She responded with the fervor of one who has recognized the value of something only after she thought it lost. This was not a dream. This was reality—Brett's lips, wet and hot against her skin.

Yet it was also a part of her dreams, something she

had experienced for months. The taste of him, the feel of him, the heart-wrenching love for him.

Was he a pirate? Yes, he was a pirate. Her pirate. She loved him and she feared him. But she feared losing him more than she feared anything else in the world except losing her sanity. She kissed him with renewed vigor.

Releasing her hold on the reins, she lifted her hands to his face. With trembling fingers she explored his familiar jawline, felt his day-old stubble of beard, traced the weathered lines at the corners of his eyes, the arch of his eyebrows, the cleft between his eyes.

When he drew their lips apart, she moved her fingers between them, tracing the outline of the precisely sculpted lips. The familiar sculpted lips.

"Delta, Delta," he whispered against her skin. "What kind of spell have you cast over me? You're like one of my mother's potions." He kissed her again, then added, "But I can't decide whether you're white magic or black."

They had stopped on the outskirts of town with the sun sinking behind them. Gradually she became aware of the calliope and realized it must have been playing for some time. Brett brushed a strand of hair away from her eyes, kissed her again, then handed her the reins.

"We shouldn't be seen returning together," he told her. "I'd hate to spoil my reputation as a gentleman with Mama Rachael. She might take you off the boat at Memphis, too."

For the first time in hours Delta thought of the showboat, of the real world. She smiled. "You probably have already fallen from her graces. You missed her ti' game."

All the while she returned the horse to the livery and

retraced her steps to the *Mississippi Princess*, she felt Brett's eyes on her, but she didn't turn around. She knew he would keep his distance. A warm, secure feeling encased her like a cocoon, knowing he was close at hand. And that warmth, she decided, was further proof that she was losing her sanity. No sane person would feel warm and secure in the arms of an outlaw.

At the docks she discovered that the calliope had already drawn a crowd. The cast of the Princess Players put the finishing touches on the set for the evening's performance. Nat looked up when she approached.

"Where's that outlaw?" he demanded. "I thought he intended to see you back to town."

"I didn't need his help," she retorted.

"You were gone a mighty long time."

She tried to sidestep him, but his next words stopped her.

"It makes a man wonder what went on."

"I'm glad you didn't say *gentleman*," she retaliated, "because a gentleman would never make such a speculation." She brushed past him, only to turn at the foot of the gangplank, her wrath growing. "Don't ever follow me again, Nat."

"I wasn't following you."

"You weren't here helping *me*, either," Zanna called, "else we'd have this set erected by now. Get back to work."

In the end Delta pled exhaustion and had supper sent to her cabin. Mama Rachael was in such a stew over preparations the Humphrieses and Menefees had made to celebrate this, her last night on board, that she spent little time trying to change Delta's mind.

"Don't wait up for me, child. Get some rest. Three days in Memphis will keep you on the run."

Delta's exhaustion wasn't physical, of course, but

125

she didn't tell Mama Rachael that. After this afternoon her feelings for Brett had become so jumbled that she knew she must try to sort them out before they met again.

While she waited for Orville to bring her meal, she wrote the piece on the Great Through Mail and began the article on Wint Felton, old outlaw, old friend. He'd had nice things to say about Brett, but old friends stuck up for old friends' sons. So what was she to believe?

Later, dressing for bed, she focused, detail by detail, on Brett Reall the man, trying to separate him from the pirate in her dream. Brett the man might be a threat, but he was alive and real and she could deal with him.

She would deal with him. First, of course, she must learn whether he was indeed an outlaw. And she must learn this before she allowed their relationship to go one step—or one kiss—further. She couldn't fall in love with an outlaw.

Why, a gambler would be bad enough. She tried to visualize the reaction of her family to such news, but found the prospect too depressing. As Mama Rachael had expressed, the isolated world of the showboat allowed a person to engage in activities that would not be tolerated in proper mainland society—such as ladies gambling in public.

Such as her announcing to her family that she had fallen in love with a gambler. Or an outlaw.

One of her brothers had been a Texas Ranger, for heaven's sake. And her cousin Cameron was with the Pinkertons. The others were all upstanding citizens. No, before one more dinner date, one more kiss, one more intimate glance, she must learn the truth about Brett Reall.

Everyone doubles, the showboat saying went. Did

that include the gambler? And if so, what was his double? A modern, nineteenth-century outlaw—or the eighteenth-century pirate in her dreams?

From outside her stateroom she heard the opening skit of the evening's performance begin. In her mind's eye she pictured Albert and Zanna and Frankie and Iona and Nat and Elyse.

She left one lamp burning so Mama Rachael could find her way around when she returned and climbed into bed. Once she settled down and tried to get her brain to do likewise, however, the gentle rocking of the showboat at its mooring became even more noticeable, and the noises from outside louder.

The last sounds she heard before drifting off to sleep were the shotgun blasts from *The Saga of Judge Noah Peale*. She visualized Albert aiming at Nat's retreating form, while a terrified Elyse huddled beneath the makeshift bar.

Amid shouts and cannon blasts, the crew of the Kingston *boarded the English vessel with little trouble. It was only after most of the thirty or so pirates touched foot to plank that Anne Bonny realized what had happened. From the corner of her eye as she battled with cutlass in hand, she watched the English captain aim a pistol at Calico Jack's temple. At the same moment a multitude of soldiers scurried from below decks, making their victory fade as quickly as a sail could collapse in a slack wind. Before she could reach for the pistol in her belt, someone grasped her from behind, and after a struggle, the king's soldier succeeded in manacling her hands behind her back.*

"Damn your scurvy hide!" she cried, only to be rewarded with a filthy rag stuffed in her mouth.

Behind the captain, aiding him Anne now realized, she saw

their latest impressment, Ned Youngblood, a talented young man she and Jack had welcomed aboard with open arms.

A talented man indeed who turned out to be the king's own. Betrayed by the hand they had fed, the life they had spared, she thought bitterly. Led into a trap which had been set with care.

And no time was to be lost she discovered, watching in horror as the soldiers led Jack toward the bow where a plank awaited. She struggled and kicked with such ferocity that, although her ankles were shackled, she was nevertheless afforded a front row view of the proceedings.

The captain of the vessel stood beside the plank, as swelled with pride as a sick boar, Anne thought, her heart bursting at his words.

"With the authority invested in me by the king, I carry out the sentence prescribed by law. For piracy on the high seas I condemn you to death, Jack Rackham, known to all as Calico Jack."

Jack stood on the plank, tall, straight, defiant. His eyes found Anne's and softened for an instant. Then his lusty laugh pierced the stillness.

"God's bones! It's been a hell of a ride!" He turned and briskly strode the length of the plank.

Tears sprang to Anne's eyes and she thought fiercely of the love they had shared, of the babe in her womb. She had not told him about the babe. The board slapped against the rail, resounding through Anne's brain; water splashed against the ship, the noises intermingling with the distant cry of a babe.

Delta and Mama Rachael stood at the rail after breakfast watching deckhands lower the gangplank to the dock in Memphis. The Humphrieses and Menefees crowded around, wishing Mama Rachael well, saying that they would see her on the return trip.

The ever-present gang of eager-eyed boys was joined

on the docks below by a growing crowd of townspeople. Delta searched for her cousin, Cameron Jarrett.

A steady hand grasped her elbow.

"Have you been to Memphis before?" Brett questioned at her shoulder.

As eager as the boys on the docks below, she looked toward him, then glanced quickly away. The sight of his lips made her queasy, revealing a stark truth—her night of contemplation had not erased the sensual longings this man stirred inside her.

To add to her dilemma, remnants of her latest nightmare nagged at her brain. Brett Reall was *not* Calico Jack Rackham from her dreams, she told herself for the hundredth time. Yet, he resembled the pirate in so many ways.

It was her imagination, she countered. Her desperate attempt to interpret the disturbing nightmares—and to explain her disturbing fascination with this man standing beside her.

"I could show you around," he offered. "Of course, it's been some time since I was here. Ten years. Likely things have changed. But I'll wager some things never change."

Some things never change. Like what? she wondered. Why did her brain play havoc with her senses when she was around him? He excited her as no man ever had. Yet he frightened her, too.

And the nightmare—

"Delta!"

She looked over the rail, spied the waving hat.

"Cameron," she called, glad to have found a reason for refusing Brett's offer. Sorry, too.

Mama Rachael offered her hand to Brett. "Thank you for the ti' games, M'sieur Reall. Perhaps on the return trip."

129

"Certainly, madame." He brushed the back of her hand with his lips.

As in a trance the old woman moved toward the gangplank. Delta followed, her heart in her throat.

Brett fell in step beside her. "You didn't mention you had a beau in every port."

She laughed, looking at him again. Again the sight of his face caused her stomach to flutter. She wished Cameron hadn't shown up. For a while, at least.

"I don't. He's a cousin."

"Kissing cousin, perchance?"

She laughed. "Come, I'll introduce you. He's with the Pinkertons."

The moment the words left her mouth the nightmare returned with full force. A Pinkerton, a king's man, what the difference? And why did she persist in thinking Brett was involved in something sinister? Why did she believe everything she heard and add to it the impact of her nightmares? Why hadn't she been able to talk some sense into herself overnight? Like Ginny often said, she really should be writing fiction rather than fact.

When she turned to invite Brett to spend the day with them he had disappeared into the crowd.

Chapter Seven

For the next two days Cameron escorted Delta around Memphis, showing her sites and introducing her to interview subjects. All the while, half her brain and all her heart remained locked as in mortal combat over her dilemma with Brett Reall.

Was he an outlaw? Was he not? And if not, why had he disappeared the moment she mentioned the Pinkertons? Was he even at this hour conducting clandestine meetings with former outlaws in Memphis?

Being with the Pinkertons, Cameron could surely discover answers to these questions in a minute. Cameron might even recognize Brett on sight. But dare she ask him? Dare she even mention Brett's name?

Mama Rachael soon took that concern out of Delta's hands. Cameron had picked them up and driven them directly to the home of Mama Rachael's friend, Maud Wadkins.

Like other ports on the *Mississippi Princess*'s itinerary, Memphis still suffered from the ravages of war. And even more recently from the yellow fever epidemics that had decimated the population, shrinking the number of inhabitants by three-quarters in the last few years.

"State of Tennessee even revoked our city charter this year," Cameron had told them. "Of course we still call it Memphis, but to the outside world, Memphis doesn't exist. Captain Kaney's helped us out by bringing the showboat to town for three days. Maybe that'll prove to folks that Memphis is on its way back."

Tall and lanky, like her brothers, Cousin Cameron had greeted Delta and Mama Rachael with bear hugs, after which he hefted Mama Rachael's trunk into the back of the hack he had driven to the waterfront.

"Where's your valise?" he questioned Delta. "Aren't you staying with the Widow Wadkins while the boat's in town?"

She tore her attention from the decks of the showboat, which she had searched in vain for a glimpse of Brett. "No," she answered Cameron, "I promised Zanna I would sell tickets for the performances."

Cameron helped the ladies onto the wagon seat, first Mama Rachael, then Delta. His hand lingered on Delta's arm. "I'll be a monkey's uncle if you don't get more beautiful ever' time I see you. It's a cryin' shame to be blood-kin to the prettiest girl in the country."

She laughed. After he positioned himself in the driver's seat and took up the reins, she leaned across Mama Rachael to tease him. "You can't use me as grounds for remaining single, Cameron. If you don't hurry and find yourself a girl, I'll be forced to find one for you."

"Go ahead," he laughed, flicking the reins over the draft horse's back. "I'm not too proud to accept your help. But from what I hear, you could use a little prodding yourself. Word is you've turned down ever' male within spittin' distance of St. Louis."

Mama Rachael adjusted her parasol. "She's too finicky. Why, you should have seen her outrunning that fine young gentleman on the boat."

"A fine young gentleman on the boat? This sounds interesting," Cameron teased, his eyes twinkling. "Tell me more."

Delta felt her face turn crimson. "Mama Rachael's the one who thinks he's a fine young gentleman. Let her tell you about him."

"Well," Mama Rachael began, "his name is M'sieur Reall. Brett Reall. He's a most handsome man. He dresses well and has the loveliest manners I've ever seen on any man, gambler or not."

"Gambler?" Cameron's teasing died at the word, and Delta held her breath for the lecture she was sure would follow. "You've picked out a gambler for Delta?"

"I don't think he's really a gambler," Mama Rachael confided. "He's too much the outdoor type, and his hands are callused like he's used to hard work. He just gambles with us little old ladies on the boat."

"Brett calls it a ti' game," Delta explained. "Ti' meaning petite. He's French or something."

"Sounds like you were wise to outrun him, Delta." Cameron chuckled. "A French gambler. Why civil war would likely break out in the Jarrett family if baby sister Delta came home with a disreputable gambling man."

"I know." Delta tried to sound lighthearted, but her heart thudded painfully against her chest.

"No need to worry," Mama Rachael retorted. "Even after he sent her roses and escorted her to dinner she refused to be nice to him."

Cameron turned the team into the residential section of town, giving Delta a respite from this tedious conversation. Delta and Mama Rachael stared in silence at the deserted streets and boarded-up residences. Many of the stately houses stood empty, their shrubbery unattended. Climbing roses grew in profusion, covering windows, adding vibrant color to the spectral ambiance surrounding them.

"I didn't expect such desolation," Delta observed. "The Widow Wadkins wrote that the threat of yellow fever had passed."

"Folks are straggling back," Cameron responded. "But of course some of these homes will remain boarded up. The fever took the lives of a great many citizens, entire families in a lot of cases."

"Maud wouldn't have insisted on my coming to visit if there was danger." Mama Rachael's sentence ended on a high tone that turned her statement into a question.

"You're safe," Cameron assured her. "I wouldn't have let either of you set foot off that boat if I thought otherwise. The plague is over, and our new sewer system will prevent it coming back. That might be something you can mention in your articles, Delta. Way I see it, your articles on Memphis will help us as much as the showboat staying in dock three days."

Maud Wadkins and Mama Rachael had been friends since girlhood. During the first outbreak of yellow fever, Maud and her daughter Hattie Louise had come to St. Louis to wait out the plague with the Myricks. When they returned to Memphis four months ago they carried Mama Rachael's promise to visit so they could return the hospitality.

When Maud's white, frame house came in view, Mama Rachael began issuing instructions. "If Hattie Louise is there," she warned, "don't either of you mention your Uncle Baylor. You know the trouble that went on between the two of them a few years back. Maud never revealed the details, but it couldn't be much comfort to Hattie Louise to be reminded of that man.''

Cameron and Delta agreed.

''Now that Kale's married and settled down, I suppose Uncle Baylor has become the black sheep of the family,'' Delta mused. She seemed to recall something about wedding plans being scrapped at the last minute, but that had happened long before she reached the age to be interested in things like weddings and beaux, so she had paid little attention.

And now her mind was filled with other things.

One other thing—Brett Reall. As preposterous as it was for her to even fantasize about a relationship with Brett, she couldn't seem to stop herself. Was it a woman's lot to inevitably think of home and marriage anytime an eligible man entered the room?

She knew better than that, of course. As Cameron had pointed out, she'd turned down a number of suitors already. She'd never found anyone who interested her—before. Recalling her promise to discover the truth about Brett before she committed herself further, Delta realized she was already committed in her heart.

But here she was, destined to spend the next few days in the company of a Pinkerton agent. With his connections, Cameron could make inquiries. He would be glad to uncloak Brett's past to reassure her, to alert her. Or to warn her off, when she already felt herself drowning in the relationship.

Her dream the night before had only made matters worse. If Brett were indeed an outlaw, alerting Cameron to his presence would be the same as turning him in.

She'd be no better than the ''king's man'' in her dream. Brett might even have a price on his head.

Would she be offered a reward for turning him in? The idea revolted her.

No, her reward would not be silver or gold. Her reward would be living forever with the knowledge that she had cost him his freedom.

But what if he deserved to be locked up? She unwillingly recalled Brett's mercurial changes in mood. What if his crimes were so heinous he was a menace to society?

Raised in a law-abiding home, she had respected justice even before she decided to become a journalist. How could she condone allowing a criminal to remain free? Her body heated at the thought of his tender kisses, at his laughter, infrequent though it was.

We are, he had said and she had felt it, too. Some ethereal cord seemed to bind them together, as though it had been their destiny to meet, to—

To what? she countered. Was she destined to play Judas to the man she loved? How could she bear such a burden?

By the time Cameron pulled the horse to a halt outside the home Maud Wadkins shared with her grown daughter Hattie Louise, Delta knew what she must do. She must find a way to gain Cameron's help without arousing his suspicions. Perhaps if he were to meet Brett—

Every time she visualized such a meeting, however, her latest dream popped vividly to mind—the king's man, the plank. She couldn't turn Brett over to the authorities. Not her. If he were caught, it would have to be by someone else's hand.

Maud Wadkins had outdone herself—alone, it seemed since Hattie Louise wasn't home—preparing enough food to feed the entire crew of the *Mississippi Princess:* roast chicken, with green beans, new potatoes, and squash, the vegetables all canned before the outbreak of fever, she assured them.

"Don't be afraid to eat or drink in my house," she added. "I boil water for everything, even bathing. I'm taking no chances on yellow fever creeping inside my door."

Yellow fever was the sole topic of conversation around the table, and Delta tried to listen, knowing that events as devastating as the plagues that had hit Memphis were invariably used as datemarks. Like the war before it, for years to come everything that happened in Memphis would be described as "before the plague" or "after the plague."

As soon as they finished lunch, Cameron carried Mama Rachael's trunk into the house. "We should be going," he told Delta. Then he winked at Mama Rachael. "Don't worry about Delta and the gambler. I have so much sightseeing planned, she won't have time to think about him."

Mama Rachael flew to Brett's defense. "You be nice to that young man, Delta."

Once they were on their way Cameron chuckled. "I think she's serious about you and the gambler."

"They're all serious about me and someone. Ginny and Hollis, included. They're so afraid I'll end up an old maid, they might be inclined to accept Brett just to see me married."

At Cameron's startled expression, she hurried to add, "I was teasing. There's absolutely nothing between us."

The first place Cameron took her was to Fort Assumption. Standing on a precipice overlooking the Mississippi River, he explained that this was the first permanent site of the present town of Memphis. "Chickasaw Indians were the first known settlers on these bluffs. Later came Europeans—the Spaniard De

137

Soto, the Frenchmen Joliet and Marquette, then La Salle, and after them the British. More recently, of course, the Yankees and Confederates fought over this land." He pointed to a portion of the river. "There's where Union gunboats sank a whole fleet of our ships." He pointed to another place in the middle of the Mississippi. "And the *Sultana* went down right there, in April of sixty-five." He shook his head. "Seems there's tragedy—or reminders of tragedy—all around us. The *Sultana* was carrying twenty-four hundred Union prisoners-of-war back home after the peace was signed. The boat exploded right out there. Most of the men were too sick or undernourished to be able to save themselves. Sad part was that the accident could have been avoided. The boat carried six times its capacity."

"How many men died?" Delta asked.

"No one knows for sure. The official count was somewhere around fifteen hundred."

From the vicinity of the docks they heard the calliope tuning up. Its mirthful sounds seemed irreverent with so much death surrounding them—the War Between the States, steamboat explosions, yellow fever.

"Life goes on, else it has no meaning," Cameron responded when she voiced her thoughts.

Delta scribbled notations for her article and later Cameron took her down to the mouth of the Wolf River. "Not many people realize it outside our immediate area, but before the war Memphis was one of the South's largest inland slave markets."

Cameron waited while she jotted down more notes. "Tomorrow I'll show you some of the things our city fathers are doing to bring this town back since the war and the yellow fever epidemics."

"You needn't go to so much trouble, Cameron. I

138

know you have work to do, and I can find my way around."

"You, trouble? Why, it isn't every day I get to squire a pretty girl about town. Besides, you're doing the city a favor, writing these articles. I will be obliged to leave you on your own the day after tomorrow, though. Business calls. But I'll return in time to see you off the following morning."

On the way back to the boat she invited him to stay for the show.

"Any chance I'll get to meet the gambler?" he quizzed.

She shrugged. A part of her wanted him to meet Brett, to settle the question of this mysterious man's identity. But another part wanted never to know who Brett was, feared learning the truth. What if Cameron recognized him? "I doubt it," she responded. "Brett keeps pretty much to himself."

"Brett?" Cameron turned a curious expression on her. "That's three times by my count you've used his given name. Could Mama Rachael be wrong about you trying to outrun this gambler?"

"Mama Rachael is never wrong," she hedged.

One good thing came of Cameron's attending the performance—he met Zanna and approved of her as a chaperon for the rest of the trip to New Orleans.

"Hollis wired me to check things out," he confessed after they had settled on the back row next to the aisle where Delta could sell tickets to stragglers. "That production manager is feisty enough to handle the seediest of gamblers."

Delta caught herself short of protesting that Brett was far from seedy.

Suddenly Cameron let out a low whistle. "Who the dickens is that?"

Following his gaze to the stage Delta watched Nat make his grand entrance. "Sh," she whispered. "That's Nat, our leading man."

"He isn't your gambler?"

"Of course not!" She flushed at Cameron's choice of words. "Brett—ah, M'sieur Reall isn't *my* gambler."

When Cameron failed to respond, she turned to see him staring at the stage, a deep frown etching his brow. "Stay away from that fellow, Delta."

"From Nat?"

"Whatever he calls himself. Stay away from him. He'd sell his own mother if the price was right."

"Nat?" she questioned again. "You must be mistaken."

He turned serious eyes on her. "I'm not mistaken. That's one dangerous man."

"Dangerous? But he's so . . . so . . ." She thought of Brett calling Nat a pantywaist. "I can't believe Nat is dangerous." She almost choked on the word, a word Nat had used to describe Brett. "Nat's meddlesome, I'll grant you, but dangerous—?"

"Delta, I won't allow you to step one foot on that boat unless you promise to steer clear of him."

"All right, I promise. Actually, I'm not very fond of him. He's too conceited. But if he's as dangerous as you say, why don't you arrest him?"

"He hasn't broken the law that I know of," Cameron admitted. "He's a bounty hunter. I'd give a plugged nickel to know what he's doing on a showboat."

How she managed to make it through the rest of the performance without giving away her distress, Delta would never know. Somehow she did. And from the rail outside her cabin later that night she watched

140

Cameron collar Nat. Standing on the wharf, while deckhands waited to raise the gangplank, they spoke at length, arguing, she suspected from their gestures and body movements. After Cameron climbed back in the hack and rode off, Nat turned to stare in the direction of her cabin.

Delta awoke the following morning in a black mood. Cameron accused her of getting up on the wrong side of the bed. The truth, she knew, was that she had tossed and turned all night wondering what Nat had told Cameron. She had no doubt what a bounty hunter was doing on board the *Mississippi Princess*. No doubt at all, only profound regret.

And fear. What had Nat told Cameron? What would Cameron do with the information? And where was Brett?

She hadn't caught so much as a glimpse of Brett since they docked in Memphis and he learned her cousin was a Pinkerton.

No one, it turned out, had seen him. Zanna stopped Delta before she and Cameron left the boat for a second day of sightseeing.

"If you see Brett in town, tell him Mrs. Humphries and Mrs. Menefee are miffed that they missed their ti' game yesterday. Tell him they've been complaining to Captain Kaney."

All morning while Cameron showed her the new rail lines, introduced her to the city fathers, took her on a ride to see the lushness of the countryside along the mouth of Wolf River, a part of her mind remained fixed on Brett. Where was he? Was Nat after him? What had Nat told Cameron? She dared not address her fears directly, but finally she managed to talk around the issue.

"You're certain you didn't mistake Nat for someone else?" she questioned over lunch at the Hotel Peabody.

"He's a bounty hunter, all right," Cameron confirmed around a bite of beefsteak.

"Maybe we should tell Captain Kaney," she suggested. "He wouldn't want a troublemaker on board." Even voicing such a concern caused her fear to mount. As desperately as she wanted Nat removed from the boat, she knew she could not arouse Cameron's suspicions.

"I don't think it's necessary," Cameron was saying. "I wrestled with that question overnight and decided to take the man at his word."

"His word? What did he say?" She held her breath, waiting to hear the worst, wondering what she would do when Cameron mentioned Brett Reall.

"He assured me he isn't on a job. Said he was taking a leisurely trip to New Orleans. When I asked about his disguise as a thespian, he claimed it wasn't a disguise. Said he'd always had a hankering to act and when he saw Zanna's advertisement for a leading man, he decided to give it a shot since he was on vacation."

"Vacation?" she whispered. Although this was what she had longed to hear, that Nat hadn't mentioned Brett, relief came slowly. She didn't for one minute accept Nat's explanation. His presence on the same boat with Brett could not be accidental. At least, he hadn't told Cameron. Whatever the reason for his silence, it gave her time to decide what to do.

"You have nothing to worry about," Cameron assured her. "I laid the law down to him last night, warned him that if he looks cross-eyed at you I'll have him snatched off that boat and thrown in the hoosegow. I'll have men come aboard at every stop down the river. If he gives you the slightest bit of trouble, you tell my man, and he'll nab the fellow.''

Delta's mouth fell open. Pinkerton agents at each port? What had she done? In thinking to allay her fears, Cameron had magnified them tenfold. Pinkertons watching the boat as they traveled idly down the river. Now her biggest concern was not whether to alert Brett, but how and when.

The latter was settled that night after Cameron returned her to the boat in time for the evening's performance.

Zanna greeted them with, ''I found Brett. He's agreed to come on a picnic with the cast tomorrow.'' She put an inviting hand on Cameron's sleeve. ''You'll join us, won't you?''

''Sorry. I have business out of town tomorrow.'' He eyed Delta then turned back to Zanna. ''You'll keep an eye on Delta and that gambler, won't you?''

''Me?'' Zanna questioned with mock innocence.

Delta cringed, wishing she could divert Cameron's attention from the gambler. But again, she dared not arouse his suspicions. ''If I didn't know better, Zanna, I'd suspect Mama Rachael of leaving you to play matchmaker in her absence.''

Zanna hugged her. ''Never. I have too much to do to meddle in other folks' affairs. Speaking of which, I'd better get backstage. We're giving the performance in our own salon tonight. Won't it be elegant?''

It was, of course, but much of the elegance was lost on Delta who remained engrossed in worry—and anticipation. Tomorrow she would see Brett. The two days since she'd seen him seemed more like months. But how would she warn him? How could she even broach such a topic? What would he say?

I know you're an outlaw. Nat's a bounty hunter. I love you anyway.

I love you anyway? Where did her brain get such foolishness? Fiction, that's all it was—all it could ever be.

The following morning she dressed with care—while her fluttering stomach told her she knew exactly what she was about—choosing a silk costume striped in shades of blue which Mama Rachael had copied faithfully from the spring edition of *Harper's Bazar*. The long princesse polonaise buttoned down the entire front and draped around her hips with revers of silk. Instead of flounces the skirt was trimmed with bands of the same material, cut with bias stripes, and yards of braid and fringe. Foregoing a bonnet, she pulled back her hair and tied it with a large bow of the same blue as her dress. She clipped on dainty pearl earrings, picked up the matching parasol, and again considered her magnificent wardrobe that was fit for a trousseau—and which Ginny had wished was one.

For several minutes after she joined Zanna and the cast on deck, however, she feared all her primping had been for naught. Brett Reall was nowhere to be seen.

And she dared not ask Zanna. Momentarily she considered backing out, but Zanna had gone to such lengths to prepare for this outing, she knew she couldn't disappoint her.

Each person was given a basket, along with the admonition not to peek until they reached their destination. On the docks several drays awaited and Zanna from force of habit, Delta knew, began issuing stage directions.

"Frankie, you and Iona climb aboard here. Albert, you go here. Elyse—" Pausing, she searched the group for Nat, but he had not arrived. "Climb in here Elyse. What do you suppose happened to Nat?"

Without waiting for directions, Delta had started to climb up beside Elyse, when she felt her basket being slipped off her arm. Familiar fingers gripped her elbow, turning her insides queasy.

Relief swept through her. She turned to smile at Brett. His smile was warm, and his black eyes flashed with a hint of arrogance, telling her unmistakably that he read her feelings like a preacher reads the Good Book.

Except Brett Reall was no preacher. He was an outlaw.

"We'll follow you," he called to Zanna, escorting Delta to a carriage behind the two drays. He helped her up, then slid onto the seat beside her and took up the reins.

"I thought you had—" She stopped herself before she blurted out her fear that he might have left the boat for good. "I mean, I thought you weren't coming with us."

"And miss a picnic?"

She cast him a wary glance. "You don't look the type."

"Looks can deceive."

They certainly can, she thought, flooded suddenly with trepidation over the things she planned to tell him today. But sitting here beside him, her senses buzzed, and soon all she could think about was the time he'd told her how much he wanted to make love to her.

"Besides," he continued, flicking the reins to follow Albert who drove the dray ahead of them, "I offered to show you Memphis."

She laughed. "I've already seen it."

"With that handsome kissing cousin?"

"There's nothing romantic between Cameron and me."

His eyes teased, but his face remained solemn. "In

that case I'm sure I can show you some things in Memphis he missed.''

The promise inherent in both his words and his tone of voice sent a thrill up her spine, a thrill she berated herself for feeling. But it did no good. Even though he kept the most proper distance, reminding her of Mama Rachael's assessment of him as a gentleman, his nearness tongue-tied her, and they rode behind the wagon without speaking.

Finally he glanced down at the basket at her feet. ''We could break away from the group and have our own picnic.''

Anticipation and panic vied for control of her senses. Her eyes darted to his. His grin revealed the truth.

She laughed. ''You're teasing me.''

His eyes held hers. ''I've never been more serious in my life.''

For a moment she couldn't tear her gaze away from his. She knew consent was written all over her face, consent and passion, and that he could read both clearly. In an effort to dissipate the charged atmosphere, she reached down and uncovered the basket.

They laughed at the same time.

''Only if we want to drink our lunch,'' she mused, studying the basket full of wine bottles.

He whistled through his teeth. ''Zanna plans some kind of party.''

And indeed Zanna had planned quite a party. They drew up behind the wagon on a grassy knoll ringed by a row of stately oak trees. Twenty yards or so away the Wolf River rushed toward the mighty Mississippi.

Brett leaned toward Delta when he drew the carriage to a halt. ''Did your cousin bring you here?''

His lips were so close to her face she felt his breath hot against her cheek. She knew if she turned her head, he could see her want for him, so she kept her eyes on the river in the distance. "No," she whispered.

"Good."

They joined the group in time to be put to work. Zanna handed Brett a corkscrew and instructed him to begin opening wine bottles. While Albert and Frankie spread cloths on the ground in precisely the spot Zanna directed, Delta, Iona, and Elyse busied themselves unloading everything from veal loaves with dozens of biscuits to cold roast beef, a ham, corked bottles of stewed fruit, cheesecakes, and even a couple of blanc-manges in their molds.

"It's a feast," Delta sighed, standing back to the admire their handiwork.

"What's the celebration?" Brett asked.

"Summertime," Zanna replied. "Settle in and get started. We have to return to the boat in time to sleep off all this wine and food before the performance tonight."

Everyone laughed and plunged in, heaping plates with a little of this, a lot of that.

Brett nudged Delta's arm. When she turned, he handed her a glass of wine. Without a word he touched his glass to hers, his eyes twinkling with silent promises. She felt her heart flutter as she sipped the cool white wine and recklessly allowed herself to consider what lay ahead for her—for them.

For him, she thought, jolted back to reality when Zanna wondered aloud where Nat could possibly have gone. Delta glanced toward Elyse, who sat doe-eyed, listlessly eating a sandwich of veal loaf and biscuit.

Delta turned to Brett.

"Don't look at me," he protested. "I don't know where your leading man ran off to."

She thought about Cameron calling Brett *her* gambler. "He isn't *my* anything," she said in a low voice.

He grinned. "A figure of speech."

Delta let him refill her wineglass, but knew she shouldn't have, since her stomach was too much aflutter to allow her to do more than nibble at her meal. Finally, Brett took the glass from her hand, set it beside her nearly untouched plate, and pulled her to her feet.

"Come on. Let's walk by the river before all this food and wine settle and you fall asleep."

She started to protest, but her hand felt too good encased in his. When they were away from the crowd, he continued, "I want you wide awake the rest of the afternoon."

She didn't dare glance at him. Her heart skipped to her throat and a longing began to gnaw deep inside her stomach; it spread quickly and she thought how she should have eaten more. She'd likely be hungry before dinnertime.

Before she knew it they had strolled several yards away from the group. Weeping willows screened the view, and Brett gently drew her to a halt. She chanced a look and discovered his eyes searing into her face. Her lips parted involuntarily. She knew he intended to kiss her.

For two days she had craved the feel of his lips against hers, of his arms around her. Who was this man who had materialized as from her dreams? Or from her nightmares?

Zanna stepped into view. "Time to head back to the boat."

Delta tried to speak, but her heart was lodged in her throat.

Brett's eyes left hers. "We'll be along in a little while," he told Zanna.

Zanna shrugged. "Fine, but—"

Delta looked at her then and smiled. She thought about Cameron approving Zanna as a chaperon. Had he mentioned it to Zanna?

"Your cousin won't be—ah, waiting for you?" Zanna questioned.

"No," Delta said. "Cameron's out of town. I'll return in time to sell tickets."

Zanna seemed satisfied. "Good. I'll count on you." She grinned. "How 'bout I leave a bottle of wine and a couple of glasses under the tree?"

"Thanks," Brett replied.

Then they were alone. The clatter of wagon wheels faded and silence fell around them. Even the buzzing in Delta's ears stilled, leaving only sounds of nature— the river rushing by at their feet, wind whispering through the willows overhead.

When Brett's voice broke the stillness, she jumped.

"Do you want some wine?" he asked.

Suddenly self-conscious, she didn't know what to say. She wanted to turn and run after the wagon. But she stood as though rooted to the spot.

"Do you?" she asked.

His eyes captured her darting gaze and held it. "You know what I want. I already told you." His eyes grew darker, more intense. "What do you want, Delta?"

As on wings of magic the weight of decision lifted and flew away, leaving her lightheaded, but certain of what she wanted. She moved into his arms.

He embraced her as though they had been separated a lifetime. When he closed his lips over hers, she seemed to melt into him, opening her lips, threading her fingers through his hair, clasping his head, pulling his face nearer, nearer.

All fear vanished. This was where she belonged. His

lips, his tongue, his arms, his body. She pressed herself closer, feeling complete. Here in his arms her life merged into one, the past and the present, daytime and nighttime. Here in his arms she was whole again.

Their tongues met, danced, delved. Their lips tasted, tempted, tormented. Passion reeled and pounded through her veins, throbbed at her throat, pulsated in the lower, intimate regions of her body, while his hands roamed and pressed and caressed.

He drew her face back, laved it with kisses. At that moment a fish jumped in the river nearby, and her nightmare flashed through her brain—Calico Jack stepped off the plank.

Fear swamped her. Fear for Brett. Fear for herself. Fear of losing him. If she lost him she would never be whole again.

"Brett, Nat's a bounty hunter."

"I know."

"You know?"

He kissed her eyes shut, then her lips. Her eyes flew open.

"But he could be hiding out here right now. He could try to—"

"Sh, you worry too much, *chère*. Pierre and Gabriel are taking care of Nat. They will keep him away from us."

Speaking, he trailed a finger over her eyebrows, down her cheek, her neck. She watched the vein in his neck throb and knew he felt the echoing throb in hers. His finger traced down her skin between the deep points of her open collar, coming finally to rest at the first button on her gown.

She stood deathly still, but her body began to tremble beneath his gentle, probing touch. Her heart beat wildly and her bosom rose and fell, drawing the fabric of her bodice tight.

He trailed his fingers over the taut fabric. Beneath it her breasts responded. Her face reddened.

"Must be some demented monk who designs women's fashions," he commented. "Hiding nothing, yet concealing everything. Drives a man crazy, wanting to see what's beneath all those layers, to touch." She felt the top button of her dress slip open. "To taste."

"Brett, what did you do?"

His fingers dipped into the top of her corset cover, and she would have sworn before a judge that her body was on fire.

"I unbuttoned your dress."

She felt him dislodged her breast, felt it rest in his palm, his hot palm. His thumb rubbed tenderly across her nipple, causing a ripple of desire to spiral down her body. She caught her breath and felt her breast expand, pressing into the palm of his hand.

"I mean, why are you running from the law?"

With deliberate slowness he bowed his head and took her breast in his mouth. She gasped at the fiery passion that flooded her with new urgency. His teeth rolled back and forth over her nipple. He suckled her breast as though to pull forth her very soul.

She grasped his shoulders, tugged him closer, felt herself drowning in the agony of wanting him.

Then suddenly he lifted his lips and began repositioning her clothes.

"Don't stop," she whispered into his tumbled hair. "Please, don't stop."

He raised solemn eyes to hers, eyes that spoke of passion as intense as her own. Scooping her in his arms, he headed for the hill where they had eaten lunch.

"We have some talking to do," he said. "Before we

go any further, I intend to answer your questions. All of them." He set her on her feet at the base of the tree, shrugged off his jacket, tossed it aside, bent and picked up the wine bottle. "Sit."

She did. He poured two glasses of wine, recorked the bottle, and sat beside her on the cloth Zanna had left behind with the wine.

"Ask," he instructed, handing her a glass of wine.

"I don't—"

"Ask whatever's bothering you. Get it all out." His liquid black eyes commanded her. "When we make love, I intend to have you here with me. All of you. Your inquisitive brain, along with the rest."

His tone of voice was brusque, but she had grown accustomed to it. The intensity in his eyes as he searched her face was familiar, too. Familiar and reassuring.

She sipped the wine. Finally gaining courage, she began with a question that had nothing to do with outlaws, everything to do with her and Brett. "Are you running away from a . . . ah . . ." She managed to shrug as though the answer didn't mean anything. ". . . a bossy wife?"

His mouth fell open. Finally he smiled. First with his eyes, like always. Afterwards his lips creased in a fine, playful line. "No."

She took a deep breath, felt it tremble in her chest. "Are you married?"

His eyes turned to stone. With a jerk of his head, he looked away at the river. "I was married once. A long time ago."

"What happened?"

He didn't answer right away, and she regretted asking such a personal question. "You don't have to answer that."

He turned back to face her. "She . . . uh, she died."

"I'm sorry."

"Like I said, it was a long time ago. I've put it all behind me—the fact that she's dead, anyway."

Delta set her wine glass aside and reached to touch his lips with her fingers.

"What else?" he demanded.

"Nothing." Her hand moved to his jaw, which she cupped in her palm. Moving closer, she leaned and placed a soft kiss on his lips.

"You wanted to know why I'm running from the law."

"Not now." She kissed him again.

"Yes, now." With one hand he brushed a wisp of hair away from her face, tenderly, in contrast to his curt command. "I was raised in the bayou country of Louisiana," he told her. "Ten years ago I left Louisiana ahead of the law. I've been in Canada ever since."

"Are you still . . . ah, wanted in Louisiana?"

He shrugged. "I suppose. If folks haven't forgotten all about it."

"Why are you going back, then, if—?"

"Because of a blue-eyed woman."

Abruptly, she sat upright.

He grinned, tugged on her chin, pulled her forward, and kissed her. "My mother," he whispered into her lips.

She scooted closer, working herself into his arms.

"I didn't commit the . . . uh, the crime," he explained. "But I couldn't prove my innocence. And I was responsible. I let it happen."

Delta kissed his lips. "That's enough, Brett. I don't need to know anything else. Not right now."

He pulled her into a tight embrace. She felt his stiff,

unyielding body against her own. Drawing back, she looked into his implacable face.

"My crime was one of omission," he said. "I should have been more aware. I should have kept it from happening. I should have—"

"Sh." She covered his face with kisses. "We won't have time for . . ." She left her sentence dangling, unable to make so bold a statement. But his startled expression told her he understood well enough.

She grinned. "Unless you've changed your mind about what you want worse than anything in your grown life." She watched his Adam's apple bob.

"Not a chance, *chère*." His husky voice sent passion flowing through her veins again.

Easing her back against the ground, his eyes followed her like a yo-yo being pulled up a string. His hand splayed against her gussied-up frame, cupping her breast, moving down to her nipped-in waist, across her hips. Then stopped.

"Delta, *chère*, you're enough to drive a man crazy. These clothes tease and tempt. They reveal everything they hide so well."

She smiled, feeling her lips tremble from the passion rising inside her. "Mama Rachael made my wardrobe, not some demented monk. Ginny calls it my trousseau."

The word was barely out of her mouth when she felt his hand grip into the flesh at her waist. His eyes hardened. "I should have suspected," he whispered. "You're on your way to be married."

"Married? Of course not."

As though he hadn't heard, he continued, "You have a bridegroom waiting in—where? Vicksburg? New Orleans?"

Reaching around his neck, she drew his face to hers. "No man is waiting for me anywhere—except here."

And when his mouth covered hers, wet and hot and increasingly demanding, she knew she had spoken the truth. This man had been waiting for her. And she, for him.

If not forever, at least for a long, long time.

That he resembled the pirate in her dream wasn't coincidental. Somehow, Brett Reall was the man in her dreams. But that bizarre, mysterious fact no longer frightened her.

Then he startled her with, "Are you sure about this?" He had already undone several buttons down the front of her gown. The revers lay aside, exposing her corset and the lacy top of her corset cover. His hand poised, lightly fingering the narrow blue ribbon that tied it all together.

"Yes."

"It's your first time?"

"Yes," she answered. But it wasn't. She had already loved him in her dreams.

"Don't be afraid," he said.

She wasn't afraid. She had experienced it all before. She knew exactly what to expect.

At least that's what she thought. In the next hour he proceeded to demonstrate how wrong she had been. With exquisite slowness he tugged at the little blue ribbon, then eased the gathers loose, allowing her breasts to lie softly against her chest.

She watched him look at her, feeling heat creep up her neck. His fingers gently teased her nipples, until she felt them harden beneath his touch. When he looked back into her eyes, she blanched.

"Don't be embarrassed, *chère*. You're beautiful. The things you feel right now are the same things I feel.

Desire. Passion. They spread through your body like lightning, but they don't fade away as fast. They grow brighter and stronger.''

While he spoke softly in a near monotone, his eyes held hers, and his fingers continued to ply her breast. Only when she began to writhe beneath him, did he lower his open mouth and cover her lips, suckling in much the same rhythm as his hand on her breast.

Just when she thought she would drown from the assault on her senses, his lips left hers, trailed downward, leaving a wet streak from his tongue along her neck, over her chest, capturing at last the tormented nipple in his mouth.

Her eyes closed tight against the rising passion, as though to better savor it. Her fingers pressed into the back of his head, crushing his face against her breast in an effort to encourage his fierce onslaught. "Brett," she breathed through abandoned lips. "Brett."

Before she fully realized what he had done, his hand had bunched her skirts and found its way beneath the layers of clothing. She knew what to expect. She had experienced it in her dreams.

But then his hand reached inside the opening of her bloomers and touched the most intimate, begging part of her. Involuntarily her hips raised, allowing his fingers to slip into the moist folds that seeped with desire. Fiery sensations spiraled in all directions from his touch.

Suddenly, her muscles tightened. *What was she doing?* Her eyes flew open. "Brett? Stop."

His hand, which had begun its rhythmic massage inside her, paused, but he did not withdraw it. Instead, he lifted his face from her breast and stared into her startled eyes.

For the longest time they stared at each other, still

as a breezeless day. Then his hand slowly began its exploration. Slipping in and out. In and out.

In and out. His eyes held hers. "Do you want me to stop?" he whispered, at length, without stopping at all.

Sensations she had never even imagined built inside her, fiery sensations, wonderful sensations, begging, pleading sensations, radiating from his stroking hand. "No." Her mouth was so dry she had trouble speaking.

His fingers probed deeper.

Her muscles tightened. "Yes."

His hand stopped. But this time his lips covered hers, kissing her in the same magical, mesmerizing rhythm, bringing life and moisture back to her senses. After a time, his kisses and her body's insistence prevailed. Before she knew what she was doing she began lifting her hips against his hand and with each lift his hand became bolder, thrust deeper, faster.

The ground swayed beneath her head. Her heart pumped to his faster rhythm. Heat and longing grew more intense with each lift of her hips, with each thrust of his hand. She felt him take her tongue in his mouth and suckle it as he had done her breast. She took his and did the same. His hand stroked faster, and she wanted it to last forever.

Then his thumb raked a place she hadn't known existed, spearing her with a new and desperate sense of longing. She felt as though she stood on a bluff overlooking a swirling river, poised to dive into the center of it.

Yet she *was* the center of it. The center and all the spiraling ripples. Ripples of fire.

And then he stopped, withdrew his hand, and lifted his lips from hers.

"Brett, what—?"

His eyes held hers, neither begging nor pleading, but intense and solemn.

"Do you want to finish?"

Her breath was so short she could manage only to nod her head.

"If you're not sure . . . if you're not positive you want to do this, we'll stop right here. Now. Before we go so far you'll always regret it."

Feebly, she wet her lips with her tongue. "I won't regret it."

He smoothed a strand of hair out of her eyes and bent to kiss her forehead. His lips lingered, heating her already fevered skin.

"I won't regret it," she repeated.

He lifted his lips and looked again into her eyes, searching now. "You aren't just saying that? Agreeing for my sake?"

She shook her head. When he still didn't look convinced, she reached her lips to kiss him. "It's new and I was skittish. That's all. I'm sure of what I want." More certain now than ever, she thought. It was so different from her dream, so real. So wonderful.

Still he didn't move. She traced his lips with an index finger. "I want it, Brett. I want you. I want you to be the first."

"The first?"

"That's all I'm asking."

With a wan smile, he returned her kiss, then eased her down again, and began where he had started before, by caressing her breast, kissing her lips. Her passion rekindled quickly this time.

This time she knew there was more. This time she craved it, begged for it. Her hips moved against his body, which he had stretched beside her.

"Please, Brett. Hurry."

He grinned at that and retraced his path beneath her skirts, wreaking havoc with her equilibrium. Finally, when she thought she couldn't stand it another minute, he withdrew his hand again and moved away from her.

"Brett—?"

He chuckled, deep-throated and husky. "Give me a minute."

She watched him fumble with his belt. Feeling her face grow hot, she looked demurely away.

"Now's no time to get modest on me," he teased. But when he eased her skirts up and moved on top of her, all jesting died in his eyes. He looked at her with such an intense, serious expression that she felt moisture brim in her eyes. "You're sure?" he whispered again.

She nodded, suddenly aware of the significance of this moment. "I'm sure," she repeated in as steady a voice as she could muster.

Without taking his eyes from hers, he fumbled through her clothing and eased himself into place. She felt him probe, hard and hot and enormous. Her eyes widened.

"Don't be afraid," he said. "I won't hurt you anymore than I have to. It will hurt a little though." He continued to stare at her, talking to her, while he eased himself deeper and deeper into her begging core. "But you're so hot and so wet and so ready," he was saying, "that it won't be bad."

She felt the world spin. His words, his face, his liquid black eyes, all merged, as she concentrated intensely on the lower regions of her body with wonder and awe and expectation.

"Relax," he was saying. "Try to relax. It's going

to hurt for a minute—now." With a quick jab he thrust his body into hers.

She tightened around him, as though she were clinging to him for safety, for security, for fulfillment.

In that moment the spinning world screeched to a halt. Brett kissed her lips, gently, not passionately. His voice droned on, but she was past understanding his words. The pain was brief, her need great, and when he didn't make a move, she did.

Lifting her hips against him, she felt his hardness slip inside her. She lowered her hips. He slipped out, out, and just before he pulled himself free, she lifted her hips again.

"Please, Brett. I need . . . I need . . . something . . . so bad . . ."

With infinite tenderness he moved into her again. "I know what you need, *chère.*"

And indeed he did.

It was as if they had dived together into the center of that spiraling river. And when they came up, it was to a bright sun and crimson flowers and a blue, blue sky. She fell exhausted against the ground, her body weak and flushed with wonderment.

He collapsed beside her, drawing her close, burying his face between her breasts. The intimacy of it brought tears to her eyes. She clung to him, so full of life and joy she thought for sure she wouldn't be able to contain it.

What had begun as a nightmare had ended in ecstasy, in fulfillment, in wholeness. Moving back she traced the outline of his lips with her fingers. She gazed into the depths of his liquid black eyes.

It took a minute for her spinning senses to recognize the change in him. As though storm clouds had gathered over the clear blue sky, his loving eyes gradually grew dim. His voice, when he spoke, was thick not with passion, but with something akin to anguish.

"God's bones, Delta! I should be shot at sunrise. What if you conceived my child?"

Their gazes held for the longest time, during which her heart stopped beating at the pain she read on his face. Suddenly the sounds around them beat up in her ears, drowning her with sorrow, and through it all came the desperate crying of a babe.

Burying her face in his shoulder, she clenched her eyelids against the return of her nightmare. Was she going mad? Totally, completely, forever mad?

Chapter Eight

Brett lounged against the rail on the observation deck, watching Delta where she stood in the doorway to the grand salon, selling tickets for the evening's performance.

She had changed clothes since they arrived back at the boat. In place of the fancy blue gown, she now wore a white shirtwaist with tucks crisscrossing her bosom and a hip-hugging black skirt with a short train that fell from a ti' bustle. The high collar of the bodice circled her neck like a wedding band and he wondered briefly whether she had worn it to keep his hands off.

At that moment she glanced his way, throwing him a radiant smile, and he knew she would deny him nothing.

She glowed. Gone was the melancholy that had haunted her blue eyes ever since he'd first seen her. He was the one who had chased it away. He knew that. He was the one who had put that smile on her lips. She was his for the taking—and he had taken.

The hunger in his body warned him he might try such a stunt again. Not that he had qualms about taking a desirable woman to bed. He certainly didn't. But Delta Jarrett wasn't just any desirable woman. And that fact rankled him.

Rankled and threatened. At first he had thought his attraction to her had something to do with her blue eyes, with the blue-eyed woman who had been slipping into his dreams the last few months. He had put it down to sexual attraction.

The innocent, yet provocative way her hips swayed when she walked, the not-so-innocent passion in her kisses stirred his body to an uncomfortable state, just thinking about them. He would have been aroused by those traits in any woman, he had told himself.

But Delta Jarrett wasn't *any* woman. The attraction he felt to her was different from anything he had experienced before. He should have been forewarned when she burst into Wint's cabin outside Cairo. God's bones! Even when he thought her out to expose him in her newspaper, all he had wanted was to smother her with kisses and take her to bed.

Then she had related the gruesome news that people were calling him a pirate. A pirate? A smuggler? No matter, either came so close to the truth as to jeopardize his entire mission. Couldn't they be one and the same? He had been furious enough to strike her for that, even though he had never struck a woman in his life. But instead of ignoring her or riding off and leaving her to find her own way back to town, as would have been his style, what had he done? He had kissed her. He grinned recalling it, thinking he'd have to ask her if she still considered him a pirate from the past.

Berating himself for not taking the situation more seriously, Brett knew he'd better face facts—tangible facts, like the sick, hollow feeling that had gripped his stomach when she called her clothing a *trousseau,* and he had for one agonizing moment imagined her on her way to wed another man.

Emotional facts, such as the joy he experienced upon

discovering he had misunderstood. God's bones! Joy? In a man who couldn't recall experiencing such a thing for ten years. Even thinking back on it, a sense of elation ebbed into his body somewhere in the region of his heart and he had difficulty suppressing it.

Delta had put it there, the same way he had put the smile on her face. But how long would her lips spread from ear to ear in the most captivating smile he had ever seen? How long, after the dangers that surrounded him surfaced? How long would her eyes remain free of melancholy? How long, when she learned the truth, the whole truth?

How long, when she discovered that her mysterious pirate was in truth a fugitive from a murder charge that would haunt him to the grave and beyond?

Oui, it was time to face facts, reality—the harsh reality that he could not live in Delta Jarrett's world and she would not be safe in his.

He tried to turn away from her, but again she cast a smile his way. A smile full of promises and hope. A smile full of . . . *love.*

He recalled the utter despair, almost anger, he had felt when she told him she wanted him to be the *first.*

The first! When what he wanted was to be the last.

And that in itself was a first—the first time in ten years he could remember wanting anything. Unable to keep his eyes from roaming her inviting form, he spun away. Staring into the black depths of the muddy Mississippi, he contemplated jumping overboard. He could swim to shore and never see her again.

Oui, he wanted her. God's bones, how he wanted her. But he could never have her, so he'd better find some way to keep that pertinent fact from hurting her.

Brett flinched when she tugged at his sleeve. "Come on, the play's about to begin."

Turning, he looked down at her, an action he recognized as a mistake the moment he got lost in her eyes.

He tried to brush it off. "I've seen that melodrama a dozen times."

"Me, too. But they expect us to be there. If we're not, they might think—" Her words stopped. He watched her drop her eyes. He recalled the way she had modestly looked aside when he undressed by the river.

The thought of it shot desire straight to the lower region of his body. He shifted his weight uncomfortably.

Seeing no way out, short of walking away from her, he took her arm and escorted her toward the grand salon. "Let's go, then. I certainly wouldn't want to ruin a lady's reputation."

Not until they were seated on the back row of golden bamboo chairs did he realize he had taken the coward's way out. He could have let her come alone.

He should have. But by the time the performance ended, he had convinced himself that this way was better. He would escort her back to her cabin and explain that he couldn't see her again. He owed her that much—an explanation—of sorts.

When the cast returned to the stage for a curtain call, the audience applauded vigorously and Delta leaned close to whisper in Brett's ear.

"Nat doesn't look at all like a bounty hunter."

Her warm, sweet breath against his ear startled him. He felt his body flex and knew he'd best make his explanation short.

"Does he?" she prompted.

Brett looked down at her, a mistake he had made once before this evening. "Does who, what?"

Her expression was serious and innocent and he thought suddenly that she had no idea of the effect she had on him.

"Nat doesn't look like . . . you know, what he is."

He smiled in spite of his promise to remain aloof. "You mean he's too handsome to kill folks for a living?"

She shook her head, setting her loose curls to swaying. With the greatest difficulty Brett kept his hands to himself.

"No," Delta was saying, "he looks too . . . too baby-faced to be dangerous."

"So does William Bonney but he's rumored to have killed twenty-one men."

She shuddered and he regretted jesting about something so serious. "Don't worry, *chère*, Nat's likely after some real outlaw. I'm only a pirate, remember?"

They slipped out of the salon ahead of the crowd and he guided her directly toward the cabin deck, where he had every intention of telling her good night—and good-bye.

He guided her by her elbow until touching her became too intimate. He dropped his hand, tried to grip his resolve, but the brush of her skirt against his leg reminded him of how close she was, of how much closer he wanted her.

She babbled gaily while they walked along the near-deserted decks. He couldn't recall her babbling before and couldn't stop himself wondering whether she would again tomorrow. Or would her eyes be filled with melancholy once more?

The sweet sounds of her voice mingled with the soft summer breeze and the gentle lapping of the river against the sides of the moored boat. He tried to close them out, to concentrate on what he intended to say to her, how he would phrase it, but like a cork bobbling on a fishing line, he felt his concentration ebb and flow. By the time they reached her cabin, he knew he had better say his piece and be gone.

"Delta, I'm sorry about this afternoon, I—"

She had stopped in front of her stateroom door. In the dim light he could make out the eighteenth-century lady and her squire painted on the top panel. At his words, she lifted her face to look at him, and it hit him in the gut—all the guilt he had been running from for ten damned years.

And here he was, apologizing to this woman again. Seems that's all he ever did. "I don't want you to think—"

"Come over here, Brett." She pulled him toward the rail. "Isn't it a beautiful sight? Moonlight on the water. It glistens, doesn't it? Looking at it now, you can't see the sandbars that wreck boats on the—"

"Delta—"

"It looks so clean and beautiful. So free of snags and sawyers—"

"Dammit Delta, hush." Before he realized it, he had grabbed her shoulders and turned her to face him. "Listen to me."

Her innocent expression further provoked him. "You can't get close to me. I can't allow you to. We can't—"

Without warning, she stood on tiptoe and kissed him softly on the lips. "We already are."

"Are what?"

"We are," she replied.

Suddenly he realized they had exchanged these words before. These selfsame words. Except it had been he who insisted they couldn't change the course they were on.

He pulled her to his chest, cradling her head against his beating heart. What the hell kind of spell did this woman weave?

Drawing away, she reached to trace the outline of his lips. He stood stock still, willing himself not to show how affected he was by her tender touch. Staring at her own lips, he recalled how they had looked after their lovemaking, full and swollen and rosy-ripe. He wished he could kiss her that way now.

"Don't misunderstand me, Brett. I'm not asking for a commitment."

His eyes narrowed on hers. "Like hell you aren't."

"I'm not."

"Don't try to bluff me, Delta. Nor yourself. A woman like you doesn't make lov—ah, do what we did today without expecting a commitment."

"Then I'm different." She studied him with a deeply sensual look. "We're different. You said it, too. There's something between us that's . . . that's unusual, mystical, even."

"I don't believe in such stuff."

"Neither do I, but it's there. And it won't go away unless we talk about it."

"Then talk," he responded in clipped tones. "I have nothing to say."

Suddenly a loud thud, accompanied by the sound of scurrying feet came from around the corner by the sternwheel. As if she had rehearsed the entire operation, Brett thought later, Delta grabbed his hand, dragged him across the deck, unlocked her door, and drew him inside her cabin.

Leaning back against the door, she relocked it. Her breath came in gasps. "That could have been Nat."

Her concern did more to unravel his determination than even her kiss had earlier. "You don't understand," he barked. "Pierre is my bodyguard. He won't let that prissy actor get near me—or you." He reached for the door handle. "I have to be going."

"Please," she said quickly. "I must talk to you. I can explain . . . well, not explain what has happened between us, but I can shed some light on it."

He gritted his teeth. "I don't want to hear, Delta."

"But—?"

"You say you don't want a commitment, well, that's exactly what you're asking for. And you can't get it, not from me. You don't even know me. You don't know anything about me. Yesterday you were terrified every time you looked into my eyes. Today we made love." His words ran out and he took a deep breath. "You should have stayed frightened."

"I know you." Her soft voice slashed guilt through him. "Don't you remember when we first saw each other? At lunch, across the dining room. Well, I recognized you."

His hand dropped from the door handle, falling slack by his side. He recalled the incident. How could he forget it? He'd even told Pierre and Gabriel how he was certain she had recognized him.

While he stood silently trying to sort his carnal emotions for this woman from his fears of whom she might be, of what she might know about him, she traipsed around the room lighting the lamps. Slowly the room took on a golden glow.

"Sit here." She indicated one of the two beds. "It's Mama Rachael's bed." She grinned, a wan, worried sort of grin. "Don't worry, I won't seduce you."

His eyes held hers for an instant before guilt forced him to turn away. "I did the seducing, Delta. Don't go thinking otherwise. I controlled that situation. You didn't have a choice."

Glancing at her, he watched her flush at his words and felt his body react, realizing that her mental images must surely match his own in every provocative detail. "I've already apologized," he added.

"Do you want something to drink?" she asked. "Captain Kaney provided us with a well-stocked bar, although,"—she glanced at him with a shy grin—"I doubt he included spirits for gentlemen."

Brett tried to smile, but he kept recalling how they had exchanged such a conversation by the river, and what he had replied, thinking what he would like to reply now. He knew what he wanted, and it wasn't a drink.

"A glass of sherry, then," he agreed.

Once she handed him the glass and poured one for herself, she sat on the opposite end of the bed facing him. She looked at him so solemnly he could read her hesitancy.

"You recognized me," he prompted. "So, who am I?"

She pursed her lips, released them, and said, "Will you promise to hear me out before you decide I've lost my mind?"

"I promise," he replied, but his brain was busy trying to decide how he would cope with her knowing the truth, the whole truth. How the hell had she learned it? She had certainly known it earlier today when she gave him the greatest gift she would ever give a man, and she had given it and enjoyed it. And she had lost her fear of him.

"Remember when I said folks were calling you a pirate?"

He nodded, striving to concentrate on her words and not on their consequences. When she finished, would

170

she throw him out the door? That's where he belonged, out . . . out of her life.

She gulped a swallow of sherry, coughed, then dabbed at her lips with the back of her hand. "Well, I had thought that, even before I heard others make the claim. Several months ago I began having strange dreams, nightmares. They weren't really nightmares while they were going on, they were dreams but they were so real I actually experienced—I mean, until this afternoon I thought I had experienced—"

"Delta, slow down. Start over. Your dreams or nightmares, what were they about?"

She looked at him, resolute, he could tell. "About the pirates Calico Jack and Anne Bonny."

Growing more leery, Brett recalled her claim that he looked like Calico Jack. "What about the pirates? What do they do in your dreams?"

"They make love," she responded.

He chuckled softly, relieved at her answer. "What's so bad about that?"

"Nothing, except—" She paused.

He watched her take another swallow of sherry before she continued.

"Calico Jack was hanged, and Anne Bonny disappeared. But that isn't all. When I came on board this showboat, my dreams started changing. Do you remember that first night when I surprised you and your friends by the paddlewheel and you—you kissed me?"

He drew a sharp breath at the reminder. *"Oui."*

"That's why I was on deck . . . dressed like that. I had awakened from another nightmare, and it was so terrifying I had to get some air. The pirates hadn't made love in that dream, they had just kissed, and she had . . . she had run her fingers over his lips, and it was all the same as between us, except the kiss in

171

my dream was soft and gentle and not rough and cruel—"

"Delta, don't."

She drained her sherry glass. He watched her grip the stem in such a tight fist he feared the crystal might crack. He wanted to take it from her, but resisted. "What else?"

"The night before we arrived here in Memphis I dreamed about Calico Jack's death. The pirate ship had been tricked into boarding a government vessel that was full of soldiers. Calico Jack and Anne Bonny had been betrayed by a government agent on board their own ship, and Anne was forced to watch him walk the plank."

Brett frowned, trying to remember how the story went. "It could have happened that way, I suppose, but as I recall Calico Jack was hanged on the island of Jamaica."

"I know. They're my ancestors. But in my dreams things are different. Do you remember standing beside me while we moored here in Memphis?"

He wanted to tell her he would remember every single time he had stood beside her, lain beside her, loved her, probably for the rest of his life. But he didn't. *"Oui."*

"The instant I saw my cousin Cameron and told you about him being a Pinkerton agent, I knew the truth. When I turned around to invite you to spend the day with us, you had disappeared."

He held her gaze for several lengthy seconds. "Then it was my loss."

"You don't understand, Brett. My dreams are a warning. My ancestors are warning me that someone needs help. Someone is in danger. Another thing—this afternoon by the river when you said that . . . uh, when you were so horrified at the thought that I might have . . .''

Her stumbling words begged for his help. Her cheeks flamed in the candlelight and he knew what she was trying to say, but he was unable to help her.

He tried to stop her. "Don't Delta—"

"When you worried that I might have conceived your child," she continued in a rush of words, "one part of the nightmare, the part that never changes, flashed through my mind. My dreams all end the same way—with a baby crying."

The sherry glass, from which he had drunk little, slipped from Brett's fingers. He watched the amber liquid spread in a widening circle over the green damask bedspread.

His eyes found Delta's. The agony on her face pierced straight to his heart. He looked away.

"What does it mean, Brett?"

Like a wounded animal, his heart struggled so hard it seemed to get lodged in his throat. Withdrawing his handkerchief from an inside pocket, he stabbed at the spilled sherry. "You tell me."

"You're the one in danger, Brett. I know it. For months I've been tormented by the knowledge that someone needed my help. Someone, someplace needed me. It's been driving me mad. That's why I came on this trip. Ginny and Hollis, my sister and brother-in-law in St. Louis, they thought a change of scenery would rid me of the dreams. But it didn't. Instead the dreams changed. Everything's clear now. You're the one in danger, Brett."

Fear and guilt boiled inside him like bile. He jumped to his feet, intending to deny any connection and rush from the room. "Why me?" he stormed, finding himself bending over her, his knees touching hers as they jutted from the side of the bed.

"Why me?" he repeated, harsh and demanding, close to her face.

Melancholy filled her eyes, searing him with a deep sense of sadness, made heavier by the tears that threatened to roll down her cheeks at any moment.

"Because you're the pirate in my dreams," she said.

"I'm not. Your dreams are about Calico Jack. He lived over a hundred years ago."

"You are. I can't explain it, but it's true. You even swear alike. *God's bones*—that's what Calico Jack says in my dreams."

"Because you heard me say it first," he countered.

"He said it first. Months ago. You are the pirate in my dreams."

"That's crazy,' he muttered, after clearing his throat to be able to utter a sound.

She reached to trace his lips, eliciting a shudder at the intimacy, at the reminder of all the other times she had performed this simple gesture.

"You are," she whispered. "You're identical to him—" her eyes left his briefly to scan his body, then she looked him full in the face again, "—in every detail."

And that simple statement, so explicit in the images it evoked, was his undoing. His lips covered hers, crushing, devouring, and the next thing he knew he lay wrapped in her arms, skin to skin, his head nestled between the soft, luscious mounds of her naked breasts.

The farthest he got from her the rest of the night was when they moved to the other bed to escape the spilled sherry. Perhaps it was the darkened room, but as the night wore on she lost more and more of her modesty. Once she told him, "I thought this afternoon was the best anything could ever be, but every time gets better.''

He chuckled. ''It's having a soft bed beneath you instead of the cold, hard ground.''

''No,'' she mumbled, ''it's having you . . . *inside* me.'' The last words escaped on a ragged breath of air while she lifted her hips in answer to his bold thrusts, drawing forth his seeds in a great trembling surge of passion.

Afterwards they clung together, damp and exhausted. Her womanly scent mingled with the faintest hint of violets in the close room, surrounding him as in a womb of her own making.

He knew he should feel guilty, but her joy prevented such a thing. He knew he should feel trapped, like a fly in a spider's web, but he didn't. And here in her arms, with her body curled into his like a cobbler's last that had been molded to fit his form and no other, he wasn't even able to question his contentment.

''Brett?'' she called once, rousing him from where he had dozed with the tip of her breast in his mouth. Stirring, like a babe he began to suckle, then as though to assure her he was instead a lover, he rolled her nipple between his teeth. She squirmed, nuzzling the soft hair at the base of her abdomen into his.

''Ready for more?'' he teased.

She wriggled against him. ''Are you?''

''I think we can manage once more before sunup, at which time, m'moiselle, I will leave you to dress for breakfast.''

''Breakfast?''

''Have you ever watched the sunrise on the Mississippi?''

She shook her head, teasing her curls across his face.

''Then this morning you will,'' he promised. ''A

175

spectacular end to a perfect night." He kissed her. "Or beginning to a perfect day."

"Or both," she whispered into his lips.

Later when he started to leave, she pulled him to her and asked a question he suspected had been bothering her for some time.

"Do you think I'm demented? About the dreams, I mean?"

Cupping her breasts, one in each palm, he bent and kissed each in turn, then he kissed her lips. "No, *chère.*. But there must be other explanations. Perhaps your family has spoken too often of the pirates. Perhaps the pirates represent other troubles you have. Who knows what goes on inside the mind while it is asleep?"

"But you don't think I'm mad?"

He kissed her again. "No. If it will make you feel better, I've had dreams of my own to worry over lately. That's the reason I'm headed back to the bayou. I've been seeing a hazy image of a blue-eyed woman in my dreams. I've never been able to make out the woman's face, but I finally decided it must be my mother calling me home."

"Calling you home?"

He laughed. "I told you I don't put stock in things like that, and I don't. The truth is, though, that my mother is a *traiteur*. Some folks even call her a witch."

Delta gasped.

Again, he chuckled. "She treats people with herbs from the bayou and potions she brews herself. She claims to have psychic powers, but I've never seen her use them. I didn't mean she was actually calling me. I haven't seen her in ten years, and well, I'm going home to see if she's all right."

Delta thought about this while she dressed. At least, he didn't think she was demented, but she could tell he didn't intend to spend much time worrying over his own safety, either.

She dressed in another gown Mama Rachael had copied from *Harper's Bazar*. This one, a mandarin yellow princesse dress, was overlaid with a sleeveless polonaise that fit like a second dress, dipping to the top of the skirt's flounce and lacing in great crisscrosses from the top of her bosom to the bottom of the skirt with a heavy white silk cord. According to the magazine, the garment was designed for the seashore, which led Mama Rachael to claim it would be appropriate for a promenade on board a steamship on the Mississippi River.

Or for a sunrise breakfast with the pirate in her dreams, Delta thought, giddy from her night with Brett. When she reached the outdoor dining area off the paddlewheel lounge, Brett's perusal fairly set her skin on fire.

"More of your *trousseau*?"

She laughed.

With his hand resting intimately at the small of her back, Brett ushered her to a table near the rail. The Mississippi River flowed ahead of them, and to one side, the docks of Memphis. Roustabouts worked around the wharf, rolling giant coils of rope, hauling crates of food on board. Chanting an ancient song whose words were lost in its steady rhythm, they prepared the steamship to embark downriver within the hour.

"The best seat in the house, m'moiselle," Brett announced, holding her chair. "I've ordered breakfast."

"Thank you, m'sieur," she laughed.

The waiter brought a silver coffee urn and filled their cups. She studied Brett so intently that he finally turned away with a wink, focusing his attention on the brightening sky.

"I invited you here to watch the sunrise."

She started to tell him she'd much prefer to watch him, but decided against it. She was determined not to break one promise she had made the night before—she would do nothing to cause him to think she needed a commitment. She wasn't fool enough to think this relationship could last. She must be prepared to take what she could get and not be heartbroken when it was over.

And she must find a way to protect him. Regardless of his opinion of her dreams, she was certain he was in danger.

They were the only two diners on deck at the moment and the hush of morning rested around them. The deep, melodic chant of the roustabouts sounded as an honor guard to the majestic sun on its rise above the horizon.

"Next time we'll get here earlier," Brett said, his eyes still on the river. Like a golden ball the sun moved higher and higher in rhythm to the roustabouts' chant. "Tomorrow morning when the boat is steamin' down the river, we'll come before dawn. It'll take your breath away."

"It already does," she whispered, knowing she spoke of the man by her side as much as of the sky, streaked with pink and gold. Sunlight skimmed the glass-smooth surface of the river, highlighting the reflections of trees and shoreline as with an artist's brush.

The waiter returned carrying steaming platters of eggs, beefsteak, grits, and biscuits and jams.

"I'm famished," she said, spreading the starched white napkin across her lap.

Brett tossed her a teasing grin. "You should be, after all the work you put in last night."

She felt a blush creep up her neck and knew she must glow like the rising sun. "Shame on you."

"Shame on you," he laughed. "No, I didn't mean that." His eyes held hers with an intense, passionate expression that turned her to jelly. "You were magnificent."

Her cheeks burned. She wanted to cover her face. But more than that, she wanted to kiss him. So all she did was stare.

"If you don't stop looking at me like that, *chère,* we'll miss the sunrise."

She had just considered telling him she wouldn't mind missing the sunrise, when she saw his face stiffen. They were seated with his chair facing slightly toward the docks, hers toward the far bank of the river.

She turned to see what had caught his eye.

"Oh," was all she could manage, seeing Mama Rachael and Cameron stride toward the gangplank.

"Your cousin, the Pinkerton?"

She nodded, lifting her arm to return the waves from below. Then fear gripped her. She turned to Brett.

"Will he recognize you?"

He shook his head.

"You're sure?" She glanced back to the deck, but Mama Rachael and Cameron were out of sight.

Brett turned her chin with two fingers. Quickly he nipped a kiss on her startled lips. "I'm sure he won't recognize me for a fugitive," he said. His eyes probed hers. "But I'm afraid he may recognize me for what I've done to you."

When his meaning registered, her eyes widened. "How?"

His fingers gently caressed her lips, then dropped to his side. "By the way you look at me, *chère.*"

"Then I won't."

"Good. I'd hate to find myself walking the plank like that disreputable fellow in your dreams. Especially now that life's beginning to have a bright side."

Mama Rachael and Cameron arrived soon after, giving Delta no chance to respond. But his words resounded through her head, bringing a gleam to her eye and a smile to her lips.

"M'sieur Reall," Mama Rachael greeted Brett, "I will miss our ti' games."

"And I, madame."

Cameron kissed Delta on the cheek, while she wondered whether she should introduce Brett, or whether Cameron would recognize the name and haul him off to jail.

Brett took charge of the situation by extending his hand. "Brett Reall, M'sieur Jarrett. Your cousin and I were enjoying breakfast on the river. We'll pull up a couple of chairs—"

"No, thanks," Cameron replied. Delta watched the way his eyes traveled over Brett. Releasing Brett's hand, he placed a brotherly arm about her shoulders and drew her protectively to his side. When he continued, still speaking to Brett, his voice sounded unduly authoritative. "I promised Delta we would come to say good-bye. That's all."

Delta grimaced. With everything that had transpired since she last saw Cameron, she'd completely forgotten his promise. What if she and Brett had remained in her cabin? What if . . . ?

"Where's Zanna?" Cameron asked her.

"Zanna?"

"She promised to keep an eye on you."

Delta's chagrin turned to acute embarrassment. "I'm sure she knows she can trust me to have breakfast alone, Cameron." Her words were intended to chastise, but she saw they didn't work, for he began to interrogate Brett.

"How far do you plan to travel on the *Mississippi Princess,* Reall? That is the name you said—Reall?"

Watching Brett with held breath, Delta knew instantly that wasn't his name. Why else would he so blithely give it to a Pinkerton?

"Oui, Reall," Brett acknowledged readily. "I'm traveling to New Orleans . . ." Leaving the sentence hanging, he shrugged as if to say—not that it's any of your business. Delta wondered why he had responded. A man wasn't required to answer direct questions like that. A gentleman never asked such questions. Then again, family responsibilities had always superseded manners in the Jarrett family.

Mama Rachael broke into the tension. "I do hope you're making the return trip, M'sieur Reall. I would so like to resume our ti' games."

Brett laughed easily with her. "So you can win the . . . ah, the shirt off my back, madame?"

While Mama Rachael continued to fawn over Brett, Cameron drew Delta aside. "Get your things together. You're coming ashore with us."

"What?"

"You could be in danger on this boat, Delta. I can't allow you to continue."

"From what?" She glanced toward Brett, then back at Cameron. "Or from whom? A gambler?"

"He isn't a gambler."

Her heart thudded to a stop. She prayed it didn't show.

"But no, not from Reall—whoever he is." He grinned. "Unless you watch too many sunrises with him."

181

Delta willed her face not to flush. "That's my business."

"Don't get huffy, Delta. I agree. Your personal life is your own business. You're a sensible woman. Ginny raised you right. Mama Rachael assures me that you are adept at keeping out of the clutches of cavaliers."

"Cameron!" She felt herself blush in spite of all efforts.

He grinned. "She also believes that this gambler is the model of a perfect gentleman, even if he does play cards with little old ladies."

Delta tried a laugh and partially succeeded. "Because he plays cards with little old ladies and lets them win," she corrected.

Cameron laughed with her, then sobered as the first whistle sounded for guests to leave the boat. "It's that bounty hunter I'm worried about, Delta. The one posing as an actor."

"I promised to stay away from Nat, and I will." She placed a hand on his arm. "This is an important trip, Cameron. I'll be one of the few journalists to record the passage through Captain Eads's new jetties. That's why I came. I can't—"

With pursed lips, Cameron stared out at the muddy river. "I have a gut feeling the fellow you call Nat lied to me the other night. He isn't the sort to spend a few weeks on board a showboat unless there was a payoff. He's after someone, Delta, and I don't want you anywhere around when he finds his prey."

"I won't be, Cameron. I promise. I'll stay completely away from Nat. But I'm not getting off this boat. Don't you understand what this trip means to my career?"

"Your career?"

"As a journalist. Captain Eads's jetties will make

news around the world. I'll be one of the privileged journalists—"

"Delta—"

"I'm going to New Orleans, Cameron. Aboard the *Mississippi Princess*. Don't worry about me."

He drew a deep breath, staring past Delta. Without turning she knew he was looking straight at Brett. She wished he'd never seen Brett.

"Tell you what," Cameron said at last, "I'll agree to you staying on board as far as Vicksburg. One of my agents there, a man named Stuart Longstreet, will meet the boat. If you've noticed anything out of line, or if Longstreet notices anything out of line, you must promise me you'll stay in Vicksburg."

She glared at him, pursing her lips.

"Your safety comes before any damned career."

Still she glared.

"Hollis put me in charge at this point, Delta. Your welfare is important to all of us."

"I know," she said at last. "I promise to be careful."

"And to get off the boat at Vicksburg if either you or Longstreet suspects trouble?"

She nodded.

"Promise?"

"Promise," she repeated, because she knew if she didn't he would never give up.

"One more thing," he told her. "I want you to wire me from every port."

"Cameron?"

"I'm serious, Delta. That bounty hunter's dangerous."

"All right. A wire from every port."

He grinned then, reminding her of her brothers. It was tough to be the only single girl with six brothers and an uncountable number of male relations to protect her.

The last warning whistle blared through the tension. Cameron glanced toward Brett, then back to Delta. His words caught her off guard. "Be careful of that fellow, too. You shouldn't trust a man who disguises himself, Delta, not even enough to dine with him on a crowded boat. You can find plenty of beaux in New Orleans."

He hugged her good-bye, then dragged Mama Rachael away from Brett with a closing question Delta knew to be a final warning.

"Kale and Carson are meeting you in New Orleans, aren't they, Delta? And Cousin Brady?"

"Kale and Carson?" Brett questioned after their visitors had left and the boat was underway. He held her chair and they resumed eating their now-cold breakfast.

"Two of my brothers."

His eyes widened in mock dismay. "And Cousin Brady. I suppose they're all as brawny as this one."

She nodded, smiling. "You remind me of them in many ways. Kale, in particular."

"Kale?"

"He's the outlaw. Or was."

Watching her over the rim of his coffee cup, he held her gaze for a long time.

Finally she changed the subject. "I thought we exorcised my nightmares last night, but now we have a new one."

The crease between his eyes deepened. "What's that?"

"Cameron is so suspicious of Nat he tried to take me off the boat. He's sending another agent aboard at

Vicksburg with instructions to remove me from the *Mississippi Princess* if he suspects danger."

"Sure it's Nat he's suspicious of?"

She cast him a worried look, not daring to tell him that Cameron had instructed her to stay away from him, too. Finally, she laughed. "I didn't look at you."

He lifted his eyebrows in response, holding a biscuit smeared with plum jam to her lips. *"Non, chère,* you did not. After breakfast perhaps we can find a way for you to amend the slight."

Chapter Nine

Love affairs, Delta soon discovered, were not easily conducted in the real world, not even isolated in the middle of the Mississippi River on a steamboat. No sooner had the waiter approached their table with a pot of fresh coffee, than Pierre appeared, his face a rigid mask.

"You are here, *mon nèfyou.*" He challenged Brett in clipped tones without so much as a glance at Delta. "Gabriel and me, we worried that you missed the boat."

Delta dabbed her lips with her napkin, careful to avoid either man's eyes. She knew her face glowed like the sun rising over the muddy waters.

"You knew very well that I did not," Brett barked. Suddenly his warm hand reached for Delta's where it lay in her lap. She felt his eyes on her face, but she resisted looking at him. He lifted their clasped hands and rested them together on top of the table. "I don't believe you and Pierre have been properly introduced, *chère.*"

She glanced at Brett, then. The smile in his eyes hadn't reached his lips, nor his voice when he introduced her to his bodyguard, a man he called Pierre.

Pierre bowed slightly from the waist. "M'moiselle."

His expression did not soften. He returned his eyes quickly to Brett, demanding, "We must talk, yes."

"Fine," Brett replied. "Pull up a chair."

"Non. Not right here."

Alarmed by the man's combative tone of voice, Delta glanced involuntarily at him. His eyes were fastened on her hand, which still lay inside Brett's clasp. She wriggled her fingers to free them, but Brett held her tighter.

"I will take myself to your stateroom," Pierre informed Brett. "Gabriel and me, we will wait for you right there."

Delta watched the big man depart with as much dispatch as he had arrived, leaving in his wake a sickening dread. She turned to see vexation written in the implacable set of Brett's jaw.

Her heart raced. "What's happened? Are you in danger?"

"Danger?" His annoyance faded to impudent grin. "No, *chère.*"

"Are you sure? He sounded so . . . so angry."

"If there was danger, Pierre would have been concerned, not angry, and we wouldn't be sitting here. He would have whisked us off this deck before we'd known what had happened." He squeezed her hand. "No, it seems we have more adversaries than your cousin, Cameron."

She withdrew her hand, lifting her napkin to suddenly dry lips. "Adversaries?"

Leaning, he pecked a kiss on her lips. "You didn't expect the world to sit by and let us fall in love, did you?"

Her stomach turned a somersault. "In love?"

He raised his eyebrows. "When a man spends the

night with a respectable girl like yourself, he'd better be prepared to call it love."

"Oh!" She looked down at her plate, frowning. "You don't think they know about last night?"

"No, *chère*. They may suspect. Probably not your cousin, but I'm sure Pierre does since I didn't return to my stateroom."

"That's nobody's business but ours."

"*Oui*, but . . . well, you must admit they have reason for concern. Your cousin wouldn't want you falling in love with some no-account gambler, would he?"

She sighed, wondering whether she should tell him that his gambler's disguise hadn't fooled Cameron, if disguise it turned out to be. "What about Pierre?" she asked, shoving her confusion over Brett's identity back into the recess she had made for it in her muddled brain. "What does Pierre have against me . . . ah, against *us?*"

He sipped from his coffee cup. "You're a journalist."

She pushed back a wisp of hair that fluttered about her face. "What does that have to do with anything?"

"I told you he's my bodyguard. He's also my uncle."

When she still frowned, he finished with, "He doesn't want you to expose me in the newspapers."

"Expose you?" Suddenly she felt like Rip Van Winkle. Had she been living in a fairy tale the last couple of days and just now awakened to the real world?

Brett drew back her chair. "I must go see what they want. Meet me for lunch outside the dining room."

* * *

Striving for levity, Brett entered his stateroom with a lively, "What's up," only to discover at once that it was the dander of his two companions.

"Your plan was to keep your *eyes* on her," Pierre accused Brett.

"That's what I've been doing."

"Along with other parts of your anatomy, *non?*" Gabriel suggested.

Brett turned furious eyes on him.

"Find someone else to occupy your time, *mon nè-fyou,*" Pierre advised. "That girl, she's too risky."

"In what way?"

"She's a journalist, *oui?*" Pierre responded.

"An' blood-kin to a Pinkerton agent," Gabriel added.

"*Oui.*" Brett told them about his meeting with Cameron Jarrett. "He didn't recognize me."

"He will check on you, *certainement,*" Pierre warned.

"Why would he?" But Brett knew the answer to that question as well as did his cohorts. Hadn't he told Delta the same thing even before Pierre put it into words?

"A respectable girl like her, I tell you, her kin will check out some no-account gambler she's spending too much time with."

Brett wet his lips, heaved a heavy sigh.

"For truth, you should lie low today and—" Pierre began.

"Lay off, don't you mean, *mon ami?*" Gabriel chuckled. "*Lay off* that fetchin' skirt."

"Keep a civil tongue in your head," Brett retorted. "If you have one." The fact that their concerns were warranted rankled him. "God's bones! We're isolated on this river. What can a Pinkerton agent do to us here?"

"We won't stay on the river," Pierre reminded him.

189

"We dock at some landing downriver this morning for a matinee. Tomorrow we arrive in Vicksburg."

"A landing? They likely don't even have a telegraph office, Pierre. You worry too much."

"And you, you protest too much, *mon nèfvou.*"

With another heavy sigh, Brett flopped on the bed, clasped his hands behind his neck, and stared up at the ceiling. "I know. I lost my head. It must have been those blue eyes and . . ." His words drifted off in thoughts of all the other charms of Delta Jarrett. Not only her soft, receptive flesh, but her bright smile and tender heart. He thought of the way her eyes had come alive, lost their melancholy.

"She's been dreaming about me," he told them. "For months." Sitting up, he stared at Pierre. "I told you she recognized me. Well, it was from her dreams— nightmares, actually. For months I've been coming to her in a nightmare, dressed like a pirate."

"Sonofabitch!" Gabriel exploded. "You believe tha' cock an' bull?"

Brett's eyes narrowed. "Are you calling her a liar?"

Gabriel bowed his neck, unyielding as always when a fight loomed.

Pierre broke in. "Eh, there, you two." He studied Brett. "Gabriel could have something, *oui.* You should give it some thought."

"Why would she make up a story like that?" Brett objected.

Pierre shook his head, as though in amazement. "Women. How fast they worm their way under a man's skin."

Brett clamped his jaws together, glaring from one man to the other, waiting for their explanations to cool him off.

"She writes for a newspaper," Pierre continued.

"She wants the best stories on the river. And you, *mon nèfyou,* would make the biggest story of them all."

Brett dropped his arms to his thighs and cradled his face in his hands.

Pierre continued to argue the point. "For truth, it was no coincidence, her turning up at Wint's back in Cairo."

Brett held his tongue.

"She might not intend to expose you, *non,*" Pierre offered, "but you must consider the possibility. You would make headlines from here to New Orleans."

"Speaking of newspapers," Gabriel broke in, "I don' suppose you've seen the mornin' papers."

Brett shook his head, still encased in his hands.

Gabriel stuck a folded paper under his nose. "Bottom right corner."

Brett stared at the headline through spread fingers: *William Trainor, Governor of Louisiana, Vows to Run the Voodoos out of his State.* Sitting up, he took the paper and scanned the article.

"This could be a trick to get you home," Pierre suggested.

"My mother isn't a Voodoo."

"Trainor, he never recognized the difference," his uncle reminded him.

Brett stared unseeing at the paper in his hand.

"He vowed vengeance," Gabriel added. "Me, I doubt he's forgotten."

"He will never forget," Brett hissed.

"One word about you in the newspapers and his henchmen would grab you before we reach the bayou."

That, Brett knew, was the truth. *"Oui,* Pierre."

"You will agree to lie . . . ah, to stick close to this stateroom, then? While we're at that landing, *certainement.*"

"Oui." As much as he hated to admit it, Brett knew they were right. "What about that bounty hunter?" he questioned. "What did you learn?"

"Gabriel searched his cabin."

Gabriel explained. "He is called Nathan Thomas, probably one of many aliases."

"Who's he after?"

"You," Gabriel confirmed.

"What do you mean, me? Brett Reall or—?"

"You," Gabriel repeated. "I foun' a wanted poster in his valise. And this advertisement from a Mississippi newspaper. The state of Louisiana's offerin' a ten-thousand-dollar reward for you—dead or alive—with a bonus of five hundred dollars if you're caught before you cross the state line."

Brett's mouth went suddenly dry. "Ten thousand, dead or alive? All these years, I've thought he wanted to watch me swing."

"There is good news, *oui"* Pierre added. "The artist's sketch, it is hazy, and ten years old. Not much resemblance to Brett Reall, gambler and Canadian gentleman."

Brett didn't show up for lunch, but Nat did. After Brett left their twice-interrupted breakfast, Delta had resisted returning to her stateroom, knowing she would only spend the morning contemplating her latest fears. Their night together huddled inside her like a precious gift, wrapped in shiny paper and tied with ribbons of fear.

Would they ever love like that again? Brett had made everything sound simple, viable. Then Cameron had come aboard with objections to Brett, and Pierre had threatened the relationship with objections to her. And there was Nat.

She had drawn Brett inside her room instinctively the night before, her one thought to protect him from Nat. To protect him? Reason told her that any man who had remained a fugitive from the law for ten years did not need the help of a woman barely out of childhood.

That's how she felt. As though she had just curled her pigtails and lowered her skirts. As though she had never been courted, never been loved.

Certainly she had never been loved.

Not even yet. Regardless of Brett's offhanded use of the word, she must not allow herself to be deluded into thinking he truly *loved her.*

But his words ran continuously through her brain: "Any man who spends the night with a respectable woman like yourself had better be prepared to call it love."

To call it love. It was the last word that echoed the loudest, and she knew she should busy her mind and her hands with other things before it took root in her brain.

Brett Reall was not in love with her.

She probably wasn't even in love with him. But her insides turned dewy at the very thought of finding herself once more in his arms.

When Nat took her elbow, she pulled away. "Come sit with me," he invited. They stood outside the lower entrance to the dining room, the same place where she had met Brett only days before for dinner.

She glared at Nat, fear swelling inside her.

"That gambler stood you up, Delta. Else he'd have been here by now."

"What makes you think—?"

"That you're waiting for him? Come on, Delta. Don't play innocent with me. I've seen you two together."

Delta concentrated on the crowd, making an effort to appear unaffected by his claim.

"Let's go." Nat encouraged her with a nudge to her spine. She flinched, but he ignored it. "If we don't hurry we'll have to sit with the old folks."

With one last glance around for Brett, she sighed and let him usher her inside the teeming room.

"I need to talk to you anyway," Nat was saying. "I met your cousin, the Pinkerton agent. Did he tell you?"

His directness took her by surprise. Distracted by what she would reply, she sat in the chair he held for her at a table with several strangers.

A couple of hours earlier, the *Mississippi Princess* had docked at the landing at OK Bend, just north of Helena, Arkansas. Captain Kaney had opened the dining room to guests from the landing, on a paying basis, of course.

While she was still wondering whether to acknowledge that Cameron had indeed mentioned meeting Nat, he asked again.

"Did your cousin tell you about our little chat?"

Waiters moved between them. "Yes," she answered.

"What did he tell you?"

Studying the thick vegetable soup, she made a hasty decision. "Everything."

Nat chortled. "Humm, that sounds promising."

"Don't count on it," she responded. "I'm not interested in bounty hunters."

"Or their prey? Aren't you interested in—?"

"What are you implying, Nat? Cameron said you're

taking a holiday. Did you lie to him? Are you instead after someone on the boat? Brett Reall, perhaps?"

"Now why would I waste valuable time tracking down a gambler?"

"You tell me."

"Brett Reall is a two-bit smuggler posing as a gambler, Delta. I have no time for either."

"Then who are you hunting?"

With movements as swift as a bird in flight, his hand disappeared beneath the table. She flinched when he squeezed her thigh.

"You."

She jerked her leg away from his grasp. "Take your hands off me."

"Come, now, Delta," he whispered in her ear, "don't tell me you're that stuck on him. That gambler doesn't deserve a peach as pretty as you."

In a flash of fury she shoved back her chair and jumped to her feet, but Nat caught her arm before she could run from the table.

"Sit back down," he urged. "Finish your meal."

She glared at him, unaware of the attention their row had called until a man directly across the table spoke up.

"Need any help, ma'am?"

She looked toward the voice, too embarrassed to see much, other than a fuzzy face.

"If this gentleman's becomin' a bother, I'll be happy to remove him."

The fuzzy face came into focus. It belonged to a blond man in his mid-twenties with the largest set of shoulders Delta had seen on a man other than Brett's uncle, Pierre.

She glared back at Nat, furious.

"Calm down, Delta. I didn't mean to offend you."

"Like hell you didn't," she seethed. But when the giant across the table made a move to rise, she responded, "It's all right. Thank you."

"A misunderstanding," Nat was saying to the giant. "Lover's—"

"Shut your mouth," Delta ordered, slipping back into her seat. "And keep your hands to yourself," she added in a stage whisper.

She concentrated on her meal, picking at the baked chicken and dressing. Nat didn't speak again until the waiter had cleared their entrees and served dessert—a bread pudding topped with brandy sauce—and coffee.

"You really interested in who I'm after?" he quizzed.

Her hand froze in midair. Instantly she wondered why she was so tense. He'd already said he wasn't after Brett. Anyone else probably deserved it.

"Not necessarily." She resumed her meal.

"I'll tell you anyway, in case you start to wonder later . . . tonight."

Turning her head, she glared at him, eliciting another chortle. "Know what, Delta? You're as easy to read as an open book. You really should work on that, being a journalist and all. Why, if you play the game right, I might give you a scoop."

"I'll find my own scoops, thank you."

"Probably not one as good as this. Not by your lonesome."

"That's all right, there are others."

But he continued to needle her, until exasperated she turned to him. "Who are you tracking, Nat. Tell me, then leave me alone."

"A murderer," he answered. "Man who murdered his wife and—well, we'll leave it at that . . . for the time being."

196

Relief began to relax her, knowing that Nat was indeed tracking a criminal, but that it wasn't Brett Reall.

"We could work together on this," Nat suggested.

"We? How?"

"I nab him, you write about it. What say we team up, Delta? First time I laid eyes on you, I knew we'd work well together."

"No thank you. I have enough interviews lined up."

"It'll be a scoop. Maybe the scoop of your life. Who knows, might make you a star reporter."

She smiled, excusing herself from the table. "I'll think about it."

But returning to her cabin she found a message that took her mind completely off Nat, the bounty hunter. It lay on her nightstand, and read: "Sorry about lunch. Meet me for dinner and dancing. Same time and place as before. B."

Suddenly her heart sang again. She hugged her arms about her waist and danced around the small room, bumping into the bed, falling back on it, laughing up at the paneled ceiling. It felt so good. So good.

She no longer had to worry about Nat being after Brett. And she didn't have to worry about why Brett hadn't shown up for lunch. She didn't have that big a claim on him, after all.

She hugged herself again. But she did have a little claim on him. Else he wouldn't have invited her to dinner.

And dancing.

And . . .

Shortly after lunch she felt the boat move as it departed the landing at OK Bend. Lighting the lamp at the bedside desk, she decided to write her last article on Memphis. It wouldn't do to arrive in Vicksburg without an article to post to Hollis. And she mustn't forget to wire Cameron so he wouldn't become suspicious. Taking out paper, pen-staff, and opening the inkwell, she set to work. But her heart fairly burst with anticipation and she had a hard time concentrating on Memphis. She wanted to finish the article before dinner, though. Tonight she wouldn't have time. Tonight she would be busy with other things.

Later, while she dressed with great attention, she recalled Nat's claim that Brett was a smuggler. A two-bit smuggler.

Surely he wasn't, she thought, striving to put it out of her mind. And in the anticipation of the evening ahead, that was not such a difficult task. She arrived at the dining room breathless, but she tried to disguise the fact by claiming to have taken the stairs too fast.

Brett's teasing perusal, however, told her clearly that he knew the reason. She watched the vein in his neck throb above his starched collar, and the thought of skipping dinner crossed her mind.

"Dinner and dancing," he whispered in her ear, seating her at the small table they had shared once before.

"Am I so easy to read?" she questioned, recalling Nat's accusation.

He took the chair opposite her and stared across the candlelit centerpiece into her glowing eyes. "Only because we're thinking the same thing."

She watched him flick the napkin out and place it on his lap. He looked back at her and continued, "But I've never danced with you, and I want to. This once."

The waiter arrived, diverting her attention with the clatter of dishes. She wasn't certain she had heard Brett's last words correctly, but the idea that she might have, sent a rush of anxiety chasing her newfound joy.

* * *

Across the table Brett took in her gown—blue lace to match her eyes—the pearls at her ears, her hairstyle, which somehow managed to be proper and seductive at the same time. He memorized her face, flushed now under his scrutiny, her eyes, cast demurely toward her plate.

From the way she picked at the roast quail he knew she was no more interested in food than he was. She wanted him. He could tell from the spots of color high on her cheeks, from the pulsating vein in her neck, from the erratic swell of her breasts as she struggled to breathe in a calm, normal fashion.

"I'm sorry about lunch," he told her. "Pierre insisted I stay close to the cabin."

She looked up. Smiled. Her eyes teased. "That's all right. I ate with Nat."

"I know."

She scanned the room, taking in the captain's table.

"He isn't here," Brett announced. "Pierre and Gabriel sent him on a mission."

Her eyes flew to his.

"Nat doesn't realize it, of course." At her frown, he added, "He received an anonymous message back at OK Bend."

"You mean he missed the boat?"

Brett grinned.

"It wasn't necessary, you know."

"What wasn't?"

"Sending him off like that. We had a talk at lunch. He isn't after you."

Brett heard her words, recalled the poster Gabriel had found in Nat's cabin. "What did he tell you?" He saw her hesitate, watched her expression turn serious.

Fear stirred in his gut. Fear of a kind he hadn't known in ten years.

"Word for word?" she questioned.

He nodded, holding his breath, waiting for her answer.

"He said he isn't after a two-bit smuggler disguised as a gambler."

Brett stared at her, momentarily taken aback by her direct answer. Then she continued.

"He said he's after a man who murdered his wife. Not Nat's wife," she explained, "the murderer's wife."

If he lived to be a hundred years old, Brett knew he would never forget the sickness that sliced through him at Delta's words, issued from her beautiful mouth, spoken in her soft, seductive voice.

He could see relief written all over her face, relief that he was not in danger from the bounty hunter. Pierre and Gabriel had argued with him all afternoon about seeing her tonight. But it was something he had to do.

He must explain to her in person that he could never see her again. Not that he agreed with Pierre and Gabriel that Delta would intentionally expose him. He knew better than that. But now they knew for certain that Nat was after him, and he had no choice but to distance himself from Delta—at once. Otherwise he would draw her into Nat's fire along with himself.

Nat's reputation for getting his man had spread up and down the river. Young though he was, Nat was an expert shot with both rifle and pistol, and an exceptional tracker. According to rumor he was as patient as Job and as cruel and conscienceless as a timber wolf.

Nat would have no scruples about using Delta to draw him out, and that Brett could not risk. Hence, the fake message calling Nat ashore at OK Bend shortly before the *Mississippi Princess* left port.

Brett didn't delude himself that Nat wouldn't immediately hire a horse or catch the rails and meet the boat in Vicksburg, but by that time Brett would have had a chance to properly end things with Delta—if ending such a relationship could ever be termed proper.

He had spent much of the afternoon cursing himself for beginning it, but seeing her now, so lovely and seductive, he knew he would never regret the time they spent together. His only regret would be in bringing her grief.

And the best way to prevent that was to get out of her life without delay. After tonight.

The music for dancing began as soon as the dining room had been converted to a grand salon, but as eager as he had been to hold Delta in his arms, once they stood on the dance floor, he found himself disconcerted. Admiring her gown again, he started to tease her about her *trousseau,* but tonight that did not seem appropriate. Instead, he tried to compliment her on her gown, but even there, he fell short.

"That's one of those skirts that ties around the thighs, isn't it?" he commented.

Her eyes widened at his public mention of her legs. "The latest fashion," she agreed, adding with a grin, "You certainly know a lot about women's fashions."

Was he blushing? he wondered, feeling the situation slip further away by the minute. Delta saved it by placing a hand on his shoulder and holding the other one up for him to grasp. "It's a waltz," she told him.

He laughed, then. "So it is. I wasn't sure you could dance in that contraption."

"Try me."

His eyes found hers, held hers. "With pleasure,

201

m'moiselle.'' Once they began to waltz about the room, his equilibrium returned, and with it came a growing unease about Delta's earlier conversation with Nat.

"So he told you I'm a smuggler?"

Her eyes told him she didn't care.

"What else did he say?"

"Nothing much."

"What kind of answer is that? Did he tell you what I'm supposed to be smuggling?"

She shook her head.

"And from where? Or to where?"

Again she shook her head.

"You aren't concerned?"

Her eyes held his. "I don't want to think about it. Not tonight."

His hand squeezed her waist. With difficulty he kept himself from drawing her body to his, from covering her slightly parted, oh-so-tempting lips with his. He wished to hell it were as easy to keep from loving her.

"What else did Nat tell you about the man he's after? The man who is supposed to have murdered his wife."

"Nothing." After a moment she added, "He said that was all I needed to know for now."

The music ended. Somehow Brett managed to stop twirling Delta and to keep them both on their feet, not a simple feat considering how his head was whirling. Zanna and Albert stopped nearby, and Brett strove to conduct a normal conversation. Fortunately, Delta's tendency to babble nervously had returned, so his reticence wasn't noticed.

After a couple of dances more, she suggested they go out on the deck. When they arrived at the rail, she stood gripping it, staring silently into the dark water.

"Are you all right?" he asked. He had followed her

down the deck until they left behind the streams of lamp light spraying, along with buzzing voices, from the various doors of the grand salon.

Turning, she stared him straight in the eye. "I've never enjoyed dancing without a partner."

"What?"

"I don't know where you were, perhaps with that blue-eyed woman from your dreams, but you weren't on the dance floor with me."

He stared dumbly, then felt his ire stir. He started to tell her that she was the one who had driven him into another world, her and her talk with Nat. He started to tell her it wasn't any of her goddamn business what was on his mind, that she didn't want to know.

But he didn't. Instead, he grasped her arms, a little rougher than he intended, and pulled her to him. His lips covered hers, his tongue possessed her, and in her passion and sweetness he began to relax.

Breathing heavily, he drew her head back a fraction. Their noses rubbed when he spoke. "You're the blue-eyed woman in my dreams, Delta Jarrett."

He felt her tremble against him, felt her breasts in all their confinement press against his chest, recalled in infinite detail how they felt unfettered against his bare skin, how they looked so smooth and ripe, how they tasted.

Moonbeams glimmered from highlights in her hair and sparkled in her eyes. Her lips parted and he watched her smile before she spoke. Her seductive voice teased.

"How long will your chaperons allow you to stay out tonight?"

He chuckled, kissing her again. "Until you run me off."

It wasn't what he had meant to say, and the moment

the words left his mouth, he regretted them. But she didn't say what he knew was in her mind, and he didn't retract the ill-thought promise.

Instead he guided her downstairs to her stateroom where they spent the next several hours as they had spent the night before, locked in each other's arms.

This time there were no secrets to tell. They had already told them all, or at least he knew she thought they had.

And there were no promises. He couldn't make them, and she evidently didn't feel the need. For that he was grateful.

He didn't tell her what he had set out that night to tell her—he didn't want to spoil their last night together. In the morning over coffee, watching the sunrise on the Mississippi, he would tell her. Afterwards he would avoid her the rest of the trip. But for the time being, this night was theirs—theirs to revel in lovemaking that must last them the rest of their lives.

Near dawn he rose from her arms. "I'll meet you in an hour to watch the sunrise."

She pulled him back. "Stay. We'll go together."

He grinned. "And give the crew and passengers your good name to play with? My wrinkled clothes would spread your reputation over the deck like spilled oil."

But he lingered at the door, hesitant to leave. He watched her pull the covers over her nudity. "Don't I get one last peek?

"A peek will cost you another hour," she teased.

Her laughter followed him all the way to his stateroom, which he entered, jacket slung over one shoulder, a whistle on his lips.

His whistle turned to one of dismay. "God's bones!

What happened here?'' The chiffonier drawers stood open, their contents strewn about the floor. The bedclothes were tangled, as in a lover's knot.

"We caught an intruder." Pierre's voice accused. Or did he imagine it, Brett wondered, dazed.

"Explain."

"We didn't take our eyes off your door for more than five minutes," Gabriel told him. "Me, I was late. Some passengers requested extra songs, and Pierre came looking for me. When we returned, your door was cracked and a lamp was on."

"Who was it?"

Brett's companions exchanged shrugs. "He refused to give his name, sure," Pierre said. "A big man, and blond."

"He came aboard at OK Bend," Gabriel added. "And—" He motioned to Pierre. "You tell him."

"He's connected with Nat somehow. And with that Jarrett woman."

Brett exploded. "Like hell!"

"You don't want to hear that, *non*," Pierre said, "but it looks like the truth. They ate lunch together yesterday, the three of them."

"Lots of people eat together," Brett stormed.

Pierre agreed. "Me, I watched them. Some kind of argument arose. The woman, she jumped up to leave. The actor held her back. The blond man challenged them both."

Brett's heart pounded faster than the pistons on the new steam engine Captain Kaney was so proud of, and none of the energy was passion, at least not the kind he had shared with Delta the last two nights. "You're crazy. Delta wouldn't . . . she couldn't be involved with them."

"Like Pierre said," Gabriel added, "we didn't figure you'd want to hear it about her. But it looks to be the truth, no?''

''No!'' Brett stormed. He slung his jacket across the room with such force it caught a lamp and dragged it to the floor. Pierre crossed the room, righted the lamp, then straightened Brett's coat and hung it over the back of a chair.

Anger raged inside Brett. Anger and fear. ''You don't know how stupid this sounds. You're accusing Delta of being involved in a scheme to bring me in for what? A damned newspaper story?'' He sneered. ''Or maybe you think she wants the reward money?''

''Me, I don't know the reason,'' Pierre said.

''You don't know shit!'' Brett roared. ''Neither of you.'' He sank to the bed and cradled his head in his hands. ''The woman's in love with me, for God's sake. She wouldn't turn me over to the authorities—''

''Or worse,'' Pierre suggested. ''To that bounty hunter.''

''We're tellin' you what we see, *mon ami*,'' Gabriel added. ''A woman, she can blind a man to the truth, *oui*. Sometimes he don' have a chance of thinkin' straight.''

''You don't know Delta.''

''We know you,'' Pierre told him. ''An' we don' want you throwin' your life away for a piece of skirt.''

''It's over now,'' Gabriel said.

Brett looked up, momentarily disoriented.

''You told her, *oui?*'' Gabriel questioned. ''That you and her were through?''

''I'll tell her at breakfast.''

''Breakfast?''

''Yes, dammit, breakfast. Now get out of here and let me change clothes.''

The two men headed for the door, but Brett stopped them before they left the room.

"What about the intruder?"

"Pierre, he threw the feller overboard," Gabriel replied, closing the door behind them.

Chapter Ten

Excitement bubbled inside Delta when she saw Brett sitting at their table outside the paddlewheel lounge. The silence was awesome. Unlike in Memphis, no roustabouts chanted this morning, no waiters scurried around the tables. A whippoorwill sang from somewhere in the distance and was answered by a mockingbird. Or was it the other way around? she wondered.

The river was a mirror of glass, reflecting the sprinkling of gold and pink from the emerging sun. Little puffs of white mist rose here and there on its surface, like tufts of cotton waiting to be picked.

The damp morning air seemed almost tangible, like cotton candy at a fair. She was tempted to grab a handful and carry it to Brett with her heart.

But he already had her heart.

At her approach he turned and she laughed, the song in her heart more poignant than the mockingbird's call. And she knew it echoed his own. His eyes held hers and she waited for them to light with a smile.

She had come to know this man so well, she thought, and to love him so much. She could always tell when he was about to smile, because his eyes lit up first. She watched for that light now, but it didn't come.

He didn't smile nor even rise from his chair when she approached, but watched her take her chair with a noncommittal sort of expression she didn't understand. The song in her heart began to fade.

Of course, he must be tired, she reasoned. They had slept little the last two nights. They both needed a good day's sleep. She smiled at that, wondering what the day had in store for them.

When his only response to her cheery "Good morning" was to turn his attention back to the river, confusion, like the cry of a hawk, replaced the mockingbird's song inside her. She followed his gaze, momentarily distracted by the spectacle.

In the short time her attention had been diverted, the sun had risen several degrees above the water, showering the dark foliage to either side of the river with golden highlights, glittering like gemstones from the dark surface of the glass-smooth river. The showboat seemed to glide through some ethereal tunnel.

"What's on for today?" she asked at last. "Or will your chaperons keep you locked away?"

He turned to stare at her briefly then, but he didn't speak until his eyes were back on the water. "We can't see each other again, Delta."

The silence around them became deafening, beating in her ears, through her brain. For a moment it seemed the only thing alive was her aching heart, and it couldn't last long, not at the rate it had begun to beat.

When she found her voice, she asked, "What happened in the hour we've been apart."

She watched him heave a heavy sigh. "My room was broken into."

"But I thought Nat—"

"Was after someone else?" he demanded, his voice fierce.

She straightened her shoulders, not so much for courage but because she suddenly felt compelled to lay her head on the table and cry. Tears rushed to her eyes. She fought them back. "You told me he missed the boat at the landing."

"He did."

"Dammit, Brett!" That got his attention. He cast her a rueful glance. No hint of a smile, hardly even recognition. "Tell me what happened," she insisted.

He focused on her then, his eyes narrowed. "You tell me who that blond man was you had lunch with yesterday."

"Blond man?"

"Don't act dumb."

"It isn't an act. Right now I feel like the dumbest person alive. And it has nothing to do with a blond man." She watched the sun inch its way higher in the sky, suddenly gripped by a haunting sense of loneliness. It was as if she and Brett were the only two people on earth, and he was saying they couldn't see each other again.

She turned to stare at him. His Adam's apple bobbed and she realized, quite by surprise, that he was struggling to contain his emotions, just as she was.

His voice became low and husky. "You aren't dumb, Delta. Just tell me who the man was."

"If you mean the man who sat across the table from Nat and me, I don't know."

"You argued with him. A person doesn't generally argue with a stranger."

"I didn't argue with—"

"Pierre saw you."

She lifted her eyes heavenward. "Pierre. Pierre. I'm sick of Pierre's interference."

She heard Brett sigh. "So am I. If I didn't know he

210

had my best interests at heart, I wouldn't listen to him."

"What did he say about me?" she demanded.

"That you and Nat and the blond man had an argument."

She pursed her lips. Angry and disappointed, she stared into the glistening water. "And you assumed we were plotting against you, is that it?"

"Not me, Delta. Pierre."

"You, too. You wouldn't be quizzing me, telling me we can't see each other again if you didn't believe every word that meddling—"

"Sh, Delta. I don't believe every word he says. But I have to know the truth. My life may well depend on it."

Sobered, she turned to study him. "I suppose what Pierre saw was when Nat . . . ah, offended me. I jumped up to leave the table. Nat grabbed my arm, and that blond man came to my rescue." She watched the side of Brett's face, saw his jaw tighten. "Look at me, Brett."

Slowly he turned. Their eyes held. Her heart beat erratically, painfully.

"I had never seen that man before in my life. We didn't speak until Nat offended me. I have never seen the man since."

He smiled, a wan, mournful sort of smile. "You probably won't see him again, either."

At her frown, he added. "Pierre found him going through my room and threw him overboard."

Her eyes flew open.

"Don't waste sympathy on him. He probably swam ashore or to a nearby sandbar."

Watching Brett turn his attention back to the river, she began to feel physically ill. Something else was

211

wrong—terribly wrong. "My sympathy isn't with him right now," she said in a soft voice. "It's with us. Are you saying you intend to stop seeing me because this stranger broke into your room?"

"No, that isn't the reason. The reason is—"

When he looked at her, his clenched jaw gave his face a rigid, distorted look. "Don't look at me like that, Delta. I warned you not to get close to me."

"Not lately, you haven't."

For the longest time he held her gaze, steady, forcefully, as though he could with a little extra effort pull the tears right out of them. Only with effort on her part did she keep from crying.

Finally he turned away with, "If you misunderstood the last two nights, I'm sorry."

Her heart beat in her throat. Curiously she pressed her hand to her chest where it belonged, willing it to return, to pump warmth and life back into her body. He had told her not to get close to him. She told him she didn't expect a commitment. So why was her heart broken?

She didn't look at him again. She knew if she did, all would be lost. And she wasn't ready to run crying to her room. "I didn't misunderstand," she told him. "But I'd like to hear your explanation, anyway."

"There are things about me, Delta, that you could never understand."

"Concerning your *two-bit smuggling,* as Nat calls it?"

He shook his head. "I'm no smuggler. I ship furs without the approval of the Canadian government, but in doing so I've helped a lot of people, including myself. I deal directly with the Indians and don't go through all the red tape that lines a lot of governmental pockets with golden fleece. They don't like it, but they haven't been able to stop me. It isn't illegal, just restricting, from their point of view.''

Listening to him, a small amount of hope began to grow inside her, until she realized that this might be the last time she ever heard his voice. ''Does it concern your ten-year-old trouble in Louisiana?'' she asked.

He spoke to the rising sun. *''Oui.''*

''But you said you're innocent. Let me help—''

He stiffened. His voice became harsh. ''Your help is the last thing I need. If my face gets spread all over the newspapers, they'd have me on the gallows quicker than an alligator can snap up a crawfish pie.''

''After all we've been—'' She paused to allow an emerging sense of anger to suffuse the pain in her heart. ''You can't still believe I would expose you in the newspapers? Not after all—?''

''No,'' he broke in. ''I don't believe it. Pierre and Gabriel do, but—''

''To hell with Pierre and Gabriel.''

He turned to her then and smiled, again a wan, sad smile. ''I know you wouldn't expose me, Delta. That isn't what this is about.''

''Then what is it about?''

This time he held her gaze while he spoke, explaining in earnest tones how it was best for both of them to end their relationship before it went any further. ''If the wrong people were to discover how much I—'' He stopped, turned back to the river, and began again. ''If the wrong people should suspect that we're close, they could use you to get to me. Do you understand what that would mean?''

''Yes.'' She followed his line of vision down the still, sleek river. The sun had now risen high enough to caress their faces with its warmth. Inside she felt as cold

213

as ice. "I'm not afraid of them, Brett. I'll do anything to help prove your innocence."

A few feet ahead of the boat a catfish jumped, breaking through the glassy surface of the river as though it had shattered a mirror. Quickly she strove to erase such a portent-filled image from her brain.

"There's no way to prove my innocence, Delta, so get that notion out of your head. No way. The most powerful people in the state believe I'm guilty, and they will stop at nothing to see justice done—*their* view of justice." Pausing he winced, then continued, "For ten years I've topped their Most Wanted list. Believe me when I say they'll stop at nothing. They wouldn't even spare the life of a . . . of a beautiful, bewitching woman."

Expressed in the most intimate tone he had used all morning, his words left her weak and practically defenseless. Gradually the significance of what he said worked through her self-pity. She couldn't abandon him, not now. He needed her more than she had imagined. Without her he would be alone. Alone, in a world filled with enemies.

"I'll stand beside you, Brett. No matter what lies ahead." At first she didn't think he heard. She started to repeat herself. "I'll stand—"

"God's bones, Delta! Don't you understand anything? It isn't only your life our relationship would threaten, but mine. If we're together they have two targets, and either way they get me. Because if they harmed you, they would know damned well I'd go after them and never let up. Not again. So, stay away from me. For both our sakes."

* * *

They docked at Vicksburg late that afternoon, and Delta spent the two days they stayed there enveloped in a cocoon of misery. For without the physical Brett Reall to chase them away, her nightmares returned, becoming her constant companion—and nemesis.

With the sun rising higher above the Mississippi, Delta had left Brett sitting alone and returned to her stateroom, where she considered secluding herself for the remainder of the trip. But she had to post an article to Hollis and a telegram to Cameron, else the family would descend upon her like a swarm of angry wasps.

So she had spent the morning finishing her article, then waited until the parade had time to form before she ventured from the security of her stateroom. She would post the article, send the telegram, and return without arranging any interviews. She could work up something on the Princess Players or the calliope to send to Hollis the following day.

Arriving on deck, however, she discovered that a representative of the mayor of Vicksburg—a Councilman Hendricks—had come out to meet the boat. Captain Kaney introduced them, and before she could resist, the overly eager, too gussied-up city salesman barraged her with details of the area's agricultural trade and figures on their river commerce.

"Along the Yazoo River and the Sunflower, as well as the Mississippi," he enthused.

Summoning her wits, Delta inquired, "What about warfage fees, Councilman?" Somewhere in her injured brain, she recalled Captain Kaney's complaints about high warfage fees along the river.

"No higher than any other port's," Councilman Hendricks exclaimed, adding, "Allow me to escort you and your party to the caves."

Casting around for a ready excuse, Delta found

none. Hendricks agreed to stop by the telegraph office and to give her time to post her article to Hollis.

At Captain Kaney's prodding, she accepted the councilman's invitation, but the instant she stepped off the gangplank, escorted by this obviously prosperous councilman, she was gripped by a great sense of longing. She should have expected as much, she rebuked, turning to scan the showboat. No sign of the beloved figure of whom she desperately sought even a fleeting glimpse.

Zanna spoke from Delta's other shoulder. "Where's Brett?"

The shock of hearing his name spoken brought a lump to Delta's throat. She dared not trust her voice to answer, so she shrugged.

"I thought you two were getting close."

Delta put on her best imitation of a smile. "No."

Zanna let it pass with no more than the comment, "When a relationship isn't going to work, it's best to find it out early." But she left the parade in Albert's charge and accompanied Delta and the councilman to the caves as though she regularly relegated such authority to others.

The depth of friendship this expressed lit a tiny flame inside Delta, but she knew the only thing that would thaw her frozen heart would be for Brett to come to her, accept her help, her love, and her presence in his life. That, she knew was not likely to happen.

The caves were impressive in the dismal way the rest of Vicksburg was impressive. Everywhere she looked, the ravages of war remained as evidence of the high cost of six weeks of bombardment—buildings destroyed, trees cut down as if by lightning, streets pocked with mortar holes, and the caves—the natural caves, hundreds of them, had been dug deeper into the clay banks by citizens seeking shelter from what Council-man Hendricks called "iron rain."

"See how they Y back from the entrances?" He motioned the ladies to peer into the back of the dark tunnels.

"The city was completely cut off from all commerce," he told them. "For six weeks the three thousand civilian inhabitants of Vicksburg, mostly women and children, lived in fear and increasing need, surrounded by upwards of thirty thousand military men. Several folks kept journals. If you care to read them for your report, Miss Jarrett, come by my office tomorrow."

By the time they returned to the boat, Albert led the cast in setting the stage for the evening's performance. As with other stops the first performance in Vicksburg would be on the docks, the last in the grand salon, the latter allowing the *Mississippi Princess* to slip quietly into the river current as soon as the guests departed, assuring an early arrival at Natchez the following day.

With half a heart Delta watched Albert and Frankie assemble the set for the melodrama.

"Vicksburg has seen so much tragedy," Zanna observed, "I hope our performance brings the citizens a laugh or two."

Then Delta spied Nat. As Brett had predicted, the bounty hunter had found his way back to the boat. Their gazes locked for an instant before his eyes darted behind her, then from side to side.

She stood perfectly still, knowing he searched for Brett. Well, let him. He wouldn't find Brett with her. But she did intend to question him about his lie. He had no business making up that story about being after a man who had murdered his wife, when it was Brett he wanted all along.

He sauntered toward her, calling, "I have a bone to pick with you, Delta."

"And I with you." Eyeing him with distaste, she stood her ground and waited for him to approach. Suddenly the lively strains of Gabriel's fiddle filled the air. As on a dime, Nat turned on his heel and vanished up the gangplank.

She pivoted in place, staring at the fiddler, who ignored her, playing to the crowd, as always.

She wasn't surprised when Brett didn't appear at dinner. She hadn't felt like going, either, but she did. In the end it was preferable to staying alone in a stateroom that reminded her so much of him.

She even considered asking Captain Kaney to move her to another cabin, but the questions such a request would raise prevented her from doing so.

Nat didn't appear at dinner, either, and since she hadn't planned to attend the performance, she gave up the idea of confronting him until morning. Then, returning to her stateroom after the meal, she found Nat lounging against her hand-painted door.

"Invite me in?"

She was tempted to slap his impudent face. "Certainly not."

"You invited that gambler in, though, didn't you? Is he in there now, waiting for you?"

"Of course not. And I'll thank you to keep such unseemly comments to yourself."

He laughed. "When you see him, tell him I'm looking for him."

"I won't see him."

"No?"

"No." Since he didn't appear to believe her, she added, "Not tonight, not tomorrow, not ever. And while we're on the subject, why did you lie to me?"

"Me? I didn't lie to you."

"You told me you weren't after Brett Reall."

"I'm not."

She ignored his denial. "You said you were after a man who murdered his wife, when all the time it's Brett's alleged smuggling—"

"Brett's *alleged* smuggling? What kind of bull has he been feeding you?"

"Nothing," she hurried to say. "Everyone knows you're after him. You aren't a master at disguise, you know."

"Everyone, Delta?" He lowered his voice, continuing in a threatening tone. "Or just the journalist who searched my room?" He grabbed her arm and shook her. "What did you do with my wanted poster? The one of Anatole Dupré?"

"I don't know what you're talking about."

"I think you do. I think you took my poster. Anatole Dupré. Does the name mean anything to you?"

"No."

He studied her carefully. "I didn't think it would. He wouldn't be that stupid. But just you wait. He'll make a mistake. And when he does, I'll be there waiting."

Suddenly from around the corner near the sternwheel came the sound of music—fiddle music. Giving her arm one last shake, Nat left with the excuse that the drama was about to commence.

The next morning Delta rose early and accompanied the councilman to the national cemetery, as planned. Again Zanna rode with them.

"I'm probably not the company you'd like, but it looks like I'll have to do."

Delta hugged her. "You're exactly the company I want."

219

The ride out of town relieved the dull headache she had awakened with. Her nightmare had returned. The same old nightmare of the pirates making love on a tossing ship, except this time it was more poignant, more personal, and she had awakened with a throbbing head.

And an ache in her heart that even the ride in the country did not relieve. While the eager councilman pointed here to a site ravaged by the war, there to a site restored to its original grandeur, she struggled to concentrate on his monologue.

The national cemetery sat on a hill overlooking the river and a broad expanse of natural parkway. Flowering shrubs and trees lent the area a peacefulness that belied the battle fought in and around these hills. The councilman paused so she could record the inscription on the gateway: "Here rest in peace 16,600 who died for their country in the years 1861 to 1865."

They followed the winding road through wooded hills and ravines. At times the roadway was cut so deeply into the earth, they seemed to be riding through a tunnel with only the vast blue sky for a roof.

The same sky that looked down on Brett, wherever he was, whatever he was doing.

On the way back to town the councilman talked about the railroads and pointed to the many fine residences that had been restored since the war. "Make us sound prosperous," he appealed, reminding Delta of Cameron's like comment about Memphis.

"The war did enough damage," she told him. "I'm looking for the bright side."

But the bright side of her private life was as hard to find as that of this war-ravaged city.

That evening she again decided to forgo attending the theatrical. But recalling Nat's unwelcome presence the evening before, she persuaded Zanna to accompany her to her stateroom before the show began.

"Is he bothering you?" Zanna questioned.

"Who?"

"Brett Reall?"

"Oh, no," Delta hurried to assure her. "I haven't even seen him since we arrived in Vicksburg. And I won't." She turned the key in her lock. "Have you?"

The moment the question escaped her lips, she hated having asked it, but she had been so desperate to see him, to hear word of him.

Zanna squeezed a comforting arm around her shoulders. "No, but I hear he ventured into Vicksburg. That man of his, the big one, was seen wandering about outside Brett's stateroom this afternoon, so he must have returned aboard. The captain's miffed that he hasn't been attending the ti' games with those little ladies."

Zanna left and, once inside her cabin, Delta lighted the lamps and poured herself a glass of sherry. Her gaze drifted over the dressing table and every other flat surface in turn, searching for a message left by the cabin boy. *Meet me tonight*, it would say. Or, *Leave the door unlocked for me*.

But of course she didn't find such a message, and tempted though she was, she did not leave her door unlocked. After bathing off in violet-scented water, she dressed for bed and sat down to write her article on Vicksburg, to post when they arrived in Natchez the following day.

The sherry warmed her inside, turning her heartache to a bittersweet reminder of the happiness she had experienced with Brett in this room. It had become a home, a haven, this room, the one place that was theirs and theirs alone. How could she bear to leave it when they arrived in New Orleans?

It was only after she risked turning out the lamps and lay snug in her bed that she realized she had spent the better part of the day anticipating this night. If she couldn't be with Brett in the flesh, she could love him in her dreams. As she was drifting off to sleep, the last vision to flit through her brain was of his beloved face. Then it was gone.

The pains started late at night, although in the eternal darkness of the cell, time was an uncertain thing. Not so with labor pains.

Although she had never experienced them before, she knew the moment the heavy pains started in her lower back that the time had come.

She'd been waiting for it, it seemed like forever.

"That's it, all right," remarked Mary Read, her fellow pirate and cell-mate. "Some things never change, like labor and death." Mary had birthed her babe a fortnight back, a stillborn, and Mary now awaited the hangman's noose along with Anne.

They would swing together, or so their jailers promised, as soon as Anne delivered the babe. Together, as they had plied the tropical waters of the Caribbean together.

Some things never changed.

Like friendship. Like death.

Anne gripped her lower belly beneath the bulge that had taken on an ever-moving shape of late, a shape that undulated inside her belly, the way the child would move in someone else's arms— soon.

Very soon. The pain lessened. She leaned back on the squalid pallet to await its return. Mary's birthing had been an education in things of the kind. The pain, the terrible pain.

It returned, convulsing, pressing, bringing beads of perspira-

tion to her forehead. Perhaps it was false, this labor, a spurious attempt to frighten her that her time was near.

But the pains continued intermittently through the next hours, how many, she had no way of surmising. When at length she felt a rush of water between her legs, she knew the time had come.

Struggling to her feet, she worked her way to the iron door of the rat-infested cell. One promise she would keep. One promise. That her babe would not die as Mary's had done. Her babe would live, but to do so, it must not be born in the squalor of this cell.

Fiercely she pounded on the iron door. "Hear me, hear me! My time has come, you miserable curs, come help me!"

No one came, of course, not until the jailer brought their meager bowls of gruel at daybreak, and by that time Anne Bonny had delivered a baby girl.

The babe cried, so Anne knew it was alive. It wailed, so Anne held it close, brushing straw and debris from its tiny damp body with trembling fingers.

Held against her the babe felt like a part of her own flesh, and when she offered the tiny thing a breast, it began to suckle. Afterwards it fell quiet, and soon its little body had been bathed by the flow of Anne's tears.

She was a mother. She had borne a babe from her womb. She had suckled her babe. That she would be hanged at daybreak for piracy on the high seas no longer mattered.

She was a mother.

They came at daybreak, to the jailer's summons, and led her away. She cradled the babe tightly against her breast, refusing to relinquish it to the grasping hands, the clutching hands of all she passed along the rock-floored corridor and out into the bright sunshine.

They led her toward a scaffold that had been erected in the courtyard. From the top of the walls and from every rooftop, people cheered. She glanced around. It was the first time she had been outside in—how long?

"Is that your babe, Anne Bonny?" someone called from the rooftop. "What're ye to do with it?"

She held the babe aloft for all to see, as though it were a wee queen born this day. And indeed it was. "Queen of the pirates!"

"Queen of the pirates!" echoed the cry. "Queen of the pirates."

Again someone tried to take the babe from her, but she held fast. Climbing the steps to the top of the platform, she tripped on the frayed bottom of her skirts, but still she held fast to the babe in her arms.

Led to a noose hanging from the center of the scaffold, Anne once more refused to relinquish her babe. She squeezed the child to her bosom with a fierceness she had previously felt only in battle, but never as strong as at this moment.

Lifting her face, she looked at the blue sky overhead. Lowering her gaze she studied the faces of those assembled, eager faces of men and women hungry to see her death, anyone's death.

The hangman tried to cover her face with a hood, but with one hand she ripped it away. And when he slipped the noose around her neck, she stared down into the wee one's sky-blue eyes, seeing her child clearly for the first time.

" 'Tis time, ma'am," came a quiet voice. A chant rose above the crowd noise, and Anne heard the priest for the first time. Vaguely she recalled him offering to hear her confession, to absolve her of her sins.

Her sins? Hers? Anguish rose inside her, fierce and hot. Lifting her head, she began to scream to the vultures on the rooftops.

"Murderers! Murderers! Don't kill my little girl!"

Someone reached for the babe.

She clutched it to her breast.

The scaffold floor moved beneath her feet. She stared into the blue eyes of her babe. The girlchild began to wail.

"Don't murder my babe! Don't kill my little girl!"

224

The Publishers of Zebra Books
Make This Special Offer
to Zebra Romance Readers...

AFTER YOU HAVE READ THIS
BOOK WE'D LIKE TO SEND YOU
4 MORE FOR *FREE*
AN $18.00 VALUE

NO OBLIGATION!

*ONLY ZEBRA HISTORICAL ROMANCES
"BURN WITH THE FIRE OF HISTORY"
(SEE INSIDE FOR MONEY SAVING DETAILS.)*

MORE PASSION AND ADVENTURE AWAIT... YOUR TRIP TO A BIG ADVENTUROUS WORLD BEGINS WHEN YOU ACCEPT YOUR FIRST 4 NOVELS ABSOLUTELY *FREE* (AN $18.00 VALUE)

Accept your Free gift and start to experience more of the passion and adventure you like in a historical romance novel. Each Zebra novel is filled with proud men, spirited women and tempestuous love that you'll remember long after you turn the last page.

Zebra Historical Romances are the finest novels of their kind. They are written by authors who really know how to weave tales of romance and adventure in the historical settings you love. You'll feel like you've actually gone back in time with the thrilling stories that each Zebra novel offers.

GET YOUR FREE GIFT WITH THE START OF YOUR HOME SUBSCRIPTION

Our readers tell us that these books sell out very fast in book stores and often they miss the newest titles. So Zebra has made arrangements for you to receive the four newest novels published each month.

You'll be guaranteed that you'll never miss a title, and home delivery is so convenient. And to show you just how easy it is to get Zebra Historical Romances, we'll send you your first 4 books absolutely FREE! Our gift to you just for trying our home subscription service.

BIG SAVINGS AND FREE HOME DELIVERY

Each month, you'll receive the four newest titles as soon as they are published. You'll probably receive them even before the bookstores do. What's more, you may preview these exciting novels free for 10 days. If you like them as much as we think you will, just pay the low preferred subscriber's price of just $3.75 each. *You'll save $3.00 each month off the publisher's price.* AND, your savings are even greater because there are never any shipping, handling or other hidden charges—FREE Home Delivery. Of course you can return any shipment within 10 days for full credit, no questions asked. There is no minimum number of books you must buy.

4 FREE BOOKS

TO GET YOUR 4 FREE BOOKS WORTH $18.00 — MAIL IN THE FREE BOOK CERTIFICATE T O D A Y

Fill in the Free Book Certificate below, and we'll send your FREE BOOKS to you as soon as we receive it.

If the certificate is missing below, write to: Zebra Home Subscription Service, Inc., P.O. Box 5214, 120 Brighton Road, Clifton, New Jersey 07015-5214.

FREE BOOK CERTIFICATE

4 FREE BOOKS

ZEBRA HOME SUBSCRIPTION SERVICE, INC.

YES! Please start my subscription to Zebra Historical Romances and send me my first 4 books absolutely FREE. I understand that each month I may preview four new Zebra Historical Romances free for 10 days. If I'm not satisfied with them, I may return the four books within 10 days and owe nothing. Otherwise, I will pay the low preferred subscriber's price of just $3.75 each; a total of $15.00, *a savings off the publisher's price of $3.00.* I may return any shipment and I may cancel this subscription at any time. There is no obligation to buy any shipment and there are no shipping, handling or other hidden charges. Regardless of what I decide, the four free books are mine to keep.

NAME

ADDRESS _____ APT

CITY _____ STATE _____ ZIP

TELEPHONE
( )

SIGNATURE _____ (if under 18, parent or guardian must sign)

Terms, offer and prices subject to change without notice. Subscription subject to acceptance by Zebra Books. Zebra Books reserves the right to reject any order or cancel any subscription.

ZB0993

GET
FOUR
FREE
BOOKS
(AN $18.00 VALUE)

AFFIX
STAMP
HERE

ZEBRA HOME SUBSCRIPTION
SERVICE, INC.
120 BRIGHTON ROAD
P.O. Box 5214
CLIFTON, NEW JERSEY 07015-5214

Chapter Eleven

Delta awoke from the dream, her body laved in perspiration, her pillow clutched to her bosom. For a time, melancholy overwhelmed her. She lay as though frozen in time and space, reliving Anne Bonny's hanging. Her arms tightened protectively around the pillow, crushing it to her body, while tears streamed from her eyes.

After a while reason returned and she began to question the meaning of the dream. Although she knew with some certainty that Anne Bonny had not been hanged and definitely not clutching her newborn infant to her bosom, the dream's portent was clear—someone was in trouble, desperate trouble.

The possibility that it might be herself dawned slowly. When the thought finally took form, she threw aside the pillow and cradled her own belly, much as the pirate queen had done in her dream. Could it be?

Could she be carrying Brett's child? The idea filled her at once with a mixture of joy and melancholy. In an instant she knew that nothing would make her happier than to bear Brett's children.

But the thought had never crossed her mind. Even that afternoon by the river in Memphis when Brett had expressed such horror at the prospect, she had not considered such a possibility.

Why would she dream of a pregnancy she had never considered? As far as that went, why did she dream of pirates and crying babies? How could she have dreamed of a man before she even met him? None of this was possible, yet obviously none of it was impossible. Certainly not a pregnancy. She could well be carrying Brett's child.

Or she could have missed the message of the dream entirely. She knew only one thing for certain—these dreams held messages, desperate messages, cries for help.

Someone was in trouble. Someone needed her.

A loud knock at the door startled her out of her stupor. Quickly she tossed aside the pillow, grabbed a robe, and tried not to hope.

But when Zanna answered her question, "Who's there?" she knew hope was yet another thing totally beyond her control.

Zanna entered the room, explaining, "We're due to dock in Natchez within the hour. I thought we could have breakfast together before then."

The image of sharing a sunrise breakfast with Brett surged like an ill wind through Delta's mind. "I'm not hungry."

"You will be before lunchtime. I'll wait while you dress. The dining room won't be crowded if we hurry."

The dining room. Not the deck outside the paddlewheel lounge. "I'll hurry."

While Zanna chattered from one corner of the room, Delta dressed hastily, concentrating on the fall of her simple brown skirt over her bustle, on adjusting the lace on her cuffs just so, on tying her hair back with a large brown ribbon.

"Come here," Zanna bid. "Let me do up your buttons in back. I don't know how a woman's supposed to dress herself in clothes like this."

"That's why I haven't worn this blouse since I left home," Delta admitted, while her brain played tricks with Zanna's fingers on her back.

Twice during the meal that followed, Zanna had to draw Delta back to the conversation and repeat herself.

"Where's your mind?" Zanna asked once.

Delta shrugged. "I didn't sleep well." But her thoughts had left her dream, at least the content of her dream. For some unexplainable reason she now felt the baby in her dream represented not a child of her own, but Brett himself. He was the one needing her help: she knew he was. The reason she had dreamed of Anne Bonny falling to her death clutching her child to her bosom, must surely symbolize the lengths to which Delta herself was prepared to go in supporting Brett.

He was a part of her life. He could deny the fact until kingdom come, but it would remain a fact. He had been part of her life for months. Seeing him, knowing him in the flesh validated her dream, convincing her beyond doubt that her life was inexplicably intertwined with his.

Whether he wanted this to be true or not did nothing to change the facts. And the thought of him facing his enemies alone was unbearable.

By the time they finished breakfast Delta's mind was set. She would go to Brett, force him to see her. Somehow she would persuade him to allow her to be a physical part of his life. Already he was part of her life in every other way.

But before she could carry out her plan, the *Mississippi Princess* arrived in Natchez and Cameron's representative came aboard.

Zanna was taken with Stuart Longstreet from the first. He wasn't as tall as Cameron. In fact, he and Zanna were close to the same height. His most visible feature was a sweeping, exquisitely groomed blond handlebar mustache. He had a ready laugh, but his brown eyes remained alert and serious. His penchant for observing large areas while keeping up a conversation, made Delta nervous. She worried that he might be searching for a glimpse of Brett.

Stuart, as he insisted on being called, was also organized, she discovered, for he had a day of sightseeing mapped out. She wanted desperately to refuse, to remain on board and find a way to get in touch with Brett, but she dared not arouse Stuart's suspicions. And she had to write articles about Natchez to post to Hollis anyway, else the family would grow suspicious.

"You can wire Cameron as soon as we get to Natchez-on-top-of-the-Hill," Stuart advised her, quick to distinguish between the disreputable Natchez-under-the-Hill, near which the boat had docked. "He'll be on pins and needles until he receives word of your safe arrival."

After retrieving her parasol and tapestry portfolio from her stateroom, Delta searched out Zanna again. "Why don't you leave the parade to Albert and come with us?"

"I shouldn't," Zanna replied. She gave Delta a quick peck on the cheek. "Have a good time today. He's a handsome man, and he appears to be more . . . ah, more honorable than *others* you've met recently. Let him take your mind off your troubles."

"I don't have any troubles," Delta objected.

"Have a wonderful day," Zanna repeated, leaving Delta dismayed. Had her feeling for Brett been so easy

228

for all to see? If so, no wonder he considered her a threat to his safety.

Stuart guided her down the gangplank, explaining about the yarn mills they would visit, and the ice factory. "Cameron was anxious for me to get you away from the wharves," he told her, glancing toward the saloons and dives along the waterfront. "Natchez-under-the-Hill is no place for a lady. Nor a man either, unless he's hunting badmen."

She felt his fingers touch lightly at her waist when they stepped off the gangplank, as though to help her keep her balance. Thoughts of Brett flashed through her brain. She turned back toward the boat, searching the decks, hoping this time *not* to find him watching her. What would he think, seeing her with another man? And so soon? Whether he cared for her or not, he would be certain to feel abandoned.

Brett wasn't in sight, of course, and the sinking feeling she experienced reaffirmed how desperate she was to see him. From the top deck, however, a figure waved in wild circles, drawing her attention.

"Have a good time, Delta."

Nat. She felt sick inside. Then suddenly she became aware of Gabriel who stood beside the gangplank playing his fiddle, an act she now knew to be a signal of some sort to Brett. She glared at him. Without missing a beat of the lively tune, Gabriel lifted eyebrows in salute, then favored Stuart with a quizzical frown.

Not only did Natchez-on-top-of-the-Hill, as Stuart called it, appear to be a more respectable place than its counterpart down under, but it was beautiful. Sitting stiffly in the carriage beside the Pinkerton agent, wishing she were back on board the *Mississippi Princess,* Delta caught her breath at the brilliant array of azaleas. Their sweet fragrance filled the air. But her spirits would not

229

be lifted more than a notch or two. Her fear for Brett had become an all-consuming plague, gnawing at her like a busy beaver.

What would this day hold for him? For her? For them? And how would she ever persuade him to let her love him?

Somehow the day passed. Delta dutifully allowed Stuart to squire her about town, first to the Rosalie Yarn Mill, then to Natchez Cotton Mills Company, both which seemed enormously prosperous. Although evidence of the war's destruction remained, she saw less of it here than in Vicksburg.

"The war was rough," Stuart replied to her comment, "especially the occupation, but we didn't spend six unrelenting weeks in the midst of one battle like Vicksburg did."

After lunch in a fancy hotel dining room, to which Delta knew she should have worn a bonnet instead of her hair ribbon, Stuart took her to the ice factory. It was a large building with a maze of pipes running every which way. The floor was littered with tin boxes, which had been filled with clear water and sunk into the floor. Men with long sticks walked along between the rows stirring the water as it froze. "We turn out thirty tons of ice a day." The foreman led them to one corner of the room, where he instructed Delta to notice the various types of cut flowers that were freezing inside the water.

"These are popular in the summer," the foreman said. "Folks like to place them on silver trays at social gatherings. Helps cool the air." He indicated several blocks in the far corner. "Those are for the *Mississippi Princess*. Captain Kaney wanted something special for the reception tonight."

Delta scribbled as fast as she could while the foreman

answered questions about the methods used to freeze the ice—"ammonia gas flowing through those pipes produces the freezing"—and to ship the ice—"pack it in sawdust," he explained.

By the time they stepped outside again, the calliope had begun to call patrons to the evening's performance. The streets were filled with people in carriages and on foot headed for the docks.

"All the performances will be on board the ship in Natchez," she told Stuart after he assisted her into the carriage.

"I should hope so," he replied, "what with the dangerous area surrounding the docks."

When he took up the reins, she expected him to head downhill toward the boat, but he turned the opposite direction.

A couple of streets over, he drew rein in front of a small building off the main square. "I've saved this little chore for last," he said, climbing down from the carriage. "Cameron indicated that you wouldn't find it to your liking, so I didn't want to spoil the day."

The sign outside the building read: Stuart Longstreet, Detective. "This is your office?"

Even before he answered, anxiety began to grow inside her. He took her hand and helped her alight, while she fought back her fear.

"What won't I find to my liking?" she asked, striving to sound casual.

He held the door, ushered her into an office that showed signs of needing a housekeeper's attention. Papers and files were stacked high on every available surface. Clearing a chair, he motioned her to it, then busied himself lighting the lamp that stood nearby.

"I take it our gambler is still on board the *Mississippi Princess?*" he inquired.

231

So he was *our* gambler now? Somehow the term held a more ominous connotation than Cameron's calling Brett *her* gambler. She shrugged. In truth she had no idea where Brett was.

Stuart handed her a sheaf of handbills. "Look through these. See if you can identify him."

Terror gripped her as Nat's accusation about the wanted poster came to mind. The papers trembled in her hands. Dare she look through these? What if his likeness stared back at her? His beloved likeness. *On a wanted poster.*

"There aren't many," Stuart encouraged, "ten at the most. I went through everything that resembled the description Cameron wired me: tall, broad-shouldered, thick black hair, dark eyes separated by a deep vertical crease, of French descent. The most likely candidate—" He paused, fingering his mustache. "Go ahead and leaf through them. I don't want to prejudice what you see with my suspicions."

She held her breath. Nothing he could say would prejudice her reaction to a photograph of Brett Reall on a wanted poster. Gingerly she began to study the pictures. Her eyes skittered across the first page. Relief followed when she didn't recognize anything about the man. Terror returned with the second page. But she didn't recognize him, either. Nor the third, nor the fourth.

"Where are these people from?" she asked, more to take her mind off what she was doing than because she desired an answer.

She didn't recognize the fifth face. Or the sixth.

"All over. We looked for someone with connections to Canada. Didn't find any." Stuart reached for the stack, withdrew a poster, and handed it to her for further scrutiny.

For a moment all she could do was purse her lips and stare at the unfamiliar face of an unknown criminal, willing her head to stop reeling, her heart to resume beating. "I've never seen that man."

She felt ill. "Why do you think Brett Reall is a fugitive? I mean, Cameron wasn't even suspicious of him."

"That bounty hunter's after someone, Delta. We don't want to take a chance on a criminal slipping into the country under our noses."

"Brett's a gambler—"

"Cameron swears not."

"Cameron only met him once."

"What kind of gambler has calluses on his hands and a face that's seen more sunshine than barroom lamps?"

She inhaled, gritted her teeth, and finally exhaled, trying to expel the awful fact that she could be responsible for Brett being apprehended by authorities.

"One that isn't very good," she suggested. "Maybe he isn't able to make a living gambling. Perhaps he has to . . . uh, to supplement his income by other means."

"In that case, it's those other means we're interested in. I've wired the name and description to the Mounties." Stuart paused to give her a look filled with portent. "I'll be traveling on board the *Mississippi Princess* the rest of the way to New Orleans."

She stared at him, wide-eyed.

"If you had identified one of these fellers—" He tapped the stack of wanted posters he had taken from Delta's hand. "—as the gambler on board the showboat, Cameron's instructions were to keep you here in Natchez until he could arrange for your passage back to St. Louis. But since you didn't—"

Delta jumped to her feet during Stuart's discourse.

233

"Cameron said? Cameron decided? Cameron's instructions—?"

"Delta, he knows his business. I can't blame him." He gave her a look that, before she met Brett Reall, might have set her heart to thrumming. Now it only irritated her. "You're a mighty lovely woman, Delta. Cameron doesn't—*we* don't want anything to happen to you."

She felt sick. Weak and sick. And frightened. "What will you do?"

"Do?"

"On board the boat? About . . . about the gambler?"

"Watch him," Stuart replied.

"I talked to Nat, the bounty hunter. He isn't after Brett," she assured him. "He's after someone else. He told me so. He even had a wanted poster with the man's face on it, and he said it wasn't Brett."

"Who is he after? Would you recognize the poster if I found it—" he motioned around the room, "—in all this mess?"

"I didn't see the poster. It was stolen from Nat's room, or so he said. He accused me of the theft."

"You?"

She shrugged. "I'm a journalist. That has a lot of people worried."

"And that's another thing that worries Cameron—and me." Stuart chewed his bottom lip, setting his mustache to bobbling. Delta wanted to reach over and yank it. She wanted to run from the room, to find Brett, to warn him.

"I really must be getting back to the boat," she said. "Zanna depends on me to sell tickets and it's getting awfully late."

It took more finagling than Delta had thought to free

herself from Stuart Longstreet. Back on the boat, he suggested they take in the afternoon sunset with a glass of lemonade on deck.

His invitation called to mind happy times with Brett, and only added to her anxiety. She must find Brett. Now she had more than her nightmare to discuss with him. Now they faced a real threat. Another one.

"Thank you, but I need to freshen up. Why don't you find a cabin boy to show you to your stateroom before dinner?"

Although Stuart carried his grip along, he didn't seem in a hurry to settle in. "We've plenty of time."

"Not on this boat. Captain Kaney runs a tight schedule. When his dinner bell sounds, he expects everyone to be dressed and ready to eat."

No sooner had she extricated herself from the persistent Pinkerton agent than she faced another problem—she had no idea where Brett's stateroom was located. Heading for her own cabin, she willed her brain to work, for she certainly couldn't ask anyone for directions.

That would only draw attention, which she must avoid at all costs. So, what did she know that would lead her to his room?

The only reference she could recall him making to his cabin was when he left her to dress for breakfast those two mornings. For a moment her emotions took over and she was lost in reflective longings so intense she felt her heart stammer.

Striving to order her thinking as she did when researching a story, she started at the beginning. The beginning.

She had first seen Brett in the dining room. No clue there.

Next the captain had introduced them at the rail outside the grand salon. No clue there.

She had seen him at dinner. Again, emotions assailed her, warm and poignant, recalling how they had bantered at the captain's table. He'd thought her an actress. Her smile faded recalling his reaction when he discovered her to be a journalist. She understood the reason, now. Or she was beginning to understand.

The next time she saw him had been on deck by the sternwheel after her nightmare. And that, she knew the moment it popped into her head, might hold a clue. He had obviously been in some sort of clandestine meeting with two men she now knew to be Pierre and Gabriel. He wouldn't have walked the entire length of the boat for such a meeting—and risk being seen either going or coming.

He would have traveled the shortest and least traveled route to and from his stateroom. Or so it seemed.

She headed for the stairway at the stern. It was narrow, dark, and thankfully empty. Not until she began climbing did she think of Nat. What would she do if he found her searching the boat for Brett?

Lie to him, of course. But Nat was becoming more and more difficult to evade.

The stairway to the observation deck, immediately above the cabin deck, opened onto the paddlewheel lounge. The moment her foot touched the deck, emotions assailed her. Then she recalled Stuart Longstreet. It wouldn't do to have him discover her mission, either. Ducking her head, she slipped around the corner and continued in the stairwell to the next level, the promenade deck.

Instantly upon gaining the promenade deck, she came face to face with Pierre. Without a word, he blocked her path. She craned her neck to see around him. The staterooms on this deck were the largest on board. They ran back to back down the center of the boat, each opening onto the passageway and rail. She had no idea how many there were. Nor where to start searching. With Pierre at this end, however, she had a good idea.

"You're lost, m'moiselle." His abruptness infuriated her.

Summoning all the determination she possessed, she looked him straight in the eye. "I must see him."

"You're lost," he repeated, his enormous bulk filling the narrow passageway. "Go back downstairs, right now."

Her brain whirred with piffle when she needed substance. In order to succeed, she would have to find a way around this brute, but all she could think of was that she wanted to spit in his face. "I must see Brett," she insisted. "It's a matter . . . an urgent matter . . . most urgent."

Mutely Pierre stood his ground.

Delta looked toward the nearest staterooms, one to her left, one to her right, each angled into a corner, separated from the rest. Could one of those be Brett's? Likely, she decided, with Pierre blocking the passageway at this particular point.

But which one? Realizing the futility even as she moved, she tried to step around the oversized guard, but as she had suspected he would, he blocked her path. Desperation overtook her.

"Brett!" she screamed to the right. Pierre's hand whipped out to stop her. She dodged it. Turning to the left, she screamed again. "Brett!"

That was all she was allowed, because the big man's arm came around her neck, turning her toward him. His massive hand clamped over her mouth. She kicked at him. Then realizing that would serve no purpose, she began to stomp on the floor. Noise. She must make enough noise that he would be forced to stop her. He could ill afford noise.

Surely this brute knew that.

Suddenly in the midst of it all, the door to the stateroom on the right opened and she saw Brett.

"Bring her in."

He spoke in a curt monotone, and she thought without reason of the ice factory and the flowers embedded in the freezing water. Somehow recalling them gave her hope. Brett Reall could put on a cold front, but that's all it was. A front.

She knew him for the gentle lover, the tender man who had shared her bed, who filled her heart.

Seeing him now, dressed in denim pants and a chambray shirt that stretched across his broad shoulders, he resembled the man from her dreams more than he ever had. He could have been one of her brothers standing there in the doorway glaring at her. He looked like them, the Jarretts, his size, his physique—except for his jet black hair and cold black eyes.

Except for the way he made her blood run hot even beneath his glacial stare.

Pierre hesitated and Brett demanded again, in a lower voice. "Bring her in before someone sees her."

Once she was inside, the charged atmosphere buzzed in her ears. Brett turned his back to her and she glanced around the room—from the bed, larger than her own, to the sofa and chairs, then back to the bed.

"What do you want?" he demanded, startling her from her reverie. Blood rushed up her neck. Had he seen her stare at the bed? Was he thinking the same thing she was? Remembering the same things?

"I need to talk to you."

"Talk."

"Alone."

"Why?"

If his question had been a dagger, it couldn't have wounded her more. As though he had pierced her heart with that one cold word, she recoiled, then willed herself to straighten her shoulders. She had not met his gaze and dared not do so now. She stared instead somewhere between the bed and the cabinet where he stood. She heard liquid splash into a glass, then into another one. She envisioned taking a glass from him, touching his hand. She clasped her damp hands tightly together.

So much time passed in silence that she feared he would refuse her request, but he surprised her by saying, "Leave us, Pierre."

"Certainement?"

Delta seethed inside. She wanted to scream, *Of course he's certain. Get out of here! Leave us alone!* Involuntarily her hands balled into tight fists. She wanted to fall on the man and drive him from the room like a shrew.

"Oui," Brett replied.

She dared not glance at either man. She stood still, struggling to bring the present into focus. She was here. She had found Brett. She had a message to deliver. That was all. But it was dreadfully important.

Somewhere in the back of her mind she heard the door close. When Brett spoke again, they were alone.

"Talk," he repeated. She heard a glass thud against the table and saw where Brett had placed her drink. She watched him motion toward it. Obviously he was no more anxious to touch her than she was him.

She picked up the glass, took a sip, and recognized the contents for whiskey. Before she thought otherwise,

239

she said, "I see your cabinet is stocked with stouter stuff than mine."

Her statement was met with silence and she instantly regretted calling the past to mind. She was here with a purpose and she must accomplish it.

"Why did you come, Delta?"

Why is your voice so cold? she wanted to cry. "You're in danger on this boat."

"How so?"

"There's a Pinkerton agent aboard. Cameron sent him. He will travel with us the rest of the way to New Orleans."

"Don't worry about it."

"Don't worry about it? What if he recognizes you?"

"He won't."

"How can you be certain?"

"He won't recognize me, Delta."

"Wouldn't it be safer for you to travel on land? Hire horses or something?"

He sighed and she chanced a look at him, still avoiding direct eye contact.

"Pierre thinks so," he admitted.

"Then why—?"

"Because I know the men I'm up against. They won't risk exposure as long as I'm on this boat. This is the safest place for me. Likely the only safe place."

Her heart thudded painfully against her ribs. Every time they discussed this nebulous threat to his life, it became more foreboding. He was in danger, terrible danger, and he admitted it to her in increments that rendered the situation increasingly terrifying.

"Nat caught me alone and made threats that he's going to get you. He said he'll wait and one day you'll make a mistake and he'll be waiting and—"

"Sh, Delta. I know what he said. Don't worry about it."

"Stuart Longstreet, the Pinkerton agent, forced me to look through a stack of wanted posters—" her voice cracked and she paused, then continued, breathless "—for a picture of you."

She waited for a response, watching him stand stoic, silent. "How can you be so calm, so—?"

"I'm not calm," he replied in even tones that belied his words. "I'm confident, though. So don't worry about me."

"I can't help it," she admitted in a near whisper.

"Yes, you can. Just stop thinking about me."

Anger fought for control inside her. "That's hard to do. My nightmares have returned."

"They're only dreams."

"Only dreams! It's you in those dreams, Brett, it's you." She almost told him about the baby, about Anne Bonny dropping to her death clutching her baby to her breast, but she stopped herself in time.

"No," he was saying, "it isn't me. You don't know me, Delta. I'm sorry if I led you on, but that's past now. Put it out of your mind."

"When forces are mounting against you on every side? Stuart wired the Canadian Mounties, for God's sake."

Again she watched him for a reaction, but he merely shrugged. Would nothing provoke this man? Nothing crack that iron-hard facade and expose the warm and gentle man beneath?

"Forget it, Delta. And forget me."

"That's impossible. I dream about you every night."

"God's bones! Stop your nonsense about those dreams. We're in real life. I'm alive, here and now. I

241

did not live a century ago. I am not a pirate. I did not fall in love with you.''

Her eyes flew to his, surprised at his words, at the vehemence with which he had spoken them. She felt as though he had reached inside her chest and grabbed her heart in his fist.

''I *made* love to you,'' he continued. ''Made love. That's physical, not mental. Carnal, not emotional. Get me out of your mind, Delta. Forget you ever knew me.''

Abruptly he turned to face the far window, staring at it even though the damask draperies were drawn tight. ''Go on now, get out of here.''

As in a trance she set the glass on the chest and opened the door. It closed behind her and she stood in the passageway a moment, breathing in the soft river air, numbed to everything else.

Suddenly from inside Brett's cabin came a thundering crash followed by the sound of shattering glass. Inside her chest her heart lurched. Tears fell from her eyes and rolled down her cheeks, while she envisioned whiskey running down the paneled wall from the glass he shattered—the same way he had just broken her heart.

Chapter Twelve

By the time the *Mississippi Princess* arrived in St. Francisville two days later, Delta had accomplished one thing: She'd channeled her unmitigated despair into determination to save Brett from the forces that threatened not only his life, but their relationship. How she would accomplish this monumental task, she had not determined. But at least thinking about it kept her from going mad.

Following Brett's brutal rejection she had returned to her cabin by the stern stairs, intending to seclude herself there for the remainder of the trip. But Zanna would hear of no such thing.

"That Pinkerton agent is on pins and needles asking about you," Zanna told her, after Delta finally consented to open the door.

"He's been sent to keep an eye on me," she retorted. "By a member of my meddling family."

"No matter why he wants to see you, Delta. He's a decidedly handsome man. You should give him a chance."

"If he's so desirable, Zanna, you go after him."

"Me? It's you he's interested in."

Knowing Zanna would not let up in her efforts to

entice her to come to dinner, Delta stuck a few pins in her wayward hair. "Come on, then. Let's see if we can't convince him he's chosen the wrong woman."

It didn't take much, for once Zanna was satisfied Delta wasn't interested in Stuart, she set her cap for him in a determined way. And Stuart responded.

Not that he relaxed his surveillance of Delta. But instead of the romantic innuendoes he had been interjecting into their conversation, he became more professional. And she was glad for it.

The extent of Stuart's dedication to keeping his eye on Brett Reall, even though the gambler had not shown his face since the Pinkerton came aboard, was evidenced in the fact that Stuart did not accompany Delta into town when the boat docked at St. Francisville.

Captain Kaney himself had arranged her interview in St. Francisville. "That's my old home turf," he told Delta. "And the lady in question is a . . . shall we say, a dear old friend. Descendent of the late naturalist and artist, John James Audubon. He painted many of his bird studies in this part of the state."

Captain Kaney, in fact, had intended to accompany Delta to Miss Eliza Strahan's plantation for tea, but an emergency in the galley prevented him from leaving the boat at the last minute. She received his message while waiting at the rail for the boat to dock.

Zanna offered to go.

"No," Delta told her. "I'm perfectly capable of finding my way." She glanced around the docks at the familiar group of boys hopping from foot to foot, eager to get on board. "St. Francisville isn't so large that I'm likely to get lost. And even if I did, I'm sure the people are friendly enough to guide me back to the boat. Or I could wait for dusk and follow the calliope."

She glanced around to where Stuart and Nat stood

apart, talking. She had seen them thus several times since Stuart joined the passengers on board the *Mississippi Princess*. Now, as on the other occasions, trepidation filled her at the sight. What had Nat told Stuart? What had Stuart told Nat? And what did it mean for Brett?

Zanna laughed, then sobered. "I'm surprised Stuart doesn't go with you. From the little I understand about his presence, it has something to do with protecting you."

Delta sighed. "That isn't all of it. Besides, what he's protecting me from isn't in St. Francisville." *It's on board this boat.*

Leaving the gangplank she exchanged glances with Gabriel, who stood in his usual spot, playing his fiddle. He was around so often, they were coming to know each other without ever speaking. At that thought her mind drifted back to the night Nat had waited outside her cabin and the strains of fiddle music that ran him off. She recalled how earlier on the docks, Nat had approached her, intending to speak. He had suddenly changed his mind and fled—at the sound of fiddle music.

Her brain began to buzz with what this meant—with the only thing it could mean. Brett had sent Gabriel to watch her. She knew she should feel piqued, but she couldn't work up her ire. Brett was having her watched, not because he would hope to discover something, not because he didn't trust her. No, that wouldn't be the purpose at all. He was having her watched for her own safety. And that could mean only one thing—he cared.

He cared for her. He cared enough to give up one of his own bodyguards to protect her.

When he was the one in danger.

Gaining the docks, she turned and stared back at the

ship. What she wouldn't give for a glimpse of him. Just a glimpse.

Strange, she thought, realizing what she was doing. Only once had she seen Brett standing at the rail, staring after her. Yet, every time she left this boat she felt his eyes upon her.

No matter that he had professed not to have fallen in love with her. No matter that he was determined in his bullheaded way to keep them apart.

She knew he didn't want that any more than she did. How could he, when every night he came to her in her dreams. Not nightmares now, since her last devastating encounter with him. Now her dreams were no longer of pirates. They were of Brett, here on this boat, in her stateroom. Of Brett and herself, making love, yes, but loving each other all the while. He could never convince her otherwise. No matter what he told her in the daytime, at night he loved her with an intensity that was almost as real as life itself.

Almost. At least the baby had stopped crying. She wondered whether that were significant, coming, as it had directly after her dream about Anne Bonny's hanging. And if so, did it carry an ominous meaning, a portent of death yet to come? Or did it signal an end of the danger she had so long feared imminent? Was the danger over?

"Hold up, Delta."

She turned at Nat's voice. Since the night he accosted her outside her stateroom at Vicksburg, Nat had kept his distance. Approaching her now, he reached for her elbow. Same old Nat, she thought, pulling away from him.

"Stuart suggested I escort you to your interview since the captain has been detained."

Delta looked for Stuart, finding him on the observation deck, engaged in conversation with a couple of men she recognized as St. Louis bankers. She waved to attract his attention, but he wasn't looking her way.

"Don't you believe me?" Nat quizzed.

"Believe you? Of course I don't believe Stuart suggested such a thing." On the other hand, her worried brain teased, if Nat were with her, he couldn't go after Brett. Briefly she considered Cameron's warning.

"If I agree do you promise not to try anything stupid?"

His eyes flirted. "I'm a gentleman, Delta. You know—"

"I know the Pinkertons are looking for a reason to pounce on you, Nat. If you lay one finger on me, they'll have that reason."

Nat grinned mischievously. "I accept the challenge, Miss Jarrett. By the end of the day you'll see that I'm much better at doubling as a gentleman than that . . . gambler."

Following Nat away from the boat, Delta's heart suddenly skipped a beat. Two horses were tied near where Gabriel entertained the crowd. Was Brett planning to come ashore? At the thought she stubbed her toe and Nat caught her arm. This time she didn't think to pull away as he continued to usher her toward the nearby livery stable. Her mind was on Brett.

While Nat went inside to wrangle with the hostler, she remained outside the large double doors, watching the steamboat from afar. Then, sure enough, after the cast had cleared the docks with the gathered crowd following in their wake, Brett and Pierre sauntered down the gangplank, ignoring Gabriel when they passed him.

She held her breath, lest the vision evaporate like mist on the river. Tears rushed to her eyes. *Brett*, she thought, *I love you so.*

He looked across the expanse of wharves. His eyes found hers, held hers for precious seconds. He loved her. She knew it. He loved her.

She smiled. He tipped his hat. A quick flick of his finger against the brim, no more, but oh it was something wonderful to see. Then he turned and mounted his horse.

Crazily, she wondered where he could be headed in his gambling attire. Why, that vest shone like a beacon in the midday sun.

"Well, what'd you know," Nat whistled beside her. "The bird has flown his coop."

Quickly she glanced away, as though she had not seen the two men on horseback. While Nat assisted her onto the sidesaddle, then climbed aboard the horse he had rented for himself, Brett and Pierre disappeared from view.

Nat had obtained directions to the estate of Miss Eliza Strahan from the hostler, and they rode out of town without seeing Brett and Pierre again.

But Delta's heart began to make plans quite apart from her brain. If she could manage to return to the boat at precisely the right time, she could see Brett again before he secluded himself in his stateroom. The odds, of course, were against two such encounters. But so were her dreams.

Nat talked on about first one thing, then another, surprising her by not mentioning Brett again.

"I haven't seen you and Elyse together lately," she told him once.

He laughed in a self-deprecating sort of way that enhanced his image in Delta's eyes. "Guess I've gone and gotten downright virtuous. It must be your influence, Delta. I couldn't see leading a sweet girl like that on, me being a bounty hunter and all. You'll have to admit that's not the most respectable of professions.''

"Then it was considerate of you not to pursue her,'' she replied, thinking suddenly of Brett's assertion that he hadn't intended to lead her on.

Camelliawood Plantation was not over two miles out of town. Its main house, a magnificent Greek-revival structure that, unlike many she had seen in towns up the river, was impeccably maintained. Magnolia trees in full bloom lined a curving drive. In front of the house, a groomsman hurried to take their horses. The grounds were abloom with camellias and azaleas and many flowers Delta could not put a name to.

Inside, imported marble vied for prominence with polished hardwoods and gilt tracings. Miss Strahan—not a day under ninety, Delta was sure—hurried to greet them, a sprightly figure gowned in regal black crepe and sporting a head full of pure white curls.

"Miss Eliza Pierre,'' their hostess commented when, after introducing herself and welcoming them to Camelliawood Plantation, she saw Delta's attention drawn to the life-size painting of a beautiful young woman. "My grandmother. She's credited with bringing Mr. Audubon to West Feliciana Parish.''

After touring the public rooms of the house, Miss Strahan escorted them through her gardens—"twenty acres of formal designs, modeled after the palace gardens in Versailles,'' Miss Strahan told them.

"These azaleas,'' she added, "are cuttings from Rosedown. Of course you know that Mrs. Daniel Turnbull of Rosedown Plantation introduced azaleas to our country.''

Delta scribbled notes, since, of course, she had not known the facts Miss Strahan seemed to feel everyone had learned in the cradle. The question foremost in her mind would have gotten them thrown out on their ears for its impropriety. How, since the devastation of the war, did Miss Strahan afford the servants to keep this enormous plantation in such exquisite condition?

The closest their hostess came to supplying an answer to the unasked question was to say that the cane crop had been good this year. Delta made a mental note to discuss the interesting Miss Strahan with Captain Kaney, who professed to being a close personal friend.

"Before we view M'sieur Audubon's studio," Miss Strahan was saying, "perhaps we should take tea here on the veranda."

Delta felt like a princess surrounded by so much luxury. At the ring of Miss Strahan's bell, servants scurried in with a silver tea service and a platter of sandwiches and crackers. Their hostess had just indicated which chairs each of her guests should take, however, when Nat surprised Delta by saying,

"I won't have time for tea, ma'am. I'm needed back at the boat to help prepare for tonight's performance." He produced two tickets from his jacket pocket. "Thank you for the tour of your magnificent home. Please accept my invitation to attend our little melodrama tonight."

Delta watched Nat's performance with a slack jaw. "I didn't realize you intended to leave so early. We haven't viewed the Audubons and—"

"You must stay, Delta," he encouraged in his most polished stage voice. "No article on St. Francisville would be complete without an account of that great artist and his works."

"But—?"

He smiled. "I shouldn't worry about finding your

way back. It's a simple matter of staying on one road, no turns to confuse you.''

Confuse me? she thought. What did he think he was doing? And she really needed—wanted—to see the Audubons.

''Of course I can find my way back.'' Although she was unable to keep the testiness out of her voice, she wasn't sorry to see him leave. She would have a much better chance of speaking to Brett when she returned to the boat without Nat by her side.

''I won't hear of you traveling unescorted, my dear,'' Miss Strahan said. ''When we finish, my coachman will drive you.''

''Thank you, but that isn't necessary.''

''Indeed it is,'' Miss Strahan insisted, sending a maid scurrying to alert the coachman. ''We'll hitch your horse on the back.''

After tea Miss Strahan led the way to John James Audubon's studio on the premises. Once inside all Delta's thoughts faded beneath the magnitude of his talent.

In addition to numerous full-sized paintings of the area's birds and plant life, several stuffed specimens of birds and small animals were set in displays that looked as natural as the wild. Delta took notes, writing hastily, while Miss Strahan explained her famous relative's methods, going so far as to claim that the artist acted as his own taxidermist.

Without warning Delta's eyes arrested on the scarlet crest of a large ivory-billed woodpecker. A wave of heat raced up her spine. Instantly she knew something was wrong. Something was terribly wrong. No baby cried this time. There was only the heat, and the fire. Red and hot. Withdrawing a handkerchief from her sleeve, she dabbed her suddenly damp face.

Miss Strahan was so entranced with her discourse on M'sieur Audubon's techniques that she failed to notice, and by the time Delta was able to break in, the calliope could be heard calling people to the boat. She grabbed that as an excuse to leave.

Riding on the seat behind the liveried coachmen, Delta fought down the fear that the boat had exploded. Many paddlewheelers exploded in the old days, something to do with the furnaces becoming so hot that steam was forced at pressures beyond the boilers' capacity. Wasn't that what Cameron told her?

That was when the boats used wood for fuel, he had assured her. Nowadays they used coal, and the temperature could more easily be controlled. Hadn't Captain Kaney explained as much the first day out?

But Brett could well have returned to the *Mississippi Princess* by now. And Zanna was on board and . . . and everyone she had grown to love. Especially Brett.

She hadn't had a chance to mend things between them. What if—?

Brett Reall listened patiently to Pierre's arguments as to why he should remain on board the *Mississippi Princess*.

"This is Louisiana," Pierre cautioned. "You're known here, sure. Wanted here. It is foolish—"

"Let me decide what's foolish," Brett snapped. He'd been short with Pierre for days now. Hell, he'd been short with everyone since Delta's visit. The tension was getting to him. Cabin fever, Gabriel called it. Perhaps. But he had an idea it depended on whose cabin he was in. Or, more precisely, who was in the cabin with him. For truth, he could ride the length of the Mississippi without ever stepping foot outside a stateroom—if Delta were there beside him.

But she wasn't. She couldn't be. He'd done the right thing. "It's more important for me to see our man here in St. Francisville than anywhere up or down the river. Tell me when Gabriel returns."

"Someone will recognize you, *certainement.*"

"Not in a gambler's garb. Hell, they've never even seen me wear a necktie." He chuckled. "This brocaded vest is so loud it'll blind them to my face, *oui?*"

Pierre grunted.

Brett slapped him on the back. "Besides, we agreed something had to be done about that bounty hunter."

"Gabriel and I—"

"Nat wouldn't follow you. It's me, he's after. Did you work out a diversion for that Pinkerton agent?"

Pierre nodded.

"Not Delta."

"*Non,* but you're supposed to forget her, sure."

"Give me time."

Riding out of St. Francisville on the horses Gabriel hired earlier, Brett inhaled the magnolia-scented air. "God's bones, it's good to be home!" But even as he spoke, he knew a good measure of his exhilaration came from having seen Delta at the wharves. Her smile warmed him yet. And her presence—as though she had been standing there waiting for him. As though they had planned to meet.

"We aren't home," Pierre objected.

"We're close enough. You can you smell it, *oui?* You can hear it, the hum of the bayou—"

"Me, I hear the sound of gunfire," Pierre responded. "The sound of a rope stretchin' across a liveoak branch. The sound of a blade slicin' bayou air. *Oui,* a blade that drips with your blood, *mon nèfyou.*"

"I'll hand you this, Pierre, you're one hell of a traveling partner. Next time I'll find someone with more *joie de vivre.*"

"*Oui,* an' get your head blown off for loving life too much."

Brett chuckled. "Don't mind me. I'm just not used to having both of you and my conscience keeping tabs on me."

"Your conscience, *mon nèfyou?*"

Brett thought of Delta. He could have had her every night for the entire trip. He would have been as safe in her cabin as in his. Hell, she'd have come to his cabin, no questions asked, no strings attached.

Except the strings they were both pulling against. She was right. Something kept drawing them together. He'd felt it again this morning on the wharf. And deep inside him, that force had spawned a great mass of need that fought like a bayou gater to free itself, to enjoy her while he could.

But it could only be for the duration of the trip, and that made it impossible. She professed not to need commitment. He professed not to want it. But the truth was, both of them did. Both of them needed it, both of them wanted it.

And that was the hell of it.

Set amidst a forest of willows and live oaks on the edge of a small creek, the little shack reminded him of shacks on the *chênières* further south—chinked cypress planks with palmetto-thatched roofs.

"Trade's been slow," André Bontura, his man in charge of operations allowed, after they had judged the place to be free of strangers.

"Have anything to do with the comin' elections?" Pierre questioned.

"*Non.* Only thing the gov'nor's interested in is runnin' the Voodoos out o' the state." Bontura wiped his brow with a filthy handkerchief and apologized to Brett. "Forgot about your *maman*."

"She isn't a Voodoo."

"Same as," Bontura responded. "In the eyes of tha' brother-in-law of yours."

"Trainor's no kin of mine."

"I thought—?"

"I never claimed him. Not even when I was married to his sister." Brett shrugged. "No love lost. He never claimed me either."

"Except now he wants your hide strung tighter'n a muskrat's pelt," Pierre reminded him.

"My question is," Brett addressed Bontura, "could we make a living out of this business if I decide against returning to Canada?"

Pierre exploded. "What did you say?"

"Could we?" Brett repeated, ignoring his uncle.

"For truth, you cannot stay in Louisiana," Pierre objected. "Except six feet under."

Brett shrugged. "Never hurts to investigate the options."

Suddenly a footstep sounded at the threshold, and the three men glanced up from where they stood.

Nat stood in the doorway, his forty-five aimed at Brett. "Dupré? That is your name? Anatole Dupré?"

Brett straightened his shoulders. "You think you've figured everything out, *oui?*"

"Close enough."

"Close doesn't count, Nat. If you haul my carcass to Trainor and I'm who I claim to be, Brett Reall, not some suspected murderer, you'll be in a peck of trouble. Trainor might be bloodthirsty, but, as I understand it, his hunger is for only one man. He wouldn't let you get off short of the gallows for murdering an innocent man.''

"I'm not stupid, Dupré," Nat said. "I'll take you in alive.''

Brett's eyes narrowed on the bounty hunter, defiant, intense. "You and who else?''

From behind Nat fiddle music began to fill the air. The sound startled Nat—only for an instant, but an instant was enough for Brett, Pierre, and Bontura to rush the door, take the bounty hunter's weapon, and haul him into the room.

"Come in, Gabriel," Brett called out the door. "Good work.''

"What d'you aim to do with this feller?" Bontura questioned.

"Me, I say we anchor him, and throw him in the bayou," Pierre suggested.

Brett studied the now mute Nat. "No need for that. All I want is to keep him off my tail until I get out of this country." He watched Pierre truss and tie their prisoner to a ladder-back chair. Bending low, Brett brought his face to eye level with Nat's.

"You see, Nat, I'm not guilty. I may not be able to prove it, but I'm not. I've never killed anyone in my life, and I don't aim to start now." His voice hardened. "So don't make me.''

"Him, he's guilty of somethin', sure," Gabriel offered. "If we knew wha', we could have him arrested and thrown in jail. That'd keep him off your back.''

"Leave 'em to me," Bontura told them. "Sheriff over in St. Francisville's a friend of mine. We'll find somethin' this heathen's done that's offensive to society.''

* * *

256

Delta fairly raced from the coach when the coachman drew up at the docks at St. Francisville. The coachman had offered to see her nag returned to the livery and she agreed with scant attention to manners. Images of Miss Strahan's lovely home and of John James Audubon's magnificent talent dimmed before the fear growing steadily inside her—fear that something had happened aboard the *Mississippi Princess*. The welcome strains of the calliope had reassured her that the boat hadn't exploded. But her premonition remained, strong and sickening. Something had happened to Brett. She was sure of it.

Zanna and Stuart waited impatiently for her to climb the gangplank.

"Where's Nat?" Zanna questioned.

"What'd you mean running off with that bounty hunter?" Stuart charged. "You should have told me Captain Kaney had been detained. I would have gone with you. Cameron'll have my . . . uh, my hide for this."

"Where's Nat?" Zanna questioned again. "The show's scheduled to start in five minutes."

"Hold it, both of you." Delta addressed each of their concerns by stating hers. "Nat said you suggested he ride with me, Stuart. I didn't believe him, but I had a good reason for letting him escort me to the plantation."

She turned to Zanna. "Right in the middle of my interview with Miss Strahan, Nat excused himself, saying you needed him to help prepare for tonight's performance."

She stared from one dumbfounded friend to the other. "Where's Brett?"

"Brett?" Zanna questioned. "It's Nat I need to find."

257

"Brett's in his cabin," Stuart responded.

"When did he return?" Delta asked.

Stuart's eyes widened.

"He left this morning about the same time Nat and I did. Didn't you see him leave the boat?"

"Son of a— Excuse me, ladies. I've been duped, but good." Stuart recovered his composure. "You think Nat's after him?"

"Why would Nat be after Brett?" Zanna questioned.

"Yes," Delta told Stuart.

While Delta and Stuart studied each other's expressions, sharing their common concern, Zanna took Stuart's arm.

"They're both grown men. Let them take care of themselves." She tugged on Stuart's arm. "What I need right now is another grown man."

Stuart glanced at Zanna vacantly, then apparently realizing what she meant, tried to draw away. "No, you don't. Not this grown man."

Zanna smiled sweeter than Delta had ever seen her. "Yes, I do. You'll make a perfect hero."

Stuart's face flushed. "No."

"But I *need* you," Zanna pleaded.

"I couldn't. I don't know the lines."

"You've seen the play. That's all that's necessary," Zanna told him, readjusting her grip on his arm.

Delta studied the pair. The rapport growing between them brought a poignant lump to her throat.

"There isn't a written script," Zanna was saying. "Ad lib. Say whatever comes to mind."

Stuart frowned. "The words that are apt to come to my mind at the moment aren't fit for the ears of women and children."

Suddenly bells started clanging and someone nearby cried, "Fire on board! Fire on board!"

With catlike reactions, Stuart grabbed Zanna and Delta by the arms and hurried them toward the gang-plank.

People began racing past them, trying to get ashore. Delta dug her heels into the wooden deck. The captain's voice came through his horn.

"Calm down, folks. Nothing to get excited about. The fire's been contained in one stateroom."

Roiled memories stirred fear inside Delta's stomach. Scenes from John James Audubon's workroom flashed through her head, accompanied by the premonitions she had experienced there. She jerked free of Stuart and started running up the deck.

"Where're you going?" he called after her.

The captain's voice came through again, continuing to try to calm the passengers' fears. "The fire has been extinguished. I repeat, the fire has been extinguished. No harm done."

While people around her paused to stare at each other, confused over what they should do next, Delta kept running.

Stuart and Zanna followed, catching her on the observation deck.

"Where're you going?" Zanna panted from behind.

Stuart came abreast of her and kept pace.

Outside Brett's stateroom, she stopped short, her hands pressed to her heart to contain its erratic beating. The door was thrown open. Smoke billowed out, but she saw no flames. Several of the crew rushed inside, then out.

She stepped forward, attempting to look inside the cabin.

259

"Don't go in there, ma'am. The room's full of smoke."

"Is there—was anyone injured?"

"No ma'am," came the reply. "The gent's a lucky fellow, though. Everything inside has been destroyed."

Stuart shouldered past Delta, demanding, "What exactly happened?"

The crewmember shrugged. "Don't rightly know, sir. Orville said he heard an explosion of some kind. Likely we'll never know how it started."

Delta's mouth felt as dry as if it had been scorched with smoke. "Where is he? The passenger?"

"Can't say for sure, ma'am. Orville here was deliverin' a dinner tray to the stateroom when the door burst open with the percussion. Flames leaped ever'where, he reported."

Delta's eyes darted around the hallway, pausing on each person in the gathering crowd. Suddenly she heard the strains of a fiddle over the escalating noise. Finding its source, she saw Gabriel standing apart from the group, playing his fiddle.

When she caught his eye, he held her gaze, steady and unconcerned. But when she tried to make her way to him, he vanished down the staircase.

Feeling a hand on her back, she turned and found Stuart staring at her with sympathetic eyes. Beside him stood Orville. Stuart drew her to his chest, patting her shoulders in a protective, comforting manner.

"Orville here says he heard a splash outside the boat when he went for help. He looked over the rail and saw the gambler swimming away."

Chapter Thirteen

Brett Reall was gone. Like a line from the melodrama, those words kept ringing through Delta's head.

Brett Real was gone. She confirmed the fact over dinner when she sat beside Captain Kaney. Although she hadn't felt like eating, she had felt still less like returning to her cabin where she would do nothing but think of Brett.

"I suppose you moved the occupants of the burned-out stateroom to another cabin," she commented to the captain over a steaming bowl of mock turtle soup, which on better days she would have enjoyed.

"As a matter of fact," the captain replied, "that gambler's gone. I got word not to expect him on board for the duration of the trip."

Although Stuart had told her the same, Delta was still unprepared to hear the words spoken. Soup dribbled from her spoon, splattering back in the bowl. "Where do you suppose he went?" she managed to ask.

"Can't tell by me," Captain Kaney retorted. "Left me in a bind, that he did. The gents expect a certain level of player for their quiet games at night. And the ladies certainly expected him to continue their ti' games. Of course, he hadn't been available for those for the last several days. Don't know what got into the fellow.''

Brett Reall was gone. She further proved the fact after dinner when she slipped off before the drama to see for herself. If Brett were still on board, she reasoned, Pierre would be standing guard. It took a good thirty minutes, but she managed to walk the passageways alongside every cabin and stateroom on the three decks that houses passengers. No sign of Pierre. She hadn't even seen Gabriel again since the fire.

Brett Reall was gone, and the melancholy that fact instilled inside Delta caused her to want to run to her cabin and bury herself in her bed.

But her bed was the last place she wanted to be when plagued by thoughts of Brett. Her bed, where they made love. *Made love.* His words, spoken in bitter tones, echoed through her pain. Yes, they had made love. But, oh, it had been so much more. For her. And for him. Now she was left with only her dreams.

And her bed was the last place she wanted to be; her bed, where she dreamed incessant dreams of him.

By the time she returned to the salon the drama was about to begin. She slipped into a chair Zanna had saved for her on the front row.

''Did Nat ever show up?'' she whispered.

Zanna shook her head, her attention trained on the stage where Frankie and Iona had begun their opening number. Frankie strummed a banjo and Iona, costumed in dance-hall flounces, warmed up the audience with a not-so-bawdy ballad.

''Stuart agreed to play the lead?'' Delta quizzed, again in a whisper, for Elyse had come on stage, looking like a birthday gift, gowned in soft blue lawn and tied up with ribbons.

262

And she sounded like an angel, Delta thought. By the time the last clear notes of "She Wore a Wreath of Roses the Night When Last We Met" faded, the audience was in tears, along with the songstress.

Sniffles turned to gasps, however, when Albert leaped onto the stage. Garbed and groomed as an exquisite villain, he knelt before Elyse, clasping both his large hands about her slender waist.

"My love, my one true love!" he cried. "You will come away with me tonight." While Elyse struggled, Albert turned beady eyes to leer at the audience. "Little does this foolish damsel know what is in store for her. I will have my revenge on that weasel of a sheriff. Hee! Hee! Hee!"

"Boo!" came a cry from somewhere behind Delta. "Hiss!" from another part of the salon. "Boo!" "Hiss!" All in accordance with the sign posted near the stage: You may boo the villain.

In the melee, a new character bounded onto the stage.

"The sheriff!" someone called. The audience applauded.

"About time you showed up," a man shouted from the rear of the salon.

"He's perfect," Delta whispered. And indeed Stuart Longstreet looked the part of the hero, six-guns drawn, wearing a white hat, vest, and a star above well-fitted denims. His blond mustache waved when he spoke; his voice carried into the audience, strong and threatening.

"Take your hands off my woman, you lily-livered, egg-suckin', cross-eyed son of a sick baboon!"

While the audience cheered, Stuart stepped out of character to doff his hat to Zanna, favoring her with a wink and a grin as bright as the dozen chandeliers in the room.

"What gallantry!" Delta whispered to Zanna. "If I may venture a guess, Stuart Longstreet is auditioning for the part of leading man in a different context than on that stage."

Zanna's face turned as red as her hair. "Do you think so?"

"Undoubtedly."

"Are you playing matchmaker? Like you did with Elyse and Nat?"

At mention of Nat, Delta's insides took a tumble. "Fortunately that didn't work out," she admitted. "On our ride to Miss Strahan's he admitted it wouldn't be right for him to pursue the courtship."

The melodrama ended with more cheers and applause. While actors dismantled the set, Albert returned to the stage and began his monologue.

"What's the story behind Nat?" Zanna whispered.

The melodrama had given Delta a respite, however brief, from thinking about the recent developments in her life. Zanna's questions brought them back in a rush of despair. "Ask Stuart."

Albert's monologue ended. Frankie and Iona returned with two chairs and a springboard for their acrobatic act. Zanna leaned over again. "I'm sorry about your gambler."

Delta pursed her lips, blinking back tears, unable to answer.

"Stuart says it's best things didn't work out between you," Zanna whispered. "He said your family would never approve of you getting involved with a gambler, or whatever Brett turns out to be."

"Stuart's right," Delta admitted. The same thoughts had tormented her for days. All her life she had done exactly what others expected. Ginny and Hollis had expended a lot of time and effort and love raising her, and she felt a heavy debt to them.

At least that debt had become heavy lately. For months she had been beset by guilt over rejecting the various suitors who presented themselves to Hollis. She had known that sooner or later she would have to choose one. And she did so want to please Ginny and Hollis with her choice.

And her brothers, too. She loved them every one. They were not saints, of course, not a man of them. But they were good men, dependable, responsible for their own actions, and dedicated to seeing justice done around them.

Even Kale, who had shot a carpetbagger back in Tennessee and afterward acquired a reputation with his gun, was a genuinely honest and upright citizen.

How would they react to a man who traveled under an assumed name, who was wanted by authorities in two countries for a crime she dared not question for fear of learning the truth?

They would give him a chance, she knew that much. They were fair-minded men. But if Brett's secret past was truly contemptible, what then? They would never approve of her marrying a criminal.

Marrying? Where was her brain? Brett Reall was gone.

Tears filled her eyes, tears of self-pity. Even if he hadn't been forced to leave the boat, she admonished herself, he would never have allowed them to continue a relationship. He had ended things that day in his cabin, forcefully and intentionally. All she had now were her dreams. Those vile dreams that were certain to drive her mad.

Applause signaled the end of Frankie and Iona's act,

jolting Delta out of her reverie. Zanna took the stage to thank the patrons from St. Francisville, who then returned to shore, while the crew of the *Mississippi Princess* prepared to shove off for its nighttime trip to Baton Rouge.

Refusing Zanna's invitation to join the cast for a midnight snack, with the excuse that she needed to prepare her article on St. Francisville before she retired, Delta headed for her stateroom.

By the time she felt the boat move into the current of the big, muddy river, she had dressed for bed and sat propped up by pillows, trying to compose her article on Miss Eliza Strahan's plantation, Camelliawood, and her famous relative John James Audubon.

Only with great effort was she able to concentrate on the lovely plantation, its eccentric owner, and the beauty of Audubon's artistry.

Her brain preferred to dwell on Brett Reall—and on the increasing loneliness she experienced as the boat traveled down the river, leaving him farther and farther behind with every turn of the paddlewheel.

The premonition engendered by the red crest of Mr. Audubon's ivory-billed woodpecker remained with her, even though the subsequent fire in Brett's cabin had claimed nothing but his belongings.

Fear for him increased with every new thought. She dreaded retiring, for this night was sure to be filled with nightmares. Or sensual dreams of Brett, which were, in truth, one and the same.

At times she wished she had never known him in the flesh, because then she wouldn't feel a physical loss. But there was no turning back, and no matter how painful the loneliness, she wouldn't trade one moment of the time they'd spent together for all the peace of mind in the world.

Glancing at the little gold locket clock that had belonged to her mother, she was amazed to discover the time nearing midnight. Reluctantly she knew she must retire. Tomorrow they would arrive in Baton Rouge and she would arrange a new round of interviews, whether she had the will to conduct them or not. Hollis would be waiting for her articles and Cameron would be waiting for her wire. And Kale and Carson and Cousin Brady were waiting for her in New Orleans. She sighed, suddenly overwhelmed by relatives, well-meaning though they were.

She had just fluffed the pillows and turned out one lamp when a knock came at the door. She paused, holding a pillow in the air. The knock came again.

Oh, Zanna, she thought. Well-meaning relatives, well-meaning friends. Where would a girl be without them? She considered calling out that she was already in bed. But which did she dread more—the nightmares she knew would come when at length she fell asleep or Zanna's well-intentioned snooping into her personal life?

At the third knock she relented and opened the door, only to stand there stunned. Her heart lurched to her throat.

"May I come in?" Brett's eyes bore into hers, and she thought crazily how they had never looked so sad.

Suddenly her reflexes returned. With haste borne of the fear she had felt for him for such a long time, she reached for his arm and drew him inside. Closing the door, she slumped back against it.

She remained that way—one hand on his arm, the other gripping the doorknob—while he stood deathly still, favoring her with such a melancholy expression she felt tears brim in her eyes and spill over.

"They said you'd gone overboard," she finally managed to say.

"For enough money folks'll say just about anything."

His voice was husky and desperate. His eyes held hers, speaking eloquently of the love he had denied feeling only two days before. For one horrible instant she thought this must be her dream. Involuntarily her hand squeezed his arm. It was warm and real.

"I've been so worried," she said.

Reaching toward her for the first time he brushed the tears from her cheeks with the back of his fingers. "I know, *chère*. I'm sorry."

Her tears stopped and in their place questions began to flow. "What about the fire? How did you escape?"

His brows narrowed. "By the skin of my teeth."

"Was it Nat?"

"No."

"You're certain?"

"Oui."

"Then who?"

He remained silent, so she did not press him.

"It's all right." Her heart began to resume its regular rhythm—regular for when she was around Brett Reall. "You're here. We'll work everything out."

She watched his jaw clench before he spoke. "Don't count on it."

She stopped short of a rebuttal, of reminding him of her dreams. He might refute them the way he had in his cabin, and she didn't dare remind either of them of that confrontation. "Anything is possible."

"Not this. I told you I was up against powerful people, Delta. You can't get more powerful in Louisiana than a governor who's been in office going on ten years and still running strong."

"But—?"

"I didn't come to argue, *chère*. We have little enough time as it is. I came because . . . the things I said the other day . . . I couldn't leave them between us."

"Leave—?"

Lifting a hand, he traced his fingers lightly across her forehead, brushing back strands of hair. "I was cruel, heartless. I didn't mean a single word of it. It tore out my heart to hurt you like that."

Her hand crept up his arm. "I know why you did it. But you're wrong to try to put me out of your life, Brett. You can't."

He grinned, a wry, sad grin. "You may be right. Perhaps you're a psychic like my mother. Stretching facts a bit, your dreams could fit my situation."

"Our situation," she corrected. She started to tell him about her latest nightmare, about Anne Bonny and the baby. Especially about the baby. But again she was reluctant to hear him discredit them. "Tell me how they fit."

His eyes turned cold. "I'm innocent, Delta. I'm innocent. But if you heard what they're accusing me of, you might think me guilty, too."

"Never," she vowed.

"That's a chance I won't take. The only thing that could make my life worse than it is right now is if you thought me guilty of such a heinous crime."

Despair washed over her like a fine river mist. Despair at the hopelessness he expressed. Despair mitigated by the hope his words instilled. He cared for her. She knew it. Together they would work things out—some way. Flinging her arms around Brett's neck, she buried her face in his shoulder. Tears seeped through her shut eyelids.

His arms came around her then, holding her tight,

close, and steady—soothing, comforting, setting her body on fire.

Finally he drew her head back and covered her lips with his own. She felt his groan rumble against her chest, quiver against her lips. She opened her mouth to his delving exploration. Her brain swirled with happiness, giddy happiness. Only moments before she had despaired of ever seeing him again. Now she was in his arms. In his arms.

She snuggled against his body, feeling the powerful evidence of his arousal warm and hard through her nightclothes. She nuzzled closer.

With a sudden swoop, he lifted her in his arms. Sidestepping the first bed, where her notebook and lead pencils were strewn, he made his way around the confines of the small room, depositing her on the far bed. For a long moment he stood over her, staring deeply into her eyes.

She had begun to wonder what he was thinking when he sat beside her, framed her face with his hands and brought his lips close to hers.

"Before we go any further, *chère*, let me correct a terrible lie." With great tenderness he touched his lips to hers, then feathered her face with light kisses, returning to her lips for a deeply sensual kiss filled with tender passion.

"I *have* fallen in love with you, Delta Jarrett. I've loved you for . . . it seems like all my life. I've never loved anyone more, not even nearly as much. I love you and I always will. And if things were different, I wouldn't rest until I'd convinced you to become my wife."

Tears rolled from the corners of her eyes. "I've loved you forever, too. At least, it seems that way." Circling her arms about his neck, she pulled his face to hers.

"So, let's make love tonight, and we'll let tomorrow take care of itself."

The words had been easy for her to say, because deep inside she knew she and Brett were meant to be together. A stirring of doubt in the back of her mind, however, told her that she wasn't quite as confident as she tried to sound.

He was dressed as she had last seen him, in chambray shirt and denim breeches, and when he didn't immediately begin to undress her, she started unbuttoning his shirt. His liquid black eyes held her gaze while her fingers fumbled with first one button, then another, until at length, she pulled the two sides apart, tugged his shirttails out of his breeches, and shoved the shirt over his shoulders.

She felt his heart throb against her palm, watched his eyes stare solemnly into hers. Holding his gaze, she played her fingers through the soft, dark hair covering his chest. Something was different about him tonight. She sensed it in the way he stared at her, as though to memorize every feature, in the way he smiled. Tonight his mouth smiled, but his eyes remained deathly serious. Fear diffused the joy she felt at having him here—in her arms, in her bed.

Pulling him down against her, she buried her face in his furry chest. "Please don't close me out, Brett. Not again. The things you said that day in your cabin don't matter. I knew you didn't mean them. What hurt was that I couldn't reach you. Please don't close me out again."

His arms slipped beneath her, drawing her close, smashing her face against his chest, where she felt his wildly thrashing heart.

After a while he sat up, bringing her with him, and began to remove her gown. When it was bunched

271

around her chest, he moved apart and proceeded to pull it over her head. At last he spoke.

"I didn't tell you the whole truth a while ago." His voice came to her, muffled by the roll of muslin he was struggling to extract from her body. Freeing the fabric at last, he tossed it aside, catching her head in his hands.

His eyes pierced hers. "I came to explain and to tell you I love you." He kissed her face, feature by feature, sending shivers down her now nude body. "But I also came to make love with you." Reaching for her hand, he guided it to the bulge at his crotch, holding her hand there in intimate communication. "You see? I'm as eager as you."

She felt her face flush, but she wouldn't have removed her hand if her life had depended on it. Gently she began to stroke her hand over the bulge, much as he stroked her. She watched his face tighten.

But this time it was an expression she recognized. Passion.

"Don't you see how easy it is?" she whispered. "Our love is great enough to drive away all our demons."

"*Oui, chère,* for tonight." His voice was husky as he set her back against the bed, dislodging her hand. When she reached to reclaim her hold, he grasped both her hands, lifting her arms above her head, where he placed them on the bed, tracing his own hands back down her arms, her shoulders, resting at length on her breasts. "We must go slow," he mumbled in his oh so familiar monotone. "I want to . . . ah, to enjoy every moment." Sweeping his hands down her body, he stretched her legs out, so she lay straight and exposed on the green damask bedspread.

Like a person devoid of sight, he began to trace her

body with his fingertips, starting at her forehead, moving across her eyebrows, her hairline, her nose, her cheekbones.

Inch by inch, she watched him feast on her nakedness. He concentrated as though he were studying a book and she wished she knew what was on his mind. His eyes followed his fingertips in sensual exploration down her chest. He gripped her breasts, fondling them until she felt her nipples go rigid and her face glow. Then his hands and eyes left her breasts, trailed down her midriff. He spanned her waist with his hands, touching thumbs in front, fingers in back. Releasing her, he ran his palms over her belly.

When his fingers paused to play through the triangle of hair at the base of her abdomen, she could bear it no longer. Already she felt as though she lay on a bed of coals. Heat radiated through her in waves of fire. She reached for his head, tried to pull him to her. Her knees came up reflexively.

"A minute longer," he whispered. "Let me look a minute longer." Before he would allow her to move, he traced his hands down both legs, even caressing her feet, bringing a giggle when he inadvertently tickled the soles.

That broke the spell. He moved back to look into her face. "God's bones, Delta. You're magnificent."

"And dying from want of you," she whispered, as he stretched beside her, lowering his lips to her breast.

Later she decided it must have been all the days they spent thinking themselves lost to each other that brought such an intensity to their lovemaking.

He devoured her, as though he couldn't get enough, suckling her breast, delving into her fiery core, stroking her face and hair, all at once.

273

"It's like the first time and the last time all rolled into one," she whispered into his rumpled hair.

Lifting his lips, he moved to her face. "The first time?" he quizzed, a teasing look in his eye.

"You were slow to get started then, too," she teased. "Making me ask all those questions, when all I wanted was this." On her last word she raised her hips higher against his probing hand, bringing a grin to his lips.

"You thought you knew it all," he recalled, pecking her a kiss.

"From my dreams," she admitted. "I was wrong. It was nothing like my dreams. It never is."

His expression sobered. She knew he was thinking about their conversation, if it could be called that, in his cabin. Suddenly he cradled her to his chest. "Ah, Delta Jarrett, there's so much more I could teach you. So much more."

His strange behavior filled her with trepidation, but she refused to think about anything but loving him— making love with him. Finally she drew back, found his lips, and rekindled their passion. When he reached for his belt buckle, she helped, their hands fumbling together with the buttons on his placket, releasing at last his rock-hard flesh into her hand.

Her heart beat fast, flushing her face, but she gripped her hand around him, holding, massaging, while he fumbled to rid himself of his clothing, after which she guided him to her aching core. Once he was embedded inside her, he stopped, staring deeply into her eyes.

"Like the first time," he told her in a husky voice that set her hips to moving. "So hot, so wet, so ready."

"So wonderful," she moaned into his lips, moving with him faster and faster, letting the rising passion chase away her anxieties.

Brett was here.

He hadn't left. He had come to her. He loved her. Together they would work things out. Together.

Together they rode the waves of passion, as the steamboat rode the mighty Mississippi, challenging the currents of life and winning. Winning.

Together. Again she felt them poised above a roiling river of fire. Again it swirled faster and hotter until at length, together they dove into its fiery midst.

And together they emerged, lifeless, yet more alive than ever before.

"I was wrong about something else that day by the river," she breathed into his ear.

Shifting to his side, he drew her with him, their wet bodies sticking, as they clung together. "What, *chère?*"

She drew back reveling in his eyes, so passion-glazed and loving. "I said I wanted you to be the first."

"I hope that isn't what you've changed your mind about," he teased.

Her mouth was dry—from the loving, but more, from the premonition that wouldn't turn her loose. She caressed his face with her eyes, loving him more than she had ever dreamed possible. "I also want you to be the last."

For the longest time they gazed into each other's eyes while the room took on a ghostly silence. The slight rocking of the steamboat reminded her of a cradle.

Whether it was a reflection of her own fear, she couldn't say, but suddenly his eyes turned cold and he clasped her to his chest with a ferocity that almost crushed the air from her lungs. Her tears fell, hot against her cheeks.

"If you're in so much danger in Louisiana," she ventured at length, "why are you returning?"

Loosening his deathlike grip a bit, he let one finger

play through her tangled hair. "I have to see my mother. You aren't the only one who has premonitions, *chère*. I've been worried about her for some time now."

"Why can't you send Pierre or Gabriel? They aren't wanted, too, are they?"

He shook his head. "But I must see for myself. I want to convince her to return to Canada with me."

Involuntarily, she felt her brain switch from reality to wishful thinking. *And me,* she thought. *Take me to Canada, too.* But she didn't dare voice such a request. Not yet. By the time they reached New Orleans, perhaps.

He sighed heavily against her. "For truth, I was hoping to remain in the bayou, but this trip convinced me I can't."

"Nat?"

"Among others," he acknowledged with a heavy sigh. "I get so homesick for the bayou country." As he spoke, he began to stroke her back in long sweeping motions. "I hate the cold, frozen north. All winter I'm cranky as a bear, thinking about the steamy bayous. And when spring brings the thaws, I don't see the icy cold rivers, but the slow-moving black waters of the bayou. I'd love to show it to you. The cypress trees drip moss. You should see the moss. It grows much heavier there than along here. A man can make a decent living selling moss."

"What's it used for?"

"Lots of things. Stuffing sofas, chairs—" he bounced a fist off the bed, "—mattresses." He kissed the top of her head. "It's wild, the bayou. You might be frightened—"

"Take me there."

She regretted the words the moment they left her

mouth. She'd promised herself to wait, not to pressure him. By the time they reached New Orleans she would have found some way to alleviate his fears for her. But this was too soon for that.

He held her so close she could scarcely breathe, so close she felt their hearts pumping as one.

"Don't ask me that, Delta," he breathed against her temple. "Please, don't ask me that."

He kissed her then, forestalling any more questions. And she returned his kisses, eager to love him again before they were forced to consider what the morning would bring.

Tomorrow they would arrive in Baton Rouge, the state capital, home of the governor. Brett trailed a hand down her body, silencing her brain with the fire he kindled inside her.

His mouth left hers, suckling a breast with such vigor it reminded her again of the first time they made love, and the way she had thought he might pull her very soul out of her body.

Well he had, at one time or another, for her soul, like her body, belonged to this mysterious man. Tracing her hand down his furry chest, she gripped the rigid evidence of his passion. At her touch, he lifted his face to hers, his eyes dark and loving.

"Ah, *chère,* what you do to me." His labored breath increased her own fervor, and she shifted to bring her body closer. He moved, too, into her, and they were together again.

Together again. For a moment she savored the sensation, wishing it could last forever. Her hands caressed his hips, trailed over his ribs, to his chest, cherishing, savoring.

Then they began to move, together, in unison, in and out, in a rhythm all their own.

"Remember I said this is like the last time, as well as the first?" she questioned.

His hips stopped. *"Oui."*

"I think it's because of the fear I've lived with these last few days. The fear that I'd lost you. I know you felt it, too."

"Sh, *chère.*"

"We've learned how terrible it would be to live apart. That makes it more intense, more—"

He crushed her lips with his, finishing their love-making in quick order. After the last spasms had receded, he kissed her still, deeply, passionately, delving, probing, leaving her limp and trembling and sated.

After a while the rocking of the boat lulled them into a state near sleep. But Delta resisted. She had missed him so badly, how could she allow herself to sleep? Again the rocking of the boat reminded her of a cradle, and her premonition returned with all its fervor.

"When we get to New Orleans," she told him, "my brothers can help us."

"Your brothers?"

"One of them, Carson, was a Texas Ranger."

He tensed.

"Don't worry," she reassured him. "He recently resigned. He married a girl in Mexico and they'll live down there for a while. He'll run her father's ranch." Delta's thoughts switched directions abruptly.

"That's an idea. Mexico." She kissed him. "Carson could find you a job. It's much warmer in Mexico than in Canada."

He ran his hands up her warm skin. "So I hear."

"Why did you go to Canada in the first place since you hate the cold. You could have gone to Mexico, or even to Texas."

"They don't speak French in Mexico or Texas. It'd be hard for an Acadian to lose himself in either place."

"I'm glad," she responded. "If you hadn't gone to Canada, you wouldn't be on this boat, and we wouldn't have met."

He chuckled. "Ah, I've convinced you to forget those dreams, *oui?*"

"Never. I . . . Well, for a moment. Now that you mentioned them, though, I know we would have met somewhere, sooner or later. It was destined—"

He stopped her with a kiss, boldly passionate. Afterwards, he considered her with a mischievous glint in his eyes. "You and *maman* are two of a kind." His expression dimmed, and when he spoke again, his voice had lost its animation. "You would have gotten along fine, you two."

With the greatest of effort, Delta ignored his choice of words. "Tell me about your mother. Is she really psychic?"

"Folks in the bayou think so. They call her Crazy Mary."

"Crazy Mary? How dreadful."

"She loves it. She's a showman at heart. But she's good at her trade, too. Folks come for treatments from all over southern Louisiana. I used to accuse her of curing them with laughter." He squeezed Delta to him, burying his face in her hair. "But she wasn't laughing the last time I saw her. Now the governor's trying to run her out of the state, calls her a Voodooienne."

Delta felt his heart beat in powerful thuds against her. His arms held her tight. His arms, so strong and warm. She snuggled against his body, fitting herself to him, relishing the texture of his skin and furry chest, concentrating on these things instead of the ordeal ahead of them. In spite of her best intentions, she fell asleep in his arms.

In his arms, where she wanted most to be in all the world.

When he was certain Delta had fallen asleep, Brett slipped out of her arms and dressed. Before leaving the room, he placed a note on her pillow, then doused the lamps, hoping with the darkness she would remain asleep while he made his escape.

Escape. The word lay heavily on his heart, as though he were escaping Delta, when that was what he wanted least of anything in the world. But in order to remain alive, he had agreed with Pierre and Gabriel on this plan of action.

Actually Pierre and Gabriel had not agreed with one part of the plan. His hours with Delta had been opposed by both men, Pierre more vigorously than Gabriel, but Pierre was like that.

He was bullheaded to a degree Brett had seldom seen in a bayou man. But that bullheadedness was more often than not outweighed by his dedication to Brett's safety and his ability to handle the dangers that had confronted them.

Pierre waited at the starboard rail on the main deck. "You took long enough, sure."

"Not nearly." Forever wouldn't be long enough with Delta, Brett thought bitterly. "Not nearly." Above them the sky was brightening in preparation for sunrise.

Sunrise—and Delta. He inhaled sharply. Everything brought thoughts of Delta. Everything would, for a long time to come.

Pierre handed him an oilcloth sack containing a few

provisions he had hastily thrown together before going to Delta's cabin. "We'll get off at the next bend, *oui,*" Pierre told him. "The bank, it is not so steep right there, and the boat, she will come closer to shore than anyplace else for several miles."

Gabriel stepped from the shadows, offering his hand. "Luck, *mon ami*. Me, I'll meet you in New Orleans. You will take care to arrive alive and in one piece."

"That's our plan," Brett quipped, then turned serious. "Watch out for her."

"It is done, *mon ami,*" Gabriel told him.

"Watch out for *us,*" Pierre amended. "If the captain asks for us when the boat reaches Baton Rouge, throw him off our trail, *oui.*"

"*Oui,*" Gabriel agreed.

When the boat was in the middle of the next big curve Pierre gave the signal and the two of them slipped over the edge of the *Mississippi Princess* into the muddy river. Brett gritted his teeth against the rush of cold water.

By the time they gained the far bank he was out of breath and the showboat was far down the river. He climbed onto the bank and stared after it forlornly. On that boat was the best thing that had ever happened to him. And he knew Delta felt the same way. The image of her waking up to find him gone, searching the boat, finally realizing she would never see him again, left him with little heart for the journey ahead.

Chapter Fourteen

Exhausted from sleepless nights and days of endless fear, Delta slept until midmorning. Awakening slowly, she glanced around the small stateroom for Brett but wasn't surprised to find him gone. In order to uphold the ruse that he had gone overboard at St. Francisville, he would have left her room before daybreak. Nevertheless, a sinking feeling enveloped her, and she wondered when she would see him again.

Then she spied the note on her pillow: "Sweet dreams, *ma chère*. B."

She reread the message three times. Weak from the relief of finally knowing beyond any doubt that she had his love, she pressed the precious message to her lips, then quickly withdrew it, lest her tears wash away his handwriting. Folding the paper carefully, she placed it in her lingerie drawer, alongside the two other messages he had sent her.

Dressing with more enthusiasm than she had felt in days, she thought about the interviews she would conduct in Baton Rouge. Hollis wanted an article on the governor and his quarrel with the Voodoos. Why not investigate, discreetly, of course? The thought that she could help Brett in the process encouraged her further.

Her night with Brett, however, was still so fresh and wonderful, she had trouble concentrating on anything other than when he would come to her again. Tonight?

Her heart sang. *He had returned to her. He loved her. He had said so.*

He loved her and everything would be all right. Aware of the danger he was in, she knew not to expect him on deck. But he had come to her in the night. And she was unable to prevent herself from anticipating another night of loving him.

On deck she waited with Zanna, Stuart, and the cast of the Princess Players while the showboat edged up to the dock and roustabouts hurried to lower the gangplank.

"My, you look pert this morning," Zanna commented. "You must have slept well."

Avoiding Zanna's eyes, Delta stared out at the dock, inhaling the heady aroma of magnolia blossoms, unsure whether she would be able to contain her joy. "Humm," she replied.

Suddenly she saw Gabriel wielding his fiddle at the end of the gangplank. Surely he wasn't signaling Brett to come ashore—not here. Surely Brett wouldn't take such a risk. When she stepped off the gangplank, it seemed to her Gabriel's tune picked up, but then it could be her own high spirits. She tossed him a broad smile and was surprised to receive one in return.

From force of habit she turned to scan the boat. No sign of Brett, of course, but she saw Stuart standing at the rail. He waved; she waved back, then nudged Zanna.

"Turn around and wave, silly." Suddenly Stuart's reason for remaining on the boat hit her. "Why isn't he coming with us?"

"Duty," Zanna answered.

"Duty?" For a moment she panicked at the idea that Brett's ruse might not have worked. "He said Brett went overboard at St. Francisville."

Zanna slipped an arm around Delta's shoulder and they fell in behind the band. Along the sides of the road growing numbers of citizens cheered and clapped. Inside Delta felt queasy.

"Orville said so," Zanna was saying, "but Stuart never believed it."

"Orville wouldn't lie," Delta objected. Forcefully she gripped her emotions. Brett could take care of himself. He'd been a fugitive for ten years, for heaven's sake. He knew how to protect himself. She should stop worrying about him.

But he had said he loved her. And that made all the difference. He had said he loved her, and one way or another she intended to help him work out his difficulties. But she had to keep him alive in the meantime.

The band played their special rendition of "Oh, Dem Golden Slippers." Cast members passed out playbills describing the matinees to be held each afternoon on the docks, and the evening performances for the next three nights.

After the free concert Albert and Frankie took the remaining playbills and began tacking them to posts and buildings around town.

Delta thought of Nat and wondered whether he would turn up here the way he had in Vicksburg after Brett tricked him into missing the boat at OK Bend. So far he hadn't. She prayed he wouldn't. Brett had enough enemies in Baton Rouge, what with the Pinkertons and the governor after him.

Zanna surprised her by offering to accompany her to her interviews. "Where to first?"

"The capitol building," Delta answered. "I'll try to

collect all the information I need in one place, so we can return to the boat in time for the matinee.''

Returning to the boat had become the foremost thought in Delta's mind. She chided herself with the reminder that Brett wouldn't come to her until dark. He couldn't. Yet she longed to return to the boat, where she knew she would *feel* closer to him.

"I know what I'll do," Delta mused aloud when they neared the capitol. "I'll interview the governor."

"That might be more difficult than you think."

"Never hurts to try," Delta quipped, already planning what questions she could ask that might help Brett. "Politicians are always hungry for press coverage, especially in election years."

"Usually," she amended in a whisper after the governor's secretary refused to consider such a thing.

"*St. Louis Sun,* you say?" the woman responded to Delta's request. Gowned in lavender print voile, her white hair pulled into a loose topknot, the secretary's appearance belied the starch beneath her soft Southern exterior. "Now why would our good gov'nor want to waste time with a little ol' paper way up yonder? His constituents don't read St. Louis newspapers."

Delta glanced around the small office, which she suspected served as an anteroom to the governor's office. Was he even now sitting at a massive desk behind those ornately carved doors?

"I thought perhaps, this being his tenth year in office," Delta persisted, "Governor Trainor might have higher political aspirations for the future."

"Higher political office? Young lady, what could be higher than servin' as gov'nor of this great state for ten years?" With the obvious intention of dismissing the intruders, the governor's secretary picked up a stack of papers, adding, "If you write about us after the election, say he's entering his second decade of service."

"What about the Voodoos?" Delta inquired without prelude.

The woman's head snapped around. "What about 'em?"

"I understand Governor Trainor is running on a platform to expel the Voodoos from Louisiana."

The woman's eyes glared from behind wire-rimmed glasses. She leaned forward, lowering her voice. "Don't you come in here, tellin' us how to run our state. Hear me? You outsiders don't understand the tribulation those natives have caused us."

"Natives?" Delta questioned.

"From Africa, same thing."

On the way back to the showboat, Zanna explained. "Voodoo queens, called Voodooiennes, are generally free black women."

"Then how could—?" Delta stopped before revealing what Brett had told her about his mother. "I heard about a white woman who's called a Voodooienne."

Zanna shrugged. "The term is bandied about rather loosely sometimes. Voodooism is a religion from Africa. Supposedly the first practitioners in Louisiana came over from the West Indies in the early part of this century. Since then they've grown into a fairly organized cult."

"I wonder why the governor is determined to run them out of the state?"

"He'll have a run for his money," Zanna predicted. "Whether they practice the religion or not, a lot of folks in this area rely on the Voodoos—or Hoodoos, as some say—for help in everything from regaining a lost love to placing a hex on an enemy."

"Have you ever heard of a woman called Crazy Mary?"

Zanna shook her head. "Is she a Voodooienne?"

Fighting back a rising sense of despair, Delta responded, "The governor thinks so." She would find a way to help Brett. She *would*.

Albert, Frankie, and Stuart had the set erected by the time Delta and Zanna returned to the docks. Delta had planned to go straight to her cabin—thoughts of that cabin had teased her all morning—but as time for the matinee was nearing, Zanna persuaded her to sell tickets.

Everyone was there, talking, working, and eating sandwiches and fruit from large trays. Gabriel stood on the outskirts, near the gangplank, playing his fiddle. She watched him put his heart and soul into the unfamiliar tune. And his body, as well, she observed. He never stayed still. If his feet weren't tapping, they were shuffling, or he was hopping around the dock with his hips swaying and his shoulders dipping. Even his hair got into the act, wisping in the breeze like his free-flying bow strings.

She wondered how he and Brett had become friends. Was Brett ever so free and uninhibited? He hadn't been since she'd known him—not even in her dreams. Since she'd known him, Brett had been continually surrounded by an aura of melancholy.

But what was he like inside? What had he been like before the governor decided to brand him a criminal?

Suddenly a great wave of poignancy rose within her, bringing tears to her eyes. She turned away so Gabriel would not see, a vow on her lips. She would set Brett free. If it were the last thing she ever did, she would set Brett free.

With effort she suppressed the ugly head of reason.

One woman could do little, she knew. But people spoke of the power of the pen, and she possessed that. And her family. Kale and Carson were in New Orleans, or would be soon. They would help her; she knew they would. After they heard her side of the story, they would help.

By the time Frankie and Iona began their opening routine, the area of the dock roped off for the performance had filled with patrons sitting on benches from the showboat, on barrels and bales of hay dragged up by neighboring merchants. A theatrical performance on the docks brought in money for all the businesses in the area.

Elyse had just ended her ballad and Albert had jumped on stage when the thunder of horses' hooves echoed down the road, stopping within feet of the roped-off area. Turning at the sound Delta caught her breath at sight of several mounted, uniformed men. Fear coiled inside her at the arrogance of their stride when they dismounted and strode toward the showboat. Since she was the closest person to where they had drawn rein, they stopped in front of her.

The leader flashed a badge—Captain J. Robb, Louisiana State Trooper. "Who's in charge here?"

"Sh," she put a finger to her lips. "The performance isn't over."

To her relief the men, four of them, quieted down. "Where's the captain of that boat?" Robb questioned, this time in a near whisper.

The fear inside her tightened. She knew better than to hope the troopers might be after someone other than Brett.

What could she tell them that would send them away without arousing their suspicions? She glanced helplessly toward Gabriel, whose eyes were fastened on the uniformed men like a fly on a spider's web. Dear God, she thought, why were her images always filled with wicked portent?

On stage Stuart had just confronted Albert. Delta watched him give what had become his customary aside to Zanna. Those two were obviously smitten with each other.

When the troopers began shifting feet beside her, she whispered, "The show's almost over. I'll go on board to see if the captain is available as soon as the curtain falls."

"Where's the curtain?" one of the men questioned.

"A figure of speech," she replied, her lungs constricted by a fear that grew larger and heavier by the moment. After what seemed like an eternity, but was in reality only a few minutes, the drama ended, the audience applauded, the actors bowed.

Delta inhaled a quivering breath. "Wait here," she told the troopers. She started toward Gabriel who still stood his ground, staring at them. If she could get close enough, she could whisper to him to warn Brett. Before she had taken more than a few steps, however, Stuart bounded off the makeshift set, reaching her side in a couple of leaps.

"What's the trouble?"

"Are you the captain?" Robb asked, coming up beside them.

Delta glanced again at Gabriel. With the performance over, patrons flocked around the actors. Some of them approached Gabriel, talking, examining his fiddle, his bow, obstructing her view of him.

"I'm with the Pinkertons," Stuart was saying as he led the troopers toward the gangplank. Delta quickstepped to stay close enough to hear them. Gabriel separated himself from the crowd and fell in behind her.

Behind her? Why didn't he dart around the group and warn Brett?

"Maybe you can help us," Robb told Stuart. "We're looking for a fellow by the name of Dupré, Anatole Dupré."

Delta's toe caught on the board connecting the gangplank to the boat. *Anatole Dupré.* Nat had mentioned that name the night he confronted her outside her cabin. When she stumbled, Gabriel caught her from behind. She turned anguished eyes to him. "Warn him," she mouthed.

He grinned. *Grinned!* Desperation flowed through her veins like ice water. Gabriel kept grinning. Suddenly she recognized his expression—the same unconcerned expression she had seen on his face the day Brett's stateroom caught fire.

Captain Kaney met them on the main deck. "No one by that name on my passenger list," he assured the troopers.

"Could be using an alias." Robb proceeded to describe this man called Dupré—tall, dark-complected, black hair and eyes, of French extraction.

Delta felt faint. Again she looked to Gabriel. Why didn't he warn Brett?

"Sounds like that damn gambler who run out on me," Captain Kaney was saying.

"Run out on you?" Robb questioned.

"He was engaged to play poker, nice little afternoon games with the ladies and more serious engagements with the gentlemen at night. Two, three days back I got word he wouldn't be traveling with me the rest of the way."

Delta held her breath, waiting for the troopers to buy the ruse that Brett had left the boat.

Then Stuart spoke up. "I have my doubts about the

man not being aboard." He turned to Gabriel. "He's a friend of yours, isn't he? Goes by the name Brett Reall?"

Delta held her breath. Gabriel shook his head.

"I've seen the two of you together," Stuart insisted.

Gabriel executed a slight bow. "Me, I talk with many passengers, my frien'. Tha' is what the good captain engaged me to do."

"You work on this boat?" Robb quizzed.

Gabriel nodded.

"Show us your cabin."

Delta felt her knees begin to buckle. This was it.

"Certainement." Gabriel scooted around the little group. "This way, please."

Stuart caught Delta's eyes. He could see her fear; she knew he could. He reached for her arm. "Leave this to us, Delta. Run find Zanna."

She pulled away. "I'm coming with you."

That was the least she could do—be there when they apprehended Brett. What she would do later, she had no idea. But she must be there when they found him. He must see her and know she would never give up.

Gabriel led the way at a sprightly pace that caused Delta to question his allegiance—until they arrived at his stateroom where he ushered them inside, allowing them to inspect every nook and cranny. Not a thing inside linked him to Brett Reall, Anatole Dupré, or for that matter to any other soul, living or dead.

"Nothing," one trooper said. Delta heard anger in his voice. Or had she imagined it? Her fear was all encompassing.

Robb addressed Captain Kaney. "We must search the entire boat. You understand, this man is wanted for murder. We have reason to believe he has been traveling aboard your vessel."

"You're welcome to search where you like, but do not disturb my passengers."

"We will need you to lead us," Robb told him.

Captain Kaney obliged, albeit grudgingly. "I tell you the man isn't aboard."

By the time the troopers left empty-handed, Delta had begun to wonder whether Brett's nighttime visit to her cabin had been a dream. Or had he left while she was in town arguing with that persnickety secretary? Whatever the reason, he hadn't been caught, this time.

She and Zanna watched the state troopers ride away from the docks with just enough time left to change for dinner. When Delta revealed her intention to take dinner in her cabin, Zanna refused to allow it.

"I know this episode upset you, Delta, but no good will come from brooding alone in your cabin."

Zanna was right, she decided. Especially since, if Brett had somehow managed to remain aboard undetected by the troopers, he couldn't come to her again until the dead of night. She shuddered at her involuntary choice of words.

"Don't be late to dinner," the captain advised them, upon returning from seeing the troopers off. "We have a special guest, aide to Governor Trainor."

An hour later Delta found herself sitting beside a rather handsome gentleman whom Captain Kaney introduced as Mr. Luis Gerard, aide to the governor. While the captain fawned over such an honored guest, Delta ate her meal in silence, trying to decide how she could instigate a conversation that would help Brett.

Finally as a waiter cleared their entree plates, Luis Gerard turned to her. "The captain tells me you're a journalist, Miss Jarrett."

Suddenly it occurred to her that she hated this man. She didn't even know him, yet she hated him—not for himself, but for what he and his cohorts were doing to Brett. "Yes," she managed to reply, watching a waiter set a dish of chocolate mousse before her.

"Perhaps you'll find the time to write something about our governor's race while the boat's in town," Gerard suggested.

Thinking of the many things she would like to write about the governor's race, and none of them positive, she took a deep breath before responding. "I requested an interview with Governor Trainor this morning, but his secretary assured me he wouldn't want to waste time with a St. Louis newspaper."

"He's a busy man," Gerard justified. "I'll see what I can do for you tomorrow. I arrange most of his appearances."

"You're his publicity manager?"

"By title, no. Jack-of-all-trades more nearly fits my job description."

"Then perhaps you can explain something, Mr. Gerard."

"I'll try."

"What is the governor's complaint against Voodoos?"

Luis Gerard choked on the wine in his mouth. After blotting his lips with his napkin, he spoke into his plate. "It's legitimate."

"I'm sure. I just don't understand it."

The governor's aide regained his balance quickly, Delta observed. The next time he spoke, he looked her straight in the eye. "What exactly do you not understand, Miss Jarrett?"

"I was under the impression that Louisiana politicians regularly consult Voodoos."

Her statement was greeted by silence, while Gerard

turned back to his mousse. "Some do, some don't," he said at last. "Trainor doesn't."

Delta let the conversation drop. She wasn't interested in Voodoos. She wasn't interested in Luis Gerard or Governor Trainor's political or personal habits, unless they related to his animosity toward Brett. But that was one subject she dared not introduce.

Gerard did it for her. "I've been told you were friends with that passenger who escaped."

"A passenger escaped?" she questioned.

"Dupré. Anatole Dupré."

"I've never met a man by that name, Mr. Gerard."

"He could have used an alias, but that isn't the point. I thought he might have revealed his destination to you, inadvertently, of course."

"If I've never met him, how could he have?"

Gerard studied her intently. "If?"

"I have never met the man you're after." Knowing she must redirect the conversation, she turned to her mousse, searching for a neutral topic.

"I hope for your sake, you never meet him," Gerard replied. "He's a cold-blooded killer. Murdered his wife and—"

The room began to spin wildly, like a giant chocolate top. Delta's spoonful of mousse dropped from her hand, clattering to her plate.

"Sir, if you please," Captain Kaney addressed the governor's aide. "This is a dinner table, not an interrogation room. We should be discussing the beauty of your state, the new jetties Captain Eads is completing down at New Orleans. That's our destination, you know. We'll be among the first boats to travel through this marvelous new gateway to the Gulf, a passage that is sure to bring prosperity to your state."

Luis Gerard ceased his questions and Delta excused

herself before she fell face-down in her dessert. She must talk to Gabriel. She must force him to tell her the truth. She must tell him about the governor's aide.

He answered her knock with a startled expression.

"Where is he?" she demanded.

He shrugged.

"Gabriel, please. Brett's in grave danger on board this boat. An aide to the governor is even now at dinner below us. He won't let up until he finds Brett."

"Don' worry, m'moiselle. He can take care of himself. Good night." With that Gabriel closed the door in her face.

If Gabriel had intended to reassure her, he failed, she thought, returning to her cabin. Her brain tumbled inside her head in imitation of the relentless revolutions of the paddlewheel that propelled them down river. After dressing for bed, she tried to settle her thoughts enough to compose an article on the Princess Players to post to Hollis the next morning, but she finally gave up and went to bed. She didn't have to post an article to Hollis tomorrow; she had done so today. They were scheduled to remain in Baton Rouge three days. Perhaps in that time she would be able to make some sense out of what was happening with Brett—

Or whoever he was. *Murdered his wife?* Her heart labored beneath the weight of such an accusation. Tears pooled in her eyes and rolled onto the pillow. Of course, he hadn't murdered his wife. He was tender and passionate and he loved her. He loved her—

Like a crash of lightning Brett's mercurial temperament flashed through her brain. He was quick to anger. She heard again the glass shattering against the wall of his stateroom. He was violent.

But he had waited until she left the room to unleash his temper.

Perhaps he had changed since—

No, no, no. Whoever he was, whatever he was, Brett Reall was not a murderer. He wasn't. She would never believe such an accusation. Never. By the time she drifted into a troubled sleep, her pillow was wet from her tears.

It was a forest filled with ghostly shapes of trees with enormous trunks and masses of gray moss that dripped from their limbs like funeral sprays. The ground was damp beneath the woman's feet, damp and soggy, with a musty odor that threatened to stifle all breath from her body. Although her breasts felt heavy, her stomach was flat, almost gaunt, and hair streamed over her shoulders and across her face, mimicking the moss that hung from the trees. It seemed an awfully long time since she had washed her hair.

Suddenly the air turned colder around her feet, and she realized she was barefoot. This seemed to be a signal, for looking around she found a small mound at the base of one of the trees. The mound was heaped with leaves and moss. A crude cross was stuck into the damp soil and stood at a drunken tilt.

The sight of the mound did strange things to the woman's stomach and she fell to her knees in the soft earth. It was a small mound, not over a couple of feet in length and narrow. From somewhere in the distant trees the sound of crooning began and the woman hung her head over the mound and began to cry. She wept for the longest time, as though she would never stop. Finally, however, she did, raising her face to the heavens which were shielded by limbs and moss. The cool night air dried her cheeks and when she opened her eyes . . .

Delta awoke with a scream. Her body convulsed as she stared at the vision from her dream, at the woman whose face remained clearly etched in her brain.

Stumbling from the bed, she reached the chiffonier, opened it, then fumbled until she struck a match and lighted the oil lamp. Holding it close to the looking glass, she peered at her reflection. The image she saw in the glass almost caused her to drop the lamp. Again she screamed, but the sound was muffled by her soul-wrenching sobs. The image swam in the tears in her eyes.

But she could still see it clearly. *The woman in the nightmare was herself.*

She had already raced from the room before she realized she hadn't changed her clothing. Rushing back inside, she cast off her nightgown and pulled on a loose-fitting wrapper without corset or petticoats, tying it securely around her waist. She shoved stockingless feet into her shoes and rushed from the room a second time.

This time she didn't stop until she reached Gabriel's door. He opened it after the first knock.

Hair flew every which way and tears streamed down her face. After a startled glance about the passageway, he pulled her into the room and closed the door.

"What has happened, m'moiselle?"

She had trouble stifling her sobs. Then when finally she did, she couldn't decide how to convince him. She watched him light a lamp and turn up the wick.

"I must see Brett. Tonight. He's in danger."

Gabriel's jaws tightened. "That is not possible, *non.*"

"Has he left the boat?"

Gabriel only stared at her.

"You must take me to him, wherever he is. He's in trouble. Serious trouble. He may even be . . . dead." Sobs shook her shoulders, she wiped tears away with the back of her hand. "You must believe me."

Gabriel poured her a glass of water, which she refused.

"Did he tell you about my dreams?" she questioned.

Gabriel shrugged, noncommittal.

"I've had nightmares for months. Brett knew about them. He said they could fit his situation—the danger he's in." She paused, afraid she had lost her cause by revealing such a thing. "Do you think I'm demented?"

After a length of silence, he answered with a solemn, *"Non."*

"Good." The relief of that brought renewed tears, which she stemmed quickly. "Good. Now I must persuade you to take me to him. Tonight I dreamed . . . tonight I dreamed about death." Speaking the words caused her hands to tremble. She clasped them together. Continuing, she stared at her hands, not daring to look at him, for fear she would see refusal in his eyes. "I dreamed about death . . . in the bayou. About a grave. A child's grave."

At his gasp she looked up to find him staring at her as though he had seen a ghost.

"You don't believe me."

"Me, I believe you, *oui.* "

"Then you will take me to him?"

He stared straight into her eyes so long she began to wonder at her own sanity. Another thought raced to her mind. "You do know where to find him, don't you?"

"Oui." Gabriel began to pace the small cabin. Back and forth. Back and forth. Finally he stopped, shrugged as in apology, and shook his head. "It is too dangerous, m'moiselle."

"Brett's the one in danger," she cried. "I must go to him."

Gabriel considered her with such a grave expression,

tears brimmed in her eyes. "He would not like that, *non*. He left me to protect you."

"To protect me?" Tears rolled down her cheeks unattended.

"*Oui.*"

"From whom?"

"From those who hunt him. For truth, I see they have found you."

Chapter Fifteen

It took Delta a few more tears and a lot more entreating to persuade Gabriel to take her into the bayou to find Brett.

"Me, I will try, m'moiselle," he finally agreed, "but I cannot promise we will make it through the swamp. We must be extra careful with the troopers about. We don' want to lead them to him, *non.*"

Returning to her cabin, she donned the clothing Gabriel had dug out of a sack and handed her with the words, "These clothes, they are not stylish, *non,* but they will draw less attention when we leave the boat."

Since she and Gabriel were close to the same size, his shirt and breeches fit her well enough. She added a pair of her own boots, then twisted her hair in a severe knot at the nape of her neck and covered it with a slouchy hat, also from Gabriel's bundle. Examining herself in the small looking glass, she desperately wished she could take a change of clothing, but Gabriel had cautioned her against carrying anything in her hands.

With minutes to spare she rushed around the cabin arranging this, that, hoping to delay the all-out search she knew would eventually take place. When the maids came in to make the bed, she wanted the room to look as though she had gone on deck. And when Zanna and Stuart came looking—

Hastily she dug out her tapestry portfolio containing her notebook and pencils. She could stuff it inside her shirt. When Zanna checked her cabin, as she surely would, the notebook would be gone, and Zanna would think she had left for her scheduled interviews. That might hold them a bit longer.

Not forever, of course, but hopefully long enough to allow Gabriel to get them out of Baton Rouge before the troopers discovered her missing.

After that—

Remorse set in at the worry she would cause Zanna and Stuart. Remorse and trepidation. What if they wired her family? They were certain to, unless—

Tearing a sheet of paper from her notebook, she scribbled a hasty message. At the top of the page she listed her interviews for the day: Magnolia Mound and the congressional chambers in the capitol building. It would take them time, precious time, to check those out. Below that she wrote: ''Zanna, please don't worry about me. I'm all right.''

They would worry, of course, but perhaps not for a while. She placed the message on the shelf beneath her looking glass and surrounded it with other belongings, none of which she could take. Her fingers lingered on her hairbrush. Surely—

No. The only thing she could stuff inside her shirt was the notebook, and she must take that.

At the door her trepidation grew, enveloping her. *What was she doing, stealing into the bayou with a man she didn't know? Had she lost her mind?*

Turning she stared at the rumpled bed. *Was she mad for chasing a dream? Demented for believing in it?*

Visions from her nightmare returned, and with them

a resurgence of her fear for Brett. She felt again the damp bayou air about her feet, the eerie tangle of moss in her hair, the moldy leaves beneath her knees when she knelt beside the grave of the babe.

Visions of that infant grave tormented her. For the first time she connected them with her earlier nightmares—with the crying of the babe, with Anne Bonny and her blue-eyed girlchild. Quickly then she left, locking the door behind her.

Gabriel waited in the stairwell behind the paddlewheel, as he had said he would. She studied the wiry shadow of the man she had persuaded to take her into the unknown bayou, feeling her arms tremble. The only thing she knew about this man was that he played the fiddle. And that he was Brett's friend.

She straightened her shoulders. Gabriel was the only person who could take her to Brett. And now she was more convinced then ever that her ancestors were calling on her to save Brett's life.

Gabriel surveyed her attire. *"Bien,"* he approved. "Like two friends, we will walk side by side down the ramp, talking. Don' stand too straight. If anyone watches, they mus' think you're a deckhand leavin' the boat for supplies."

"What about you?"

He held up his fiddle case. "Me, I leave ever' morning at this time, sure. I take myself to the livery an' hire two horses."

"Every day?"

He nodded. "Come, we will go now. The passengers, they should be asleep, but if we pass anyone, keep your eyes down. The sky is still dark, sure. Even a frien', he won't recognize you unless you look him in the eye."

She followed him, amazed at his proficiency. Amazed and relieved.

Since he had instructed her to carry on a conversation, she began by asking, "You leave the boat every morning at this time to hire horses for Brett and Pierre?"

"*Oui.*"

"What about yourself?" They reached the gangplank and walked down it, side by side. She felt her legs wobble on the unsteady walkway, although this morning she knew it could well be fear that weakened her knees.

"Me, I return to the livery for a third horse when I need one," Gabriel was saying.

They stepped onto the docks. "You played your fiddle by the gangplank as a signal?"

"*Oui.* Me, I took myself into town to look for those who might be a threat."

"How do you recognize someone who's a threat?"

"Ah, that is not easy, *non,*" he admitted. "Especially here in Baton Rouge. Here we must consider ever'one a threat."

The sky was already brightening in the east when they strolled across the docks. The only lights were the government beacons on poles. The air hung heavy with magnolias.

Delta had to force her limbs to match Gabriel's leisurely pace, for anxiety made her want to run for her life.

She noticed how his eyes continually roamed the area from side to side and far ahead.

"What kind of training have you had?" she questioned.

"Training?"

"As a sentry," she explained. "You seem to be adept at seeking out spies."

"The war," he replied, then added, "an' a lifetime of looking behind me, *oui.*"

His offhand statement brought a return of Delta's earlier concern at putting her safety in the hands of this stranger. She wanted to ask him from what crime *he* was running, but she didn't. She had come this far; for Brett's sake she couldn't turn back. Besides, his answer would likely only serve to frighten her more, and she was sure to need all her wits to get out of town.

When they approached the livery, he instructed her to wait outside at the end of the building, where she envisioned being set upon from every side until he returned, leading two horses.

They rode north, keeping to the leisurely pace Gabriel had set in crossing the wharf area. Delta's anxiety rose.

"If anyone is watching won't they know we're leaving town?"

"They will see us ride north, sure," he replied. "But the bayou is south. We're following my morning routine. Me, I search the livery an' talk with the hostler about strangers who rode in overnight. Then I take myself through town, watchin' for anyone who even smells like a government man. For truth, in this town anyone could be a threat."

Suddenly Delta thought of Nat, who had insisted he saw through Brett's disguise. "What happened to Nat?"

The moment she asked the question, she bit her tongue, wishing she could take it back. Nat had called Brett a killer. So had the governor's aide, if Brett were indeed Anatole Dupré. She didn't necessarily believe either of them, but if this man riding beside her, a friend of Brett's, called him a murderer, she would have to consider it. Gabriel would know the truth.

"Don' you worry yourself about him," Gabriel responded. "Nat, he's taking a ti' vacation. He'll turn up one day, for truth."

The road from the docks led through town and out a ways. When it forked Gabriel guided them eastward, along a trail he said would double back and reach the river well below Baton Rouge, near the steam-powered ferry. They rode through areas of lush green foliage and soft summer scents. She breathed a sigh of relief, reassured about Nat, thus about Brett. But inside she knew there was more than enough trouble ahead to keep her on edge until they found Brett.

She would like to hope that once she found him, her fears would be resolved. She knew this might not be the case.

Back on the docks shadows receded beneath the brightening sky to reveal the figure of a man who rose from his haunches, watching the pair of horsemen ride away from the livery.

The one with the fiddle he recognized. That friend of the gambler's. The other wasn't large enough to be the gambler himself, and certainly not his bodyguard. Reason told the man that nothing was amiss. The stranger accompanying that fiddler was likely a deckhand he had taken along for company.

But reason did not always hold true. And Trainor would brook no miscalculations where Anatole Dupré was concerned. The man dropped his cigarette to the earth at his feet, then ground it out with the ball of his booted foot.

This he would have to report. He consulted his

pocket watch. Perhaps he should wait a while longer, see if the fiddler returned at his usual time. Trainor wouldn't take kindly to wasting time and effort on a false alarm.

Zanna met Stuart outside the paddlewheel lounge for a late breakfast. He rose when he saw her coming and placed a tender kiss on her lips.

"Where's Delta?" he questioned, drawing out her chair.

"Asleep. I knocked, but lightly. She's been so upset over this business with Brett that she probably didn't sleep much last night." Zanna sipped the coffee the waiter set before her. "Do you think he's gone for good?"

Stuart stared into the muddy water three decks below them. "For her sake, I hope so."

"You sound as if you believe Gerard's story."

"If that gambler is indeed Anatole Dupré, murdering his wife isn't the half of it. Dupré's the most wanted man in Louisiana, has been for ten years. Perhaps the most wanted man in the entire country."

Zanna's eyes widened while he spoke. She glanced around the near-deserted deck, then asked in a whisper. "What else did he do?"

"He's wanted for murdering his baby daughter at the same time."

Zanna's coffee cup clattered against the saucer when she set it down. "That can't be true." She pursed her lips between her teeth. Her eyes searched Stuart's. "Can it?"

He shrugged. "To my knowledge no one has positively identified Brett Reall as Dupré. But if that's who he is, he's extremely dangerous."

"Then I hope he's gone," Zanna sighed. "For Delta's sake. And I hope she never learns the truth."

"From what Cameron says about Delta's family," Stuart told her, "Reall or Dupré or whoever the hell the man is had better be gone for his own sake. The Jarretts stick together against any and all adversaries. And believe me, they're a formidable lot."

"Uh-oh. Speaking of formidable lots, look who's coming." Zanna sat facing the docks. Stuart turned at her words. Together they watched Luis Gerard, the governor's aide, accompanied by half a dozen state troopers, dismount and hitch their horses at the rail near the boat. As in single stride they approached the *Mississippi Princess.*

"Looks like we might have trouble." Stuart scraped back his chair. When Zanna made a move to rise, he helped her. They watched Gerard and the troopers disappear as they stepped from the gangplank onto the main deck of the showboat.

Stuart took Zanna in his arms and kissed her. She felt herself responding as she had longed to do for days. At thirty-five she had given up hope of finding a romantic kind of love, thinking such was reserved for young women with stars in their eyes. The most she could hope for, she had told herself over and again, was to marry some old widower with gout or some younger widower with a houseful of children.

Neither alternative appealed to Zanna, who finally decided she would rather spend her life directing dramas than living one. But Stuart Longstreet had set her heartstrings to strumming.

At first she had refused to admit as much, thinking it impossible that he could feel the same way she did.

Lifting his face, he grinned. "Hold that thought."

"What—?" She felt her face flush.

He stared hungrily into her eyes, sending tingles racing down her spine. *"That* thought." He kissed her again. "I had a pleasant morning planned for us, but looks like it'll have to wait until we see what the governor's men want."

"We have reason to believe our fugitive may still be on board," Gerard was responding to Captain Kaney's inquiry when Stuart and Zanna reached the observation deck where the captain had stopped the obviously irate governor's aide and his band of state troopers outside the main dining room.

"If he is, we'll find him," the captain vowed.

Zanna listened, concern growing, while Stuart confronted Gerard. "What's happened to cause you to believe this?"

"His man, the fiddler, is still watching the town," Gerard replied. "One of my informants told me he saw the fiddler and another man leave the boat just before daybreak."

"Another man?" Captain Kaney questioned.

Gerard nodded. "Wasn't Dupré, though. The man was too small to be either Dupré or that bodyguard of his."

"Pierre," the captain supplied.

"Whatever he calls himself, we believe both Dupré and his bodyguard are on board this ship."

"If it is Dupré," Zanna interjected.

Gerard glared at her. "It's Dupré."

"How can you be certain?" she persisted. "Unless you've seen him face to face, of course."

"The Governor has spies about. He has been assured the man traveling on this vessel under the alias Brett Reall is none other than our most wanted fugitive, Anatole Dupré."

Captain Kaney led them along the passageway toward the staircase. "Might as well start at the top and work our way down," he was saying.

Gerard barked commands, instructing three of his troopers to stay alert for anyone trying to escape down the gangplank or overboard on the river side.

"Why is the governor taking such a personal interest in this fugitive?" Zanna questioned, skipping to keep up with the lengthening strides of the determined men.

Gerard favored her with another glare. "Dupré murdered Governor Trainor's sister and her infant daughter."

"Sister? You mean Brett—ah, Dupré was married to the governor's sister?"

"I trust that explains our urgency," Gerard barked.

Indeed, Zanna thought, and the danger Delta would be in should she find herself in the middle between Brett and the governor's men.

Zanna followed the men another few steps, not wanting to draw attention to her new concern. Finally, she managed to divert Stuart's attention while the remainder of the entourage continued to the promenade deck.

"I'm going to alert Delta," she whispered.

"Good," Stuart responded. "Stay with her. She'll need you when this comes to light."

Failing to rouse Delta by repeated knockings, Zanna finally chased down Orville, who reluctantly unlocked the door to Delta's stateroom.

"The maids have already cleaned these rooms," Orville said in response to Zanna's stunned glance about the tidy cabin.

"Oh, yes," she mumbled absentmindedly.

"If you want I can light a lamp," he offered.

Zanna nodded, already headed for the wardrobe. Delta's clothes still hung on the rod inside the chiffonier, others were folded in neat stacks in the drawers.

Then beneath the looking glass among Delta's toiletries she found the message Delta had left for her.

Reading it, Zanna began to breathe easier. Delta had gone to her interviews. She glanced at the last line, a smile forming on her lips. "Zanna, please don't worry about me. I'm all right." How like Delta. Always so considerate.

It wasn't until Zanna showed Stuart the note later that its significance began to dawn on her. She found him, along with the captain, Gerard, and three of the troopers, descending the staircase from the promenade to the observation deck.

"Why didn't you stay with her?" he quizzed in a whisper.

"She's gone to her interviews."

"Hope that satisfies you," Captain Kaney was saying. "The man's nowhere around. Neither one of them. Not Reall nor his man Pierre."

"I'm satisfied, Captain," Gerard replied. "For now. But you must remember, Dupré's a fugitive from justice and a danger to the public. If you or anyone aboard this vessel see or hear anything about him, you are bound by law to contact us immediately. Anything less would be considered harboring a fugitive. I will await your report on the identity of the deckhand who went ashore with that fiddler."

Gerard departed in a flurry, leaving two troopers behind, "To interrogate that fiddler when he shows up," he explained.

After the captain left them alone, Stuart turned to Zanna. "How did Delta take the news?"

"I didn't see her. She had already left for her interview but she left this note."

Stuart took the paper. Zanna watched him study

Delta's itinerary, printed at the top and the note scribbled at the bottom. "Where did you find this?"

"On her dressing table."

He stared into space a moment, chewing a corner of his mustache, then turned serious eyes on Zanna. "Why would she leave a message locked inside her stateroom?"

Zanna shrugged. "I guess she . . . uh, figured I'd worry when she didn't turn up this morning."

"Then why didn't she look you up before she left the boat?" he quizzed. "According to this her first appointment wasn't until ten o'clock. She would have had plenty of time to talk to you before she left."

"She might have been running late," Zanna excused, fumbling for an explanation. Now that Stuart had put the question into words, it bothered her, too. "I told you how distraught she's been lately."

"This isn't logical. If she expected you to worry about her, she should have taken measures to reassure you. She wouldn't force you to break into her room to find a message. Why didn't she give the message to Orville or to some other crew member?"

Zanna's anxieties grew with each new idea Stuart introduced. "They didn't find Brett?"

He shook his head.

"They're sure he's that murderer?"

"They seem to think so."

"I'm going to the capitol building. That's Delta's first interview."

Stuart took her arm. "I'll come with you."

Zanna didn't realize until after they had paid fruitless visits to both the congressional chambers inside the capitol building and Magnolia Mound, Delta's second interview, how glad she would be to have Stuart along.

And for a completely different reason than she would have thought before Delta turned up missing.

Stuart Longstreet possessed a very level head in emergencies. An hour after leaving Magnolia Mound, they had visited the livery and every other place along the docks, asking after Gabriel and the deckhand who had accompanied him off the boat. The most they could learn was that Gabriel had hired two horses, as he had done every other morning the boat had been in town. Riding through town, however, they found no trace of him.

"And since he hasn't returned to the boat," Stuart summed up their findings, "we can only assume that he left town in the company of a deckhand Captain Kaney can't place."

"A deckhand just Delta's size," Zanna replied, adding, "if we're to believe the description of Gerard's informant."

Stuart grunted. "We have to believe it. And I have to wire Cameron, bad as I hate to break such news. He'll get the Pinkertons involved. Next thing is to alert Gerard." He took Zanna in his arms. "Try not to worry. We'll do everything we can to find her. With such a dangerous fugitive involved, the Pinkertons will cooperate with the governor. We'll locate this man— Brett Reall, Anatole Dupré, or whoever he is."

Two days after leaving the showboat Brett and Pierre reached bayou country. They had crossed the Mississippi on a ferry north of Baton Rouge, then headed west toward the Atchafalaya River. Dressed as roustabouts, they hoped to get a head start on those whom they knew would soon be in pursuit.

Much of the country they crossed was cane country,

broad flat expanses with few places to hide. Brett wondered whether Delta would interview any of the many sugar cane planters between Baton Rouge and New Orleans. He could show her—

Abruptly, whenever his mind strayed to Delta, he forced his thoughts away. Someday, when the raw wound of leaving her had healed, he would think about her, he promised himself. He would spend hours recalling every nuance of her voice, imagining every luscious inch of her body; he would dwell on the red streaks in her hair when the sun caught it just right, and the way her eyes turned to blue fire when they made love. Someday he would allow himself such luxury. But that someday would not be soon in coming.

He began to regret having made this trip, and except for the urgency he felt to see his mother, he would have turned back.

But to where? he wondered. Where was his life headed? What lay in store for him? Ten more years of running? And after that, ten? The futility of it began to gnaw at him.

The war-defiled countryside did nothing to lighten his mood. Everywhere great mansions stood neglected, a testament to the war, their slave quarters in need of whitewashing, their fields unplanted.

When at length Brett and Pierre reached the forest beyond the acres—*arpents*—of level fields, Pierre challenged his companion's dark mood.

"Me, I've listened to you bellyache about missin' the bayou for ten years. For truth, we are here. You should start enjoyin' it, *oui?*"

Pierre poled the pirogue and Brett looked around. The rich black soil, the warm smell of humus, the dark, almost purple still waters. Pierre poled in and out among the swollen cypress trunks and their stumps which folks said looked like gnarled knees—*boscoyos,* they were called. The tall trees had far-reaching arms that spread wide, shutting out most of the sunlight. Their branches dripped with even more moss than he had recalled, long and thick and curly, like Delta's hair except for the color.

These waters had been home. He'd known them intimately, as one would know the woman he loved. And without the woman he loved beside him, they seemed cold and empty and foreign. He cursed aloud into the hushed bayou.

"I might as well be guilty, for all the good my innocence does me."

By nightfall the second day they arrived at the Bayou Teche home of his cousin Marcellus Broussard, where Brett slept, exhausted, for two days.

When he awakened, Marcellus and Pierre had gone into the swamps to check traps, leaving word for Brett not to set foot outside the house until they returned.

"A precaution," Angie, Cousin Marcellus's wife, told him. He had found her in the kitchen washing dishes through the window. And the poignancy of such a simple sight—a woman standing inside the kitchen, reaching through the opening to wash dishes on the small shelf attached to the outside of the house— brought a reminder of how long he'd been gone.

"I haven't seen a *tablette* in ten years," he told her, indicating the shelf.

She dried her hands while he spoke and by the time he finished she had crossed the room and thrown herself, laughing, into his arms. He swung her around, knowing this was what he had missed the most—family.

"Welcome home, Anatole." Releasing him, Angie dished up a heaping plate of jambalaya and set it on the split-cypress table. "Sit yourself down an' eat."

She poured thick, black coffee into two cups. "Me, I'll fill you in on the family. What do you want to know first?"

Brett glanced around the room, absorbing the atmosphere of being home. "How's my mother?"

"Bien."

"Is Trainor bothering her?"

Angie's lips tightened at the name. *"Non.* We tried to persuade her to come here and live among family, but she refused. Said she couldn't go off and leave the ones who depend on her cures."

Brett smiled. "She's aged, *oui,* in ten years?"

"Oui. But not so you'll notice. She's spry—in body and mind." Angie laughed, her black eyes alight. "Ah, she will be happy to see you, for truth. She's talked of nothing but you for months. She even held a séance, trying to contact you."

Brett laughed. "I should have suspected as much. I've been dreaming about a blue-eyed woman—"

The words, once spoken, called Delta so vividly to mind that he stopped in midsentence, all thoughts erased by the vision of her face.

Angie reached across the table and patted his arm. *"Non,* don' think about her, Anatole."

"I wasn't." He knew Angie didn't believe him, but he didn't press the issue. He wasn't ready to explain that another blue-eyed woman had entered his life, because she hadn't. Flitted through was a more apt description of the brief relationship he had shared with Delta.

He finished eating while Angie fulfilled her promise to catch him up on the family—births, marriages, and deaths. He listened to her words, spoken in the half-English, half-French dialect of the bayou country, imagining how those of whom she spoke must have changed in the ten years since he'd seen them.

"Five children?" he quizzed at one point, after she related the size of hers and Marcellus's family.

She laughed. *"Oui,* an' another on the way, but Marcel, he doesn't know it yet."

Brett finished eating with Angie's lilting voice filtering into his soul, welcoming him, bringing a false sense of well being and security. After she took his plate, he went to stand in the doorway looking out at the side of Cousin Marcellus's property. Like all homes along the bayou this house fronted on the water, with the bulk of the property extending behind it. To either side were the homes of Marcellus's brothers. According to custom, Papa Broussard had given each son a slice of land when he married, a narrow rectangle less than an *arpent,* with room for a house near the bayou and fields behind it on the fertile prairie that was safer from flooding.

"That's Cousin Ardon's house," Brett remembered aloud, nodding toward the house to the south. "And Cousin Octave is north of you."

"That's right, *oui.* You will see them all tonight at the *fais-do-do."*

Brett surveyed what he could see of Cousin Marcellus's property from the kitchen door—chicken coops and a well, with a barn and hog pen beyond. All the while his brain played with a persistent topic—not how good it would be to attend a down-home dance after all these years, not how good it would be to see his family, not even the pretty girls he could dance with—no his brain returned to Delta and to how much he wished she were here to attend the *fais-do-do.*

"What's this about me staying indoors until Marcellus returns?'' he asked, more to get his mind off Delta than to learn the answer.

"A stranger was seen in town," Angie told him. "A *marchand* selling clothes, sure." She smiled. "But now that we have you back, Anatole, we won't chance losing you, *non.*"

Which turned out to be the way everyone in the family felt. The surveillance required before they would allow him out of the house to attend the dance and the guards posted around the area while they were there would have done the Pinkertons proud.

Thoughts of Pinkertons brought Delta to mind. Delta—her blue eyes that would be filled with melancholy again by now, her thick brown hair that felt like corn silk between his fingers, her satiny smooth body that warmed his soul and fired his passions. *Delta.* How long would it take to get her off his mind?

The dance was held at the house of Papa Broussard. The large front room had been emptied of furniture, except for a table at the far end, heavily laden with specialty dishes of the women in attendance. The feet of the table legs were wrapped with kerosene-soaked rags to ward off ants. Strange, Brett thought once again, how it was the little things that reminded him how long he'd been away and how much he had missed his home.

"Smellin' tha' filé gumbo makes me hungry to get to Crazy Mary's," Pierre observed. "For truth, your *maman* makes the best gumbo in the world."

Brett stared at the gumbo, willing himself not to retch. Even after ten years the thought of gumbo reminded him of the cabin, of gumbo splattered over the bodies.

They stood on the *galerie*, visiting with cousins, while the band played in true 'Cadien fashion—the slurring notes and irregular beat reproduced faithfully by an accordion, a fiddle, a harmonica, a washboard played with a spoon, and triangles—called ti'fers.

"Gabriel, he would be home right here," Pierre observed of the music.

"*Oui,*" Brett agreed, but speaking of Gabriel brought thoughts of Delta. "He'd better keep his eyes on her," he muttered.

Pierre slapped him on the back. "For truth, *nèfyou,* there are plenty of girls here tonight to take your mind off her."

And, indeed there were. Pretty girls. He watched them flirt, some precociously, some shyly, some with a boldness their parents would be ashamed of. Or should be. Those girls reminded him of Nicole. And Nicole reminded him of trouble.

Nicole *was* trouble, even in death. She had been from the beginning, but he had been too blinded by her saucy beauty and citified ways to see the barrenness inside her brain, inside her heart.

Not that his family hadn't tried to warn him. They had. Cousins, aunts, uncles, even his mother. But in the end, he had married her anyway.

His gaze drifted over the men in the room. Was there a man among them who hadn't slept with Nicole at one time or another? Both before and after she married the bayou man, Anatole Dupré?

And William Trainor, damn his black soul, considered the Duprés trash. Not good enough to marry his sister. He was ashamed of the bayou man and of the *traiteur* who had borne him.

He'd finally come full circle, though, Trainor had, condemning his sister along with her in-laws. That was when Trainor decided to run for public office. Nicole's promiscuity did not enhance his reputation with the highfalutin folks he needed to win a statewide election.

Oh, he'd tried to bring her home. Her and little Olivia. But Nicole had refused to go. Not that she loved her husband, she loved only herself and the life she had created beyond the grasp of her sophisticated family. Even pregnancy had not slowed her down.

Nor had the baby. Crazy Mary cared for Olivia whenever Brett had to be gone. And that really maddened Trainor. Kin of his being reared by a *traiteur*— or as he insisted on referring to Mary Dupré, a Voodooienne.

God's bones! Brett cursed under his breath. How he wished he'd never heard of William Trainor or Nicole or— He shook his head to clear the unwanted thoughts. He'd dealt with losing Nicole. For truth, he'd never had her to lose, and he had accepted that fact long before her death.

But his daughter was a different matter. Little Olivia's death had been brutal and senseless. He had never learned to think about it without becoming enraged.

And Trainor blamed him. God's bones, how could he think any man capable of murdering his own flesh and blood? But Trainor believed it still. Those papers Gabriel found in Nat's cabin proved the governor was as eager to see him dead today as he had been ten years ago.

Ten thousand dollars, dead or alive. And five hundred extra before he crossed the state line. Trainor didn't want him back in the state. Why, the governor didn't even want the satisfaction of seeing his sister's murderer swing, as Brett had believed for ten years. Ten thousand dollars! Before he crossed the state line.

Before he crossed the state line. This shed a whole new light on the situation. Trainor didn't want him back in the state. Was willing to pay big money to keep him out. Why? What possible harm could he, Anatole Dupré, bring a man who'd been governor for ten years? What harm? What was Trainor afraid of?

The dance wasn't half over when an idea struck Brett. And it was so abhorrent it brought chills to his arms, even here in the damp muggy bayou. He grabbed Pierre by the arm as soon as the big man came off the dance floor.

"I know where to find the answers."

Pierre blinked to focus on the meaning of the cryptic statement.

"I know where to begin searching for the murderer. First thing tomorrow, I'm setting out."

Chapter Sixteen

Delta had never seen anything like the bayou in her life, had never imagined such a place, not even in her nightmares. It was wild and eerie, and although it teemed with so much life she thought it might explode, she found it somehow peaceful—as though she had left the violent world of murderers and bounty hunters and government agents far behind.

She hadn't, of course, and so she sat tensed in the pirogue, while Gabriel poled them along the twisting canals. Sunlight filtered through a canopy of cypress branches, glistening in iridescent splendor on the oily water surrounding their enormous gnarled trunks. Streamers of gray moss shot through with sunbeams hung from the broad tree limbs, giving the entire area a party atmosphere, as though paper decorations had been strung from all the trees. The moss reminded her of a story Hollis told about the time he had ventured into an underground cavern where rock formations hung in profusion from the ceiling, glistening when light touched them. Like a giant cave, the bayou seemed isolated from the real world.

The dark water looked thick and heavy, earth-steeped, as though it would stain her fingers if she dared dip them into its deceptively still surface. Which she didn't since the water fairly simmered with the life in and upon it—catfish and gar, bullfrogs and crawfish, shrimp and terrapins. And alligators. Their knobby backs protruded here and there above the murky surface of the water. Occasionally she spied a lengthy snout resting on the bank. She had yet to encounter the whole body of one of these fearsome creatures, or even an open mouth.

To either side of the canal, on what she took for solid ground, the soil bubbled with the life beneath its surface. She doubted such land would support a person's weight. She certainly wouldn't want to attempt to walk on it.

Overhead and around them the entire forest resounded with a symphonic concert of caws and chirps and a distant tap-tap-tapping.

"Ivory-billed woodpecker," Gabriel responded to her question. She smiled at the thought of something familiar in this alien world, envisioning the bird M'sieur Audubon had left stuffed at Camelliawood. But the woodpecker's tap-tap-tapping sounded so much like an army of troopers marching through the bayou that she expressed her worries aloud.

"If there were intruders in the bayou," Gabriel assured her, "the birds, they would tell us. Their songs would not welcome, *non.* They would sing a warning."

She gazed around, awed by a sense of timelessness. A menagerie of birds went about their cheery business high in the overlapping branches of cypress trees. "They aren't afraid of us?"

"We belong."

We belong? Perhaps Gabriel, but certainly not she herself. She relaxed a bit after that, however, imagining the cacophony above and beyond and to either side of them as sentries—watching, waiting, ready to warn of danger.

Gabriel stood at the back of the hand-hewn boat they had bought from a fisherman upon reaching the bayou. He plied the long pole, pushing it against the bottom of the stream, propelling them lazily along, keeping to the main canal for the most part, occasionally turning this way or that into one of the many fingers that trailed off in any and all directions. She tried to concentrate on the trip, striving without success to determine what he used for markers.

Gabriel had proved to be a proficient guide. Leaving Baton Rouge they had stopped some distance before reaching the ferry, turning the horses loose to find their way back to the livery. Using gold coins, which she feared neither of them looked prosperous enough to possess without raising questions, he had encouraged the ferryman to take them across the Mississippi without waiting for more passengers. Afterwards he led them across the acres and acres of sugar cane fields without encountering a soul.

Time and again she recalled his cryptic response that he had learned his skills by watching his backside, and each time she thought of it, she wondered what kind of fool she was.

But they had arrived at the bayou without mishap, and he procured the pirogue using the same approach as with the ferryman, except the pirogue hadn't cost them as much gold.

He talked little, responding to her requests in the terse manner she had come to expect. He was uneasy around her; she knew that without him saying so. She wondered whether he was uncomfortable around all women or whether it was their particular circumstances that made him so now.

She thought she might feel better if she knew the source of his uneasiness, but realized all too well that wasn't necessarily the case. It would do her no good to inquire, she knew, since he either rebuffed or responded with the briefest explanation to her every inquiry, as when she had finally managed to find the courage to ask him about Brett.

"Is he Anatole Dupré?"

To which Gabriel had shrugged. "Me, I'm taking you to him, m'moiselle. He is the one to answer your questions, sure."

But his reticence only served to heighten her fears and her fears began to smother her from the inside, as the thick, sultry air of the bayou seemed bent on smothering her from without.

She fanned her loose shirt against her chest. "How do you determine where to turn from one canal to another?" she asked, suddenly needing human conversation to strengthen her tenuous grip on reality.

"Depends," he replied. Finally when she had almost given up on a conversation, he added, "For truth, the bayou changes quickly. The big river, he rearranges the map ever' spring with floods and silt from above. An' loggers, they dredge new canals to float out cypress trees. Since I've been gone nothin' looks the same, *non.*"

"Then how are you navigating?"

"By feel—an' direction. Me, I might take ourselves up a dead-end canal before we get where we're headed."

Delta chose to ignore the consequences of such a development. Surely Gabriel would know how to get them out of a dead-end canal. "Where are we headed?"

"To my family, first. Can't chance goin' straight to Crazy Mary's."

"Won't the troopers know to watch your family, too?"

He grunted. "The troopers, they don' like the bayou. They won' find enough brave men to do more'n stake out Crazy Mary's place, sure."

"Will they harm her?"

He chuckled *"Non.* They're afraid of her powers, *certainement.* That's the reason Trainor wants to run the Voodoos out of the state. He don' want to share power with them."

She thought of a dozen additional questions to ask him, but before she could decide which topic might be most fruitful with this close-mouthed man, he nosed the pirogue onto a bank that looked fairly solid.

"Step easy," he cautioned, offering her a hand after he jumped to the bank. "For truth, it isn't as solid as it looks."

For the next hour or so she followed him through the forest, putting each foot exactly where he told her. And here in the deep woods, Gabriel came alive. Gripping her hand firmly, he pulled her in and out, this way and that, reminding her of the way he danced around the docks playing his fiddle.

Not until he had named all the trees they passed, "Water hickory, locust, tupelo," and many of the plants, "palmettos, salt cane, oyster grass, cattails," did she realize what he was doing. What she had taken to be a recitation of local fauna for her sake, was in fact a homecoming ritual. Gabriel had come home, and his joy was plain to see.

"How long were you in Canada with Brett?" she called to him.

"Five years."

Five years. Brett had been away ten. How she prayed he made it back to his beloved bayou country.

By the time they reached higher ground, the forest had changed to pine trees, tall and majestic. Then they left the forest behind all together, emerging onto a prairie.

She paused to look back. "It's beautiful."

"Oui," he agreed, adding, "bayou folk think so. *Anglais,* they usually don't see it that way."

She came up even with him, matching his stride. Ahead of them beyond a plowed field she saw a row of houses. She looked back at the forest again. "It felt as if we were the only two people in the world, like we were traveling through the Garden of Eden."

"Oui." This time he studied her with a mixture of curiosity and warmth, bringing a sudden rush of tears to her eyes.

And the tears reminded her of Brett—of her nightmare. In the distance children rode a horse, a woman hung clothes on a line. Was it her tears that called the nightmare to mind with more clarity than in two days? Or was it the return to civilization that signaled the resumption of her mission? And intensified her fears for Brett.

After their first stunned reaction, Gabriel's family fell into welcoming him with such enthusiasm that Delta began to fear they wouldn't let him leave to complete the journey. And they welcomed her, too, after he explained who she was and why he had brought an *Anglaise femme* into the bayou.

Their hesitancy to accept an English woman when they thought she might be involved with Gabriel would have worried her, had she not had weightier things on her mind. Would Brett's family see her as an outsider, an *Anglaise?* Surely, after they worked everything else out, they wouldn't be faced with his family's rejection of her because she was *English.*

As the evening wore on, she began to wonder whether Brett's family was as large as Gabriel's—twelve brothers, five sisters, all married with children. And they all lived close by, along with uncountable numbers of uncles, aunts, cousins, godparents.

Causerie, or nightly visiting, Delta soon learned, was a time-honored custom along the bayou.

"Every night except Monday," Gabriel explained. "Visiting on Monday is sure to bring yourself enemies."

This particular evening everyone from up and down the bayou chose to visit the home of Gustave and Verina LeBlanc, Gabriel's parents, to welcome Gabriel home to the bayou—and to gape at the *Anglaise* he brought with him, she decided, from the curious glances she received all evening.

They sat on the *galerie,* which was like a deep and wide front porch with an overhanging roof and stairs leading to the second floor *grenier,* a sleeping room for the bachelor boys in the family. The *galerie* fronted the bayou, so visitors, if they did not live close enough to walk, poled up in their pirogues.

Mountains of food filled the table—jambalaya, crawfish prepared several different ways, étouffée, a huge pot of filé gumbo, and gallons of black coffee—café, it was called.

The food was delicious, if spicy, and it reminded her of the night Brett flirted with her at the captain's table, asking if she liked spicy things. That had been the first meal they ever shared, the time he learned she was a journalist. Now she understood why he had seen her as a threat.

Since the conversation around her was carried on in French, which she didn't understand, her mind was left free to wander, and wander it did.

For the first time in days she thought about her own family—Ginny and Hollis back in St. Louis, waiting to hear that her trip had rid her of those debilitating nightmares. She hoped they never learned the extent to which those dreams had developed. With luck she would be able to find Brett and travel to New Orleans before anyone became too worried about her. She thought about the children, especially the twins, Jimmy and Joey, and her promise to find them a pirate.

A pirate. Brett Reall. A tremor of fear coursed down her spine, and she clasped her hands about her arms. A pirate. She prayed that was all he was and nothing more—nothing worse.

When she thought about Brett, her mind stopped wandering and became mired as in bayou mud. Where was he tonight? What was he eating tonight? Was he still free?

Still alive?

She finally gave up and went to bed on a pallet in a back room she would share with three of Gabriel's sisters. Earlier in the day they had taken her in hand, fixing her a bath and providing her with a loose-fitting cotton dress, of the kind they wore. She hadn't seen a single corset or bonnet since she arrived. With nothing else to sleep in, she lay down in the dress, smoothing the material beneath her to minimize wrinkling.

"Me, I'll wake you early," Gabriel had told her after translating the sleeping arrangements from his mother's French.

Delta had nodded. Then her eyes sought his. "Do you think he's all right?"

Gabriel had shrugged, then grinned. "Ah, Delta, you are the dreamer. Go to sleep and dream sweet dreams of him, sure."

Lying alone now in the back room that smelled

328

sweetly of cypress, sounds of the family reunion drifted to her—Gabriel's voice and his fiddle, an accordion played by someone else. She visualized again the warmth in Gabriel's eyes and heard his teasing good night wish. Delta, he had called her. Dream sweet dreams, he had said.

After days of silence or terse replies, he had suddenly called her by name and wished her sweet dreams. She tried to imagine what could have changed his opinion of her, finally deciding it must have been when she called the forest beautiful. He was a strange man, a private man, like Brett. Did Brett have the same deep feelings for this country? For his family? If so, how had he been able to stay away ten long years? Only something truly terrible—heinous he had called it—would have kept him from such a family, from this land he loved.

Her body ached from the unaccustomed walking they'd done the last two days, and before she realized it, she was drifting off to sleep. Then Gabriel's voice came from the porch. He spoke in French, so she didn't understand his words.

Except for the name he spoke.

Anatole Dupré.

Brady Jarrett lived in a two-story townhouse on Toulouse Street one block from his Chartres Street Tavern. The house was designed with an upstairs *galerie* rimmed with fancy iron grillwork and a central courtyard with fountain and a myriad of blooming flowers.

Ellie and Aurelia Jarrett sat in the courtyard enjoying the warm spring afternoon, while their husbands Kale and Carson tried their hand at mixing proper Southern-style mint juleps.

"Brady told you not to add so much sugar." Carson reached across his brother Kale, grabbed a handful of mint leaves and began tearing them apart.

"That's not the way Brady said to do it," Kale objected.

From the table their wives looked on in amusement. Even though Aurelia still spoke little English, she and Ellie had become instant friends and their journey to New Orleans from Summer Valley, where Ellie and Kale lived, had solidified their relationship.

"Here comes Cousin Brady, now," Ellie told the men. "You can ask him yourselves."

But one look at the ashen-faced Brady Jarrett and both women jumped from their chairs and ran to help him. Unlike most of the Jarretts, Brady was neither very tall nor very trim. Perhaps his years running an eating establishment, had resulted in his portly figure.

"Cousin Brady," Ellie questioned, taking his arm to lead him to a chair at the wrought iron table, "are you ill?"

Aurelia gripped Brady's other arm. While Ellie seated the man in one of his own iron chairs, the bolder Aurelia loosened his silk tie and began to unbutton his starched collar.

"Are you—?" Aurelia looked helplessly to Carson, then back to the stricken man. "Are you choking on food?" she asked in hesitant English.

Brady smiled at her successful attempt. "No, my dear." Shifting in the chair, he inhaled a deep breath that stressed the buttons on his already tight vest. He lifted a hand, fluttering a telegram from his pudgy fist.

Kale and Carson had by now joined the group at the table, and Kale took the paper.

"It just arrived," Brady explained as though he were out of breath.

Kale pursed his lips as he read. The group watched his jaws clench. His face turned pale. The telegram trembled in his fingers. "Sonofabitch." The word whispered through his lips.

Ellie rushed to Kale's side. "What is it?"

"Delta—"

"Delta what?" Carson took the telegram from Kale's limp fingers, while Kale found his voice and told the ladies the spirit of the message.

"It's from Cameron. Delta's turned up missing from that showboat. She may have been . . . kidnapped."

While he spoke. Aurelia had busied herself pouring Brady a glass of lemonade, which she now handed him. "Drink," she instructed.

Ellie gasped at Kale's words. Her eyes held his. "Delta?" she questioned. "Our dear Delta?" Clasping her husband about the waist, she buried her face in his chest. His arms trembled when they came around her. In her mind Ellie saw Delta as she had last seen her, laughing and enjoying herself at the ranch. She saw Delta's blue eyes, the same blue as Kale's. Perhaps because of all the Jarrett children they alone had blue eyes, Kale and Delta had been even closer than the others.

Carson tossed the telegram to the table and Aurelia moved to his side, slipping a comforting arm around him. For a moment the only sound in the courtyard was of the slight breeze rustling the leaves of the crape myrtle trees and water gently splashing in the fountain.

Brady found his voice and related the rest of the message to the women. "Cameron's agent in Baton Rouge reported it. Seems no one is sure exactly what happened. She may have gone off on her own or she may have been kidnapped. Either way the man involved is a criminal."

331

Tears fell silently from Ellie's eyes.

"Who is this man—Anatole Dupré?" Carson questioned.

"Most wanted criminal in Louisiana," Brady explained. "You may have heard of him in the Ranger service. They're sure to have searched for him clear across the country. Even in Texas and beyond."

"What did he do?" Aurelia asked.

"Murdered his wife and daughter," Brady told them bluntly.

The women gasped at the horror of Brady's words.

"Must've been from an important family," Carson observed. "Telegram says Cameron has offered the Pinkertons help to the Governor of Louisiana."

"Governor Trainor," Brady confirmed. "Way I understand it, Dupré's wife, the murdered one, was Trainor's sister."

"Delta didn't run off with a murderer," Ellie said. "He had to have kidnapped—" Her voice faltered and she pressed her lips together. Kale tightened his hold on her.

"Cameron's on his way to Baton Rouge now," Brady assured Ellie. "Says he's to meet his agent there and strike out after her."

"Is there any way we can get started from this end?" Carson asked.

Brady shook his head. "No telling which way the trail leads. Dupré's been missing for ten years. He could've struck out for anyplace, carrying along a hostage to make sure no one stands in his way."

"Well, I'll damned sure stand in his way," Carson barked. "How long will it take us to get to Baton Rouge?"

"By train, four hours or so, depending on the stops."

Carson glanced around the courtyard as though looking for an answer to their distress. "Do you know the schedule?"

"I'll send Maynard." Brady rang the bell for his houseboy as he spoke.

Kale hadn't said a word during the preceding exchange. Finally Ellie moved out of his embrace to study him more closely. They read each other's thoughts, for one thing was foremost in their minds—Delta must be saved.

Ellie took Kale's hands and held them in hers. She turned them over and looked at them from all sides, hands that had not held a gun for nearly a year now. Not since his fight in the darkened cavern beneath their house had almost resulted in his death.

Not since their wedding night when he promised her he had put his guns away forever—

Or until together they decided the cause was just.

"You must do it," she told him.

He nodded, lowering his face to kiss her tenderly on the lips. "For Delta."

Carson, meanwhile, picked up the telegram and studied it. "Wire Cameron," he told Brady. "Tell him to wait for us at this Riverside Tavern where he plans to meet his agent. It'll take us longer to get started that way, but if it's the only way to pick up that bastard's trail, then we'll have to do it."

Aurelia tightened her hold on Carson, reminding him that she probably understood only the rudiments of what had transpired, so he turned to her, explaining in Spanish. "You and Ellie stay here with Cousin Brady, angel. Kale and I'll return with Delta."

"And that criminal will finally pay for his terrible deeds," she answered.

"For all of them."

"For Delta, most of all," Kale vowed.

The house Brett had shared with his wife Nicole was located on a small finger of Bayou Teche, twenty miles south of his cousin, Marcellus Broussard's home. And that house was where Brett determined to begin his search for the truth.

The more he considered the situation the more he believed he was onto something.

"If you're right, *mon nêfyou,*" Pierre had cautioned, "you will need proof, and lots of it, *certainement.*"

"Oui. That is why I must go back. The proof is there. In that house. I feel it."

Pierre scoffed. "Yourself, you didn't *dream* it, like that little blue-eyed—?"

"Hush your mouth, or *yourself,* I'll knock out your teeth," Brett warned, then added with a sheepish grin, "even if you are twice my size." He turned serious again, his voice grave. "Those dreams held more truth than fancy, and they terrorized Delta."

And they brought us together, he thought. That, in the end, was the purpose of this last-ditch attempt to prove his innocence. Now he had a reason beyond himself to clear his name.

For ten years he'd lived under the threat of being convicted for a crime he had not committed. For ten years he had believed what his mother told him, that his innocence could not be proved, that without the real murderer in custody, the governor would see Brett hang for the crime.

All of which had been true at the time. Even though the facts were the same today, he realized how gullible he had been. If Nicole had been killed by a jealous suitor, as everyone believed, that man would have faded into his previous life in the bayou, and sooner or later he would have been found out. After the number of men Nicole slept with and led to believe she really loved, no one had been able to keep quiet the fact that he had murdered her.

Except for the murder of the child, he thought. That was enough to seal a pair of lips into eternity. Brett clenched his eyes tightly over the vision, which, though it was ten years old, still remained so vivid he could smell the blood and see the cold, lifeless body of his beloved little daughter.

Why would a jilted suitor murder a child? For fear of being discovered, his mother had said, and Brett had taken her word for it. His mother had insisted his own life was in danger, not only from this depraved suitor, but also from the distraught brother of his murdered wife, the demented governor of the state. Governor William Trainor who hadn't had a civil thought for his sister since she ran away to the bayou.

Crazy Mary claimed not to know the killer's identity, and unless they could prove who murdered Nicole and Olivia, they could not disprove Brett's role in the murder. So for ten years Brett had lived in hiding, as though duty-bound to save his life from a governor who sought his death in revenge for the murder of a sister he had long ago learned to hate.

Five years ago when Gabriel joined him in Canada, he brought word from Crazy Mary that it was still unsafe for him to return.

Year by year the chance of exposing this demented killer, thereby clearing his own name, became less and less probable. Brett had accepted it—until now.

Until Delta became such an all-consuming force in his life that he knew he would rather die at the gallows for a crime he hadn't committed than to live without her. He had to prove his innocence. He could offer Delta nothing less than that—his proven innocence. And to do so, he must expose the killer.

The moment Brett's intentions became clear, Pierre had objected. "Ah, in the bayou, things, they change fast. That house, it might not be there still."

"We'll ask Cousin Marcellus."

"If it's there, that house, it would not have stood empty all this time," Pierre had reasoned. "Someone, they will be living in it, sure."

Brett had merely nodded, thinking, as the music from the *fais-do-do* floated in energetic drifts of sawing fiddles and whirling bodies.

"Trainor, he knows you're back," Pierre told him. "Maybe he expects you to go there. Maybe he has the place under surveillance, *oui.*"

"The house still stands," Cousin Marcellus confirmed later that evening after Brett and Pierre followed the family home across the bayou.

Before dawn the following morning Cousin Marcellus went ahead of them in his pirogue, while Cousin Ardon and Cousin Octave traveled through the forest on foot to determine whether the state troopers had the place under surveillance.

As prearranged Brett and Pierre followed a couple of hours later in a pirogue, first Pierre poling, then Brett. Brett drank in the longed-for atmosphere of the bayou, feeling overwhelmed by actually being back. He scanned the forests of hardwoods to either side of the canal, wondering whether mink and otter were still plentiful, whether muskrats still brought top dollar, whether the market for moss had held steady since the war.

The air hummed with life, both the creatures who exposed themselves to the men, and those who burrowed into the liquefied earth. Overhead branches of the cypress trees rustled with activity, caws and calls, all repeated by the persistent mockingbird, until the air rang with their sounds.

A cottonmouth slithered over a cypress knee and a bullfrog kroomped from a nearby stand of reeds. Here and there knobby bodies of alligators protruded from the still black water.

He was home, back in the bayou after ten long years. He was home. And this time he was going to stay, at least long enough to clear his name.

Afterwards he would find Delta. He would find her, and if she would have him, they would decide where to live, what to do. A woman of her gentle upbringing would likely feel threatened by such a wild place.

He scrutinized his surroundings, absorbing them, as his body absorbed the steamy heat. It wouldn't matter where they lived, not to him. He could love the bayou and not live in it. But he wasn't at all sure he could love Delta Jarrett and ever give her up.

Reaching the landing, Brett hopped out of the pirogue, then stopped, studying the mud-chinked, split-cypress cabin, the home he had shared with Nicole. Some home.

The house itself wasn't bad. In the tradition of most homes built by the Acadians along the bayous of Louisiana, the house rested on cypress stumps well above the soggy land. That wouldn't keep it from flooding in season, but the raised foundation lifted the house out of reach of most crawling things.

He perused every detail from the palmetto-thatched roof extending low over the deep *galerie* to the window behind which he knew to be the bedroom he had shared with Nicole. He waited for emotion to assail him, but it didn't. The demand to hurry did, however, to hurry and to succeed.

"We have brought ourselves here," Pierre grumbled. "Now what do we do?"

Cousins Marcellus and Ardon met the men at the landing. "The Heberts who used to live in a shack down the way have moved into the house," Marcellus explained. "Madame Hebert agreed to let you see the inside of the house. Octave is keeping watch north of the clearing. Ardon will go south, and me, I will take the bayou."

Brett and Pierre approached the house, with Brett still wondering what he intended to do. He was going by feel, and suddenly felt foolish for coming here.

"Follow me," he told Pierre. "I'll speak to the residents, then we'll look around."

"Ah, *nêfyou*, what do you expect to find right here?"

"Something to spur my memory."

The lady of the house stood on the *galerie*, providing the first thing beyond the house itself to spur Brett's memory. The last time he'd seen Madame Hebert had been the night of the murders, when he'd run to their cabin, desperate, searching for answers.

The Heberts had seen nothing. Had heard nothing. He still recalled how their hollow eyes had riveted on his blood-soaked clothing.

Madame Hebert greeted him, then followed them silently across the *galerie*. Brett stopped on the threshold leading to the living room. From there he could see through the house to the closed kitchen door at the rear. He tried to clear his mind, to recall that night so long ago. Not the part about finding them, that he would never forget. He focused on what could have transpired in this house before the murders. What could have happened here? For so long now, all he'd recalled, all he'd allowed himself to recall was the splattered gumbo. He strove to move beyond that mental barrier.

The bodies had been cold when he arrived home after dark, and Nicole had clearly been expecting a visitor. That was what led to the theory that she had been murdered by a rejected suitor—she was home, awaiting the arrival of a lover, folks said. But to Brett's knowledge Nicole had never entertained men in their home. He'd have to give her credit for that—he had never come home and caught her red-handed, not in their own home, not in their own bed.

And Olivia had been home that night. Brett recalled going over all these questions with his mother. Nicole never left Olivia home alone, so if she had been planning to go out later, she wouldn't have picked Olivia up from Crazy Mary. Brett had gone there first instead of coming directly home, so sure had he been that Nicole would be out and Olivia would be waiting for him at his mother's.

The deep pangs of sorrow that always filled his heart when he thought of Olivia slowed his investigation further. Olivia, only three years old, had never had a chance.

Beautiful, blue-eyed Olivia. He clenched his jaws and entered the front room. Pierre stepped inside after him, followed by Madame Hebert. The house was neat as a pin. Brett almost complimented the lady on it. Nicole had never kept the place straight, much less clean. He walked through the front room, stopping at the door to the kitchen. As was the custom in Acadian homes the kitchen door was kept closed except during mealtimes to keep heat from escaping into the rest of the house. The bayou was steamy enough without adding man-made heat.

Behind this door was where he had found Nicole and Olivia. In the kitchen, which was always closed off except when cooking or at meal time. In the kitchen, when he couldn't recall Nicole ever willingly preparing a meal.

The gumbo proved she had been cooking though—for a visitor, local opinion held. He glanced around the room, at the table, the *tablette,* the cabinets, the cookstove. Nothing unusual. Everything ordinary, familiar.

His eyes fixed on the spot where he had found them, on the floor near the *tablette,* while Olivia's little blue eyes swam in his vision. He reached for the door frame to steady himself.

Angrily he had questioned his mother's assertion that Nicole was preparing dinner for a guest. "She's never cooked a meal for a man in her life," he had stormed. "Nor for Olivia."

"You must calm yourself, Anatole," Crazy Mary had said. "You are in danger, *oui.* Grave danger. They will arrive soon to arrest you. You will never be able to prove your innocence. Never. They will hang you for this, *certainement,* if you live to go to trial."

"That isn't the way of justice, *Maman,*" he had retorted. "They must prove my guilt."

"*Non.* This time you will have to prove your innocence."

Retreating from the kitchen, Brett retraced his steps to the front room, then to the room opening off it, the bedroom, which he had saved until last.

The furniture was different. An iron bed, where theirs—his and Nicole's—had been a moss-filled mattress on the floor.

He thought of Nicole, from a proper home, reared with luxuries. Nicole, who preferred the rugged life of the bayou, the rugged men of the bayou.

That was what had attracted her to him in the first place, but her interest hadn't lasted beyond a week or two of marriage. As soon as she discovered that he wanted a regular home and family, she told him how things were going to be.

He had even tried to persuade her to return to Baton Rouge. But she would have none of it. Nor had she wanted them to go their separate ways. On hindsight it would have been better had he gone into the swamps to trap and never returned.

His biggest regret, however, was Olivia. Dear, beautiful Olivia, who never had a chance. That was his fault—his for fathering her, his for allowing her to remain in the same house with her mother.

Abruptly he turned, bumping into Pierre, and left the room. On the *galerie* he stood, staring out at the bayou, at the bearded cypress and tupelo trees, at the wilderness beyond, the country he had loved since childhood. He had been wrong to come here. Nothing had been gained. Nothing. Gathering his wits, he thanked Madame Hebert.

"I have often wished I could have done something to prevent the tragedy, livin' so close," the old woman surprised him by saying. As if in an effort to confirm that she had tried to help, she asked, "Did your *maman* send you the stickpin I found after we moved here?"

Brett frowned at her, not understanding, then shook his head.

"We have not been to Crazy Mary's," Pierre explained.

"*Bien,*" Madame Hebert said. "When you go there she will give it to you. I knew you would want to keep it, since it matched the gold locket little Olivia always wore."

Again Brett thanked the woman, although he still

341

wondered what she was talking about. After conferring with his cousins he and Pierre climbed into the pirogue.

Brett took the pole and did not speak again until they had traveled several miles through the misty bayou wilderness.

"*Maman* knows more than she's told me," he said aloud, surprising even himself.

"Crazy Mary?" Pierre questioned. "Why would she keep anything from you."

In his mind Brett saw the gold locket Madame Hebert mentioned, the one Olivia always wore around her little neck. "Because she knew what I would do if I suspected the truth."

Chapter Seventeen

One sight of Crazy Mary, and Delta knew where folks got her appellation. It wasn't so much the woman's looks—she was nice looking, if a bit strangely garbed. A tall woman, somewhere in her late fifties, her wrinkled skin stretched like fine tanned leather over prominent cheek bones and a wide forehead. Her hair was black, streaked liberally with gray, and pulled into a tight bun at her nape. But there ended all resemblance to little old ladies with buns.

Crazy Mary's bun was pierced with several stickpins crowned by colorful wooden figures. Large gold hoops hung from her ears. She wore several strands of beads around her neck—gold, glass, and one made with dozens of tiny bells. Her clothing was different, too, from what city women would deem proper—a long, full skirt of bright colors and a blouse with no collar and scant sleeves.

Delta had scanned the forests to either side when they approached the house.

"My cousins, they are watchin'," Gabriel had assured her.

She relaxed a bit, studying the house to divert her mind from the dangers around them. It looked like the houses of Gabriel's relatives, except for being raised above the ground on stumps. Inside, however, she now saw nothing even vaguely familiar. Crazy Mary sat cross-legged on a carpet on the floor, surrounded by a ring of lighted candles. Pebbles of various sizes were strewn about the carpet, as were small dishes filled with colored powders and dried objects, the identities of which Delta refused to speculate on. From outside the house she had heard singing, and when they stepped through the open doorway, she discovered Crazy Mary to be the source. The strange woman sat with her eyes closed and her face lifted to the rafters, crooning.

Although the room was otherwise unlighted, the dozens of candles provided both an undulating light and a smoky haze. The air was heavy with the sweet odor of incense. Gabriel and Delta stood in the doorway unnoticed, until Gabriel interrupted the woman's crooning by clearing his throat.

The blue eyes that flew open startled Delta. Blue eyes full of life and joy—and something that spoke instantly of wisdom.

"Gabriel," the woman cried, rising immediately to hug him. "Me, I didn't know you were comin'." A frown, which reminded Delta of the way Brett's brow creased between his eyes, etched her leathery face. "How could I have miss' such a thing?" She circled his upper arms with long slender fingers and examined his face with candid approval. "You have not chang', *non*, and yet you have. You are the same, yet, for truth, wiser."

"Let me introduce you. Madame Dupré this is—"

Delta's heart stopped on the name Dupré—the first proof she had encountered of Brett's identity.

"Me, I know this *pichouette*," Crazy Mary interrupted Gabriel. Taking Delta's hands, she spread them palm-up on her own hand and began to stroke them, all the while staring intently into Delta's eyes. "Her name is Anne Bonny."

Foremost in Delta's mind for hours—days, actually—had been one concern: Was Brett at his mother's home? Now with Crazy Mary's astonishing remark, even concern for Brett vanished.

"No," Delta managed to say. At the same time, however, her brain returned to a fear she had put aside the last few days—her own sanity. She wasn't Anne Bonny. Yet, how in the world did this strange woman know to connect the two of them?

Crazy Mary continued to stare deeply into Delta's eyes, disconcerting her. She tried to look away, but found herself unable to. Finally she said, "Anne Bonny was my . . . ah, a distant ancestor." *Very distant,* she thought, feeling her hands begin to tremble in Crazy Mary's grasp.

"Come, then, *pichouette,* we mus' discuss how I could have made such an error." Crazy Mary drew Delta inside the ring of candles. As if on second thought, she glanced at Gabriel, motioning him to follow them inside the circle of candles. "Sit yourself, Gabriel. You have help' Anatole in his trouble, *oui.* You mus' witness the truth."

Delta's heart thrummed to a stop. *Anatole Dupré.* Now she knew the truth of it. Brett Reall was Anatole Dupré. Soon she would learn the rest, the final truth—his crime, his guilt or innocence. Yet, at the moment the question she most wanted answered was whether he was still alive . . . and free.

"Is he here?" she managed to ask.

Crazy Mary shook her head. *"Non,* he is on his way, for truth. Me, I was workin' on that when you arrive'." She frowned, shaking her head in obvious confusion. "I don' understand. I have such difficulty contacting Anatole. I never experience' such difficulty before."

Smoke from the candles began to sting Delta's eyes. Her mouth felt parched, not from the smoke, she knew, but from fear.

Hadn't Ginny always told her that fear of the unknown was the worst kind of fear? The unknown. Brett's unknown past. Panic welled inside her. She didn't want to know the truth. She wanted to run from the house. To find him. To hold him. To love him.

Crazy Mary squeezed her hands. "You are a troublesome young woman. You kept me from reachin' my son."

"Me?"

"Oui," Crazy Mary studied Delta with a warm, congenial expression that belied her strange accusation. "You are not Anne Bonny, sure?"

"Anne Bonny was a pirate who lived and died over a hundred years ago," Delta told her.

Crazy Mary's eyes expanded to form two blue disks in her leathery face. "For truth! I knew I heard tha' name before." She frowned. "You say she is your kin?"

Delta nodded. "She was my great-grandmother several times removed. My name is—"

"Don' tell me." Crazy Mary held up both hands to ward off Delta's words. "Me, I will discover your name. Already I know why you brought yourself here."

Delta stirred nervously. This conversation was becoming more bizarre by the minute. She began to wonder whether the "crazy" in Crazy Mary didn't stand for demented instead of strange. "You know why I'm here?"

"For truth. You love my son."

Tears rushed to Delta's eyes at the simple truth of that statement. Whether it was a mother's intuition or the result of psychic communication didn't matter.

"For truth," she whispered, feeling a tear roll down her cheek and lodge at the corner of her mouth. She touched it with the tip of her tongue and tasted the salt. That much at least was reality.

"Don' be sad, *pichouette*. Anatole, he loves you, *oui*. He will arrive soon now."

Delta pressed her lips between her teeth, too frightened, too confused to utter a sound. Crazy Mary began crooning beside her. "Your name is . . . I almost have it. *Oui*. It is . . . Me, I can almost see it."

Delta scarcely dared breathe.

"Your name is . . ." the strange woman's words drifted off. "It is somethin' about this country—Levee? Jetty? Swamp?"

Delta's confusion turned to distress.

"Delta." Crazy Mary opened her wide blue eyes, a self-satisfied expression lighting her face. "Your name, it is Delta, *oui?*"

Whether it was the incense, the smoke from the candles, or the bizarre events transpiring in the room, Delta felt as though she had left the real world behind. "Delta Jarrett," she supplied.

Crazy Mary's eyebrows shot up. "Me, I could have discover' it for myself. Ah, well, it will save time."

Gabriel, obviously unmoved by the preceding demonstration, spoke up. "You say that Delta, she interfered with your attempts to reach Anatole?"

Delta heard the name slip effortlessly from Gabriel's lips. *Anatole.* Would Brett ever be Anatole to her?

"Oui." Crazy Mary explained. "Ever since Trainor got on his high horse about the Voodoos, I tell you, I

347

know somethin' mus' be done about the man. I start' tryin' to contact Anatole several months ago. But I kept gettin' interference.''

"Interference?" Delta asked.

"Pirates. A man and a woman. Just when I was close to making contact with Anatole, the pirates would flit through my brain. Now I understan', it was your kin.''

Delta failed to see what was apparently so clear to Crazy Mary, but she admitted, "They've been interfering with my life, too.''

"How's tha'?" Crazy Mary demanded.

"I've dreamed about them for months. Strange dreams about Anne Bonny and Calico Jack.'' She hoped the woman wouldn't ask for details. How could she discuss the substance of the dreams with Gabriel present? Or for that matter, with Brett's mother? Again she felt a blush spread across her cheeks. Had Brett's mother dreamed the same dreams?

"Tha' explains it, sure.'' Crazy Mary was nodding energetically, an act that set the little bells around her neck to jingling. "I did not dream of the pirates, but they flitted in and out of my brain. Tha' explains everythin'.''

"Not to me,'' Gabriel admitted.

"Nor to me,'' Delta added.

"You have heard of soulmates, *oui?*''

A lump formed in Delta's throat. She nodded.

"You mean two people whose souls belong together?'' Gabriel questioned.

"*Oui.* Me, I interrupted their search—Anatole's and Delta's souls searchin' for each other. The pirates were tryin' to keep me out of the way.''

Suddenly Delta recalled Brett telling her that under any other circumstances he wouldn't have believed her

348

nightmares. She wouldn't have believed them either, except they had been happening to her. Now, she felt the same doubts about Crazy Mary's extraordinary explanation. Souls searching for each other? And other souls running interference, as it were.

But she had dreamed those dreams. And she had been mysteriously attracted to Brett, and he to her. *Soulmates*. Regardless of how bizarre the concept, it fit exactly the way she felt about Brett.

"There's more to the dreams, though," Delta told Crazy Mary. "They weren't pleasant. They were about death. That's why I left the boat to find Brett . . . ah—"

"Me, I know who you mean," the strange woman assured her.

"For some time now, I've believed that my dreams were a warning—no, a plea, that my ancestors were prompting me to help someone who was in danger. Soon after I met Brett I decided he was the person they wanted me to help."

"Tha' is not uncommon, *non*," Crazy Mary commented.

Although Delta felt it was uncommon to the extreme, she didn't say as much. "For months my dreams were the same, the same scene between the pirates. Then I met Brett and the dreams began to change."

"You are right. Your ancestors used the dreams to guide you, *certainement*."

"One part of the nightmare always remained the same, though," Delta revealed. "All except two dreams ended with a child crying."

Crazy Mary tensed beside her. "*Oui*, a warning for Anatole."

"The pirates had a baby," Delta explained. "Calico

349

Jack hanged without learning about the baby. In my dreams, Anne Bonny was hanged holding her infant daughter in her arms.''

Crazy Mary hung her head, staring toward the flickering candle flames. "The pirates are not restin' easy,'' she said at last. "They never had a chance to grieve, *non.*"

"The baby lived,'' Delta said. "She's considered the matriarch of the Jarrett family. Our impetuous nature is supposed to have come from her, our blue eyes from Calico Jack.''

"Outside space and time,'' Crazy Mary explained, "things we don' resolve on this earth sometimes become intermingled. Tha' is what happened here. It is connect' to our present problem, sure. How much did Anatole—Brett, as you know him—tell you about his difficulty?''

"Only that he's wanted for murder, that he's innocent, but that he can't prove his innocence. He said he didn't want me to know the details because . . . because the crime was so heinous I might believe him guilty and he . . . he didn't want that.''

Crazy Mary was nodding her head, listening, Delta supposed, although she had trouble deciding when the strange woman sitting beside her was operating in the present or off in a trance.

Finally Crazy Mary spoke. "It is time you know the truth. All of it. The truth I have kept lock' in my heart all these years.''

Delta caught Gabriel's startled expression across the room. Neither of them said a word.

"Anatole, he is right,'' Crazy Mary said. "He is innocent, but he wouldn't have been allow' to prove it. Nicole, his wife, she was murdered at their home down the bayou. Olivia,'' Crazy Mary paused, and when she continued, her voice cracked with emotion, "their tiny daughter, Olivia, she was murdered, too."

Delta's stomach churned in violent rejection of Crazy Mary's words. "Brett's daughter?" No wonder he hadn't wanted her to know.

"How could he have been accused of such a thing?" Delta questioned. "Why couldn't he prove his innocence?"

"Him, he was set up, for truth," Crazy Mary stated unequivocally. "Nicole was a whore. From the beginning she was no accoun'. She was never a wife to Anatole, or mother to Olivia, *non*. She took herself aroun' the bayou with any man who would go with her. It was like she had to sleep with ever' man in Louisiana, not once but over and over. And she wanted Anatole to know about each and ever' one of them, sure."

"Why did he put up with it?"

Gabriel answered. "When you know him better, Delta, you'll understand. Me, I always wonder' why he married her in the first place."

"She was like that before they married?"

"*Oui*," Gabriel hissed.

"Nicole, she had a way of exciting men," Crazy Mary explained, "of makin' each man feel like a man. Afterwards, I tell you, she was just as good at tearin' him down."

The room reeled in Delta's fear-blurred vision. Brett's daughter murdered? And him accused of the crime? With difficulty she brought herself back to the present, to the solution rather than the crime. "Why couldn't Brett prove his innocence?"

"The set up was plan' perfect, *oui*. And executed perfect," Crazy Mary explained. "Anatole was off trappin'. He had sold his load of muskrat pelts and was returnin' home. Ever'one at Greer's Landin' heard

351

him say he was on his way home. Ever'one heard him say he expect' to fin' an empty house. Ever'one knew what he meant. Nicole, she never stayed home nights. Come sundown she would take herself off to a *fais-do-do* or to a rendezvous with some new man.''

''But you said she was murdered at home,'' Delta objected.

''She was. It was the perfect setup. Accordin' to say-so spread aroun' the bayou, she stayed home tha' night to welcome Anatole from his month-long trappin' trip.''

Delta's brain whirred with Crazy Mary's story. She'd thought the worst thing that could happen would be to discover that Brett was Anatole Dupré. Now that fear had been realized, and it was worse than any nightmare.

''The story told 'round the bayou was tha' Anatole, he caught his wife with another man,'' Gabriel added in a monotone. ''No man in the bayou would have blamed him for the killin', except for . . .''

''Except for Olivia,'' Crazy Mary completed. ''The perfect setup, sure.''

''But who could believe Brett killed his own child?'' Delta questioned. ''Why couldn't he have searched the bayou for the murderer? It must have been someone who knew her, who knew where they lived.''

''A rejected suitor with wounded pride,'' Gabriel said. ''So the story was told. My cousins, and Anatole's kin, they have look' for the murderer for ten years.''

Crazy Mary squared her shoulders. ''The murderer, he wasn't from the bayou, *non*. Nicole wasn't from the bayou, either,'' she told Delta. ''She was sister to our gov'nor, William Trainor.''

''Dear God,'' Delta whispered on breath that seem

crushed from her lungs. "No wonder he's still after Brett."

"The gov'nor, he is still after Anatole," Crazy Mary said, "because he murder' his own sister and niece. He cannot afford for Anatole to return an' draw attention to the case. Tha' is the reason he wants to run me out of the bayou. A few months ago I decide' the time had come for the truth. We cannot allow such a man to escape punishment any longer, sure."

Delta sat stunned. "What about Brett?" she asked. "The odds against him proving his innocence after ten years will be insurmountable."

"It was Trainor, *certainement?*" Gabriel questioned in a voice that revealed his surprise to be as great as Delta's.

"*Certainement,*" Crazy Mary declared, then added, "But I have no proof that would hold up in court."

"Trainor, does he know you suspect him?"

"He wonders, sure. He has always wonder' what I know. Lately he has become more frighten'. According to say-so, he will run for United States President next time. If tha' is true, I tell you, he cannot afford to leave anyone aroun' to link him to the crime."

Delta's brain flew to a new worry. "He will kill you."

Crazy Mary laughed at that. "*Non, pichouette.* Trainor, he claims not to believe in my powers, but he won' take a chance. The *Anglais,* they are as frighten' of the otherworld as bayou folk. With good reason." She finished with an oath.

Anglais? Delta flinched at the term, though she knew Crazy Mary had not intended it as a slight. Like Gabriel's family, Crazy Mary's contempt for those they termed "English" was obvious. But for some reason she didn't seem to include Delta in that group. Perhaps, like Delta, Crazy Mary considered it inconsequential under the present circumstances. At worst, it was another hurdle she and Brett would have to cross, after they crossed those looming ahead.

Brett's daughter had been murdered! The pain of it brought tears to Delta's eyes. "How old was Olivia?"

"Three years," Crazy Mary told her. "Nicole, she had no interest in the child, so I kept Olivia when Anatole went into the swamps to set his traps. Me, I should have been suspicious tha' day. Nicole never came for the child. It was always Anatole who pick' her up. But tha' day Nicole came early. I should have been suspicious. I hated to allow tha' *bébé* to go with her own mother. But I did, sure. I had no choice. Nicole she said she had a message from her brother, the governor. That she wanted Olivia to see her uncle. I even gave Nicole a pot of filé gumbo for their dinner."

"You knew," Gabriel breathed. "Yet you never told Anatole."

"I never tol' a soul," Crazy Mary said. "If I had, Anatole, he would be the next one to die. If he knew Trainor was at tha' house, he would have charge' the man like an angry bull alligator. And he would have been killed."

"My dreams make more sense," Delta said. "In the last one . . ." She clasped her arms, warding off not the premonition now, but the stark ugly truth of the matter. "My last dream was of a grave." Her eyes found Gabriel's. "That's when I awakened on the boat and convinced you to bring me here. I dreamed of a grave, a child's grave, near the bayou, and of a woman kneeling over the grave crying. And when I awoke I realized the woman in the dreams . . . was myself."

Gabriel stared at Delta, wide-eyed and solemn.

Crazy Mary reached for Delta's hands. She began rubbing them like before.

"Don' worry, *pichouette*. Tha' grave in your dream did not belong to your own *bébé*."

Delta felt her face flame at the suggestion. "No," she managed, shaking her head. But recalling the dream, her fear returned. "I thought it belonged to Brett."

Crazy Mary gripped Delta's hands more tightly. Then she turned to Gabriel. "You left guards aroun' the place, *oui?*"

"*Oui.*"

Crazy Mary rose, pulling Delta to her feet. "Come, both of you. I will show you the *bébé* in your dreams."

Holding Delta by the hand, the tall, strange woman led them across the small clearing that surrounded her cabin and into the woods beyond. They walked silently, Delta numbed by the revelations of the past hour.

Revelations that Brett was indeed wanted for the murder of his wife, and not only his wife, but an infant daughter. The correlation between her dreams and what she was beginning to know as reality filled her with both awe and fear.

They stepped lightly on the damp, soggy ground, which was littered with leaves. The musty odor of decaying nature rose around them. The forest thickened, filled with ghostly shapes of cypress and tupelo and sycamore trees.

Light filtered in thin streams through the masses of gray moss overhead. She looked up expecting to experience the same secure feeling as in the pirogue with Gabriel, but was suddenly chilled by the realization that this was in fact a reenactment of her nightmare.

The sweeping gray moss resembled funeral sprays.

355

By the time Crazy Mary halted at the base of the largest of two enormous oak trees, Delta knew what to expect. A chill wind touched her cheeks—or was that from her dream, as well?

Suffocating with the fear of what was sure to follow, Delta glanced down, and there, as she had known it would be, lay a small mound covered with leaves and moss.

Crazy Mary's voice penetrated her dream world. "This is Olivia's grave. The other is Nicole's. Trainor would not allow them to be buried in the cemetery with his family. Me, I am happy for it."

Releasing Delta's arm, Crazy Mary knelt to the ground. As though her movements were being controlled by some force outside herself, Delta watched the woman straighten the wooden cross at the head of Olivia's grave.

"Ah, such soft earth. I mus' find a way to keep this cross straight, for truth."

Suddenly overcome by the awful reality of it all, Delta fell to her knees. Tears poured from her eyes, dripping to the leaves below. Finally she covered her eyes with her hands and wept. Her head reeled with the ultimate meaning of her dreams and of her presence here. This was the baby who cried in her dreams. Brett's daughter. Brett's murdered daughter. Little Olivia.

Soulmates. Yes, she and Brett were soulmates. And now that they had found each other they would spend the rest of their lives together—as long as Brett remained free and alive. If he even arrived here without being apprehended.

Sobs shook her shoulders. She was conscious of the presence of Gabriel and Crazy Mary, conscious of a need to gain control of her emotions. But she was powerless to shake the sadness that kept her on her knees as if it were a yoke pressing on the shoulders of an ox.

At length she felt hands on her arms, warm hands that reminded her of the way Crazy Mary had taken Gabriel by the arms and looked into his eyes.

"Chère?"

The hands pulled her to her feet, while her brain weighed the word and the voice, and her heart leaped to her throat. She turned in Brett's hands, faced him, stared into his magnificent eyes. In spite of all her efforts, tears continued to roll down her cheeks.

"You're safe," she whispered, still standing with her hands gripping her arms. "Dear God, you're safe." Her words stirred fears inside her, realistic fears that he would not be safe for long.

He stared at her as if he had seen an apparition, scanning her face, her body, the loose-fitting dress Gabriel's sister had loaned her, returning to her face. "You crazy *femme*. You shouldn't have come here." But his tone was soft and belied his words. Suddenly his expression sobered. "Now you know it all."

"Oui." The word escaped on a sob.

With that they fell into each other's arms. Her heart beat so fast she was sure it would play itself out. Brett was here. He was safe—for the time being anyway. She tightened her arms around him and felt his hands on her back, stroking her, holding her near. When he tried to move her head back, for a moment she refused to lift it off his chest. She never wanted to let him go.

But when she lifted her face and felt his lips, soft and tender, on her own, she knew *this* was what she wanted to feel forever. *Soulmates.* What a glorious word. They were soulmates, and so much more.

Finally a measure of sanity returned and she glanced around for Gabriel and Crazy Mary.

"They're waiting at the house," Brett told her. When his eyes strayed beyond her shoulder, she turned in his arms, allowing him to view the grave of his daughter, and beyond it, that of his promiscuous wife.

She slipped her arm around his waist, holding him near, and felt his heart beat fast against her shoulder.

"I never knew where they were buried," he whispered, dropping to his knees in the same spot where he had found Delta.

She knelt beside him, still holding him close. "Olivia had blue eyes," Brett whispered. "As blue as yours, like *Maman's*. That's the last thing I saw of her, those little blue eyes shining from her cold, lifeless body."

Delta held him tighter, feeling his chest rumble with unshed tears.

"I couldn't put them out of my mind," he said. "For ten years I've been haunted by those blue eyes, wondering what I could have done to prevent her senseless death."

Suddenly he turned toward Delta and clasped her head between his palms. He peered solemnly into her eyes, as if searching for the truth. "I'm going to expose the person who did this, *chère*. Do you understand?"

She blinked to hold back a rush of tears. *"Oui."*

"Do you understand what it will mean for us?"

"I understand that I love you and that you love me. And that I'm going to help you solve this problem so we can be free to live the rest of our lives anywhere we want—together." She moved forward in his grasp and kissed his lips. "Come, let's go talk to your mother."

Chapter Eighteen

Within four hours after Cousin Brady, accompanied by Ellie and Aurelia, drove Kale and Carson to the New Orleans depot, the two brothers arrived at the Waterfront Tavern in Baton Rouge.

The lives of these two brothers had taken vastly different courses, Carson's to the Texas Rangers, Kale's to the outlaw trail. Now they had both changed their stripes.

Following his marriage to Aurelia Mazón in Mexico a few months earlier, Carson had resigned his commission in the Texas Rangers to run the Mazón family ranch in Mexico.

Kale had settled down, too, marrying Ellie, widow of Benjamin, the oldest Jarrett brother, after solving Benjamin's murder in Texas.

Both men thought they had hung up their weapons for good. But neither had counted on their little sister, Delta, finding herself in a peck of trouble in Louisiana.

"I still can't figure it," Kale said for the umpteenth time since leaving New Orleans. "That Dupré had to have kidnapped her. Delta wouldn't have run off with the sonofabitch."

"Nope," Carson agreed. "Not Delta. And there

isn't a tree in Louisiana high enough to hang the bastard from, not so's he'll swing through all eternity."

Kale consulted his pocket watch. "Two o'clock. What time are we expectin' Cameron?"

"This afternoon."

"It is this afternoon."

"Barely. I'm itchin' to get on this trail same as you, Kale, but there's not a hell of a lot we can do until Cameron arrives."

Fifteen minutes later Stuart Longstreet entered the Waterfront Tavern and approached Kale and Carson.

"Cameron wired me to meet you here. I'm the agent he sent to look out for her," Stuart admitted to Delta's brothers. "Hate the turn of events." After he brought them up to date on the case, Kale and Carson barraged him with questions.

"You're sayin' Delta ran off with some fiddle player instead of a gambler?" Kale quizzed, his tone caustic.

"The fiddler is a friend of that gambler who the troopers think is Dupré," Stuart explained.

"They don't know?" Carson questioned.

"Nobody knows, to my knowledge. A member of the theatrical troupe on board the *Mississippi Princess* was a bounty hunter by the name of Nathan Thomas. Seems he was on the trail of this Anatole Dupré. He told your sister as much. Gerard speculates Delta went along with the fiddler in search of a story."

"Like hell she did," Kale stormed.

"Not Delta," Carson confirmed. "Who's Gerard?"

"Governor Trainor's aide. He's conducting the governor's end of the manhunt. It was the governor's sister—"

"We heard all that," Kale informed the Pinkerton.

"You searched Delta's cabin on that showboat before it took off for New Orleans?" Carson quizzed.

Stuart nodded. "With Zanna's help. She's the artistic director of the theatrical troupe. She and Delta became close friends. Zanna believes Delta left the boat of her own accord."

"She doesn't know Delta very well, then, if she thinks Delta's that foolhardy," Kale told him.

"Zanna thinks Delta's in love with Reall."

"Who's Reall?" Carson prompted.

"Brett Reall, that's the name the gambler went by."

"He's one and the same with this Dupré?" Carson questioned.

Again Stuart shrugged. "Some folks think so. Me, I don't know. After I came on board he kept pretty much to his cabin, so I didn't get a chance to observe him."

Kale and Carson studied each other, then stared separately into the dusty space of the tavern.

"Delta's not some wet-behind-the-ears kid," Kale commented to no one in particular.

"She wouldn't fall in love with a gambler, certainly not with a murderer," Carson said.

"Unless he duped her," Kale argued. "Men are good at that."

They finished their beer, and still Cameron hadn't shown up.

"Train from Memphis won't arrive for another hour," Stuart told them. "You two best find you a bed to lie down in. It might be the last shuteye you get for a while."

Kale and Carson had just agreed that might be the best suggestion they'd heard in some time, when Luis Gerard arrived with word that the governor wanted a word with "that woman's kin."

"That woman has a name," Kale snapped. "It's Delta. Miss Delta Jarrett."

"We'll be happy to meet with the governor," Carson told the aide. "Long as it can be accomplished within the hour. After that we're off on a manhunt."

The governor, according to his persnickety secretary, had rearranged his busy schedule to accommodate the brothers. His secretary ushered them through the carved double doors, holding her skirts to the side as though their denim and buckskin might contaminate her.

"Wonder if she'll clean the carpet after we leave?" Kale hissed to Carson after they'd entered the ornate office.

Governor Trainor was a man slight in build and in manners. Instead of rising to greet the two men, he merely nodded to a pair of leather wing chairs.

"Gerard tells me you're willing to cooperate with us in bringing this killer to justice."

Kale and Carson mumbled in agreement. "Yes, sir."

"Sure are."

"Then sit and let me fill you in."

The brothers took the indicated seats, which faced the governor's mammoth cherry-wood desk. The governor eyed them from beneath heavily thatched black eyebrows.

"Dupré's a devil. Dangerous as a man can get. He has a lot of family in the bayou who can be expected to hide him, so stay alert for names like Broussard, LeBlanc, Fontaine."

Kale and Carson listened, nodding, trying to record the specifics.

"Bayou folks think highly of Dupré's mother. According to them she can perform miracles. I happen to know she can't, but regardless, this puts you up against odds of a different kind. Her name's Crazy Mary. She's a Voodooienne, a witch.''

The expressions on the brothers' faces changed from solemn attentiveness to wary suspicion.

"Sonofabitch," Kale hissed.

"A witch?" Carson questioned.

Trainor smiled, the satisfied smile of a man accustomed to dominating others. "I don't believe in such nonsense, but most folks in these parts do. You have to take that into consideration when you're dealing with bayou folk.''

Carson expelled a whispered oath. "A murderer and a witch. I'm ready to wake up from this nightmare.''

Trainor continued. "Gerard will act as my lieutenant, leading a company of state troopers. I want the two of you to stick close to them. Don't go initiating things on your own. Understand?''

Carson nodded.

"No," Kale objected. "I don't give a tinker's damn about this Dupré or his mother, witch or not. We're here to find our sister, hopefully before she comes to any harm. If we have to strike out on our own to do it, you can be damned sure that's what we'll do. She's our sister. We call the shots.''

Trainor's eyes narrowed to slits. Veins stood out on the backs of his clenched fists.

"Understand?" Kale barked.

Trainor leaped to his feet. "You insolent cowpoke. What did I expect from a couple of Texans?" He flung an arm toward the door. "Get out of here. If you want to search for your sister, you will do so under my terms or not at all. And if you disobey my instructions, understand this—my troopers will be under orders to shoot first and shoot to kill.''

Kale and Carson headed for the door, but Trainor

called them back with another warning. "If you love this sister of yours half as much as you say, you'll co-operate with my men. We're going to get Dupré. One way or another. The woman that bastard killed was *my* sister, and the child, her baby daughter, was my niece."

Arms entwined, Delta and Brett retraced their steps along the leaf-strewn path to his mother's house. The moment they stepped into the clearing, however, Delta stopped short, as though her feet had suddenly become mired in bayou mud. Apprehensively she glanced around the clearing.

Brett urged her forward. "We're safe for the time being. Gabriel's cousins, my cousins, and Pierre are all out there keeping watch."

Tightening her grip around his waist, she took a ten-tative step. Surrounded by danger as they were, all she wanted was to throw herself in his arms, to hold him and to have him hold her until, like a storm, the danger had passed.

But this was one storm they could not wait out. As surely as they stood here together, it would come. If they didn't defend against it, it would destroy them.

Brett's pace quickened when they neared the house. He dragged Delta up the steps and into the front room, where the first thing she noticed was that the candles and other paraphernalia had been removed from the center of the floor. Crazy Mary rushed to greet her son.

Releasing Delta, Brett swept his mother in his arms, laughing and hugging her. Wordlessly he began to dance her around the room to the beat of some un-heard tune.

Delta stepped back beside a grinning Gabriel to watch this suddenly exuberant Brett. His unrestrained laughter echoed in the otherwise hushed room. He continued to twirl his mother in faster and faster circles, missing the furniture by scant degrees.

Crazy Mary laughed with her son, gaily, as though no cloud hung over their house, over their lives. Her eyes stared intently into his, causing Delta to wonder what transpired between these two people who appeared to be in such intimate communication.

Watching them, Delta was suddenly struck by the truth. It was not Brett Reall she watched dancing with his mother to some silent tune in a shack filled with herbs and potions on a lonely Louisiana bayou. This was not Brett Reall, suave and cynical impostor. It was Anatole Dupré, an uninhibited bayou man who bore no more than a stark physical resemblance to the man with whom she had fallen in love. She had never heard Brett laugh like this, had never seen him dance with such abandon, his guard down, relaxed, happy.

The dance did not end abruptly, as it had begun. Rather, it wound down slowly. After a couple more passes around the room, the dancers halted, still gazing into each other's eyes. Brett held his mother at the waist, while she lifted a hand to smooth back a shock of hair from his forehead, her expression serious, loving. Methodically, as though she were sightless, she traced his features with rough, willowy fingertips, all the time crooning, "Anatole, my Anatole."

Yes, Delta thought, here was the real Brett—Anatole Dupré, not the murderer they made him out to be, but a beloved son, a son who loved in return.

As though she had drunk her fill from a long, refreshing drink, Crazy Mary suddenly dropped her hands and her gaze. Her solemn expression turned to one of mischief. "Eh, Anatole, you are proud of me, *oui?*"

Delta's heart skipped, watching the familiar frown line crease Brett's forehead. Her fingers fairly itched to touch him.

Crazy Mary turned to Delta, reaching for her hand, drawing her to them. "For bringin' you this lovely *pichouette.*"

Brett slid an arm around Delta's shoulders and gathered her to his side. "In case you haven't noticed, *Maman*, Delta Jarrett isn't a little girl." His words teased, but his serious eyes held Delta's and her heart throbbed in her throat.

"Hurrmph!" Crazy Mary laughed. "I call her what I like."

"*Oui, Maman.* I see you have not changed in ten years." He winked at Delta, continuing to tease his mother. "You claim to have brought us together? Aren't you taking credit for an awful lot?"

"Me, I deserve it. Without my help, you might not have met in this lifetime."

Delta listened to the peculiar exchange, unsure how much of it she believed even after all that had transpired. But she didn't really care, since for whatever reason they had met and fallen in love.

"It was the dreams, *oui,*" Crazy Mary was saying. While she continued to explain how her attempts to contact Brett—Anatole, she called him—were interrupted by his and Delta's souls who had been struggling to meet, Brett's hand left Delta's shoulder and moved to the side of her head, which he guided to his chest. Beneath her cheek his heart thrummed quite as erratically as her own.

"The pirates an' me, together," Crazy Mary acknowledged.

"The pirates?" Brett stroked Delta's hair.

"For truth," Crazy Mary insisted. "Delta's dreams about the pirates caused her to take passage on the showboat—and to believe in you, once she met you, even though others advised her not to."

"I experienced a few dreams myself." Brett squeezed Delta's head tighter against his shoulder. "Dreams of some wispy blue-eyed woman."

Crazy Mary's eyes lighted with success. *"Bien."* She beamed at Delta. *"Oui,* I brought her to you. The blue-eyed woman in your dreams."

Brett laughed. Delta felt the rumble in his chest before it exploded from his throat. But when he pulled her face away from his chest and looked down into her eyes, she saw not humor but love. "I don't care who takes the credit, long as I get the girl," he whispered before planting a quick, all-too-chaste kiss on her lips.

Oblivious, Crazy Mary smiled at Delta. "Together we got him home, *oui?"*

Brett gripped Delta's head, pressing it firmly back to his chest. *"Oui,"* he acknowledged, serious again. "Now we must discuss the consequences."

Crazy Mary nodded sagaciously.

"First, let me warn you," he added. "I've come back to clear my name, and I need your help, *Maman."*

Delta's eyes found Gabriel's, just before Brett turned her by the shoulders and peered into her eyes as intently as he had looked at his mother when they danced. One hand left her shoulder and caressed her face.

Tears pooled in Delta's eyes, but instead of blinking to stop them, she let them spill over and roll down her cheeks. "I have a plan." She spoke quickly, lest he interrupt with objections. "We can leave here tonight. With your cousins and Gabriel's cousins for guards, we can escape the bayou. I know we can. We can return to Canada and—''

His thumbs wiped the tears from her cheeks, his eyes pleaded with her to understand. *''Non, chère.* I must clear my name. I want to be free. For us.''

Crazy Mary took Brett by the arm, much as she had done Delta earlier. ''Come. Sit yourselves down. We will discuss the difficulty, sure.''

They sat around a rough-hewn cypress table that was littered with dried plants Delta took to be herbs. Before sitting down herself, Crazy Mary poured coffee for all of them—the same thick, black café they had been served at Gabriel's home. Then she proceeded to tell him the story she had related to Delta and Gabriel earlier.

Brett's first question after his mother finished her tale was voiced in a monotone. ''You've known it was Trainor all along?''

The strange woman nodded. ''Suspected,'' she corrected. ''Not *known* so it could be proved.''

Without warning Brett jumped to his feet, sloshing coffee from every cup at the table, reminding Delta of the old Brett from the showboat, the man of mercurial temperament who was quick to explode. He braced his hands on the table's edge and glared across at his mother. Delta watched, torn between the agony she felt for him and empathy for his mother.

''When you sent me off ten years ago, you knew who the murderer was?'' His voice ricocheted from the thin, single-board walls like a cannon shot. Delta imagined it carrying through the gaps between boards all the way to the bayou, all the way to Baton Rouge and into that stuffy little office of the governor's persnickety secretary.

"Anatole, you could not have prove' your innocence."

"I never had a chance to try." Kicking back his chair he began to pace the floor.

"I tell you, my son, you could not have prove' it, *non,*" she repeated.

Brett raged on. "I've been living in hell for ten goddamn years, and you sit here, knowing all the answers." He stopped to glare at her again. "What right did you have? Tell me that. What right did you have to make such a decision for me?"

Mary Dupré didn't give a hint at being crazy. She sat tall and straight, solemn-faced, neither defensive nor apologetic. Delta watched her, awed by the woman's strength. "Me, I am your mother."

"And I'm your son, your only child," Brett charged. "I deserved the truth."

"Brett—" Delta began.

He turned stormy eyes on her. For an instant his rage ceased. His eyes caressed her face, almost worshipping in their tenderness, but in their depths she saw ten long years of pain and loneliness—and guilt. *Dear God, how she loved this man.*

Abruptly he turned away. Facing a rear window, which was shuttered against the governor's spies, he crossed his arms over his chest. Delta watched his shoulders tremble with his great inner struggle.

"We had no time to find evidence, Anatole," his mother explained. "Trainor, he would not have allow' us time. The troopers, they came no more than an hour after you left. Me, I convince' them you had gone the opposite direction so you could escape, sure."

"Escape? I'm innocent, goddammit," he spat. "I deserved a chance to prove it."

Crazy Mary repeated her reasoning. "You would

369

have had no chance, my son. Don't you know sendin' you away was the hardest thing I ever did? You had three years with Olivia, yet losin' her broke your heart. You had been part of my life for twenty-five years. *Oui,* you were my only son, all I had. Your life was worth ever'thing to me, even if it meant sendin' you away forever.''

"All right," he conceded. "I had to go away for a while. But why ten years? Why not one or five or—"

"You would have had no chance before now, *non.* Trainor, he had no soft underbelly.''

"And he has now?" Brett challenged. "Trainor wants me as badly now as before. I'm still number one on his Most Wanted list. And the evidence, if there ever was any, is ten years old.''

Delta watched Crazy Mary thread her long, worn fingers in and out between each other, making what Ginny told the children was a church with a steeple and a door. Then tearing down the structure, she rebuilt it and tore it down again, speaking, explaining to her son.

"Don't mistake what I say, Anatole. Me, I love you as much as ever, sure, but the time has come to stop that man. He is too powerful. His threats, they don' bother me. It's the principle. Drivin' people away on a whim. No man should be so powerful. Today it is me, or those he calls Voodoos. Who will it be tomorrow? And tomorrow? With ever' success he becomes more powerful.''

"And you want me to be the sacrificial lamb?"

Crazy Mary's eyes followed her son, as he crossed the room and sat again beside Delta.

"I tell you, no one else holds such a black-black secret over him.''

"Non? He has come this far, murdered his own sister

370

and niece, and done nothing else a man could hold against him?''

Crazy Mary shrugged and in that innocent gesture Delta found a word that described this strange woman: elegance. Not the kind of elegance found in fancy drawing rooms or governor's mansions, but an elegance of spirit. It shone like a star in all she did—in her words, in her gestures, in the manner she accepted her son's accusations, in the way she had danced with him and gazed into his eyes, in the way she had straightened the cross on her granddaughter's grave. Mary Dupré was a woman of elegance.

''A man who *can* speak against him?'' Crazy Mary quizzed. ''Or a man who *will?* Like you say he prob'ly has committed other crimes. But me, I have seen no one willin' to call his hand.''

Brett stared into the empty depths of his coffee cup. ''He sets his traps as carefully as I.''

Rising, Gabriel carried the heavy pot around the table refilling cups. ''Your traps are for pelts to earn your living, *mon ami*. Trainor's traps, they are for people who get in his way.''

Brett rested his elbows on the table, threaded his fingers through his hair and supported his head. ''How did Nicole get in his way? Or Olivia?''

''Me, I don't know the truth.'' Crazy Mary tried to explain her theory. ''Nicole's lifestyle embarrass' her family, sure. She would have been a big-big problem, her brother runnin' for gov'nor.'' She paused, finding her son's eyes. ''Olivia, who can say what prompt' such a tragedy? Perhaps he didn't expec' her to be home.''

''Or perhaps Trainor, he wanted to cut all ties with the bayou,'' Gabriel offered.

"Never mind the reason, the bastard deserves to die for that alone," Brett hissed.

His words fell like stones in the ensuing silence. Suddenly he reached for Delta's hands, grasping them, holding them against the tabletop. His eyes found hers, piercing into her soul. "Ah, *chère,* you found yourself a real nightmare, coming here."

"It's where I want to be."

"For truth," he muttered derisively.

She moved her hands until she was clasping his. "With you. That's where I want to be. Wherever that is. Whatever it means."

"I told you what it means."

She attempted to smile, but knew she didn't quite succeed. "We're already halfway through. We know who did it."

His hands tightened their grip, but she watched his eyes soften. His mouth moved into that thin line of a smile she recognized from the showboat. She knew now how that smile could explode into laughter. And now that she knew, she wondered when she would ever hear him laugh again—and what ghastly occurrences they would face before she did.

Brett turned at last to his mother. "How d'you propose I stop him?" He winked at Delta. "You could drive him mad with nightmares, like you almost did Delta."

"Me, I did not bring Delta those nightmares," Crazy Mary declared. Turning solicitously to Delta, she asked, "You know tha', for truth, *pichouette?*"

"For truth," Delta responded with verve, eager to reassure this woman who had so recently been berated by her son.

"Whatever we do," Gabriel put in, "one thing's clear. We have to prove Trainor's guilt. If we try the innocent-till-proven-guilty approach, you, *mon ami,* will fin' yourself swingin' from the nearest oak limb, *certainement.*"

Delta flinched, and Brett tightened his grip. "Then we'll prove it," he snapped.

"First thing we do," Crazy Mary said, "we mus' get Trainor to the bayou, away from his own surroundings." She ran a finger back and forth along one of the long grains on the table top. "We get him out here, *oui,* then we scare the truth out of him."

"The man won't scare easy," Brett warned. "Else someone would have tacked his hide to the barn door long before now."

"It won't be easy, *non,*" his mother agreed. "But we mus' try, even if we don' succeed."

Delta's mouth went dry.

"We'll succeed, *Maman,*" Brett responded, but Delta suspected his show of optimism was for her benefit.

Crazy Mary continued to plan. "We'll gather folks from up and down the bayou for a séance. That will worry him, *non?*"

"I wouldn't bank on it," Brett argued.

"*Oui,* if we set him up first, like he set you up, Anatole. We'll convince him the devil's out to get him. That'll loosen a man's tongue, for truth." She rose and refilled their coffee cups again, speaking all the while. "Gabriel, you and Pierre will go to Baton Rouge and spread the *gris-gris.*"

Again Brett doubted. "It'll take more than a few bags of tricks to frighten Trainor. We need evidence— or something he thinks is evidence."

"For truth," Crazy Mary agreed. "A special kind of *gris-gris.*" Rising again, she rummaged through one of the cabinets at the far end of the room, returning with a small wooden box. When she withdrew a gold chain, Brett's eyes fastened on it.

She held it forth, but Brett made no move to touch the small charm that dangled from it.

"Olivia's," he muttered.

"Oui, it was aroun' Olivia's little neck," Crazy Mary agreed, "when they brought her here for burial."

Delta watched Brett purse his lips between his teeth. After a long moment, he reached for the chain, cradling the charm in the palm of his hand, studying it, lost in dreams.

Or nightmares? Delta wondered. When he looked up, tears glistened in his eyes.

"It belonged to Olivia." He held the charm for Delta to read the inscription: *Olivia. May 9, 1866.* "The date of her baptism," he explained. "This is the crest of the *respected* Trainor family. This particular charm has been worn by the oldest daughter in the Trainor family for generations. It belonged to Nicole. When William Trainor saw it around Olivia's neck at her baptism, he became enraged, said it besmeared the family name for her to wear it."

"A baby girl?" Delta whispered, unable to contain her shock.

Brett nodded, still staring at the charm that swung from his fingers. "How will this help?"

Crazy Mary withdrew another item from her box. A gold stickpin for a man's tie.

"Madame Hebert said she found it," Brett said, his voice confused now rather than accusing.

Delta looked closely at the crest on the stickpin.

Brett explained. "The Trainor family crest, same as on the charm. There were two of them, the stickpin and the charm. Nicole never wore her charm. I suspect the only reason she put it on Olivia for the baptism was to anger her brother. William Trainor was never without his.'' He squinted at his mother. ''How did it come to be in my house?''

''No one knows for sure,'' Crazy Mary acknowledged. ''Madame Hebert brought it to me. She found it lodged between two boards in the kitchen when they moved from their shack into your house.''

Brett inhaled, holding his breath behind pursed lips.

Crazy Mary continued. ''Earlier, the afternoon of the funeral to be specific, M'sieur Hebert had seen someone approach the house.'' She turned to Delta. ''That was before the Heberts moved into the house themselves.'' She continued her story. ''When he went to investigate, he saw William Trainor through the open *tablette*. Trainor was on his hands and knees searching for something. When he heard M'sieur Hebert, he hurried to his feet, mumbled something about paying respects to his sister by visiting the scene of her death.''

Beside her, Delta felt Brett exhale his pent-up breath. His fist connected with the table of a sudden, setting the cups to rattling. ''It all adds up,'' he fumed. ''Trainor was at the house that night; he had the troopers on me before anyone could have reasonably known about the murders; he didn't stay for the funeral, but turned up at the house again that same day, searching the floor; later Madame Hebert finds this.'' He squeezed the stickpin in his fist. ''It all adds up. If I'd known one of these things, just one—''

''You would have gotten yourself killed,'' Crazy Mary interrupted.

Brett breathed in and out in great heavy drafts.

''And you wouldn't be here today, sitting at my table with this lovely *pichouette* by your side . . .'' she added.

375

Without looking at her, Brett reached for Delta's hand, clasping it as tightly as he had the stickpin a moment earlier.

". . . with the chance to clear your name, at last," Crazy Mary finished.

For the longest time silence reigned about the table. Finally Brett asked. "How will you use these things?"

"I won't use them alone," she explained. "We'll cover Trainor with gris-gris, like dirt on his coffin." Gathering momentum, she spoke to Gabriel, planning aloud. "You will take these things to the Voodooienne in Baton Rouge, *oui*. Olivia's charm, it goes in a little sack with some dirt, to be left among Trainor's underclothes in his dressing room. I'll cook up a bowl of *congris* to set under that oak tree in front of Trainor's fancy house. Somewhere I have a dried toad to place inside his pillow. Dirt mus' be sprinkle' aroun' a line of pebbles tha' will lead to a pluck' rooster with nine silver pins stuck in its breast. The rooster, he mus' be hung in a tree in Trainor's backyard."

Delta listened, her despair growing. "I don't doubt your powers," she said at length, "but how can Pierre and Gabriel accomplish all this without the governor discovering them. His servants will see—"

"It is his servants who will aid us," Crazy Mary explained. "Me, I've been in contact with a true Voodooienne who counts several of the gov'nor's servants as clients. They will do anything she tells them and keep their mouths shut. For truth, they would be afraid not to."

Delta's eyes swept the room, taking in the rows of brown jars and the bunches of dried herbs. Her head swirled with all she had seen and heard, with the necessity to free Brett from the hold Governor Trainor had on his life. But she felt caught in a vortex of something strange and mysterious. They were play-acting, when they needed to face reality. What would her family, whose feet were planted firmly on the ground, think of attempts to solve a person's problems by black magic?

"Don't worry, *chère,*" Brett told her. "*Maman* knows about these things. Most people, even if they don't believe in psychic powers, are frightened enough of their own death to fear black magic. *Maman* doesn't practice black magic, but she knows those who do. She can pull this off, if anyone can." He fingered the little gold charm. "I still don't understand—"

"William Trainor, he believes we buried Olivia with this charm aroun' her neck." Crazy Mary's voice sent a chill down Delta's spine. "Trainor, he came here for the funeral, *oui,* but he did not remain for the burial. Now we know he went back to that house to search for his lost stickpin." She smiled at her son. "Me, I know you do not believe such things, Anatole, but before they close' the coffin, somethin' told me to take this little charm from aroun' Olivia's neck—for you. Now I understand, it was not for a keepsake, for sure. When Trainor finds this charm in a sack of dirt, he'll think it came from her grave, *certainement.*"

"Graves are used to put curses on people," Brett explained, although by this time Delta had decided their explanations were falling a little short. She would never understand such things. She was almost afraid to try.

"Pierre and Gabriel, they will take themselves to Baton Rouge, *oui.* They will leave the *gris-gris* with the Voodooienne," Crazy Mary planned. "The following morning they will arrange for Trainor to find a warning—from Olivia, I think—written in chicken blood on his back doorstep. It will instruct him to find his matching piece of jewelry on her grave. He will bring himself out here, right quick."

"Won't he know the stickpin can't prove his guilt?" Delta questioned.

Crazy Mary nodded. "But he will want to shut me up, sure. An' he won' know what proof I have of his guilt. That he mus' bring himself to the bayou to discover before—"

"You mean he'll come out here to kill you?" Delta questioned, aghast.

Crazy Mary grinned. "Don' worry yourself, *pichouette*. He would be afraid to kill me because of my powers. An' he will find it hard to engage others to do this foul deed for the same reason."

"She will be guarded well," Gabriel added.

"I tell you, by the time we finish with William Trainor," the strange woman predicted, "tha' man, he will be so confuse' and frighten' he'll confess and not even know it, sure."

The plan seemed awfully weak to Delta, but she held her tongue. Gabriel on the other hand appeared satisfied. He scraped back his chair. "Me, I'll go find Pierre. Sooner we start, the sooner we finish."

Brett rose. Pulling Delta's chair back, he took her in his arms. "You'll be safe here with *Maman*. We won't be gone over a day or two."

"Non," Crazy Mary objected.

Brett cocked his head, waiting for his mother's explanation.

"You Anatole, you aren't takin' yourself to Baton Rouge. Half the state is lookin' for you, an' the other half would turn you in for a bayou song. You mus' hide till we're sure Trainor is on his way."

Brett opened his mouth to object, but Gabriel cut in. "I agree. Gaston and Carl can take you down the bayou to tha' cabin on Fontaine's *chênière,* unless they know a better place.''

Again Brett objected, but again he was overruled.

''Anatole,'' his mother argued, ''you will listen to your *maman, oui?* We can't chance the troopers capturin' you before we get Trainor to the bayou, *non.''*

''Listen to your *maman,''* Gabriel teased. ''If you want to come out of this with your hide on, keep yourself low till we're ready for you.'' He grinned. ''You, too, Delta. If you stay here, Trainor's spies might get wise. You mus' go into hidin' with Anatole.''

Chapter Nineteen

They didn't leave Crazy Mary's cabin until dusk, having determined that to be the safest time for Brett to travel. As Gabriel put it, "Trainor's men, they won' wander aroun' the swamps after dark, for fear the Zombi'll swallow 'em up."

In the hours remaining before dusk, Crazy Mary sacked the *gris-gris,* which, Brett explained, was "paraphernalia used in casting spells or warding off evil or illness or even in effecting white magic, such as warming the heart of a lover or persuading a stingy husband to spend his money."

Delta tried to remain open-minded about these things, but so much hung in the balance—Brett's life, their future. Whatever else witchcraft could or could not do, she prayed it would elicit a confession from William Trainor.

Crazy Mary bustled around the cabin preparing things Delta had never seen or heard of—black devil oil, conjure balls, and a mixture of herbs and oils she took from the little brown jars and placed in tiny black paper sacks. Once, she put them both to work: Brett, to making feather crosses; Delta, to writing William Trainor's name on several scraps of paper.

"This piece of cloth—" Crazy Mary held up a scrap of material that was so brown it looked burnt, "—it has been soakin' in bayou mud two weeks. Trainor, he will think it's from a shroud." She dropped the material in the sack, then added several other ingredients, naming each in succession—one dried lizard, the wings of a bat, the little finger of a—"

"Sh, *Maman,*" Brett interrupted. "Go easy on the details until Delta gets used to us." He drew Delta close, holding her face in his hands, and kissed her tenderly. "You all right?"

She smiled. "I don't care how strange it sounds if it works."

Fortified by several bowls of Crazy Mary's gumbo, Pierre and Gabriel prepared to leave for Baton Rouge carrying burlap sacks filled with the *gris-gris.*

"Save me some of tha' gumbo," Pierre told his sister-in-law. "I tol' ever'body in Canada you make the best gumbo in Louisiana." He turned to Brett. "You, Anatole, you keep yourself in hiding till someone comes for you."

Brett agreed with qualifications. "Timing's important, so be sure you come for us before Trainor gets here."

"*Oui.*" Pierre glanced at Delta. "Both of you stay right here in Mary's cabin till dusk, then keep yourselves on that *chênière* till someone comes."

"Someone you recognize," Gabriel added.

Brett grinned. "Get out of here, both of you. Let's get this show started."

The two men lingered a few moments longer, heightening Delta's anxiety. Their reluctance to bid Brett farewell bespoke their concern for the outcome of this charade.

And that after all was what it amounted to. She

thought perhaps she might relax if she knew more about Governor Trainor. How susceptible would he be to black magic? The plan was to draw him to the graves where he would expect to find evidence of his guilt.

But instead of hard evidence, he would find his gold stickpin . . . and Brett—or, Anatole Dupré—who, according to the plan, would elicit a confession from the governor. A simple plan. Far too simple. Delta worried over that.

When Crazy Mary showed them another little box in which she had placed Trainor's stickpin, Delta began to tremble.

Brett pulled her to his chest and held her tightly while his mother explained, "This goes in a hole in the grave under a black candle. When Trainor comes to fin' the evidence, we'll catch him."

A simple plan, Delta thought again. Too simple.

Watching Crazy Mary resume her task, Delta recalled Hollis mentioning witchcraft and Voodoos before she left St. Louis, and his comment that no one up there believed in such things.

Well, folks down here certainly believed in them. At least, she hoped they did, one person above all others—William Trainor.

While Brett helped his mother gather supplies to take to the *chênière,* they talked of the bayou, of who was still living, who had died, who had moved away, of how the trappers were faring, how her work was going. He was different from the man she had fallen in love with on the showboat, almost another person. No longer the sophisticated gambler whose speech was groomed for city ears, he spoke the dialect of the bayou, much of which Delta had trouble interpreting.

He didn't laugh with total abandon again, nor did he again berate his mother for having kept this dreadful secret from him these ten long years. He seemed comfortable and very happy to be home in the bayou cabin with its strange furnishings and even stranger inhabitants. Reacclimating himself, he tried his hand at recalling names of the herbs that hung from the rafters in bunches, drying—sassafras roots and palmetto and arris and saffron.

Yes, she decided, this was a new man, or at least a side of the man she had not seen before. This was Anatole Dupré. Where was Brett Reall? *Who* was Brett Reall?

From time to time he drew her into the conversation, questioning her knowledge of various herbs and potions, explaining when she didn't know the answer. At those times, when his eyes found hers, she saw Brett's eyes, and when, on occasion, he passed her in search of some new thing with which to test her, he would plant a soft kiss on her lips.

With Brett's lips.

Once Crazy Mary went out back with hatchet in hand. Delta watched from the window as the woman adroitly caught a chicken, laid it across the chopping block, and proceeded to chop off its head.

Brett came up behind Delta, enclosed her in a tight embrace, and nuzzled his head against hers, while together they watched his mother at her task.

"This must be worse than your most frightening nightmare," he said.

She felt his arms around her, felt his breath against her cheek. Covering his arms with her own, she snuggled back against him. "It's better than my best dream, being in your arms." She turned in his embrace and looked into his earnest eyes.

His lips descended quickly, tenderly claiming hers, leaving her weak and trembling. She wondered whether it was desire or fear that weakened her most at this moment.

"What is the *chênière* where we're to hide?" she asked.

"An island," he responded, letting his lips drift over her face. His breath fluttered loose wisps of hair about her temples. "The word means oak. These inland islands take their name from the oak trees that struggle to grow on them. There's a cabin, at least there used to be. It won't be fancy. Likely it won't even smell very good. It's in muskrat country. Trappers use it in season, other times it's abandoned."

"We'll be safe from the troopers there?"

He nodded, nipping kisses to her lips.

"And from the Pinkertons?"

"The Pinkertons?"

"They're certain to have joined the search now that I'm gone," she confessed. "Stuart will have wired Cameron, and Cameron wouldn't sit around and let me disappear without conducting a search." Her heart began to pound as this new fear took root and began to grow at an alarming rate. "I've led them right to you, Brett. How could I have been so foolish?"

"Without your help I've managed to get enough men after me to make life more than difficult. You haven't done any harm. Except to yourself." His eyes turned stony. He drew her to his chest and cradled her head in his hands.

Gabriel's cousin, Carl, came at dusk, and they left with him, loaded with provisions Crazy Mary insisted on sending along.

"We aren't going away for a week, *Maman,*" Brett objected, but he obligingly took the sacks of food and bedding and placed them in the bottom of the pirogue. Delta sat facing him, while he took the stern, picked up the pole, and shoved off, following Carl's boat. Crazy Mary had stayed inside, hoping to draw less attention to their departure.

But when Delta saw the curtain flutter at the window, her stomach gripped in knots. Crazy Mary was watching for a last glimpse of her son, hoping—Delta was certain—that it would not be the last.

No one expected this scheme to work, she thought suddenly. Not Pierre or Gabriel. Not even the *witch* who was supposed to cast the magic spells.

They headed down the bayou, just the two of them in the pirogue. But they were not alone. Gabriel's cousins escorted them in pirogues through the still, black waters, and Brett's cousins guarded them from the forests to either side.

Fear coated her body with a sheen of sweat. She studied Brett through the shadowy mists. "What are our chances?" she whispered, afraid to speak louder.

He held her stare for such a long time she knew he interpreted her meaning, but when he spoke it was to lighten her mood. "For what, *chère?* A night alone in the bayou, us? *Bien,* I would say. Very, very good."

The thrill his jesting raised along her spine was enough to alleviate some of her fear for this man, who had been her lover for months now in one guise or another. If they were to be set upon at any moment, she should at least savor the time they had left.

"That, Brett Reall, is a matter too serious to joke about."

"Who's joking?"

She glanced from side to side, taking in the pirogues of the LeBlanc men, then looking deeper into the forest where unseen eyes of Brett's cousins, the Broussards, watched and protected them.

Brett chuckled. "They won't remain at the *chênière.*

Not if I have to skin and stretch each one of their hides myself.''

The full moon rose, filtering moonlight through the dense foliage above them, casting the lacy cypress leaves and dripping moss as eerie shadows across the pirogue.

Night sounds surrounded them, amplified by the darkness. Delta tried to relate the bird calls, the ka-roomps of bullfrogs, the sudden splashes in the water here and there to the trip she and Gabriel had taken through the bayou in daylight, but this journey seemed to be on another planet, so different was it from the other.

Brett stood silently at the rear of the small boat, moving it, guiding it with the force of his pole. He followed several yards behind Carl's pirogue, which led the way. His quiet presence soothed her jitters to no more than a troubled flutter in the pit of her stomach. Anticipation of spending the night alone with him stirred in a small corner of her mind.

''Brett—'' She had intended to ask him how much farther to the *chênière,* when another concern crossed her mind.

''What do I call you? Anatole sounds so strange, so unlike *you.* ''

He chuckled. ''I've gone by Brett so long I have trouble with anything else, too. Except for Gabriel and Pierre no one has called me by my given name in ten years.''

She watched his solid black form maneuver the boat through the still waters. ''You're Brett to me,'' she said at length.

''Then that's what you should call me, *chère.* ''

''I will. Brett will be your ti' name.''

The trip took an hour, more or less, and even that

caused worry. Were they far enough from Crazy Mary's cabin to be safe? Close enough to return in time to confront William Trainor, saying the governor fell for the ruse and ventured into the bayou?

When their pirogue nudged the bank beside Carl's, Brett jumped out, pulled the boat to level ground, and reached for Delta. Moonlight cast its silver brilliance over the small island, giving it the appearance of a stage set whose outer limits were ringed by the darkness of the theater. She tried to identify something, anything as being familiar, from her own world, but except for the small cabin sitting on stumps, she didn't see another familiar form.

"Where are all the oak trees?" she asked suddenly.

Beside her Brett chuckled. "Only the strong survive on a *chênière*. There may be a few oaks left, the survivors. You'll see, come morning."

Carl, along with Gaston who had by now anchored his own pirogue alongside the other two, helped Brett carry the supplies to the cabin. Carl came out holding his nose.

"Me, I'd sleep out here in the open," he suggested. "No tellin' what those trappers left behind."

"Don't light a fire," Gaston cautioned. "Not at night so's the light can be seen on shore, sure."

"We'll make pallets on the *galerie*," Brett agreed. "*Maman* sent crab cakes and crawfish pie we can eat cold."

Carl and Gaston left after reiterating Pierre and Gabriel's warnings not to leave the island until someone they knew returned for them.

"Couple of days, your *maman* thinks," Carl said.

"Don't you go gettin' impatient and take yourself away from here," Gaston warned.

Standing on the *galerie*, Delta watched the two men

shove their pirogues into the bayou waters and disappear into the darkness beyond the circle of moonlight. When she turned, Brett was staring at her.

The moon was in her eyes, casting him in silhouette like a black, lifeless statue.

"Do you want—?" he began.

"You know what I want," she whispered, rushing to his arms, which came around her, crushing her to his lean, hard body, holding her against his racing heart. He covered her lips with his own.

He kissed her deeply, passionately, his desperation echoing hers. Finally he drew her face back and laved it with kisses.

"Now I know what real fear is," she told him. "It was worse than any nightmare, thinking I might never see you again." Her words called to mind her last nightmare, and she tightened her grip on him. "Except if you were dead. I thought you were—"

"Sh, *chère.*" He kissed her trembling lips. "We're together now. We'll be together forever." Finally he released her. "We have two days before we see another person. Why don't we eat and fix our pallet and then—" he nipped her lips, "—then we can get down to business."

While Delta unpacked the basket of food, Brett shook out quilts his mother had sent. He spread them on the *galerie* floor close to the staircase leading to the *grenier*.

"Fortunate *Maman* prepared us to camp out. She must have seen the state of this cabin in a trance." He shook out the mosquito netting, fastening it to the *grenier* stairs and the wall to form a tent above the mattress of quilts he had spread for them.

"She saw?" Delta questioned.

Straightening, he studied her.

388

"Do you think she really *saw* this cabin?" Delta asked again. "I mean, could she see . . . us?"

In two steps he reached her, taking her in his arms, laughing. "My modest *chère*. You don't want my *maman* looking in on us?"

"I don't want anybody looking in on us."

He squeezed her to him. "Neither do I. To answer your question, no I don't think she can see us. Not unless we're standing right in front of her." He kissed her. "But don't tell her I said that."

Delta laughed, but when Brett began to run his hands down her body, she sobered, looking out at the black wilderness surrounding them. "What about all those kinfolk of yours and Gabriel's?"

Grinning seductively, his hands cupped her breasts. "Must have been some amorous muskrat trapper who built this place. Come morning you'll see. The *galerie* fronts nothing but water as far as the eye can see." His lips nipped kisses along her neck while he spoke. "Tonight you'll have to trust me." Moving his lips to hers, he mumbled, "Do you?"

She trembled with anticipation. *"Oui."*

His hands left her breasts, tracing over her midriff, splaying across her belly. "Where'd you get this dress?"

"From one of Gabriel's sisters," she whispered, because her heart beat so furiously she could hardly speak.

"I like it." His husky voice sent shivers down her spine.

"I thought you would, since it wasn't designed by a demented monk."

With a groan of satisfaction, he unfastened the button at her neck and stripped the dress over her head, his hands skimming her intimately in the process. Next

389

he removed her slip and bloomers, leaving her trembling and nude and burning with want.

But when she reached for his shirt, he held her back.

"Let me look at you." As he had done in her stateroom, he began with her hair, stroking and admiring his way down her body, until fire raged inside her.

"Brett, please—"

"Let me look," he whispered. His thumbs teased her nipples until they stood erect in the moonlight. Leaving them, he stretched his fingers around her waist, touching thumbs in front, fingers in back.

Suddenly she realized what he had done that night in her stateroom. He had memorized her body, thinking he would never see it again. And now? What was he thinking now?

"Brett, I'm frightened."

He spread his palms over her stomach, then moved his hands around and clasped her buttocks, slipped below them, circling again, tangling fingers in the triangled mat of curls, dipping inside her heated, weeping core. "Ah, *chère*, don't be frightened. Not tonight." Slipping his fingers in and out, his lips tasted hers, then moved down her neck, leaving a wet trail to dry in the sultry air.

When his lips tugged at her breast, her head swayed, and she reached for his shoulders to steady herself. She felt his mouth leave her breast, trail down her chest. He dropped to his knees, laving her belly with his tongue, stoking the heat inside her to almost unbearable heights. She watched moonlight glint in silver beams from his black hair. She saw his head drop lower, felt his tongue trail down her belly, felt his lips touch the curly patch of hair.

One of his hands went around her, cupping her buttocks, drawing her to him. Her nails bit into the flesh

390

on his shoulders when she felt his mouth against her, kissing her, caressing her, his tongue darting in and out in hypnotic rhythm.

"Brett . . . ?" she murmured, feeling herself on that cliff again, staring down into the spiraling river of fire again. She shut her eyes against the brightness. "No, Brett . . ." she murmured, even as her hands slipped to his head, even as she pressed his face against her, filling her with agony. Sweet, fiery agony.

But still he loved her with his mouth, his lips stroking, his tongue darting and teasing, dipping and tasting, devouring her.

She felt herself leave the precipice, as though she were being hurled into space. Below her swirled that fiery river. "No, Brett . . ."

Still he loved her, until she never wanted it to stop. But it did. She felt her body convulse against him, felt him redouble his sweet assault, felt herself plunge at last into that fiery river.

When she surfaced, he was retracing his path to her lips. Her breath came heavy, in gasps. When his face reached hers, he stared long into her eyes, his breathing as labored as her own.

"That was making love." He grinned, sweeping her in his arms. "Now let's try it another way."

He deposited her on the pallet inside the mosquito netting, and began stripping off his own clothes. "Did the mosquitoes eat you up?"

"No," she whispered, feeling him lie down beside her. Their pallet was in shadows, so she couldn't see his face, but she heard him laugh.

"Ah, *chère,* you were buzzing too loud to hear them." His lips found hers, and she snuggled into his embrace, feeling his rigid arousal, hot and demanding against her belly.

Boldly moving her hand between them, she grasped his arousal, stroking him with a tight fist.

His breath quickened. "Ah, *chère, non* . . ."

Her kisses deepened and she knew what he was feeling, knew how wonderful it was, so she didn't stop. Finally she shifted her hips until she could draw him to her, guiding him with her hands until she felt him plunge to her depths. Afterwards she clung to him, and they rode the crests of passion together, until at last they lay sated and wet in each other's arms.

In each other's arms. Suddenly she recalled thinking the same thing on the boat, the night he went overboard. He had returned to her that night, she'd thought forever. But he had known even as they loved, that he was leaving.

Fear gnawed inside her, bringing her recently spent emotions to life. Two days on this island, and after that, what? She tightened her hold on him, felt tears rush to her eyes.

"What is it, *chère?*"

"I'm so frightened."

"I know. But it's almost over. Two days."

"Then what?"

He lay still in her arms. She felt his heart steady and strong against her. In two days would it still beat with life and love?

"Let's take these two days for what they are," he suggested. "A gift. Two days alone on a deserted island. What more can we ask?"

She snuggled into his embrace, her fears unassuaged. She knew she should try to pretend all was well, for his sake. But she was so afraid of losing him.

"I would go away with you," she said into his chest. "We could lose ourselves somewhere, anywhere, as long as we're together."

He stroked her hair, his fingers tangling through its length. "I have to clear my name, Delta. I can't live with you without clearing my name."

"It wouldn't matter to me."

"Someday it would. Someday you would get tired of running, tired of hiding. I have to clear my name. I've known that for some time now."

"Since when?"

He pondered the question, then answered with a chuckle. "I suppose since that first night on the showboat when we dined at the captain's table."

His answer startled her. Lifting a hand, she traced the outline of his lips with her fingers.

"When you told me you had six brothers," he continued, "I knew I'd better clear my name before I met them or my name would be black as bayou mud."

Cameron arrived on schedule at the Waterside Tavern where he found two impatient cousins biding their time with his equally impatient agent, Stuart Longstreet.

"It's been a coon's age," Carson said, shaking Cameron's hand.

"Sorry for the circumstances."

"Let's get this show on the road," Kale said. "What'd you have to go on?"

"I just left the state house," Cameron told them. "The troopers are ready to ride, with or without us. I could tell, from talking to Gerard, that the governor wants us along." He eyed his two cousins. "Seems he doesn't trust the two of you not to strike out on your own. He's ordered his troopers to keep you in their sights."

"That bastard," Kale fumed.

Carson flipped coins on the table to pay for the drinks and picked up his hat.

Before they could leave, however, two men entered the tavern. At the sight, Stuart let out a low whistle and headed toward them. He confronted Gabriel with a harsh demand.

"Where's Delta?"

Gabriel and Pierre exchanged glances.

Stuart motioned toward the group he had just left. "Come over here. I want you to meet some fellers." The introductions made, he faced Gabriel again. "Let me repeat the question. These two Jarretts are Delta's brothers, the other a cousin. They're mighty anxious to hear what you have to say."

"You're damned right we are," Kale barked.

Carson eyed the newcomers. "We were just headin' over to the state house. Why don't you boys come along and tell your story to the governor?"

"The troopers are fixin' to ride out after you and that murderin' sonofabitch who kidnapped Delta," Kale added.

"No one kidnapped Delta," Gabriel told them. "She's fine."

"What'd you mean by fine?" Carson challenged. "Where is she? We know damned well she didn't ride off with some criminal who disguised himself as a gambler."

"*Non,*" Gabriel admitted. "Sit yourselves right here, an' we'll explain."

"The troopers are ready to ride," Cameron objected.

"Hear me out," Gabriel encouraged. "You might decide to join us instead of ridin' with the gov'nor's henchmen, *oui.*"

Each man eyed the other, then by mutual, if silent, consensus, took his seat.

"Be quick about it," Carson commanded, his glare conveying more clearly than words, his doubt that Gabriel would be able to convince this group of anything.

Pierre and Gabriel sat facing the Jarretts and Stuart Longstreet. Gabriel did the talking.

"Me, I'm the one she rode off with."

Kale scraped his chair back; Carson shot a restraining hand to his brother's arm; Kale settled back down, but remained tensed, ready to strike at a moment's notice.

"When Pierre here and Anatole slipped away from the boat below St. Francisville, Anatole, he left me behind to see after Delta."

"To see after her? Why?" Kale challenged.

"So that gambler is the murderer?" Carson questioned.

"He is Anatole Dupré, *oui*, but he is not a murderer, *non*."

Not a man across the table showed a sign of believing Gabriel's claim.

"Delta brought herself to my cabin two nights later in Baton Rouge," Gabriel continued. "She had a dream tha' convinced her Anatole, Brett she calls him, was in danger, dead, maybe. The way she described her dream, I thought so, too, for truth. Either way, me, I knew Delta was in danger on the boat. Those who hunt Anatole, who have hunt' him for ten years, they are evil men. They would stop at nothin', *non*, not even at takin' an innocent woman hostage, to draw him out of hidin'."

"Time's wastin'," Kale barked. "Where can we find Delta? Are you prepared to lead us to her?"

"Delta's in hidin' with Anatole."

"Will you take us there?" Carson questioned.

Gabriel perused the men.

"We're set to ride with the troopers," Cameron warned.

"The troopers, they will kill Anatole, and if they think she is a threat, they will kill Delta along with him, *certainement.*"

"Delta's no threat to anyone," Kale said.

"She knows the truth," Gabriel said simply.

"What truth?" Carson demanded.

"The truth about who murdered Anatole's wife and child ten years ago."

Even Kale withered at that. Cameron sank back to his chair, and Carson challenged Gabriel. "Tell us your side of this story, and be quick."

Complying, Gabriel sketched the story beginning with Nicole's promiscuity, ending with Anatole learning the identity of the murderer only the day before.

When he finished, the men from Texas sat in dazed silence.

Carson found his voice first, but he was unable to hide his skepticism. "You say this Anatole's mother, the witch, is putting a hex on the governor of Louisiana?"

"I tell you," Gabriel said, "Trainor, he's a wicked man. He will stop at nothin', and him, he thinks nothin' can stop him."

"That's the first thing you've said I can take as gospel," Kale responded. He looked at Carson. "You saw it, too. Trainor's a manipulatin' sonofabitch."

Carson nodded.

"What makes you so sure this witch can stop the man?" Kale questioned.

"Crazy Mary, she's no witch," Pierre defended. "She's a *traiteur*."

"What can she do?" Carson prompted.

"She can convince Trainor that she will reveal the truth," Gabriel responded. "When he goes to the bayou to stop her, he will find planted evidence on his niece's grave. Then Anatole, he will step out of the woods and force a confession."

"Where will Delta be while this is going on?" Kale asked.

Gabriel and Pierre exchanged glances.

"Delta, she will be safe. I guarantee it," Gabriel assured them. "The bayou, it is filled with our kin. No harm will come to Delta, *non*."

"Why can't we get her out before the action starts?" Carson inquired.

Gabriel stared hard at Delta's brothers. "She wouldn't leave if Saint Peter brought himself down from heaven and took her by the hand. She intends to stay with Anatole, sure."

Pierre shifted his bulk for greater emphasis. "They are in love, m'sieurs."

Kale and Carson exchanged worried looks, then they turned to the Pinkertons beside them.

Stuart shrugged. "I told you what Zanna said."

"I should have known," Cameron berated himself. "I should have taken her off the boat at Memphis. I didn't like the looks of the feller, but I had nothing to base it on, and Delta promised me to get off at Natchez if there was trouble."

Gabriel shook his head. "This situation, it developed, m'sieur. No one could have stop' it, *non*. It was, I tell you, meant to be."

"Wait a minute," Kale barked. "I don't cotton to

all this Voodoo talk.''

"Believe it or not—" Pierre returned.

"Let's get this straight," Cameron cut in. "You're asking us to tie in with you. You say if we go with the troopers, they will likely kill both this friend of yours and Delta."

"Oui," Gabriel agreed.

"If we come with you, what happens?"

"We will be there when Anatole confronts the gov'nor. With all of us as backup, especially with the Pinkertons behind him, Anatole's case will carry more weight."

"How do we know we aren't starting another Civil War down there in the bayou?" Stuart questioned. "What if the troopers start shooting and we shoot back?"

Pierre shrugged his massive shoulders.

"That is a chance, *oui,*" Gabriel admitted. "But it is not likely. Me, I suspicion tha' when the gov'nor confesses, the troopers will back off. Nobody likes the bastard, *non.*"

"Trainor, he plans to run for United States president next," Pierre added.

The decision was difficult—for Cameron and Stuart, to go against the law in pursuit of justice; for Kale and Carson, to know that whichever way they chose could be the wrong one for Delta. In the end Cameron and Stuart decided to ride with the troopers, where they could handle a volatile situation, should one arise.

"Know this," Kale told the two bayou men, "if you turn up liars, you're alligator meat. All the cousins in this country won't be able to save your sorry hides."

Gabriel and Pierre nodded.

"One thing about it," Carson remarked while he

and Kale tightened their cinches before riding away from the tavern with Pierre and Gabriel, "the governor's made his plans for us clear as rainwater."

Kale grinned. "Shoot first and shoot to kill."

Chapter Twenty

Delta awoke to a morning hush that was at first lulling, then, when she found Brett gone from their mattress on the *galerie*, terrifying.

Hastily she slipped into her clothing. Then she saw him standing at the edge of the small, flat island, hands in his hip pockets, staring out at the swampland that stretched endlessly before them. The sun was just beginning to show its glorious face. From the woods surrounding the island on three sides came the distant call of morning birds.

Delta remembered Gabriel's claim that a person could distinguish between the friendly chatter of bayou birds and the sounds they made when danger approached. She had thought of them as sentries. But would she recognize the difference? She started across the island, glancing fearfully toward the woods, then back to Brett, who stood gazing out at the rising sun, still as a statue.

A myriad of fears tangled inside her head, trapping her happiness at being with him again, the way swamp vines trap a running man. Were troopers out there even now watching and waiting for their chance to capture Brett? Were his cousins still around, alert, guarding them? Were Gabriel's kin still at their posts?

Just before she reached him, Brett turned to see her, and his eyes lit up with an infectious joy. Kissing her tenderly, he gathered her to his side. When he spoke. it was to the rising sun.

"Do you realize, *chère*, this is the first morning in ten years I've awakened and not wondered who murdered my family."

Slipping an arm around his waist, she studied his profile, strong, proud, and so very dear to her heart. And yet so different from the cynical man she had met on board the showboat. She rested her face on his chest and felt his heart beat against her cheek—the heart of Anatole Dupré.

"I'm free," he whispered to the breeze. With a hand he lifted her chin, gazed long into her blue eyes. His voice gained strength. "I'm free of that terrible burden, Delta. Free."

His eyes shone brighter. His smile animated his entire face. Without warning he swept her in his arms and swung her around in a circle, singing, "Free, free, free!" By the time he set her on her feet, her head was spinning. She held to him for support, and he kissed her long and hard, until she swayed against him, returning his kisses with utter abandon.

But her brain would not be easily calmed. She even began to consider that this new man, this Anatole Dupré, might be possessed of an impetuous nature. His joy and his words echoed through her mind, tempered by the truth—the truth, that he wasn't free. Not yet. And they could, at this very moment, be surrounded by the enemy.

Suddenly she dislodged her lips and buried her face in his chest, clinging to him. "I'm so frightened."

Gently he lifted her face, cupping it in his hands. "We're safe here on the *chênière*," he reassured her. "It's like the eye of a storm. Every year hurricanes strike this part of the country. They blow in a fierce circle, leaving a hole in the center, a space of quiet, still air—the eye of the storm. We've passed through the first side of the storm—getting here in one piece. When Trainor takes the bait, we'll leave and enter the other side. It may be fierce, but it won't last long, and like in a hurricane, the second side will blow from the opposite direction—our direction. This time Trainor's at the disadvantage; we hold the cards."

The rising sun shone on his face, highlighting his coal black hair, his black eyes. Stretching out of his grasp, she kissed him, unable to share his optimism, unwilling for him to know it.

But he guessed. "We have two days alone out here, *chère*. Why don't we make this an adventure we'll want to tell our grandchildren about?"

Later she considered the fact that he always knew how to win her over. How could she refuse to be happy in the face of his own joy? Rummaging through the sacks his mother sent, they found coffee, several tins of food Delta didn't recognize, some camphor to chase away mosquitoes, a couple of palmetto hats to keep the sun off their heads, even a change of clothing for each of them.

"Look, a dress," Delta cried, holding up a one-piece cotton garment similar to the dress she wore. "I think I'll change and wash these things I have on."

Brett glanced up from where he knelt on the floor, withdrawing the coffee pot, a large cooking pot, and several utensils. Setting everything aside, he rose to his feet.

His eyes sparkled. "I think I'll help you."

Before she could move an inch, he grasped her around the waist. Dancing her about the porch, he began to skim her dress up her body. His clothes followed. Lifting her in his arms, he deposited her on the mattress, drew the mosquito netting around them, and proceeded to love her as avidly as he had the night before, as tenderly as on the riverbank in Memphis, with as much passion as in her stateroom on board the *Mississippi Princess*. And when at length they lay damp and satisfied in each other's arms, breathing heavily in the sultry air, she knew she lay in the arms of Brett Reall.

Afterwards she fixed coffee in the pot over a fire he built in a pit that had been used numerous times in the past.

"No use trying to clean up that cabin," he commented. "Especially in this heat."

But watching him wander around the *chênière*, she decided his reasons for wanting to spend all their time outdoors had more to do with being home in the bayou than with anything else.

"You missed it very much," she commented with a lump in her throat.

He turned to take the cup of coffee she handed him. His eyes told her the truth. He sipped the coffee, then finally grinned mischievously. "Not bad."

"I watched Gabriel's sisters make café at the *causerie*."

"The *causerie*? For truth, you're beginning to sound like a *bonne bayou femme* yourself."

"I still have a lot to learn," she admitted.

"Ah, *ma chère*, I will teach you everything."

His earnestness caught her off guard. He sounded so certain of their future. How could he be? She strove to lighten her mood. "To dance the *fais-do-do*?"

"For certain."

"To pole a pirogue?"

"For certain."

"To—?"

Suddenly he tossed his tin drinking cup to the ground and caught her in his arms. "I said *everything*." His lips closed over hers in a deep, delving, delicious kiss that set her heart to racing with sheer passion.

Lifting his lips, he stared lovingly into her begging eyes. "For truth, Delta Jarrett, the more I have of you the more I want."

She felt herself tremble in his arms. Her fingers traced the lips of her pirate. But when she started to kiss him, he released her, caught up her hand, and tugged her along.

"Later, *chère*. Right now, there's another lesson I want to teach you." Stopping by the *galerie*, he took up a pile of netting, then led her toward the slow, still water along the backside of the island.

"These little streams are called *coulées*," he told her. "We're going to set crab nets so I can teach you how to make the best jambalaya anyone's ever tasted."

She laughed. "Is it like your mother's gumbo?"

His eyes dimmed for a moment. Would he ever rid himself of the image of that gumbo splattered across the bodies of his family? Somewhere deep inside he began to think it was possible. With Delta Jarrett by his side, anything was possible. With Delta in his heart, there would be no room for hatred or misery. *"Maman* can fix you gumbo. I'll make you jambalaya."

She hugged him. "You'll make me happy."

That evening after she had eaten her fill of the bayou man's jambalaya, which she was sure must match his boast of being the best in Louisiana, after she had watched the sunset on the bayou snuggled in the arms of Anatole Dupré, after Brett Reall had loved her again on their mattress on the *galerie,* they lay in each other's arms, content and happy. And proud of themselves for not allowing the events that lay ahead to dampen their pleasure at being together.

He had asked her to tell him about her trip through the bayou with Gabriel. "You weren't frightened?" he quizzed when she finished.

She shook her head. "Well, maybe a little. It was so wild and new. But deep in the bayou, there's a sense of—I'm not sure what to call it—of timelessness, perhaps, or peace. I told Gabriel I felt like we had traveled through the Garden of Eden."

"I'm surprised," he admitted. "Most—"

She snuggled closer. "I know. Gabriel told me that most *Anglais* don't like the bayou." Sweet heat traveled deliciously up and down her spine with every stroke of his hand. "Do you think I'll ever be accepted here?"

Pulling her face away from his shoulder, he kissed her soundly. "We are, *chère.* We're together. Our lives are as one. But that doesn't mean you have to live in the bayou."

"I want to."

"Ah—" He began, shaking his head.

"I do," she insisted. "I'm sure I'll learn to love it—almost as much as you do. But will your people ever accept me?"

He kissed her again, deeply, a kiss that expressed all the love and passion he had pledged to her. "For certain," he whispered against her skin. "I will see to that."

The following day he took her at her word, beginning to teach her everything about the bayou that appeared within reach of their small island—the muskrat runs, the mounds where the little animals lived, the most likely places to set traps.

Anatole Dupré, bayou man. She studied him closely, loving him more each moment. Her bayou man.

Even the ground beneath their feet, which trembled more in some places than others, became part of her education.

"Prairie tremblante, it's called." He explained how in some places only a foot or two of mud and plants floated on several feet of liquid mud. "I'm a bit rusty. Time was when I could take out at a run and never hit a weak spot. Me, I'm not certain I could do that today, not without falling through."

He had shown her the pointers—alligator grass, cane, cattails. Each one indicated where the ground was solid or weak. She had learned the difference. At least, she thought she had, until the second afternoon when Brett had gone to haul in their crab traps for the last time. Crazy Mary had speculated it would take two days to entice the governor into the bayou, and Brett wanted to be prepared to return to his mother's cabin at a moment's notice.

Delta had remained on the *galerie,* preparing their packs for this journey that would end their idyllic flight from reality.

Suddenly fear, cold and debilitating, overwhelmed her. What lay ahead for them this day? And afterwards? A chill of foreboding sped along her spine and she wanted to be with Brett. Every instant that remained for them, whether it be a lifetime or this one afternoon, she wanted to spend with him.

Racing from the house her only thought was to be with him, to touch him, to look at him, to hear his voice. She took the path he had taught her to use, she was sure of it.

Until the ground gave way beneath her feet. Without warning her body plunged through the thin layer of sod like a hot knife through butter. Her arms flailed out. She opened her mouth to scream, but before she'd uttered more than "BRE—" she clamped her lips closed.

She couldn't scream, not with their little island nestled so closely to land on three sides. Brett had said Gabriel's family and his own cousins were keeping watch, hidden in the dense growth of the forest. But what if the troopers were near? Or Trainor's spies?

Grasping tufts of grass in both fists, she was able to stop her downward plunge before her shoulders slipped through the opening made by her body. Cold water and mud closed in around her legs, plastering her thin dress about her hips.

Brett would come back along this trail. All she had to do was hold on. At the thought she pressed herself closer to the ragged edge of ground and dug her elbows into the grass.

Brett would come. If she could hold on, he would come. She looked around, trying to decide where she had gone wrong. Palmettos ringed the island in several places. That's where she made her mistake, she decided. She had taken the wrong side of the palmettos. He wouldn't be able to see her from the path, but she could hear him. She would hear him, and she would call out in a normal voice.

A mosquito buzzed around her face and she started to swat it away, only at the last moment recalling her tenuous hold on the ground. Around her, other sounds of the bayou came into sharper focus. The bayou teemed with life, both above water and below.

She wriggled her feet at the thought. What lay below the surface? Crawfish or shrimp or—alligators? She had no idea which animals lived where—or who ate what. As much as she had learned about the swamps the last two days, she was now confronted with how little she knew. Her ignorance began to play on her mind.

Even if she were able to hold on until Brett came along the path, did she dare? Again Ginny's remonstrations about her fanciful imagination came to mind. She wiggled her feet. Cold liquid swished between her toes and around her ankles. She didn't feel anything alive.

Yet.

Quickly she began to scramble. Digging elbows into the ground she heaved her body at the same time, lifting herself by inches. On the first attempt she lost as much ground as she gained when she relaxed her arms to try again.

The next time she held on, even though the rough grass and torn earth scratched her arms and her muscles began to ache. The third time she raised herself to waist level. After that it was easy. At length she pulled her feet through the jagged opening.

Dragging herself several yards away from the hole, she lay crumpled on the ground, struggling to catch her breath and steady her jangled nerves.

Just as she rose to her feet, Brett came up on her. "God's bones!"

Their eyes held, his anxious, hers contrite.

"I was coming to be with you, but I took the wrong path."

He jerked her roughly to his chest, unmindful of her muddy clothes. "Delta, *chère*, you could have been drowned."

When her heart stopped racing, she pulled away, conscious of her filthy condition. Ruefully, she examined her dress that hung in shreds and clung to her body with a thick layer of ooze and sprigs of vegetation. Reaching a hand, she wiped mud off Brett's shirt.

"I made a mess."

"*Oui.*" He chuckled, running a finger down her chest, then holding it up, covered with mud. Then before she knew what had happened, he grasped her dress at the neck and ripped it away. "No use trying to save this one."

Shocked at finding herself standing nude in the broad open daylight, she attempted to shield her body with her arms.

"No need for modesty, *chère.*" He shook his head in mock concern, examining her from head to toe. "For truth, your endowments are well hidden by a layer of bayou mud."

Over her protests that she would get him muddy, too, he swept her in his arms and carried her to the cabin. "We'd better get you cleaned up before Carl comes."

The reminder of their limited time showered her with enough trepidation to chase away the residue of fright from her plunge through the *prairie tremblante*.

Outside the rear of the cabin Brett stood her on her feet beneath the tank of the cistern, where, after unhooking a pipe, he directed a stream of clear cold rainwater over her skin. She stood stock still while he bathed her with his hands. By the time he finished, her trepidation had vanished, replaced with an equally urgent, but vastly different emotion.

Before it was over she had stripped his muddy shirt off and washed it in the stream of water, soaking his pants in the process. Regardless, he again picked her up in his arms, this time to carry her to the *galerie* where he deposited her on their pallet and closed the mosquito netting around them.

"Ah," he breathed heavily, "we're away from those pesky insects."

She laughed. "I believe they bother you more than me."

"You mean because this is my favorite place on the *chênière?*"

She nodded, grinning.

"Then you aren't as smart as I had you figured, *chère.*" Settling down beside her he let his hands follow his gaze down the length of her freshly washed body. "This is what calls me back." He tweaked an already rigid nipple, then idly traced his fingers along the valley between her softly mounding breasts, moving downward to the patch of dark curls. "And this." His teasing hand moved lower. "And this."

When she arched her body toward him, he retraced his path. With splayed palm, he swept a hand beneath her, bracing her shoulders, lifting her closer to him. "And this," he muttered just before his lips claimed hers.

Afterwards, lying in his arms, the glow of lovemaking dimmed, leaving her with a heart-rending ache. "They'll come for us today," she whispered.

"They should."

"You mean if the plan works?"

He nodded.

"What if it doesn't?"

The crease between his eyes deepened and at length he replied, "We'll think of something else."

"We could stay here," she suggested. The fear inside her began to grow. Suddenly it was larger than the fear she had felt while trapped in the trembling earth. With the greatest effort she resisted clinging to him, crying, begging him not to try such a reckless scheme as tricking the governor and exposing himself to the state troopers and the Pinkertons.

He didn't need to hear her fears. He needed her support. But his hand on her breast had stilled, and she knew he felt her runaway heart.

"You would get tired of my cooking, *chère*."

"I can cook."

"There's not much to choose from on this island. As much as I love the bayou, this island isn't big enough. I love the meandering courses, the wild swamps, the boundless wilderness—the freedom." His hand traced her body while he spoke, mesmerizing her with both his voice and his touch.

"And I love you," he whispered, kissing her soundly.

Her arms flew around his neck. She pulled him close, remaining silent only by pressing her lips firmly between her teeth.

But worries overwhelmed her. "The governor doesn't believe in black magic. Your mother said so."

"Trainor may not believe in black magic, but he believes in the power of the spirits," Brett assured her. "Living in this country, he's seen proof. And his constituents believe in the power. Besides it won't matter what he believes, if his constituents believe him guilty. That fact alone should send him to the bayou. He has to be certain *Maman* hasn't spread her suspicions around. And that she doesn't have proof of his guilt."

Involuntarily Delta shuddered. With two fingers, he lifted her chin. "It's a chance, *chère*. But a chance I must take." He kissed her. "For us."

"For us," she whispered, wishing there were some other way, a way that wouldn't expose him to danger from so many forces.

411

Carl came at dusk and Delta soon discovered how dangerous Brett considered their mission.

"I want you to ride with Carl," he told her.

She stared from his pirogue to the one poled by Gabriel's cousin.

"To where?" she demanded. In the dusk she watched the cleft between his eyes deepen.

"Carl will bring you to *Maman's* after it's over."

"Like hell!"

"Delta," he admonished. "Get—"

Before he could order her not to, she stepped into his pirogue and seated herself on the wooden bench, where she waited with arms folded across her chest. Around her she heard noises of the men loading Crazy Mary's bedding and other supplies. She concentrated on the shallow bottom of the pirogue.

Finally she felt it dip when Brett stepped on board. Then she felt his hands on her shoulders. He knelt before her.

"It's for you own good, *chère.*"

"My good is with you."

He lifted her chin, forcing her to look at him. "I want you out of the way when I confront Trainor."

She glared at him, willing tears not to roll down her cheeks.

"I don't want to have to worry about you."

She bit her lip, knowing she was losing the battle against her tears. "Then don't," she snapped. "I'm not the one they've been after for ten years. And I'm not stupid. I won't get in the way. I wouldn't dare do anything to cause you to have to think about me instead of Trainor and his dozens of troopers and the

Pinkertons and— But—'' She stopped when she felt a tear spill down her face, then another, and another.

Brett caught them with his fingers.

"I must come with you," she pleaded. "I must be with you. After we get there, I'll stay with Carl or Gabriel or anyone you say, wherever you say, but I must come with you."

He stared at her a long time, then bent and kissed her tenderly. Finally he stood, motioned Carl, and they shoved off.

She rode tensed and quiet, wishing they could talk, but afraid to break the silence around them. At length Brett did.

"Our chances are good."

She stared at his blackened form standing at the back of the boat. "For what?" she whispered, recalling the way he had dodged this question days before. She couldn't see his smile, but there was laughter in his voice.

"For a long and lusty life together, *chère.*"

Hot tears poured down her cheeks and her heart felt as though it might pump itself out. All she could do was grip her hands tightly about her arms and pray he was right.

Gradually she began to hear noises in the distance.

Brett swore softly. "Sometimes I think they're right to call her *Crazy* Mary." Delta turned to see a great blaze in the distance.

"What's going on?"

The noise grew louder—music, singing, shouting, beating drums, stamping feet. The bayou teemed with life, but tonight it was the human kind.

Before the pirogue could approach the landing near Crazy Mary's cabin another of Gabriel's cousins hailed them from shore.

"Over here."

Brett poled into the reeds.

"What is it?" Delta questioned. The fire leaped into the sky and seemed to come from close by. The noise became deafening. Above and intermingled with the drums and stamping of feet on the bare ground, came the sounds of ringing bells and chanting voices.

Brett took her arm, edging her into a thick stand of reeds. "A Voodoo ceremony," he whispered directly into her ear, which was the only way she could have heard anything other than a shout.

Carl nudged his boat alongside Brett's and jumped ashore. "Crazy Mary's called out *les petits habitants, oui,*" he joked.

"Who?" Delta asked.

"That's what the *Anglais* call us bayou folk." Carl slapped Brett on the shoulder. "For truth, us bayou folk are all out tonight, *mon ami*. When this is over, Anatole, we expect you to throw a *fais-do-do,* sure."

"Count on it," Brett quipped. He nodded toward the sounds. "How do we get around this?"

"We don't. We'll go through, less chance of bein' noticed that way. Stay in the middle; we'll surround you." Taking a kerchief from his pocket, Carl tied it around Brett's head.

Delta's brain whirred. Her mouth was dry. He looked like the pirate from her nightmare.

Brett grasped her hand. "Stick close until I tell you, then Carl will take you someplace safe."

"And nearby," she added.

He squeezed her hand. *"Oui."*

Carl restrained Brett with a hand to his arm. "The place, it is ringed with troopers."

Delta tensed. Her feet stopped in midstride.

Brett tugged on her hand. "Don't let them spook

you. You don't look anything like that journalist who ran off with a gambler.''

"But you look like—" *Anatole Dupré,* she thought.

They moved into the pack of dancing, drinking people. Someone passed a bottle to Delta, and Brett whispered in her ear. "Take a swig. I doubt *Maman* would allow them to use anything—" he paused, shrugged, and she saw him grin in the dancing light, "—anything truly offensive.''

She glanced at the mouth of the jug, then back to him.

"Try to fit in," he encouraged.

Lifting the jug, she took a swig of something that tasted like watered-down whiskey. "A ti' drink," she whispered, but he couldn't hear for the noise.

Since he had begun to dance around in imitation of the other dancers, she tried it, too. All around her bodies swayed. Her loose-fitting bayou dress matched the garments worn by the other women, except for a few who wore long flowing robes.

Then she spied Crazy Mary. Garbed in a long white robe belted in purple, Brett's mother danced alone on a platform near the bonfire. On her head she wore a kerchief that was tied in such a manner that numerous points protruded from her head like spikes. Around her neck she wore strand after strand of necklaces, some of gold, some silver, some glass. Emanating energy and power, Crazy Mary looked every bit the witch—unearthly and strangely beautiful.

Delta stared transfixed. "I thought she wasn't a Voodooienne," she called into Brett's ear.

"She isn't. Voodooiennes are free women of color, but she's banking on Trainor not making the distinction. The Vodu is that snake in her hand.''

Delta's breath caught in her throat. From all sides dancers jostled her, but she paid no heed.

"She's dancing with a snake?"

"Not just any snake," Brett said. "That's supposed to be the holy serpent."

Delta's eyes widened.

"According to Voodoo legend the first man and woman were blind and the snake gave them sight, so he became the god of the Voodoo religion."

Delta glanced behind her to see if any troopers had heard. Looking back to the center of the ring, she watched Crazy Mary toss the snake into the crowd. The dancers cheered. From below someone handed Crazy Mary a bowl, which she held to the heavens as though blessing it, afterwards drinking a long draft of its contents. Again the crowd cheered.

Crazy Mary began to chant. The crowd joined her. Since the words were French, Delta had no idea what was being said, but beside her Brett picked up the song.

"You've done this before?" she shouted in his ear.

He shook his head.

"How do you know the words?"

Drawing her to his side, he spoke close to her ear. "Because that isn't a Voodoo chant, it's a bayou song. I've been singing it all my life."

"But what if—?"

He squeezed her hand. "Even if they recognize the song, they won't know the difference."

They made their way slowly through the writhing, chanting, dancing people. Delta cast about, searching for those who, like herself, might look out of place. She had no idea what the governor looked like, but he was certain to stand out in this gathering.

"Are they sure he's here?" she questioned Brett.

He nodded.

416

On the platform Crazy Mary drank again from the bowl, then handed it down.

"Pass it around," came the cry. "Pass it around."

"What's in the bowl?" she asked.

"Blood. Remember that chicken she killed the other day?"

"Chicken blood?" She shuddered. The idea that the bowl might make its way around to her with even a drop left in it became a nauseating possibility. *"Old* chicken blood?"

Brett chuckled. "What happened to that adventurous journalist I met on the showboat?"

Delta glanced right and left at his remarks. "She would never have drunk old chicken blood."

"Never?"

She shook her head.

"Not even to save the hide of an old reformed pirate?"

Around them some of the men and women began dancing together. Delta slipped her arm around Brett's waist and moved closer to his side. "Perhaps not *never,*" she admitted. "But I hope I don't have to."

He pressed her tightly against him, maneuvering her through the throng, which had by now formed into a writhing line that inched its way toward a cauldron bubbling on the bonfire. Each person who danced by dropped something into the pot.

"What are they doing?" she demanded, worried now lest they be discovered because they had nothing to add to the cauldron.

"That's the Voodoo brew," Brett explained, then added as if he had read her thoughts. "Don't worry, we'll slip through the crowd. That was *Maman's* purpose in assembling such a large group, I suppose. We can move around unnoticed."

Not until they reached the other side of the gathering did Delta realize that they were no more than a hundred yards south of Crazy Mary's cabin, the opposite direction from the graves.

Suddenly the reality of their purpose here tonight worked its way through the frenzied fantasy surrounding them. Delta watched Brett scan the crowd. His traveling gaze came to a halt. She saw him glare across the gathering at a man who looked as out of place as she felt—black suit and tie, complete with starched collar. A choleric expression reddened his pale face.

William Trainor? Instinctively Delta knew that citified man must be the governor. So, he had come. Like a knife wound to the heart, she knew the dangerous part of their plan had now begun. Until now they had been skirting the issue, much as they had skirted the dancing Voodoos. Now they faced it.

As she watched, afraid to take her eyes away from the slight, balding man, a second man approached him from out of the crowd. They spoke.

Delta gasped. Her hand flew to her mouth before she blurted out his name.

"What?" Brett questioned.

"That's Cameron. Talking to—"

Brett shrugged. "You knew to expect him."

"I didn't expect him to be on speaking terms with the enemy." Her thoughts quickly formulated into a plan of action. "I'll talk to him. Perhaps if—"

"No." Brett's arm left her shoulders. He grasped her tightly about the upper arm. "Everything's set in motion, Delta. We can't change the plan now."

Carl nodded toward the governor. "He's been edging around all night. Give him a few more minutes, and he's yours."

"Then take Delta," Brett told him. He squeezed her

shoulders again, drawing her near. When she looked up, his eyes were serious. "Go with Carl. I'll find you when it's over."

They stood still as death, while the music and the chanting throbbed around them, beating up in her ears, closing out all the things she wanted to say, choking the words in her throat, damming the tears in her eyes. She nodded.

Carl took her by the arm. Brett moved away. She caught his sleeve.

When he turned back, she smiled. "Don't worry about me. I promise not to play a meddling journalist."

He winked, then turned and disappeared into the crowd.

She allowed Carl to lead her away from the clearing, her mind gyrating in much the same way as the dancers. Trained from an early age to trust her family, everything inside her cried to run to Cameron. Only with the greatest effort did she resist. Brett was right. The plan had been set in motion. Any change she made could cause it to fail.

And failure meant death, death for Brett. Desperately she strove to quiet her racing heart. Dozens of worries filled her mind. Questions buzzed like angry bees inside her head, but she dared not ask them now.

Carl led her into the dense woods beyond Crazy Mary's house, along a route she decided must parallel the path to the graves. The undergrowth was thick and soon they were in total darkness. With no more than a tug, Carl indicated she should kneel. She complied.

Where was Brett? She hadn't seen where he went, but she knew he must be close by—somewhere closer to the graves than she and Carl, she prayed. She wanted to ask but dared not make a sound.

She wondered where Gabriel and Pierre were, but she dared not ask that, either. The troopers were all about; there must have been a couple of dozen at the Voodoo ceremony. She had seen none of them around the woods, but she didn't doubt that if a ruckus arose, they would converge on the area like a horde of hungry alligators.

And then there was Cameron. Had Stuart come, too? Had they brought a force of Pinkertons? Obviously they were here to aid the governor. How far would they go to that end? Anxiety gnawed at her stomach. She clenched her hands into fists and gritted her teeth to keep them from chattering.

She never had been good at sitting things out.

Brett distanced himself from Delta as quickly as he could. If he were discovered, he didn't want her connected to him in any way. Gaston, Carl's brother, whispered something in his ear and thrust a jug of whiskey in his hand.

Brett nodded—then waited while Gaston distracted the nearest trooper—before lifting the jug to his lips and staggering drunkenly away from the clearing. By the time he reached the nearest stand of trees, sweat had broken out along his arms.

Fear. He had lived with it off and on for ten years. Tonight he must make fear his ally. For Delta's sake. And for his own.

Slipping quickly through the trees, Brett skirted the graves and hid behind the giant oak tree that marked Nicole's grave. Setting the jug aside, he withdrew the knife at his waist and fingered its blade. He carried it only as a last resort, but if push came to shove, he wouldn't hesitate to use it.

For two days he had pondered over what to do should Trainor fail to take the bait, and the knife had presented itself as the only solution. Unless he confessed, Trainor alive would always be a threat—to Brett and to Delta. If he used it, of course, they would be forced to live in hiding the rest of their lives. But unless Trainor confessed, they would have to do that anyway.

Footsteps crept stealthily down the path. Brett stood poised, alert. Away from the bonfire his night vision improved, aided by a shaft of moonlight that pierced the oak branches and fell in a scattered beam between the two graves. A small flickering light, the black candle, he supposed, burned at the head of the small grave, just beneath the listing wooden cross.

Although Brett could not see clearly, he could identify forms. And he would recognize William Trainor in the fires of hell, he thought, watching the governor approach the graves. Trainor peered clandestinely over each shoulder, then fell to his knees at the head of the little grave. Flinging the black candle aside, he began scratching in the earth beneath it.

Brett's stomach contorted. For a moment he thought he might be sick. But there was the sick man—sick to the depths of his soul. Any man who would murder his own sister was sick. But the man who would murder an innocent child was evil through and through.

Brett fingered the knife. The urge to kill another human being struck him a powerful blow. He fought it down.

Trainor's digging hands suddenly stopped. Brett watched him stare into the hole he had made, then begin to dig more energetically. Again Trainor stopped. This time he scooped a box out of the earth and tore into it.

Brett stepped into the clearing. "Looks like your luck just ran out, Trainor."

The governor started. His eyes searched Brett from top to bottom, then riveted on Brett's face. "You ignorant bayou scum." He dropped the box and fumbled for something at his belt. "I've got you now." His threat, emitted through a constricted throat, lost much of its emphasis.

Brett kicked the gun out of the governor's hand before it cleared his belt. His knife blade glinted in the shaft of moonlight. "Pick up the box and look inside."

Trainor glanced down at the little wooden box, which had fallen open on top of the small grave. Brett watched the man's hand twitch, watched him recoil from touching the box.

"Pick it up—unless you're afraid to."

"You ignorant bastard," Trainor spat. "You think you can scare me with all this hocus-pocus? Think again. I have two dozen state troopers around that witch's house waiting for my signal." When he attempted to rise to his feet, Brett kicked again, this time knocking the governor off balance.

"I said look inside the box."

"It's a trick," Trainor accused, regaining his balance. "A trick played by that Voodoo witch you call a mother."

"Then why did you fall for it?"

"I didn't."

"Why are you here?"

"To put a stop to her sacrilege."

"Ah? Then why didn't you send your troopers? I've known you a long time William Trainor. I'd wager that, except for their funerals, the last time you personally came into the bayou was to murder my wife and daughter."

"Wager all you want. You can't prove a thing."

"No? Look inside that box."

Trainor's gaze wavered, but again he stopped short of touching the box. Using the toe of his boot Brett nudged the box closer to the man's hands. When he did so, the stickpin fell out. Moonlight reflected off it.

Trainor stared at the piece of gold as though under a spell.

"Now tell me you don't believe in witchcraft."

"That's what's wrong with you people." Disdain dripped from Trainor's voice. "You rely on witchcraft, when you should use your brains. Not that you have any. I'll—"

Brett ignored the man's outburst. "That's the stickpin bearing your *illustrious* family's crest. The stickpin you lost in my kitchen the night you murdered my wife and daughter."

Trainor's hand darted toward the stickpin. Quickly he jerked it away. "That's absurd. You can't prove such a thing."

"No? Madame Hebert saw you at the house that night," Brett lied. "And the day of the funeral, M'sieur Hebert saw you groveling on your hands and knees, searching for something on my kitchen floor."

Trainor reached for the stickpin. Without examining it, he clutched it in his hand. "The only thing this proves is your ignorance," he retorted. "Yours and that Voodoo queen's."

"Call us any name you want, Trainor, except one— murderer is *your* epitaph."

Trainor snorted. "You think so? You think this is evidence against me?" His eyes darted right and left, taking in the dark forest that encircled them like the void of space encircles a star, isolating them, lending an aura of privacy, of secrecy. His eyes fastened on

Brett. "If you want to hear it, all right. Yes, I killed that whoring sister of mine. Was I to leave her alive to ruin my chances for a respectable public service career? Think about it Dupré. I did you a favor."

"You framed me," Brett returned. "You murdered my wife—whether we loved each other isn't the issue—and you murdered my daughter. A child, Trainor. An innocent child who never had a chance to do you wrong."

"She saw me."

Brett gripped his emotions. All he wanted at the moment was to bound across the grave and strangle William Trainor. To hell with the knife. He wanted to *feel* life ebb out of the man. But Delta was out there somewhere, waiting, watching. Delta, and his own future. And this time he would do everything right.

"So you admit murdering Nicole and Olivia?"

"I wouldn't have killed the child, Dupré. Not if she hadn't seen it all. I didn't count on her being home when I sent word for Nicole to meet me at your cabin. I didn't set out to kill Olivia. I'm not depraved."

Brett tightened his grip on the knife handle. "You're the only person in this world who could believe such a thing."

"No." Trainor stood, straightened his spine and his tie, and smiled broadly at Brett. "You're the only person in the wold who will ever hear those words. I don't have to kill you. I have two dozen men to take care of the task. But I figure the voters would like a good old-fashioned hanging." He glared across the graves. "In the meantime if you dare utter one word of our conversation, I promise you, your mother will be the first to pay. And that girl who left the boat with you will be next."

Brett's stomach bunched in knots, but he returned

the governor's insolent smile with one of amusement. "Don't count on it." He lifted his hands, motioning to each side. "You can call me bayou scum all you like, Trainor, but I doubt you'll ever call me ignorant again."

Trainor stared, aghast, as several men stepped into the clearing. He turned to run, but before he could move two paces, other men stepped from the woods.

Even Brett was surprised at the number of witnesses, some of them strangers. Then Delta tore through the brush and threw herself in his arms. He held her close to his aching heart.

"Is it over?" she asked.

"Oui, chère, it's over."

Behind them Cameron Jarrett took charge of the prisoner, aided by Stuart Longstreet, Carson and Kale, and Gabriel and Pierre.

Lifting her hand Delta traced Brett's lips with tender fingers. "I was so frightened for you."

He winked. "Me, too." Then he kissed her, deep and passionately, a kiss full of tenderness, replete with promises.

Finally she drew apart, turning her attention to the tiny grave. "To think how this all began."

Brett knelt beside the grave and began filling the hole Trainor had dug. Delta straightened the cross.

Brett glanced across at the grave of his wife, then back to Olivia's. "They can rest now."

She thought of Calico Jack who had hanged without learning about his babe. *Rest easy,* she whispered, *we have mourned for you, too.*

Beside her Brett crossed himself, then grasped Delta's hand and pulled her to her feet. Above them the sky began to lighten with the coming dawn. He kissed her tenderly. "I was wrong to say we couldn't begin again. With this new sunrise we have a second chance."

Her heart pumped with love and thanksgiving and hope. She lifted her lips to his, feeling his heady passion ease the tension of the last few days.

Suddenly two hands grasped her shoulders, pulling her arms from around Brett's neck.

She turned startled eyes to the perpetrator. "Kale?" She looked to the man beside him. "Carson?"

Her brothers swept her with worried looks. She watched their expressions harden; as one they transferred their attention to Brett.

Delta reacted intuitively. Struggling in Kale's hold, her only thought was to shield Brett from whatever ominous designs her brothers had in mind.

But Kale retained his grip on her shoulders. Turning her around, he headed her down the path. "Run on back to the clearing, Delta. We need a word with his feller—alone."

Chapter Twenty-One

Two days later Delta sat in the courtyard of Cousin Brady's New Orleans home with her sisters-in-law, Ellie and Aurelia, sipping lemonade and in general being pampered by Cousin Brady's servants. Brady, accompanied by Cousin Cameron and her brothers, Kale and Carson, had escorted Brett to the New Orleans District Attorney's office, where Brett's name was to be finally and forever removed from the state's Most Wanted list.

"They're probably grilling Brett about some part of his past right now," she fretted. A servant set a silver tray piled high with pastries and fruit in the center of the wrought iron table. Beyond the table a fountain splashed and around them mockingbirds sang from crape myrtle trees. Bougainvillea, camellias and magnolias bloomed in abundance. After days of grueling travel through the bayous of southern Louisiana, this was paradise. And yet without Brett, it seemed barren.

"They mean well," Ellie assured her.

"*Sí*, they do," Aurelia added. "But I remember how I felt when my brother interfered between Carson and me." She laughed. "I reminded Carson of that last night. He knows better than to ruin things for you and Brett.''

"They both do," Ellie added.

Delta studied both her sisters-in-law. Ellie, she had loved immediately upon meeting her in Texas almost a year before. Aurelia, she had just met, but she could see why Carson had fallen in love with her.

"It isn't easy being their baby sister," Ellie consoled. "They want only the best for you."

Delta cast her eyes heavenward. "The best." How well she recalled what these two overprotective brothers wanted from her. That scene in the bayou would remain etched in her brain forever.

"They hardly greeted me before they lit into Brett."

"It's their way," Ellie defended. "Business first."

Delta inhaled the perfumed scents of Cousin Brady's garden. Ellie and Aurelia were right, she knew. Her brothers had seen Brett as a threat to her best interests, and they had tried to dispatch that threat the same way they attacked all problems, forthrightly.

She could still see the pale light of early morning glint from Kale's implacable blue eyes when he pulled her out of Brett's embrace. Expecting an adversary, she had been startled to see her brother, and not just one brother, but two of them, glaring at her as though she had taken up with the devil himself.

Both brothers had swept her with their eyes. Then, obviously deciding she was unharmed, had lit into Brett. Before Delta had had time to intervene, Kale had spoken.

"Run on back to the clearing, Delta. We need a word with this feller—alone."

She recognized Kale's tone—a curt command—before his words registered. When they did, she struggled back to Brett's side. He had just fought one major battle; how dare her brothers confront him before he had a chance to draw a peaceful breath.

Draping his left arm around Delta's shoulders, Brett had extended his right hand to Kale. "Anatole Dupré."

"We know who you are. What we'd like to hear is—"

Carson interrupted Kale by accepting Brett's offered hand. "Carson Jarrett, Delta's brother. This here's Kale, another brother."

Brett shook hands with Carson, then again offered his hand to Kale, who looked at it long and hard.

"What I want to know," Kale demanded, "is did you kidnap or in any other way wrong my sister?"

Delta gasped. She clutched Brett around the waist. She felt his steady grip on her shoulder, heard his voice, gentle but firm.

"Why don't you ask her?"

When Kale transferred his belligerent scowl to Delta, she had straightened her shoulders, somewhat assuaged by the feel of Brett's chest against her arm. "He most certainly did not kidnap me, nor as you say *wrong* me in any way. He's . . ." Stopping, she looked up at Brett. His serious expression fueled her anger at her brothers. "I left the boat of my own accord. He didn't even know I'd left. He would have stopped me if he'd known. But I came because I had to be with him." She tightened her hold on Brett. "I'm here and I will stay here forever. Even if he hadn't been able to clear his name, I would have never left him. Even if you and every other Jarrett in the entire world try to take me away, I'll stay—"

"Delta," Carson interrupted. "We're not trying to take you anywhere. I mean, we just want to make sure you're all right."

"I am."

"Fine," Kale told her. "Now, run along and let us talk to Dupré."

Carson had placed a restraining hand on Kale's shoulder. When he spoke, Delta thought she heard a trace of humor in his tone. "Settle down, brother. I've seen these tactics used before. They didn't work then, and from the looks of things they won't work now."

"They certainly won't," Delta had retorted.

When Brett cleared his throat, the sound drew their attention as if it had been a cannon shot.

"I understand your concern," he began. Holding Delta's gaze, he winked. "As you see, your sister hasn't been harmed. And like she said, we're together and we intend to stay together." His expression had turned solemn then, delving into the depths of her blue eyes. "Will you marry me, Delta Jarrett?"

Like Ginny had often said, Delta possessed a fanciful mind. She'd fantasized about the man of her dreams proposing to her. But she could never have imagined it like this. Never could she have seen herself standing in a swamp in the state of Louisiana with two of her brothers fighting mad at her side and the sky coloring with a new sunrise overhead, while the man of her dreams gazed into her eyes with such love and passion that it shut out every thing else—Voodoos, murdering governors, dastardly nightmares, even truculent brothers.

She had met Brett's lips as they descended. Her arms flew around his neck, her lips opened to his. He kissed her soundly, firmly, teasing her with a quick thrust of his tongue before he drew back, an amused look on his face.

Loosening her hold, she traced a finger around his lips, conscious only of the fact that she had performed this gesture innumerable times—to the pirate in her dreams, to Brett Reall, to Anatole Dupré—and they were one and the same man, the man in her dreams, the man she would live with forever.

"*Oui,*" she whispered into his lips.

Carson had cleared his throat at that, and Delta jumped. Brett winked at her mischievously. "I told you why I needed to clear my name, *chère*. Seems I was right."

Noises from the rear of Cousin Brady's townhouse announced the return of the men. Delta jumped from her chair and rushed to meet Brett.

"How did it go?"

In answer he grabbed her by the waist and swung her around the brick courtyard.

"The *Mississippi Princess* is docked down at the wharves," Cousin Brady announced. "I'll send Maynard to fetch your trunks, Delta."

Brett set Delta on her feet. "Why don't I drive her down to the docks?" Although his question was directed to Brady, his eyes remained fixed on Delta. "She might like to assure Captain Kaney and the crew that she's well and safe." He shrugged. "And I should make amends for running out on them like I did."

They took Cousin Brady's carriage, with her cousin offering to send a dray to fetch her trunks if she wanted him to.

The early afternoon air was softly humid and redolent with the perfume of numerous flowering plants. Brett took the reins and Delta sat beside him, idly smoothing Aurelia's dress over her knees.

"Fortunately Aurelia and I are near the same size,"

she mused beside Brett. "Otherwise I'd have been forced to remain at the house until we got my trunks."

He transferred the reins to one hand and drew her toward him with his other. When he was satisfied she was as close as she could reasonably get and still allow him to drive the carriage, he lifted his arm and draped a wrist over her shoulder. *"Oui,"* he answered her observation. "Your trousseau awaits you."

She giggled, suddenly feeling giddy and free for the first time since they had met. The street they traveled gave way to a double-rutted road that traveled beneath a canopy of oak trees. She looked around.

"The docks should be behind us."

Brett flicked the reins, encouraging Brady's fine team. *"Oui."*

Curiosity bubbled inside her. An image of the picnic they shared in Memphis came to mind. "Where are we going?"

"Does it matter?"

Resting her cheek against his shoulder, she shook her head, letting the texture of his broadcloth jacket rub against her face. "Not as long as we're together. And alone."

"That's what I thought, too. It's been a while."

"Too long."

They traveled in silence, letting the feel of each other simmer inside them, the anticipation build.

"There won't be much time," he allowed at last, slowing the team before steering the carriage off the road. She inhaled the heavy scent of magnolias when they started down an unkempt one-lane road, finally emerging in front of a magnificent old Greek revival home.

She sat up and looked at it. Dilapidated as it was, its former grandeur shone through. Brett set the brake and jumped down, threading the reins through the iron ring on an ancient hitching post. When he came to her side of the carriage and held his hands up she slipped eagerly into his arms.

He kissed her once then turned her to face the house. "What do you think about it?"

She studied the structure before replying. From the overgrown shrubbery to the sagging shutters it looked hopelessly in need of repair. But an elegance was there, hidden by neglect, beckoning some enterprising soul to come to the rescue.

"It needs a little work," she responded.

"*Oui.*"

The practicality of Ginny's and Hollis's upbringing pierced through her romantic nature. "It would cost a lot of money to do the job properly."

"*Oui.*"

"And a fortune to furnish it and run it as a home."

He nudged her toward the door. The sound of rusty hinges echoed through the three-story foyer. Delta surveyed the once-elegant entrance, turning a full circle to take in the sweep of the grand circular staircase.

"I bought it," Brett announced.

Abruptly she turned her attention to him. "You what?"

"I signed the papers this morning." He held up his hands to ward off her objections. "But with one condition." His eyes searched hers. "That you like it as much as I do."

"You bought—?" She turned another full circle on her heels before meeting his intense gaze. "You bought this?"

He nodded. "The house, the outbuildings, the cane fields and sugar mill, and several hundred additional *arpents*. The property fronts the Mississippi and backs up to the bayou.''

''But we agreed,'' she objected. She watched the familiar crease form between his eyes.

''What did we agree?'' he asked.

''That it would cost a lot of money.''

He grinned. *''Oui.'*

She stared beyond him to the dark, empty rooms. ''And that it would take a fortune to repair it and furnish it and—''

''Oui.''

''And to run it.''

He nodded.

''But where—?''

His frown stopped her. ''Do you like it?'' he demanded.

She held his gaze, watched him beg her to like this house. ''Of course I like it, but that doesn't mean anything.''

''You do like it?''

''Oui,'' she whispered.

Without warning he scooped her in his arms and danced around the dusty, marble-floored rotunda. ''Then it's yours.''

''Brett,'' she demanded. ''Where did you get the money? How will we ever pay for such a . . . a palace?''

He laughed. ''The fur trade has been lucrative, *chère*. I have enough funds to pay for the house and anything you want to do to it or put in it, and to run the plantation for a couple of years. After that we should have the hang of things and be able to support ourselves on sugar.''

She buried her face in his shoulder and tried to still her racing heart. What he said made sense, yet everything had happened so quickly her head swam and she could force no coherent thoughts. For once in her life facts seemed more important than fantasy.

"It will take an awful long time to repair things."

Brett set her on her feet, took up her hand and led her through the mansion, all twenty-nine rooms of it. Every room had a marble fireplace and elegant chandeliers and hand-carved moldings. Upstairs the rooms across the front of the house had enormous windows that looked out upon once-lovely gardens, and beyond to the mighty Mississippi River. Their river.

"Brady said there's a townhouse down the street from him that's available," Brett told her. "We can lease it until things are ready here, if you agree."

Suddenly she began to laugh and once started she couldn't stop. Brett stood back, folded his arms across his chest and watched her, an anxious look on his face.

Finally he said, "If you don't like this place, there are other plantations for sale up and down the river. This one seemed to offer the most in terms of making a living—"

Her laughter stilled. "I love this place. It's wonderful." Stepping closer she rested her hands at his waist and looked pensively into his eyes. "Your plans are perfect. But you've forgotten something."

She watched the truth dawn in his eyes. Slowly he lowered his lips and kissed her. *"Non, ma chère,* I have forgotten nothing." Taking her hand, he led her down the stairs and to the carriage. "I'll explain on the way to the showboat. Tomorrow is the opening of the jetties. You can't miss getting your byline on one of the biggest stories of the decade."

Not until they returned to Cousin Brady's several hours later did Delta realize what she had forgotten.

"Captain Kaney invited all of us to ride through the

jetties on board the *Mississippi Princess* tomorrow," she told her family.

Ellie and Aurelia were excited. Even Kale and Carson agreed readily, although Kale expressed reservations.

"The only time I'm comfortable around that much water is when it's to water cattle. Guess I've taken one trail herd too many across a swollen river."

Cousin Brady asked about her trunks. When Delta confessed that she had forgotten, he inquired, "Shall I send Maynard to fetch them?"

"No." She cast a wistful glance to Aurelia. "If you have something I can borrow to wear tomorrow."

"Sí."

The gown Aurelia offered Delta the following morning was one of the loveliest dresses Delta had ever seen—yellow tissue taffeta with bouffant sleeves and a skirt so wide she knew it would cause a stir.

"It's magnificent," she sighed. "But I don't need anything so grand."

"This is a big day for you," Aurelia objected. "You are the only female journalist to report on the opening of the river. You must wear a significant gown."

Delta began to suspect just how significant the gown was, when she entered the courtyard an hour later and instead of a compliment, Carson favored her with a puzzled expression.

"How significant is this gown?" she whispered to Aurelia.

Aurelia smiled grandly.

"Carson doesn't like me wearing it. Why?"

Aurelia shrugged. "He won't mind, not really. It's just a dress. I mean, it was the gown I wore when we got married, but—"

Delta's eyes flew to her new sister-in-law. "Your wedding dress?"

Aurelia shrugged. "*Sí*, but I brought it to wear to important functions." She hugged Delta. "You look beautiful in it. After all you've been through, you deserve something special today."

Tears filled Delta's eyes. She hugged Aurelia. "Oh, Relie," she said, using the nickname Aurelia insisted everyone except Carson call her, "I'm so lucky to have you and Ellie for sisters."

"We're lucky to have you, too." Aurelia looked across the courtyard to where Carson and Kale talked with Brett. "Those men are going to get on well. It's sad we'll live so far apart."

The evening before Brett and Delta had told them about the plantation, inviting them all to return for Christmas. "Even if we haven't completed all the work," Delta had said, "there's plenty of room for pallets." She smiled at Ellie and Kale. "As I recall we were supposed to attend a wedding in Texas last Christmas."

Ellie grinned and Kale responded. "I managed to take care of that little matter well ahead of time." His gaze rested on Brett and Delta. "Speaking of weddings, when're you two plannin' to tie the knot?"

Delta blushed.

"We'll let you know," Brett promised.

The docks buzzed with activity when they arrived in two of Cousin Brady's carriages.

"It's like Christmas, New Year's, and the Fourth of July all rolled into one," Kale commented.

"Better not mention the Fourth of July around here," Brandy cautioned. "Folks aren't far enough away from the conflict to celebrate being back in the Union."

Delta clutched Brett's hand and felt excitement build to excruciating levels inside her. Bunting draped all the boats in the harbor, but the *Mississippi Princess* was the grandest of all. A banner strung between the two smokestacks proclaimed the showboat to be the official representative of Captain Ead's hometown of St. Louis. The calliope played and Delta waved to Zanna, who leaned over the rail on the promenade deck searching the crowd.

Pulling Delta by the hand, Brett led the Jarrett entourage toward the gangplank, where he stopped, and Delta gaped.

There stood Gabriel, playing his fiddle as he had done at every stop along the way. She rushed over and hugged him, causing bright red spots to flower on his cheeks. Drawing back she noticed Pierre, whom she greeted with a less demonstrative hug, and was surprised at the enthusiasm he showed in returning her greeting. When she faced Mary Dupré, regal in a colorful gown adorned with bracelets and necklaces and tiny bells, Delta's composure slipped. Tears sprang to her eyes.

Brett's mother reached with a lacy handkerchief to dry them. "There, there, *pichouette,* don' cry, *non.*"

Delta introduced Ellie and Aurelia and Cousin Brady to Brett's mother and friends and together they all trooped aboard. Captain Kaney, flanked by Zanna and the Princess Players, greeted them on the main deck. He shook hands with Brett, kissed Delta on the cheek, and issued a robust welcome to their guests.

"Come aboard, folks. History is being made today."

It wasn't until they were steaming along in the midst of a procession of ships that stretched as far as the eye could see in both directions that those around them

438

began to suspect they might have more in store for them this day than the opening of the jetties, as important as that occasion was.

The captain led them to the promenade deck, where he invited them to help themselves at the buffet set up along the wall. Waiters moved among the crowd serving champagne. Zanna gave the first clue when she distributed flowers, roses for all the ladies—Ellie and Aurelia and Brett's mother each received corsages. Delta's was a bouquet, at least four dozen, she decided, thinking suddenly that if there were time she could count them to calm her nerves.

There wasn't time, of course.

Carson made the first guess. "Now I know why Aurelia loaned you her wedding dress," he whispered in Delta's ear.

She laughed. "Relie didn't know. It was a coincidence."

They stood in the middle of the open deck with other passengers milling on either side, talking, laughing, sipping champagne. The boat churned along the narrow channel. Captain Kaney stepped to the end of the prow, motioning Brett and Delta to follow him.

"Ladies and gentlemen," he called. Brett slipped his arm around Delta's waist. She knew she was trembling. He bent over and kissed her cheek, lightly, tenderly. Then the captain continued.

"Gather 'round. We've some official business to take care of before we reach the jetties."

Delta looked into Brett's eyes, wondering whether they were doing the right thing. Around them she heard feet shuffling.

"What's happening?" Ellie's voice questioned.

"Hell, it looks like a—" Kale began.

The band drowned out his voice, with a brass rendition of "The Wedding of the Lily and the Rose."

Before the last strains died away, Captain Kaney's voice boomed above the surrounding confusion. "We are gathered here today to witness the marriage of these two fine young people—Anatole Dupré, known to many of us as Brett Reall, and our own lovely journalist, Delta Jarrett."

The service took only a matter of minutes, all of which Delta spent worrying over whether Brett was marrying her because he wanted to, or because he felt coerced by her brothers. The deck swayed beneath her feet. The last few weeks played through her brain, as familiar in their despair as the lines of Zanna's melodrama.

"Kiss your bride," Captain Kaney instructed.

Brett turned her with hot palms to her bare shoulders. She lifted worried eyes to his. He frowned.

"Are you sure—?" she whispered.

His lips effectively halted her words; his kiss, hot and sensual, answered her question. She leaned into him, feeling secure and protected, and very, very loved.

At length, she became conscious of hands clapping around them. Gabriel's fiddle took up a lively jig. Brett lifted his lips. "Madame Dupré," he whispered against her skin.

Her eyes searched his. All she wanted was to hold him, to kiss him, to love him. And he knew it, she could tell.

He winked. "Later, *chère*."

Carson was the first to claim a kiss. "You're a beautiful bride, Delta." His voice cracked when he added, "I'm glad you wore Aurelia's gown."

"I'm glad you married her," she told her brother.

Kale came next, shaking Brett's hand, then grabbing Delta in a rough bear hug. He held her back and gazed into her blue eyes, eyes the color of his own. "Guess we laid that old worry to bed," he told her. He shook Brett's hand, then turned back to Delta. "There's no curse on our blue eyes."

She clasped Brett tighter. "I think they're lucky," she told Kale. "We may be the luckiest ones of all."

Brett kissed the top of her head. "Ellie and I are the lucky ones."

The calliope struck up the familiar, "Oh, Dem Golden Slippers," drowning out any chance of conversation. Horns from boats both ahead and behind them blared, and the *Mississippi Princess* began its historic entrance into the channel created by Captain Ead's jetties. Delta turned her attention, as much of it as she could, to taking notes for an article on the new passage. Brett stood beside her, tall and proud.

From the third deck of the showboat they looked out upon the broad, flat terrain. In most places it was hard to distinguish between land and water and sky.

"James Eads is an engineering genius," Captain Kaney proclaimed, while his pilot steered the bulky showboat through the narrow man-made pass.

"For truth," Brett agreed. "I'd have doubts about poling a pirogue through these marshes."

Once the showboat cleared the channel and turned around in the basin, Cameron approached Delta with congratulations. "When do you figure on finding time to write that article?" he teased. "How 'bout I wire Hollis not to expect it for a fortnight or so?"

Delta blushed, but recovered quickly. "Would you wire him when you return to shore? Brett and I are leaving on the boat in the morning and I won't have a chance."

"Sure thing."

441

"Tell him . . ." She thought a moment. "Tell him to tell Joey and Jimmy that I'm bringing them a pirate."

He shook his head in mock despair. "What happens to this career you were dead set on pursuing?"

"I may still. Cousin Brady knows the publisher of the *Picayune*. He offered to introduce me after we get settled."

"And babies? How will you work and run that mansion and raise babies?"

Delta caught Brett's eye from across the deck. He winked and her spine tingled. She started to tell Cameron he'd left out her most important role: *loving her husband.*

Instead she patted her cousin's arm. "Don't fret, Cousin Cameron. You know the old saying, 'Where there's a will, there's a way.' "

Cameron hugged her. "I'm happy for you, Delta. Long as you're sure this is what you want."

"I'm sure." Her eyes twinkled. "When we get to Memphis, I'll see about putting Mama Rachael's matchmaking skills to work for you."

He laughed. "She is pretty good at it, isn't she?"

Somehow Delta made it through such suddenly mundane things as the first jetty passage and visiting with her family, family she wouldn't see again for a very long time.

Once she spied Zanna and Cameron in conversation, and when she asked Zanna about it later, Zanna blushed. "Stuart is meeting the boat at Natchez. Cameron said Stuart's taking some time off and wants to travel to St. Louis with us."

Pierre and Gabriel were eager to discuss the new plantation and the roles they would play in running it. Delta liked them both, she realized quite unexpectedly—even Pierre, with his stern countenance. His job had been to protect Brett, and he had performed it admirably. He hadn't liked her at first, but she couldn't blame him. When all was said and done, she had endangered Brett's life.

After an hour or so of nonstop visiting, Brett insisted she eat something, so they filled plates and stood together at the rail watching the ship steam into its berth at New Orleans. Together, where they belonged.

Together, where they had always belonged.

Delta got teary-eyed when it came time to bid her family farewell.

"Take care of her," Kale warned.

"Oui," Brett said.

"She may be your wife," Carson added, "but she's our little sister—" He left the statement hanging. No sense issuing threats. The facts were enough—they loved Delta and were willing to take on anyone who harmed her.

But from the hearty way Kale and Carson bade Brett good-bye, Delta figured those two had been won over.

Pierre and Gabriel prepared to leave. They escorted Crazy Mary, who hugged her son, then Delta. "You, *pichouette,* you're the one he should have married the first time, sure. Then we wouldn't have had all that trouble."

Delta hugged her. "If all those terrible things hadn't happened, I would never have met him."

Crazy Mary's eyes brightened. "Me, I would have arrang' it. I wouldn't let you wander the spirit world pining for each other, *non.* "

Gabriel hugged Delta, then shook hands with Brett. "When you bringin' yourselves home, you two?"

Brett shrugged. "Since Cameron fixed things with the Mounties, we don't have to return to Canada, but I'll need to close down operations along the river." He glanced at Delta. "We'll stay a while in St. Louis with

Delta's family. It may take us a couple of months to get everything settled."

When the two men turned to escort Crazy Mary toward the gangplank, Brett called to them. "Contact Bontura up in St. Francisville. Tell him to advise Nat of the truth and set him loose."

Delta tensed beside him. "Do you think it's safe?"

Brett chuckled. "For me, *oui*. Maybe not so safe for the next fellow Nat goes after."

Delta thought about it. "Zanna might take him back as leading man for the Princess Players." She looked across the gathering at Elyse, lovely and lonely as ever.

Brett's eyes followed hers. He chuckled. "Not a bad idea. Nat made a better actor than he did a bounty hunter, anyway."

The ship bucked against the rushing current, rocking the bridal bed where two lovers lay locked in a heated embrace.

"Ah, ma chère," he whispered, "you are as passionate a bride as you were a lover."

"And you, my husband, are as lusty as the pirate in my dreams or the gambler on board the showboat."

He belted out a laugh as he plunged again and again into her receptive body. "God's bones, Delta! You have led an exotic love life."

He drove his hungry body faster and faster into hers, until at length she felt them dive together into that swirling river of fire. When they broke the surface it was to a blue sky veiled in bayou moss and the sweltering heat of a summer's night. She drew him to her bosom, holding him in sweat-laved arms. "For truth, my love, you have become one man, and I at last am whole."

"We are," he whispered into her tangled hair. "We always have been. Now we will be forever."

Author's Note

I leave the truth about Anne Bonny and Calico Jack Rackham, if truth about pirates can ever be separated from fiction, to others. Delta Jarrett's dreams are fictitious. However, Anne Bonny did deliver a girlchild while she and fellow-pirate Mary Read were in prison. (Mary also delivered a child, and it may have been stillborn.) Although Jack Rackham was Anne's lover most of her pirate life, facts vary as to whether he fathered her child. The law in those days provided for women pirates, if pregnant when captured, to deliver their babies before being executed.

Delta's brothers, Kale and Carson, have appeared in their own stories. Kale and Ellie's love story is found in *Sweet Autumn Surrender*, released by Zebra Books in October of 1991; Carson and Aurelia's in *Silver Surrender*, June, 1992. The next book in the *Jarrett Family Sagas* will feature one of the twin brothers, Rubal Jarrett.

My husband always cautioned our sons not to make a mistake they would have trouble dealing with when they grew up. Someone should have warned Rubal Jarrett of such. After meeting Molly Durant at a dance a year before, he is unable to get her off his mind. Intending to pursue a courtship, he returns to East

Texas only to find Molly in a peck of trouble and blaming it all on him. It takes all his wits and intervention from an unexpected source to woo this lady who has inherited a dilapidated boarding house, five young siblings, and valuable property from which the timber has been stolen. To make matters worse, she's engaged to marry the local banker. Look for Rubal and Molly's story at your bookstore in a few months.

In Delta's story, as in previous books, I've used settings readers can visit today, either in person or vicariously through further reading. If you're interested in taking a steamboat excursion down the Mississippi River, contact one of the steamboat companies headquartered in New Orleans. Chambers of Commerce are always a good place to begin such inquiries.

If you prefer to read about the trip or the bayous of Louisiana, I suggest:

Life on the Mississippi by Mark Twain
Tales of the Mississippi by Ray Samuel
The Bayous of Louisiana by Harnett T. Kane

I close with a special word of thanks to a dear friend and exemplary writer, Nancy Goodnight, for her help with this manuscript.

WHAT'S LOVE GOT TO DO WITH IT?

Everything . . . Just ask Kathleen Drymon . . . and Zebra Books

CASTAWAY ANGEL	*(3569-1, $4.50/$5.50)*
GENTLE SAVAGE	*(3888-7, $4.50/$5.50)*
MIDNIGHT BRIDE	*(3265-X, $4.50/$5.50)*
VELVET SAVAGE	*(3886-0, $4.50/$5.50)*
TEXAS BLOSSOM	*(3887-9, $4.50/$5.50)*
WARRIOR OF THE SUN	*(3924-7, $4.99/$5.99)*

Available wherever paperbacks are sold, or order direct from the Publisher. Send cover price plus 50¢ per copy for mailing and handling to Zebra Books, Dept. 4286, 475 Park Avenue South, New York, N.Y. 10016. Residents of New York and Tennessee must include sales tax. DO NOT SEND CASH. For a free Zebra/ Pinnacle catalog please write to the above address.

HISTORICAL ROMANCES BY PHOEBE CONN

FOR THE STEAMIEST READS, NOTHING BEATS THE PROSE OF CONN . . .

ARIZONA ANGEL	(3872, $4.50/$5.50)
CAPTIVE HEART	(3871, $4.50/$5.50)
DESIRE	(4086, $5.99/$6.99)
EMERALD FIRE	(4243, $4.99/$5.99)
LOVE ME 'TIL DAWN	(3593, $5.99/$6.99)
LOVING FURY	(3870, $4.50/$5.50)
NO SWEETER ECSTASY	(3064, $4.95/$5.95)
STARLIT ECSTASY	(2134, $3.95/$4.95)
TEMPT ME WITH KISSES	(3296, $4.95/$5.95)
TENDER SAVAGE	(3559, $4.95/$5.95)

Available wherever paperbacks are sold, or order direct from the Publisher. Send cover price plus 50¢ per copy for mailing and handling to Zebra Books, Dept. 4286, 475 Park Avenue South, New York, N.Y. 10016. Residents of New York and Tennessee must include sales tax. DO NOT SEND CASH. For a free Zebra/ Pinnacle catalog please write to the above address.

DESIRE'S EMBRACE

"There's something between us, Delta Jarrett. Something that's been going on a long, long time. I feel it, and you do, too."

With studied slowness, he lifted her arms and placed them around his neck, then slid his own around her shoulders. Gradually, gently, giving her all the time she needed to pull away, he drew her closer. But she didn't pull away. Such a thing never entered her mind.

When his lips touched hers, she reached to meet them. And this time, they set her on fire. This time they were soft and kind, turning her melancholy into something so poignant, tears again filled her eyes. She tightened her arms around his neck, feeling her tensed muscles relax even as her body sprang to life with a thousand different sensations—sensations that were all new, yet deeply familiar at the same time.

Consumed by a sense of anticipation, she opened her lips to his and returned his rising passion with passion of her own. . . .

SEA FIRES (3899, $4.50/$5.50)
by Christine Dorsey

Spirited, impetuous Miranda Chadwick arrives in the untamed New World prepared for any peril. But when the notorious pirate Gentleman Jack Blackstone kidnaps her in order to fulfill his secret plans, she can't help but surrender—to the shameless desires and raging hunger that his bronzed, lean body and demanding caresses ignite within her!

TEXAS MAGIC (3898, $4.50/$5.50)
by Wanda Owen

After being ambushed by bandits and saved by a ranchhand, headstrong Texas belle Bianca Moreno hires her gorgeous rescuer as a protective escort. But Rick Larkin does more than guard her body—he kisses away her maidenly inhibitions, and teaches her the secrets of wild, reckless love!

SEDUCTIVE CARESS (3767, $4.50/$5.50)
by Carla Simpson

Determined to find her missing sister, brave beauty Jessamyn Forsythe disguises herself as a simple working girl and follows her only clues to Whitechapel's darkest alleys . . . and the disturbingly handsome Inspector Devlin Burke. Burke, on the trail of a killer, becomes intrigued with the ebon-haired lass and discovers the secrets of her silken lips and the hidden promise of her sweet flesh.

SILVER SURRENDER (3769, $4.50/$5.50)
by Vivian Vaughan

When Mexican beauty Aurelia Mazón saves a handsome stranger from death, she finds herself on the run from the Federales with the most dangerous man she's ever met. And when Texas Ranger Carson Jarrett steals her heart with his intimate kisses and seductive caresses, she yields to an all-consuming passion from which she hopes to never escape!

ENDLESS SEDUCTION (3793, $4.50/$5.50)
by Rosalyn Alsobrook

Caught in the middle of a dangerous shoot-out, lovely Leona Stegall falls unconscious and awakens to the gentle touch of a handsome doctor. When her rescuer's caresses turn passionate, Leona surrenders to his fiery embrace and savors a night of soaring ecstasy!

Available wherever paperbacks are sold, or order direct from the Publisher. Send cover price plus 50¢ per copy for mailing and handling to Zebra Books, Dept. 4286, 475 Park Avenue South, New York, N.Y. 10016. Residents of New York and Tennessee must include sales tax. DO NOT SEND CASH. For a free Zebra/ Pinnacle catalog please write to the above address.